♦ THE ♦
MESA OF
FLOWERS

THE MESA OF FLOWERS

❖

by Harold Courlander

CROWN PUBLISHERS, INC., NEW YORK

Inquiries should be addressed to Crown Publishers, Inc., One Park Avenue, New York, N.Y. 10016

Printed in the United States of America
Published simultaneously in Canada by
General Publishing Company Limited

Designed by Shari de Miskey

Library of Congress Cataloging in Publication Data

Courlander, Harold, 1908-
Mesa of flowers.

1. Indians of North America—Southwest, New—Fiction.
I. Title.
PZ4.C863Me   [PS3505.0885]   813'.5'2   76-54720
ISBN 0-517-52937-8

TO MY TEWA AND HOPI FRIENDS.
ALTHOUGH THIS STORY IS FICTION
IT COULD NOT HAVE BEEN WRITTEN
EXCEPT FOR THEIR GENEROUS SHARING
OF THEIR TRADITIONS AND REFLECTIONS
ON THE WORLD AROUND THEM.

AUTHOR'S NOTE

LET US IMAGINE, IF WE CAN, THAT VAST REGION OF THE SOUTHWEST lying between the Rio Grande and the Colorado River as it was four or five centuries ago, when small groups of people wandered there as minute figures in an aged landscape. Families and clans drifted one way and another, building camps or villages in the shelter of cliffs and buttes, resting a year or two, or perhaps many years, then drifting again through the awesome terrain to other cliffsides or mesa tops where they made new settlements. They built their houses, baked pottery and grew maize in a wilderness so wide that they might travel weeks or months without seeing signs of other humans. The land dwarfed them. Not yet had these people persuaded themselves that man was the creator, owner and disposer of nature. They had not lost the perception that mankind was merely one of many kinds, and that they had to share the world with living brothers cast in the forms of bear, deer and antelope.

Elsewhere, in distant parts of the world, there were humans who felt old and wise, who had fathomed the secrets of their mountains, deserts and lakes, who had roads leading from one familiar place with a name to another with a name. But here it was different. When a family or a clan ventured across the great land, it did not always know what lay at the end of the journey. Rumor or legend sometimes gave them landmarks, but others who may have passed this way left no trails. Sometimes the wanderers gravitated to a canyon and made a village of volcanic blocks, stone or sunbaked clay. Sometimes they followed a river course until an event, a whim or a prophecy turned them in another direction. Here and there a village was built and abandoned as if it were a casual thought, a way station on an invisible and unending road. Some who journeyed went into the wilderness and disappeared, leaving no record except, perhaps, a pictograph or two on sunbaked rock. Today pottery shards and eroded ruins mark the passage of these people on their journeys and migrations.

What impelled them back and forth through this country of broken tablelands, rock formations, buttes and sparse water? We suppose that when drouth came they sought new places to grow their corn. Perhaps, also, they had not yet outgrown the urges of nomadic hunters. But it seems that there was something else. The myths and recollections of their descendents describe some of the journeys as fulfillments of prophecies, or as flights from dissension and evil, or as searches for places where the people could live in moral balance with one another and in spiritual harmony with the land around them. They valued the beauty of mountains, flowers, growing corn and goodness of heart. They were not unknowing of nature, for already they had mastered the arts of survival in a land whose character had been shaped by the desert. Yet their struggle for physical survival did not shut out their need for larger meanings and their quest for larger answers. Their religious feelings told them whether they were doing right or wrong. They sought to perceive what lay behind the world observed by the senses. They relied heavily on legends, visions, rituals and insight to guide them on their way. They also followed rumors and natural signs in their quest for moral achievement.

Man armed with myth, aware of his smallness among those awe-inspiring geological monuments that dramatized the antiquity of the land—what was it like for him in those days as he moved across the unspoiled and unconquered wilderness? Perhaps we can glimpse something of that experience in this narrative of the Grey Fox People and their journey to find a place whose name had been told to them, but whose location was only vaguely pointed out by signs in the sky. If you yourself happen to be of the Grey Fox Clan, do not suppose that this story must be about your own people, for different groups claimed the grey fox as their insignia, and some of them surely disappeared while passing across the wide valley of time. Yet it is a story, nevertheless, in which many clans of the Southwest may recognize some fragments of their traditions and their past.

H.C.

Now we sit in our kiva in a canyon whose name we never heard before we arrived. We take warmth from our fire. We discuss the meaning of life. When we were in our last village we could not foresee anything, only that there would be a journey. What we see now is only where we are and where we have been. Today, sitting here, we are like the body of a tadpole. Its tail thins off into the past. The tail is the story of where we have been and where we came from, and what has been told to us by our grandfathers and grandmothers. The body is here and the tail is there; but tomorrow and the days of our grandchildren, we cannot see them at all because they are invisible. In time to come our grandchildren will sit like this, and we will be the tail of the tadpole. Let us give them a good story to remember. We must remain in balance with everything around us, and in harmony with ourselves. Otherwise we will disappear in the wilderness.

—Limping Deer, to the Grey Fox old ones

TWO COYOTES MOVED ALONG A RIDGE ON THE FAR SIDE OF THE river. They paused briefly to look at the cluster of stone slab houses that cast long sunrise shadows, then trotted on. Small desert birds foraged in the brush for insects, and a crow gave its first call of the day. Limping Deer, sitting on the roof of his dwelling, arose stiffly and stretched his legs. He scanned the morning sky as he had been scanning the sky of the night, still searching for an unusual sign, but he saw nothing but two puffs of pinkish white cloud resting on the horizon. The cool of night was already returning to the house of Desert Spirit from which it had come. Limping Deer descended by ladder to the ground and walked slowly to the riverbank to gather an armful of driftwood for his fire. He returned, mounted again to the roof, and descended by a second ladder into his living quarters. His wife, White Moccasin, was at work with her firebow. She greeted him, saying, "How was the night?" Limping Deer dropped the firewood by the

1

hearth and brushed his grey hair back from his face with the back of his hand. He said: "The night did not say anything. It was merely night, like all other nights. Each star was in its place. Coyotes cried to the Desert Spirit. Nightbirds gave their calls. As the sunglow came, Morning Star shone brightly and then closed her eye. That is all."

When White Moccasin's fire was burning, she set her flat breadstone on its four corner stones and gave it time to heat. Then she spread corn batter over the smooth surface with her fingers. Almost instantly the batter turned into wafer-thin piki bread, which she quickly peeled off, rolled up and put aside to cool. Again she spread batter on the breadstone. Limping Deer sat cross-legged on the floor next to the blanket on which Falling Snow, his grandson, was beginning to stir. Limping Deer pulled gently on the boy's arm, saying, "Get up, young one. Leave your dreams behind. Birds are already gathering food. Grandmother Coyote is out hunting, and Grandfather Deer has taken his tribe to their grazing place. Let us eat piki so that we have strength to work in the field." Falling Snow sat up and rubbed lingering sleep from his eyes. Like his grandfather, he now watched White Moccasin's corn batter being transformed into rolls of piki. When the bread cooled, the three of them sat silently and ate their morning meal.

Then Limping Deer arose, took his hoeing stick and went out to tend his corn. As he loosened the earth around the stalks whose ears had not already been picked, he occasionally glanced to see if one or another of them had some unusual form that could convey a message to the people. He stopped to ponder over a mole hole. He studied bird and rabbit tracks among the stalks. He listened to the faint sound of the running river, and paused now and then to watch an eagle soaring over a distant butte behind which the sun rose in the late summer. An errant breeze blew through the field and he listened to the creaking of cornstalks as they rubbed against one another. But he saw nothing and heard nothing that answered the question, "Where shall the people go when they leave this settlement at Bend-of-the-Water?" The air became hot. Desert Spirit had opened the door of the room where warmth was stored. The desert sweltered. Limping Deer returned to the village and sat against a wall in the shade. He heard corn-grinding stones, and smelled the smoke of a pottery fire. He was dimly aware of the ache in his legs from bending in the field, and he remembered that once, long ago, his body had not complained about the work it had to do.

Limping Deer had lived through many corn harvests. His sun-darkened skin was deeply weathered, and his knuckles were swollen and twisted by the years. It seemed to him that life was merely a journey without any ending. Three times within his memory the people had gone out into the wilderness and come to places where they built new houses, made new grinding stones and baked new pottery, and planted their corn. The first time, in the days of his grandfather, it was brilliant colored lights in the sky that said, "Go in this direction and find what awaits you." The people left their village, travelling northwest, and settled at another site to plant their corn and rear their children. The second time, the sign was a large bear that walked through the village and went westward and disappeared. So the people abandoned their houses, their pots, their heavy stone tools and their fields and travelled to the west. Again they settled, this time on a high bluff. But moving sand blew across their fields and covered their corn, and a soaring hawk pointed their way into the wilderness once again. They journeyed once more to the west until they arrived at the Western River, and here, at the spot they named Bend-of-the-Water, they settled anew and cultivated their corn and beans.

It was now near the end of their fourth summer at Bend-of-the-Water. As the people began to harvest their corn they discovered that the ears which heretofore had been blue had changed color and become speckled, and they understood this to be a sign that they must prepare to resume their journey. But the direction of their migration was still a mystery, and they awaited the signal that would guide them. Meanwhile, they prepared. The men hunted. They dried strips of meat and stored them away. The women ground meal and made corn cakes that would not spoil. They repaired skin water bags and made new forehead straps for their carrying baskets. They hung strings of peppers to dry outside the houses from the protruding ends of roof rafters. A party of men had been sent to a certain place eight days to the south to get a new supply of salt.

Night after night the old ones of the village had taken turns holding vigil for some kind of sign. Limping Deer had resolved that if no sign was visible to him on his watch he would go into the wilderness and seek a vision. And so he now went to the round underground kiva in the center of the village, entered through the opening in the roof, and sat on the earthen floor. Soon other old ones, wise in the mysteries of life and the history of the people, came and joined him. Limping Deer put tobacco in his stone pipe and lighted it with an ember. He puffed several times, letting his thoughts fuse with the smoke, then he passed the pipe to the old one sitting next to him. Each man puffed in turn, and when the tobacco was burnt out Limping Deer said: "My brothers, my nephews, my children, we are in harmony with the spirit of the world. Let us begin." Yellow Corn took a buzzard feather from a storage place in the wall. He placed cold ashes on it and held it before Limping Deer's mouth. Limping Deer blew some of the ashes away. Yellow Corn went from man to man, each of whom blew on the feather until at last the ashes were gone. He said: "As these ashes have been blown away, so have our thoughts of malice, anger and selfish actions. Buzzard, the Cleansing One who has given us this feather, he has helped us to make our hearts clean. Thus we help Limping Deer in what he is about to do."

Limping Deer said, "Brother, children, nephews, today I am going out in search of an answer." One of the old ones answered: "May you succeed. Bring us your dream if you only dream. But if a true vision comes to you, bring us what you see." They chanted a prayer to Desert Spirit, and the force of their singing entered into Limping Deer and strengthened him. He put on the ceremonial waistcloth he himself had woven when he was a young man, and the deerskin moccasins he had made when he was initiated into the fraternity of the wise old ones. He put a few drops of water on the dried pigments placed before him, and with his forefinger he traced black lines across the bridge of his nose and his cheekbones. After that he made white braidlike marks on his legs. They sprinkled sacred cornmeal on his shoulders and put a single eagle feather in his hair. When this was done, he departed from the kiva.

Walking to the east, Limping Deer soon left the village behind. He went on until the sun began to slide into the west. He came to a tall split rock out of which a piñon tree was growing. There he sat down and began to empty his mind of all things. He closed his eyes and chanted a song imploring the Spirit of Creation to grant him a vision. He felt the heat of the afternoon sun, and below him he sensed the warmth of the Earth Mother. He heard the voices of Coyote and Wolf. Later, when the sun slid out of sight and darkness spread across the land, he heard Owl and other birds of the night. The stars opened their eyes, and he watched them follow their course. There was the cluster that people called the Suitor. Limping Deer clearly saw the young man chasing three maidens across the sky, and remembered his own youth. Not far away from the Suitor were the stars called Limping Deer, after which he had been named, and yet another group known as the Warriors. In time he closed his eyes, but he did not sleep, and he opened his eyes again just as the forehead of the sun became visible.

He began to hunger now, but most of all he thirsted. He knew that there could be no vision until he emptied himself of physical sensations, and so he struggled to put out of his mind thoughts of water, food and searing heat. His eyes rested on the piñon tree growing from the split rock. He admonished himself, saying, "Be like the piñon, which ignores heat, hunger and thirst. May the sun be soothing, may thirst comfort me." Again the sun disappeared in the west, and again it rose in the east, and at last, on the fourth morning, Limping Deer felt nothing. He saw the desert around him with his true eye. Whereas it had seemed empty of life when he first arrived, now he saw all kinds of living things there, going and coming. Under the piñon tree was a spring of water where the animals came to drink. Whereas when he first came the small butte to the south was nothing but arid rock, now it was covered with trees and flowers. As the animals spoke to one another, Limping Deer discovered that he understood their speech, and some of them greeted him as they passed. The sun no longer moved in its course across the sky, but remained motionless overhead. Everything was bathed in brightness.

A large grey fox came and stood before Limping Deer, looking at him as if he had something to tell him. At last the fox removed his animal skin and became a man. "Let us smoke the smoke of harmony," he said. He lighted a pipe, puffed on it, and handed it to Limping Deer. The two of them smoked, passing the pipe back and forth. Grey Fox said, "You have come, you have cleared your mind of man-thoughts, and now you see the world truly." Limping Deer answered, "Yes, uncle, it is so." Grey Fox said: "I have two things to tell your people. First, you will be known hereafter as my children, for I have adopted you. Second, the sign you are looking for will soon be seen in the sky." Limping Deer said, "I have heard. I will remember."

Grey Fox arose and put on his fox skin. He departed, and as he did so the brilliant light began to fade and soon the desert was in darkness. Once again there were the sounds of the night birds. Little by little Limping Deer became aware that his body was shivering. When the sun showed itself again he looked for all the living things he had seen, but they were not there. The spring was also gone, and the butte of flowers was once again nothing but barren rock. Limping Deer understood that the spirits of things as they really were had come to him. He arose with effort, for his legs were cramped and numb. His tongue was parched and swollen, his lips were cracked and flaked. It was only the power of his will that carried him slowly back to the village, and when he arrived there people came and walked him to the kiva. He descended the ladder into the kiva and drank a little water, and after that they washed the dust and sand from his skin. Lying on the earthen floor, he fell into a deep dreamless sleep.

Three old ones — Yellow Corn, Crying Wolf and Badger Boy — sat against the kiva wall and chanted while he slept. They chanted the story of the people, beginning at the beginning when humans emerged from the center of the earth:

> *"Ah-heh! Who are we? Where did we come from?*
> *The day the earth opened, we emerged.*
> *Ah-heh! The earth is our mother.*
> *Thus we were born.*
> *Father Sun cast his rays on our mother,*
> *And she swelled and gave birth to the people.*
> *Corn Spirit then gave us maize.*
> *Water Spirit gave us rain.*
> *Desert Spirit gave us secrets of the wilderness.*
> *Ah-heh! So it was that we began.*
> *We built our houses at Red Cliff.*
> *We lived there until Serpent Spirit spoke to us.*
> *Serpent Spirit said go forward to the Mesa of Flowers.*
> *We departed from Red Cliff not knowing which way to go.*
> *We settled again at Cottonwood Spring.*
> *How long we lived at Cottonwood Spring is not known,*
> *For we forgot Serpent Spirit's advice.*
> *Then the earth trembled and the cliffs fell,*
> *And we journeyed toward the setting sun*
> *And made our dwellings at Badger Spring.*
> *There we lived on until our corn changed color,*
> *And from Badger Spring we went northward*
> *Until we came to Canyon That Is Blue.*
> *There we lived on until Serpent Spirit came again,*
> *Saying, 'This is not the place of which I spoke.'*
> *And so we departed from Canyon That Is Blue."* . . .

The three old ones chanted until the song brought them to Bend-of-the-Water, then they fell silent for there was nothing more to recount. It was late evening when Limping Deer awoke. White Moccasin brought him food, and he ate. He said to the three old ones: "My brothers, my nephews. I was in the desert four days. And on the fourth day I saw the world with a true eye. The barren butte was in flower, a spring flowed where there had been only sand, and all our animal brothers were there. A great thing happened. Grey Fox Grandfather came. He took off his fox skin and we smoked together. Ay! He had something to say! Call the kiva brothers together. I will speak of what I saw, and they will test the truth of it."

Crying Wolf, who was the village caller, went from the kiva to find the men whose knowledge of things reached into the past. He stood on a high rock that rose among the dwellings and called out the names of those who were wanted. The old ones came out of their houses, entered the kiva and sat silently. They smoked, and then Limping Deer told them all that had happened. When he came to the end of his account, some of the kiva brothers questioned him about the world that had been revealed to his eyes. Had he truly seen these things, or had he merely imagined? What did Grey Fox Grandfather look like when he removed his fox skin? What language was spoken by the animals? Was it night or day in that true world of which he spoke? To each question, Limping Deer gave an answer. Sometimes he closed his eyes and was silent for a time as he sought to re-create the scene in his mind. In the end, all were satisfied with the reality of the vision. They agreed to regard themselves as children of the Grey Fox. But they said, "Still, we do not know what kind of a sign to look for, only that it will appear soon in the sky."

So they arranged for a sky watch, with each man taking his turn, some by day and some by night. Three days passed with nothing remarkable to note, only soaring hawks and puffs of clouds here and there. But when the sun set on the fourth day it was redder than usual, and it seemed to hover on the horizon a long time before it disappeared. Shortly after darkness came there was a shower of shooting stars, fiery white arrows flying northward. The people watched in wonder, knowing that this was the message for which they had waited so long. They went to their houses to make ready for the journey. The women filled their backpacks with cornmeal and dried meat, and filled their skin water bags. The young men sorted out the tools and weapons that they would carry. The old ones met in the kiva, where they chanted sacred songs and prayed until a certain constellation became visible through the entrance in the roof. Then they spent the remainder of the night making prayer feathers. When the grey false dawn arrived they placed the prayer feathers on a bowl of cornmeal and gave it to one of the village's fastest runners with instructions to place it at the site of the split rock and the piñon tree where Limping Deer had seen the world truly.

As the runner departed into the desert, Badger Boy, entrusted with recording the experiences of the people, went to the tall rock back of the village on which had been inscribed the details of their arrival at Bend-of-the-Water. With his flint point and palm hammer he incised the head of a fox. Below the fox head he cut a series of stars with flaming tails. And underneath these symbols he made a spiral of four complete turns, each representing a year, and at the end of the line he made a zigzag going north, showing the direction of the new migration. He returned to the kiva, saying, "It is done." After this the people waited for the runner to return from the desert. When at last he appeared over the eastern ridge, the people prepared to move out. The women helped one another place their heavy baskets on their backs and adjust the forehead straps. Babies were secured in their cradle boards. The men carried their hunting and fighting weapons, bags of tools and flint points and skins of water.

At last Limping Deer said: "My children, now we begin our new journey to the place called Mesa of Flowers. How far it is I cannot tell you. What we know is only what has been said by our fathers and our grandfathers. It was Serpent Spirit who told us of the place. He warned us not to forget. After the people settled at Cottonwood Spring life was good to them and they forgot their teachings. The old ones said over and over, 'It is time to continue the journey,' but the young said: 'Is it not good here? Why should we go on? Serpent Spirit, does he really exist? We have never seen him!' And finally the earth shook and the mountaintops fell and our village was destroyed. In this way Serpent Spirit spoke to us after a long silence, and we resumed our way. He gave us time to rest at Badger Spring, and again at Canyon That Is Blue, also at other places, and finally here at Bend-of-the-Water. Now the flaming arrows in the sky tell us that what we are looking for is to the north somewhere. Surely we are coming to the end of our journey. So let us have strong hearts. Let us begin."

The people departed from Bend-of-the-Water in a long line. They followed the riverbank until it veered to the west, then they moved north into the desert wilderness. The stone slab houses of the village stood deserted. Storage rooms within the houses still had ears of maize in them, and blackened cooking pots sat on the hearths. Heavy grinding stones lay where they had last been used. Standing atop the tall rock on which the record of the migration had been inscribed, a lone grey fox watched the people disappear among the northern buttes.

In the late afternoon of the first day, two scouts in advance of the main party came back to report that they had found a spring at the base of a small butte a short distance ahead. The people agreed that they would camp there for the night, and the scouts guided them to the place. There the backpacks were set down and the women began to prepare the evening meal. Water was dipped from the spring with small pitch-lined basket dippers. Meanwhile, Yellow Corn and Badger Boy walked along the base of the butte to see what it had to tell them. Badger Boy picked up a broken bit of pottery, saying, "Ah-heh! The Water People have been here!" He passed the potsherd to Yellow Corn, who examined it carefully. "Yes," Yellow Corn said, "here is the figure of a tadpole." Farther on they came to a cluster of crudely made houses, roofless and partially filled with drifting sand. Badger Boy's eyes turned to the rock wall against which the deserted hamlet huddled. At last they saw what he was looking for. "Here is where they made their mark," he said, pointing to weather-worn inscriptions partially hidden by a spreading cactus. He cut some of the cactus away with his flint knife. There was the sign of the frog, and to the side of it a series of short parallel lines. Next, a cloud symbol, and underneath it growing corn. Then a winding spiral, meaning arrival, and an unwinding spiral meaning departure. That was all.

Badger Boy said: "The Water Clan People camped here for a season. There were twenty of them. They grew corn, then they went on." The two men returned to where the others were resting. They said: "This is an old Water Clan village. They left their marks on the pots and the rocks. They rested here for a summer to replenish their corn. Where they were going, the signs do not say. Perhaps to the north or the west." Limping Deer reflected. He said: "Yes, it seems that we follow their trail. To arrive at this place they must have been going northward. Perhaps they also were seeking the Mesa of Flowers." Badger Boy said: "Many seasons have passed since they were here. The houses are drifted with sand and the signs on the rock are weathered."

As darkness fell, the people sat close to their fires, for Desert Spirit had opened the door of the room that held the cool winds. After they had eaten, Falling Snow said, "My grandfather." Limping Deer replied, "My grandson." Falling Snow said, "Grandfather, tell us about the Water Clan People."

Limping Deer sat with his eyes closed for a long while. The people knew he was setting his mind in order and discarding discordant thoughts, and they too remained silent. At last, his eyes still closed, Limping Deer sang a snatch of song. He opened his eyes, saying, "That is the beginning of the Water People's song. I heard it long ago, but the end of the song did not stay with me. The words were burned away by the heat of many desert summers. This much I know. The Water People came from a distant place in the south, beyond certain mountains and forests. Where did they come from in the beginning? It is not said in the song, I am sure of that."

Limping Deer paused, deep in thought. Then he went on: "I do not know if they came from the womb of the earth as we did. Yet as surely as the sun and the earth are the father and mother of all living creatures, so it must be for the Water People also. It is said that they came from somewhere in boats with houses built upon them. They lived a long time in their houseboats, until the winds brought them to the shore. From that place the Water People migrated to a certain canyon. There they settled and built a village. They lived on. Their corn, beans and squash grew well. They were not molested by enemies. There was harmony. Yet in time they came to regard their good life as a gift they had given to themselves. They forgot the ones who had created them and sent them on their sea voyage. They began to think of themselves as creators. They forgot that their corn was the offspring of the sun and the earth. The young began to ignore what the old ones remembered. They used the kiva for gambling instead of for sacred things, and aged people who were sick or crippled were left to find their own way to go on living."

Limping Deer closed his eyes again and meditated for a long time, until at last Falling Snow said, "My grandfather, what happened then to the Water People?" Still, for a while, Limping Deer did not continue. When at last he began to speak again it was as if he were seeing in the darkness what others could not see. "So it happened, it is said, that Water Serpent brought the village to an end. I cannot tell you if Water Serpent is the same as our Serpent Spirit in another form. But Water Serpent began to shake inside the earth, and he tore the underground rivers apart. The water poured out of the ground and washed the village away. Then Water Serpent came out and spoke. He said: 'You people have forgotten the meaning of life. You must leave this place where I have given you so much. Abandon it. It has become evil. Travel toward the star that does not move. You will live in the desert and again learn the meaning of life. Whenever you need corn, stop and plant. When you have harvested your corn go on again.' They said to Water Serpent: 'Where are we going? What is our destination?' And he answered: 'When the time comes, I will give you a signal. First, however, I want to learn what kind of people you are.'

"So the Water Clan People departed from their village. Like us, they have been travelling a long time. They have broken into small bands. They wander. But all are looking for the place where Water Serpent will tell them to settle. Perhaps they have already found it, I cannot say. Perhaps it is the same Mesa of Flowers that we are looking for, but I cannot say it is so. This is what I heard in my youth, and I tell it as I remember it. Only a learned man of the Water Clan can say how much of this story is true."

The people slept on the ground in their blankets. When morning came they refilled their skin water bags, took up their loads and resumed the journey. That day their scouts discovered an old shrine, a wind-hollowed rock in which a bowl and prayer feathers had been placed. The bowl was plain, without any markings on it, so they could not surmise who had left it there. After that they encountered no signs of human passage. The horizons were far away, and all the land around them seemed as if no humans had ever been there before. The only living things they saw that day were some eagles soaring so high that they seemed as small as swallows. That night when the people sat at their fires it was Yellow Corn who was asked to speak of eagles.

He began slowly, saying, "All creatures are our brothers. The bear, beneath his skin, is our brother. The fox also, and the coyote and the deer. The animals are closer than we are to the Spirit of the World. For this reason when we kill a deer we always say to it, 'I am sorry, brother, I do not want to do it. Be generous. Be forgiving, and when your spirit goes to the spirit world, take my prayer with you.' But the living eagle can rise high into the sky where no other creature can go, into the Endless Space which is the home of Sun and Moon. It is the eagle above all others who surely can carry our prayers to the Spirit of the World. It is for this reason that we make our prayer feathers of eagle down. Each tiny breast feather of the eagle is so precious that men are willing to undergo great dangers in climbing the cliffs to reach the nests of eagles. The outward form of the eagle is a deception. To understand what the eagle is, one must see him truly. As for what we see when we look at Eagle, that is not the spirit of Eagle. His spirit is not different from our own. We are a brotherhood. When he comes to us in a dream, Eagle speaks our language. This is not the mystery. The mystery is why, being brothers to one another, we look so different. It has been told by my uncles who were old when I was young that when an eagle and a man together see the real world truly they recognize that no differences exist between them.

"And so it was when our ancestors in the country of the Eastern River—from where we began our own migration—were on a long journey in the desert wilderness. Two children, a boy and a girl, were lost. They could not be found and were given up for dead. After hunting for the children many days, the people continued their journey. But the two children were not dead. They went here and there in the desert. They were hungry and thirsty. And a mother eagle watched them from above. She brought them food and placed it on the ground for them to eat. She went away and returned with water in her beak, from which they drank. Each day she came to feed them, as if they were her own true children. In time the children understood the real nature of the eagle. They saw that they and she were the same. And one day when the eagle flew away after feeding them, the children ran after her. Their arms became wings, their feet became talons, their mouths became beaks. Now they also were eagles, and they followed the mother eagle into the sky and lived with her there. So it is until now that if we capture a young eagle we carry it in a cradleboard as if he were a human child, for in the spirit world of which we are a part there is no difference between us."

The next morning before the journey was resumed one of the girls reported seeing a rabbit, and it was decided that there should be a hunt to replenish their meat supply. The young people went out with throwing sticks. They began in a line, those in the center going slowly, those on the ends moving more rapidly. In time the line became a shallow arc, and when someone called, "Bend the bow!" those in front went more rapidly yet, making the arc deep, as if an invisible hunter had drawn his bowstring. Gradually the two ends of the curve came together, making a circle. After that they all came together at the center, but they saw that they had caught nothing, so they began again at another place. This time they stirred up two rabbits, and the young hunters rained throwing sticks at them. One rabbit was felled, but the second broke through the circle with several boys in pursuit. The rabbit went into a hole beneath a large rock. One of the boys put his twist stick into the hole and twisted until the split ends became entangled in the rabbit's fur. When he pulled it out a struggling rabbit came with it. The hunt continued, but the game they sought was scarce, and when they returned to the camp they had only four rabbits to show for their efforts. It was not much. Limping Deer said: "We must have fresh meat. Let some hunters go on ahead of us to look for deer."

Three young men volunteered. They took their bows and, running at a fast lope, disappeared over some low hills that lay to the north. The main party continued its march, but it had to stop while the sun was still high in the western sky because a young woman was in childbirth. The people made camp at the foot of a small butte. Limping Deer was concerned about water, so scouts were sent to the west where some cottonwood trees had been seen. The baby was born, but the searchers for water did not return that night. When the sun was overhead the next day, they came holding up full water bags as a signal that they had found a spring. So instead of going north, the people went west to replenish their water. They rested by the spring that night, and the next morning they resumed the journey northward. Several days later they saw a thin column of smoke somewhat to the east of their course, and they made their way in that direction. They found their three hunters waiting for them with the carcass of a deer. They divided the meat, so that many families had a little of it, and fresh venison was eaten that night.

Afterwards the hunters were called on to tell the story of the killing of the deer. One of them said, "I could tell the story, but I leave it to my elder brother, Walking Bear." The second hunter said: "I too leave the telling to Walking Bear. If he does not tell it right, I will prompt him." So Walking Bear began, addressing himself at first to Limping Deer and the other old ones and then, as he became involved in the tale, turning his eyes to the others who filled the circle around the fire: "My father, my uncles, something happened when we went to seek a deer. If I tell it wrong, my brother hunters will speak and you will know if I tell falsely. If I said merely, 'We followed a deer and killed it,' that would be the way it usually is, and you would ask no questions. But it was not that way, because we think that witchcraft entered our lives. However, listen, you children of the Grey Fox, and judge this matter yourselves.

"The morning we began our hunt we went northward, as you saw. We went here and there, one way and another, seeking game tracks. We thought, 'Surely one does not catch deer in a place like this.' We sought growing trees, or green grass and a spring. We were discouraged. We said, 'Let us look for badger, or let us shoot a hawk, that is better than nothing.' Then in the distance we saw a small canyon.

We went there, thinking, 'Perhaps it is a place where small game lives.' As we approached we saw that the cliffs of the canyon were bluish-green, and that there was much grass growing in the valley between. Now we were encouraged. We thought, 'Yes, here we will have success.' We entered the canyon. We heard human voices. We saw two naked boys running in the grass playing stick ball. They hit the ball, they ran after it. We came to them, saying, 'Is there a village in the canyon?' They laughed at us. They said: 'There is no village. This is Grandmother's canyon. There is only Grandmother's house.' We said to them, 'We do not see any house.' They said, 'Over there, beyond the rocks that look like corn ears.'

"We went to the house. We called out. A voice answered: 'Come in! Come in!' We went up the ladder to the roof. We descended into the house. Old Grandmother was grinding corn. She was very old. She said: 'Sit down, rest a while. You must be tired.' We sat down. She said, 'How goes the hunting?' We said, 'Grandmother, how do you know we are hunters?' She said: 'You carry your bows in your hands, not slung on your backs. Also, no one but hunters ever find their way to this remote place.' We said: 'Grandmother, can you survive alone so far from other people? This is a hard desert around you.' She laughed and answered: 'Young men, when you are as old as I am you will know much more about the secrets of existence than you do now. Here I have everything I need. Those boys, my grandsons, find game for us whenever we need it. They collect firewood for our fire. But let us talk about such things later. First let us smoke.'

"She lighted her pipe, she smoked. She passed the pipe to us and we also smoked. Her tobacco was very strong. It made us feel weak, as if we were eagle down floating in the air. She said: 'Do not fear anything. I am not a witch.' We answered, 'No, Grandmother, we are comfortable, and the tobacco has brought us into harmony.' She asked us, 'Why are you here?' We answered: 'We are the Grey Fox People going northward to the Mesa of Flowers. The three of us were sent ahead to find game, but we have seen no deer or antelope in this country.' She said, 'Why are you looking for the Mesa of Flowers?' We answered: 'Our wise men have spoken of it. It will be the end of our migration. We were at Bend-of-the-Water, and shooting stars told us to come this way.' Grandmother said: 'Yes, others also have passed by here looking for the Mesa of Flowers. Some have reached it, but others were lost in the wilderness.' We asked, 'Grandmother, is the Mesa of Flowers really there in the north?' She answered: 'Yes, it is there. But it is a hard journey. Some of your old ones will not still be living when you reach it. You Grey Fox People, you should know that there are difficulties in your way. There are dangers. There are tribes ahead that are not friendly. They do not grow corn of their own, and if they become hungry they take what others have grown. To get what they want they are willing to make war. Also, there are sorcerers. They perform mystic deeds without concern for what is good or bad. They go unnoticed among the people causing dissension and bad hearts. At the Mesa of Flowers, there are people living there already, and no one can say if they will accept you.' She went on this way, telling us of dangers.

"Then we asked her, 'Grandmother, tell us where to find game in this country.' She answered with these words: 'Yes, when you leave the canyon go to the east. You will come to a small mound with piñon trees growing on it. Pass around the mound. Beyond it is a wash. Follow the wash to the north. In time you will arrive at a grove of cottonwoods. There, most certainly, you will find something.'

"We thanked Grandmother. We departed. As we left the canyon we saw the two boys still at play. We arrived at the mound and passed around it. We followed the wash to the cottonwood grove. Standing there as if he were waiting for us was this deer. We killed him. We apologized to his spirit. Then we brought the meat here to wait for you. That is all. If I have told it falsely, let my companions say what is wrong with my story." The two other hunters said, "As Walking Bear told it, that is the way it was."

The people reflected on what the hunters told them. They sensed the presence of a mystery. Yellow Corn said: "It is something to think about. But where was the witchcraft in it?" Walking Bear answered: "Why, I mentioned witchcraft because it seemed unnatural. There were many things that made us wonder. The old woman living this way in the wilderness—why should she do it unless some village had exiled her for sorcery? And the tobacco we smoked, it was not like any other tobacco. It was very strong. It had the power to make us listless. She spoke of dangers ahead of us. How could she know such things?" Limping Deer said: "But was there any evil? Did she cause any misfortune to lie on your trail? It seems that all she did was to tell you where to find game." Walking Bear answered: "Yes, my father, it seemed this way to me also. But is it not something to think about that the deer was waiting for us when we arrived at the grove, and that it did not run away but stood motionless until we killed it?"

"Yes, my son, it is something to think about," Limping Deer said.

"Where is the grove where you found the deer?" Walking Bear an-swered, "Not far, just a short running distance beyond the high ground there." Limping Deer and Yellow Corn went to the high ground and stood looking in the direction Walking Bear had indicated. When they returned, people asked them, "Did you see the cottonwood trees?" Yellow Corn replied: "No, we could not see them. Perhaps there is a haze in the air." Walking Bear protested, "Before we came down from the place where you were standing, we looked for the last time at the trees and we could see them clearly." Yellow Corn said: "My nephew, go and look again. Perhaps our eyes are growing dim with age." Walk-ing Bear ran to the high ground. He stood looking, and when he re-turned he said to Yellow Corn: "My uncle, I cannot see it now. It must be the haze, as you say. Perhaps the long afternoon shadows have thrown darkness over it."

That night the deer was divided, and as the people sat at their fires Limping Deer spoke to Badger Boy, saying, "Have you pondered over things?" Badger Boy answered: "Yes, I have thought about it. It could only have been Ancient Grandmother." Limping Deer addressed Yellow Corn with the same question, and he answered, "Yes, surely it was she." The other elders were queried, and they all gave the same answer. People began to gather around Limping Deer's fire. Falling Snow said, "My grandfather." And Limping Deer replied, "My grand-son." Falling Snow asked, "My grandfather, can you speak of Ancient Grandmother?" Limping Deer said: "Have you never heard of Spider Old Woman? She is the same. She has many names. We also call her Earth Old Woman, sometimes just Grandmother. It was she who helped the people after they came from the belly of the earth. The two young boys, those who always seem to be playing stick ball, they are also known by many names, but our people call them the Warriors." Falling Snow said, "I have heard of Spider Old Woman and the War-riors, but that was long ago at the beginning of things and the people of that time are dead." Limping Deer turned to Badger Boy, saying, "Let the young ones hear truly about Grandmother."

Badger Boy closed his eyes to see clearly what he was about to tell. At last he said: "It is true. Ancient Grandmother was there at the beginning when the people emerged from below. She spoke to the peo-ple and gave them guidance. She told the old ones how to put the sun and the moon in the sky. She sent us to the Eastern River, and there we settled. Our old ones have told us that when their fathers were at war, the Warriors came to help them. One carried lightning in his hand, the other held thunder, and with these weapons they destroyed our enemies. Earth Grandmother is called Spider Old Woman because she sometimes takes the form of a spider. You have seen the hole the spider makes in the ground. Down below, if one could enter so small a hole, a person would find Grandmother performing ceremonies in her kiva. Her kiva is deep in the earth because Grandmother is the Earth Spirit. Long before we emerged from down below she had many sons and daughters, and each of them was in charge of a particular thing. Corn Spirit, Water Spirit and Desert Spirit were some of her children. They live on, like Grandmother and the Warriors. We believe that Grandmother came here to help us. By now she may have descended into her kiva to rest until, somewhere, people are in need of help. Even in her kiva she works to give people the things they must have to live. The earth is our mother. It provides everything—corn, beans, peppers, clay for our pots, stones for our tools and the points of our weapons, plants from which we weave our cloth, reeds with which to make baskets, water to drink. As we came from the earth, so does everything that we know except the sunlight and the clouds. It is an old woman who provides for us, our Earth Grandmother. Perhaps we shall meet with her again some day. Meanwhile we shall make prayer feathers and leave them at the next spider hole we see as a mark of our gratitude for her help."

Limping Deer and Yellow Corn nodded their assent to what Badger Boy had said. But the youngest of the three hunters spoke, saying, "My uncle." Badger Boy replied, "My nephew." The hunter said: "About Grandmother I understand. But the boys, how can they be warriors? They are young, they run naked and play stick ball. What enemy would fear them?" Badger Boy answered: "My nephew, I do not wonder that it perplexes you. What we see when we look at a thing is only part of what is there. The heart of a thing is hidden from the eyes. The form of a person is only the shadow cast from within. The shadow cast by the Warriors is that of young children. We know that they can discard these outward appearances and reveal themselves in another form. Just as men can become bears, and bears men, so these grandsons of Earth Grandmother can be seen as boys at play or fierce men of war. In one form they are creators, in another form they are destroyers. As creators they made the buttes and mountains after the people emerged from the underworld. It was they who made the salt beds and turned marshes into dry land so that it could be walked upon. The desert is merely another aspect of the marsh. This is what the two boys saw when they looked around them in the wilderness. Young eyes see truly that one thing can also be another thing; that a companion can be an antelope, or an antelope a companion; that a mountain can be a hardened ball of mud thrown down by a giant. As children the Warriors saw what the world needed to make it more beautiful, and they created these things.

"It has been told to us," Badger Boy continued, "that once the Warriors also created people. They were living in a certain place with Grandmother, and they became lonely and yearned for companionship. So they went to their spring, and out of mud they made many small houses, and people as well. They made a complete miniature village there. They called their little human figures Reed People, after the reeds that grew by the water. Because their yearning for companionship was so great, and because the force of their thinking was so strong, the Reed People came alive and the village became real. So if you should ever meet a person of the Reed Clan, remember that it was the Warriors who created him. Like children, the Warriors see clearly what is just or unjust. If a strong enemy attacks a weak village, the children become angry. They transform themselves into something fearful to see. They have red and black war paint on their faces, eagle feathers in their hair, and flashing lights in their eyes. On their legs are rattles that give off fierce sounds, and in their hands they hold fiery bows. The elder Warrior hurls lightning and the younger dispatches thunder, and the enemy loses heart and flees. It seems to us that our hunters saw them, in their youthful form, in the canyon with the blue walls. It is something to remember."

There were exclamations of wonder when Badger Boy finished. People wanted to know still more about Grandmother and the Warriors, but Limping Deer looked into the star-filled sky and said: "It is late. See, the Suitor is already overhead. Tomorrow we must journey again, and who knows how it will be? So let us rest. Yet before we sleep, let us speak of Coyote." This was for the young ones, to give them peaceful thoughts for the night.

"We speak of Uncle Coyote, who has been in the world since the beginning, Coyote the inquisitive one who watches us from a distance. He was here when the people emerged from below. But before the people emerged, there were only animals in this land. The animals liked beauty around them, so they decorated the earth. They put streaks of color on the rocks, they made leaves for the trees, and sometimes they made a lake or a waterfall. They caused grass and flowers to

grow and put tassels on the corn. They made many things to put here
and there, not always knowing where they would place them. One day
they made small crystals like those we sometimes find on top of the
ground. They made a pile of them. Night came, they slept. Of all the
animals, only Coyote did not work at such things. But he always
watched the others from a distance, because he was curious.

"And so when the animals slept, Coyote came to examine their
work. He picked up a crystal and smelled it. 'It is not edible,' he said,
and he threw it away. He examined another. 'This is nothing,' he said,
throwing it farther than the first one. Every crystal he picked up he
found to be worthless. One by one he scattered them, throwing them
on the ground or into the air. When at last he was through throwing
the crystals he went away. But the crystals that Coyote had thrown into
the air, they went up into the sky and gave off light. It was our people
who put the sun and the moon into the sky after they came from the
center of the earth, but it is Coyote whom we must thank for the stars.
Those crystals that he placed there shine like fiery eyes in the night. So,
as we see, even a worthless person can give something to the world."
The children's faces were turned skyward as they contemplated the
great work of Coyote. Now the people moved slowly away from Limping Deer's fire. They went to their blankets and slept.

When daylight came, the people travelled again. The scouts went
ahead in the morning and returned in the evening. They told the people what the land looked like, whether they had seen signs of game,
and if there were any springs that they could count on. Many days
passed this way. One morning as the scouts were about to leave the
main party, Limping Deer saw the mute wishfulness in Falling Snow's
face. He said to Falling Snow, as if admonishing him, "Is it not time
for you to go ahead with the scouts? You are almost a man now." Falling Snow answered as if he had received a reprimand, "Yes, my grandfather, it is time." Limping Deer said: "Very well, go and learn. Let
nothing escape your eyes and ears. Listen to Red Sky and Young
Antelope, for they know much. Whatever they tell you to do, do it,
and I will hear about everything when you return." White Moccasin
put piki and dried corn pudding in a carrying bag for Falling Snow. He
took it and went to join the two men, who were already at the edge of
the camp waiting for him.

They looked at him silently for a moment, then began to run toward
the north. Falling Snow enjoyed the running. And if Red Sky and

Young Antelope had much to teach him, still they did not have to tell him how to run. They moved at an easy all-day pace, Red Sky in the lead, Young Antelope following, and Falling Snow in the rear. The boy had the urge to go faster, to show these men what running really was, but he knew it was not a game. He wanted to earn respect, and so he timed his strides with theirs.

They paused briefly at the crest of a tall dune from which they could see in all directions, and then they went on. As the sun moved higher into the sky Falling Snow's legs began to grow heavy. In the beginning he had felt as light as a bird, but now he had to exert himself to keep the pace. For the men, the running was nothing but stride after stride. Falling Snow began to understand the meaning of being a scout, but he did not allow his exertion to show in his face when, occasionally, Red Sky or Young Antelope looked back at him. His mouth grew dry but he did not reveal it.

At last, when they came to the upper rim of a high bluff overlooking a dry wash, Red Sky stopped and scanned the countryside. He looked closely at Falling Snow. He said, "Little brother, what have you seen since we left the camp?" Falling Snow answered: "Why, I saw nothing but unpeopled land. There were two coyotes, and an antelope grazed on a distant mound." Red Sky said: "Yes, but I saw eight coyotes, and there were three antelope, one on the mound and two below. You did not see the desert tortoise? We almost stepped on him. You did not notice the snake sunning on the rocks? The lizard trails in the dust? The gopher holes? The grey rabbit crouching in the brush?"

Falling Snow's spirits fell as he heard the gentle rebuke. He said, "I may have seen some of these things, but I didn't think they were important." Red Sky said: "When a man is scouting, everything is important. The safety of the people depends on him. Everything your eyes see and your ears hear must be gathered and stored in your mind, just as corn is stored away in the granary. When you need it, it will be there. You, your mind was on the running, thinking, 'I will show these big cousins of mine that I too can run.' Your eyes were too much on the trail. Forget your feet, they will go by themselves. We run not for the running but to see what dangers may lie ahead of the people." Falling Snow was not happy. He said: "Yes. I hear what you say. I understand." But that was not yet the end of it, for Young Antelope spoke, saying, "Little brother, can you tell us where we have been and where we are, counting each thing as a knot in a counting cord?" Falling Snow answered haltingly: "We went out of the camp northward. We passed a small field of cactus. We went between two buttes. We halted at the top of a tall dune. From there we went on, first running downhill, then uphill. There was a ridge in the west, and beyond it I saw the peak of a mountain."

"Yes," Young Antelope said, "such things we have seen, but many knots in your string are missing. Let us think now of what we saw from the crest of the dune. The sand and rocks stretched toward the place of the rising sun, and there were three small dunes in that direction. And in the direction of the setting sun, there were four small dunes clustered there like a family sitting around a cookpot. Thus we distinguished the tall dune on which we stood from other tall dunes. And beyond the dunes in the west there was a small valley along the edges of a wash that descended from higher ground to the north. At one place there was a little green and a tree was standing at the edge, meaning that one might find a spring there. And those buttes we passed, from where we stood on the dune we could see meandering threads of grey going to their tops, that is to say trails, but whether such trails were made by humans or animals we do not know. All such things we count as knots in a string so that when we return and the old ones ask us, 'How is the trail?' we can speak with knowledge." Falling Snow could answer only, "Yes, big brother, I have heard."

The scouts ate a little piki and moistened their mouths with water from their water bags. Falling Snow did likewise. Then they were running again toward the north, turning east or west to go around difficult ground when necessary. They came to a smooth dome-shaped boulder, and there they stopped and examined the ground. Red Sky said: "A worn trail. Perhaps there are people living nearby." Now they moved forward slowly. Falling Snow could scarcely see what the scouts discerned as a trail, but after a while he began to notice the slight depression and the faint polish left on the stones by wear. He was elated that he, also, could see the marks left by human feet in the wilderness. They came to a place where the trail passed through a split rock, and on the walls there they saw that people had written a record of their passage. There were symbols meaning clouds and rain, and underneath them was a growing cornstalk. A little beyond they found a large figure, whether monster or man they could not tell. In one hand he held a bow, in the other a jagged bolt of lightning. When they emerged from between the rock walls they moved cautiously, their eyes touching on even the smallest features of the landscape.

Red Sky stopped, saying, "There it is." Nestled at the foot of an eroded butte was a group of stone houses. A thin line of smoke mounted into the sky from a pottery fire, and they heard the faint sound of human voices. Red Sky said, "Let us find out who these people are and whether they are peaceful."

They went forward crouching, sometimes crawling, until they heard a cry from the top of the butte. They saw two men standing there waving to the people in the houses below. Young Antelope said: "They have discovered us from their guard post. Let us stay here to see what happens." Red Sky said, "Perhaps they will send a war party out." They waited, but they could not see what was going on in the village, so Red Sky suggested, "Let us go forward a little farther." They crept carefully to a rise of the ground, from where they were able to see the main trail to the settlement, and they saw a group of men with bows and lances coming toward them. Red Sky said: "They are eager to defend the village, or else they are warlike and do not have a heart for peace. Let us go back and tell the people. It is for them to decide what to do."

They went running southward again, loping with long strides. Falling Snow felt the ache of his legs, and he struggled to disguise his fast breathing. When the sun began to slide down behind a ridge in the west they came to a small cave eroded out of a cliffside. There they ate some of the dried corn pudding they carried in their knapsacks and lay down on the rocky floor. As he drifted into a sleep of exhaustion, Falling Snow heard Young Antelope say, "You run well, little brother." It filled his heart with gratitude.

It seemed that he had just closed his eyes when he felt Red Sky shaking him. The sun was not yet visible, but the sky was becoming light. Again they were running. Falling Snow's muscles were stiff, but his eyes roamed the landscape, taking everything in and storing it away like corn. Now he recognized features of the land mentioned by Young Antelope the day before, and he wondered how he could have missed them. As they passed over the large dune he saw clearly what was to the east and west. He recalled Young Antelope's words, "You run well, little brother," and they lightened the weight of his body. He was almost unaware of the running. They stopped only once to rest, and after that they did not stop again until they met the people coming through a small valley. Everyone crowded close around the scouts, sensing that something important had been found. Red Sky did the speaking.

He said, addressing Limping Deer but speaking loud enough for all to hear, "My father," and Limping Deer answered, "My son." Red Sky said: "We came to a village. How many houses, we could not tell, perhaps thirty, perhaps more. We could not see everything. Men at the guardpost above the village gave an alarm. A war party came out. We do not know what kind of people they are. Whether they wanted war or peace, we could not tell. We returned quickly to let you know what we saw." One of the old ones asked: "Was there nothing more? Were there any signs on the rocks?" Red Sky answered: "There were signs, but who knows who placed them there? We saw the markings meaning rain and corn, and there was also a monster holding lightning in his hand. That was all. There was no record signifying any particular clan." Another asked, "What was their language?" Red Sky said: "We did not hear it. We were too far away." Someone asked, "What was growing in their fields?" Red Sky said: "On our side of the butte there were no fields. We could not see anything growing." To the question, "Was there anything else to be seen?" Red Sky said, "Only the smoke from a pottery fire."

When there were no more questions to be asked, Limping Deer turned to Falling Snow, saying, "My grandson, you went, you came back. That is good." Young Antelope said: "He runs well, like a man. He has the heart of a scout." Limping Deer said again, "That is good."

The people continued the journey until darkness fell, and when they camped that night many of them gathered around Limping Deer's fire to talk about the village that lay ahead. Yellow Corn said: "We have heard from the old woman in the canyon that somewhere out there are sorcerers and other hostile people. Let us think of the old woman as Earth Grandmother, for surely it was she who spoke to our hunters. Let us think of her warning. Let us go slowly. When we arrive within sight of the village, let us stop and confer. We will learn what to do. If we sense that all is not well, we can turn westward and later on go north again." But someone objected, saying, "They have seen our scouts already. They know we are coming. So let us go westward now and avoid them altogether. For we are only a small people, and who knows how big they are?" A man said: "There was only a single pottery fire burning. It cannot be a large village." Red Sky answered: "Yes, only one fire, but there seemed to be many houses. We could not see everything. There may be dwellings on top of the butte as well."

At last Limping Deer said: "Let us sleep. Let us dream a little. Let us have good thoughts, strong hearts, and eyes that pierce the outward appearance of things. When we arise in the morning we shall know what to do." So the people returned to their fires and slept. But Limping

Deer, Yellow Corn, Badger Boy and some of the other old ones sat talking late into the night.

The sun came up sluggishly, and its first rays cast a reddish glow over the land. Desert Spirit had already called back the cool night air and sent out hot winds. Limping Deer spoke to the people as they prepared to leave the encampment. He said: "My children, the fiery arrows in the sky pointed our way for us. They did not say, 'Go this way, go that way,' they said to go north. We will turn aside only if we have to. Who lives in the village ahead we do not know. Perhaps they are good cousins. Let us find out. When we know who they are we shall know what to do. Let us think of those people the old ones tell us about. They went on a journey. They went north, they went south. They went east, they went west. They tried one direction, they tried another direction. The desert claimed them. They disappeared in the wilderness forever. But we have been told that we will find a peaceful life at the Mesa of Flowers. That is where we are going. So let us begin again and find our way to that place." So once more the people moved northward.

After they had crossed the large dune darkness came. They camped again, and went forward at the next rising of the sun. By midday they could see the eroded butte that contained the village. They found a small spring, and there they set down their loads. The men took their lances and bows and proceeded through the split rock. When they reached the high ground they saw a party of warriors astride the trail.

Yellow Corn called out: "Fear nothing, we are peaceful people. We are merely passing by." One of the village warriors called back, "Who are you and where do you come from?" Yellow Corn answered: "We come from the south, many days away, and then from the east, farther still. We are called the Grey Fox People. Who are you who live here?" The village man said: "We are mixed people. Some are Blue Fox and Arrow clans. Some are Antelope and Coyote clans. What do you want here at Red Rocks Place?" Yellow Corn answered: "We did not know of Red Rocks Place. Our scouts discovered your village, that is all. Where is your chief?" The man answered: "He is not here. He remains in the village." Yellow Corn said, "We want to sit with him and smoke." The man said: "Wait where you are, we will send a runner to tell him. If the chief says no, then you and your people must turn away."

The runner departed, the Grey Fox People waited. When the runner returned, two of the village warriors advanced, saying, "Are your bows unstrung?" Yellow Corn replied, "Yes, our bows are unstrung." The man said: "Very well. Our chief is called Long Arrow. He says, 'Let two of their old ones come and smoke.' " Yellow Corn said: "That is good. But how do we know what you will do with us once we are there? Leave two of your warriors here with our people as a pledge." The village spokesman said, "Yes, we will do it. Here are two young men. Here is Crow That Walks, he is Long Arrow's son. Here is Walking Buffalo, he is my nephew. They will stay. We mean no harm to you, and these young men are a pledge."

And so Yellow Corn and Limping Deer followed a party of the men into the village. They passed between rows of dwellings which, like those of the Grey Fox People, could be entered only from above. Women and children stood on the rooftops to watch. When they came to the central court, Limping Deer and Yellow Corn saw that there were two kivas, both with ladders protruding from their openings. They passed the first one, and when they stepped onto the roof of the second their guides said. "Our chief is waiting here."

From below they heard a voice calling: "Enter, do not hesitate. Let us meet." Limping Deer and Yellow Corn descended the ladder. The person who sat waiting for them in the kiva was an old one. He said, "Sit down, let us smoke together." He handed them a freshly lighted pipe. They smoked silently until the tobacco was consumed. Then Long Arrow said: "Cousins, let us speak of things. We see that you are not looking for war. Then way have you come?" Limping Deer replied: "We are on a journey, and our signs take us north. We did not know that your village was here. We came upon it unexpectedly. We thought: 'Surely the people who live in this place have much knowledge of this region, while we know very little.' We thought, 'These people appear to be peaceful. Should we not pause for a moment in our life's journey to exchange words with them?' That is why we are here. From your language we take you to be cousins. Your speech is somewhat different, yet we recognize everything. That is good. We think you may have come to this place, as we did, from the east."

Long Arrow said: "Yes, from the east and the south. It was in the time of my father that this village was settled. Once our people had other settlements in the south, but a drouth came and dried up our fields. So we departed from those places. Some of us went toward the Eastern River. Some went toward the Western River and beyond. Some came north. We were scattered. The Blue Fox Clan and the Arrow Clan came to Red Rocks Place. Later we were joined by people of the Antelope Clan and the Coyote Clan. Now when our sons and daughters are ready for wives or husbands they have a choice of three clans. We are in balance."

While they talked, a woman brought them fresh melons to eat. Then, after they had spoken of many things, Limping Deer asked: "Do you know of the place we are going to? It is called Mesa of Flowers. Our old ones told us that it is there we will complete our journey and make our final village." Long Arrow pondered. He said: "Yes, we have heard of such a place. It is far. We have never seen it: but it is said that flowers grow all around, even in winter. We have heard that others are already living there, the Bear Clan, the Bow Clan and the Flute Clan. Perhaps you are too late. They may not accept you." Limping Deer replied, "It does not matter if others are there already, for it was promised that everyone would live there in harmony and balance."

Long Arrow looked at the ground and was silent for a while, at last saying, "West of here, not too far, perhaps a half day's running, there is a valley with a stream. It is a good place. I saw it many times when I went hunting as a young man. Why don't you people settle there? We will get to know each other. Your young men may find wives here, and our young men can choose from among your daughters. In this way we can unite our families and both of us can flourish." Limping Deer said: "Our journey has been a long one, if we count our days from the beginning. It is not good to settle down knowing that our destination is still ahead of us. Yet I will speak to the people about it. Meanwhile we will rest a while at our camp. When we have talked about it in council, you and I will meet again." "Yes," Long Arrow said, "that is good. Let us smoke together many times. Let us make decisions with deliberation."

Limping Deer and Yellow Corn returned to where their party was waiting for them. The two young men from Red Rocks Place who had stayed to guarantee their safety, Crow That Walks and White Buffalo, rejoined their companions and turned back to the village. When the Grey Fox party arrived at their encampment, Limping Deer reported: "We met with the chief, Long Arrow, in his kiva and we smoked. The village is peaceful, it is not looking for war. Their young men came out thinking we might have had bad intentions, but they saw that we had peaceful thoughts. Now all is well between us. Let us camp here for a few days and recover our energy. Let us build up our shelters a little and sleep a few nights under cover. Meanwhile, Yellow Corn and I will discuss things in council."

So the people began to make lean-tos to cover them, and that night they sat around their fires later than usual because they knew they would not have to travel the next day. A circle of older men sat in council at a fire distant from the others. There Limping Deer and Yellow Corn reported in detail on their visit to the village and the conversation with Long Arrow. When they spoke of Long Arrow's description of the valley and stream to the west, and his suggestion that the Grey Fox People settle there, a warm debate was launched. Some thought the invitation should be considered, but others said: "What about the place where we were going? Again and again we said we were going to the Mesa of Flowers. Now some of us are saying, 'Let us rest like thistledown falling to the ground.' Is this the prophecy of our grandfathers?"

At last Limping Deer brought calm to the discussion, saying, "No one has said, 'Here we stay.' No one has decided anything. We merely consider the matter. Many have spoken their opinions one way or another way. Let us ponder on what we have heard and sort things out. When we have done this we will know the answers to our questions." On that note the council ended and the people slept.

The next morning Long Arrow and a party of village men came to the camp with corn and squash. Among them were some youths, including Crow That Walks and White Buffalo, who already had friends in the camp. The young men sat apart while the old ones talked, letting their eyes wander wherever girls were cooking or walking back and forth. The girls looked at the young men only furtively, and pretended not to be aware of them. Long Arrow also took note of the girls in the encampment. And before he departed he said to Limping Deer: "We have young men in our village who have no wives. You, also, are there no Grey Fox young men without wives, or young women without husbands?" And Limping Deer answered: "Our children are dear to us. Before we speak of such matters let us first learn more about one another." Long Arrow said: "Yes, there is much to know. We have many things to speak about. Tomorrow come again with some of your old ones. Your old ones and ours will smoke together. That is a beginning."

On the following day six elders of the Grey Fox People went to the village—Limping Deer, Yellow Corn who had medicine for curing, Crying Wolf who was the caller, Badger Boy who inscribed the people's history on the rocks, Yellow Bird who once had talked with Desert Spirit in a dream, and Still Water, the people's war chief who had special knowledge of snakes. They arrived at Long Arrow's kiva and heard him call from within, "Enter, enter and be welcome." They descended to where Long Arrow was sitting with elders of the village. The Grey Fox men sat down in a place reserved for them. Long Arrow filled his pipe and lighted it with an ember from a small fire. He puffed four times and passed the pipe to Limping Deer. Slowly the pipe moved around the circle. Because there were so many in the circle, the pipe had to be refilled and lighted again, and when at last it came back to Long Arrow he put it aside and said, "Cousins, tell us about your journey." The Grey Fox People told of their travelling and of the old village they had left behind in the south. They also spoke of their hunters and the encounter with Spider Old Woman. At last Yellow Corn said: "You, cousins, we want to hear who you are and where you came from. Perhaps long ago our trails crossed each other's."

Long Arrow said: "Yes, let me speak of where we came from and other such things. The origin of our people is this: In the beginning there was nothing in the world but land. There were trees, flowers and grass, but no humans or animals. The Sun Spirit was not happy that there were no people, and so also was the Earth Spirit. So the sun fertilized the earth, and there grew three giant reeds of a kind never seen since that day. Out of one reed when it was ripe there burst forth water, which flowed different ways and became lakes and rivers. Out of the second when it ripened there burst coyotes, badgers, deer, antelope, wolves, bears and all the other animals we know. From the third reed there came people. Because the waters arrived first, they are sacred to us. Because the animals came second, they are our elder brothers and sisters. We people were the last to come, therefore we have humility in everything. When we hunt we have to kill creatures who were here before us, and we always ask their pardon as we bend our bows. If Sun and Earth had given us another way we would not kill them at all. But if we have to make war on humans to defend ourselves we do not ask their pardon, because neither of us is elder to the other. Yet we honor bravery, and of the enemy that we kill, if they were courageous in battle we take their hearts and bury them, saying as we do so, 'You, brave heart, if you had been born among us you would be our brother.'"

Long Arrow paused and closed his eyes to put his thoughts in order. Then he said: "We here are of four clans, the Blue Fox, the Arrow, the Antelope and the Coyote. I am a Blue Fox person, so of that clan I am free to speak, but the stories of the others are their own, and only the old ones of those clans know the true story of all their years on earth. Yet how they came to get their names is known to all of us. The

Coyote Clan, now, in ancient times they were wandering in the wilderness, and while they were going from place to place a woman gave birth to a child. It was afflicted with some grief that could not be soothed, and it cried and would not give up its crying. It cried in the daytime when people were on their journey, and it cried at night when other children slept. Its mother nursed it often, and its older brothers and sisters brought it small toys to hold. One brought a blue feather, one a pine cone, and another carved a doll from a cottonwood root, but the child did not end its crying. One day the child's father discovered a coyote den with little ones in it. He brought a coyote puppy, and when the child grasped the creature's fur, instantly the crying came to an end. The child grew and the coyote grew and they played together as brothers. From this the people understood that they had a special relationship with coyotes, so they called themselves the Coyote Clan.

"The Antelope People, so their old ones say, took their name this way: They too were in the wilderness at that time. A child was born to a young girl who had no husband. She placed the baby in an empty coyote den and prayed to Desert Spirit to take care of it for her. Desert Spirit heard her prayer and sent Grandmother Coyote to find the child. Grandmother Coyote found it, but she was old and had no milk to give. So she carried the child to the antelope who were living not far away, saying, 'This small one was abandoned by the humans. Can no one here give it milk? I myself am too old.' And one antelope that had just given birth to a child of her own said, 'Yes, I have enough milk for two. I will take care of it.'

"Now, the people from whom the child had come moved on from place to place, but their corn did not grow well, and after four years they turned back and came again to where the child had been abandoned. The child's mother had been grieving for it, though because of her prayer to Desert Spirit she believed it to be still alive. So she went searching, and she came upon an antelope herd running in a valley. She saw a small boy running with the antelope, and she knew that the child was hers. But the antelope ran swiftly and she could not catch them. She went back and told her people about everything, and they came with her and saw the boy running with the antelope. He was one of them now. Because of this the people took the name Antelope Clan.

"The Arrow Clan, before it had a name, was wandering in the wilderness seeking a home. The people did not know which way to go. They followed many false signs that took them nowhere, until one day they found an ancient arrow lying on the earth where it had been uncovered by the wind. They saw that it was pointing eastward, and so they went that way until they came to a green valley, and there they built their first village. Thereafter they called themselves the Arrow Clan, and it is said that their old men living in a settlement distant from here preserve the ancient arrow along with other sacred things.

"I myself am Blue Fox Clan," Long Arrow said, "and what I tell you of this clan I heard from my mother and my aged uncle, so it is truly told. When the people born of the third great reed scattered, they went in many directions. Some went southward, and where they settled is not known to us. Some went north and west. We do not know where they came to rest, but it is said that they changed their language and their manner of dress, so that if we were to meet them today we would not know one another. Our own people travelled toward the sunrise. For numerous seasons we did not encounter any other humans, because it was a land that had been known only to our elder brothers, the animals. As we travelled we saw a blue fox travelling ahead of us. It seemed that he was leading us somewhere. At first the people laughed at the thought that such a thing could happen, for who ever heard of a fox leading people? But each morning we saw the blue fox in the east, running before us as if he were one of our scouts. The people became used to it. When they arose in the morning they looked for the blue fox, and he was always there.

"One day the blue fox turned away from the east and went north. The people began to argue. Some of the people said, 'Let us continue toward the sunrise sky and be rid of the fox.' Others said, 'The fox has been our guide. If he goes north now there must be a reason. Let us follow him.' We could not agree, and so our people split into two parts, one going eastward, one going north. Those who followed the blue fox were the ancient grandfathers and grandmothers of my own people. They followed the blue fox to a small valley with trees and grass at the foot of a great hill of rocks out of which a spring was flowing. People asked, 'Is this the place?' but no one knew the answer. They camped. When the sun rose in the morning, the blue fox was gone, he was not with us anymore, and so we understood that we were to stay there and build our settlement. We called the place Rock Spring, and we called ourselves the Blue Fox Clan because it was our elder brother, Blue Fox, who had revealed things to us."

When Long Arrow was finished speaking, Limping Deer said: "If I have called you cousin, it is because all men are cousins if they are not evil toward one another. Yet we are surely closer than cousins. The blue fox and the grey fox are brothers, and it was the grey fox that gave us our name. I will tell you now how we became the Grey Fox People." Limping Deer told of his vision in the desert, when the true world was revealed to him. Long Arrow exclaimed, "A-heh! Our clans are related!" Yellow Corn exclaimed, "A-heh! Our clans walk together!"

Then Yellow Bird of the Grey Fox delegation spoke. He said: "We have heard many things about the difficulties that lie ahead of us. We have heard that there are villages of sorcerers called Yayatu living out there. If you know of such people tell us something so that we may know how to deal with them." Long Arrow answered: "Yes, we know of the Yayatu. Here we call them Yayaponcha. Some of these people have a village north of here a few days' running. Only once have we seen them here at Red Rocks Place, when three of their men came to trade belts and leggings for tobacco. Although they seemed rough and unkempt, they did nothing to offend us. There are some who say the Yayaponcha practice sorcery. Others say that they are merely wild and uncivilized. Perhaps we are too young to know about such things. Yet my uncle, Sleeping Bear, has knowledge of the Yayaponcha, for his life has been long and he knows much about the comings and goings of people in this country. Let him speak if he cares to tell you anything."

Sleeping Bear, an old one with crippled legs and blind eyes, spoke in a high-pitched cracked voice, saying, "Where the Yayaponcha lived before they came to this country we do not know. But it is said that long ago they came from the underworld. When certain tribes and clans emerged from the belly of the earth and departed from the place of their birth, the opening was still there where they came out from below. In time a group of witches and wizards emerged at the same place, and they were called Yayaponcha, a word whose meaning I do not know. Because they were evil, no good spirit helped them and they did not know which way to go. So they wandered, first to the east, then to the south, then to the west, and then to the north. Wherever their corn grew they rested a while, but these people did not value serenity, and they moved one year to one place, one year to another in search of ways to put their evil talents to use. It is said that they came one time to the house of Earth Old Woman and asked for her help. But Earth Old Woman understood who they were, and she said to them: 'You speak as if you were of good heart, but I see that your hearts are bad. You have chosen evil ways, so who can help you? Go out, find your own trails. Wherever you go, people will reject you. You are alone in the world.'

"The Yayaponcha were angered to hear Earth Old Woman speak so, and they said, 'Let us kill her and be done with it.' But when they looked for her in the house she was not there, having turned into a spider and gone down into her kiva in the earth. So they went on. Sometimes they encountered humans, and by their medicine they turned people into dogs or performed other cruel acts. There were years when the Yayaponcha broke up into bands and went in different directions. It has been told, though I never heard it from anyone who saw it, that the Yayaponcha once came to a village with full storerooms of corn. The Yayaponcha made magic and caused the corn to fly from the storerooms into their own camp, after which they went away. It was told to my father by a person who had seen them that they can put life back into a body that is cold. It was told that every sixteeen days they would take one of their own people and throw him from a cliff, breaking his bones and causing him to die. When the body was cold they would carry it into their kiva, and after placing a blanket over it they would cause it to breathe again. Many such things were done by the Yayaponcha. They could point a finger at a distant mountain and cause writing to appear there.

"As for those Yayaponcha people living north of us, they speak a language somewhat like our own, but they have many strange words that we do not understand. We recognize them by this and also by their hair, which is not trimmed like our own but left to grow long and tangled. This is everything I know about these people, as it was told to one and passed on to another. I have invented nothing, but if others have invented I can not say. If I have said wrong, it is because I know no better, but our young people know even less." Yellow Bird said, "I thank you, brother, for sharing your knowledge of the Yayatu with us. They are surely something to avoid."

Then Long Arrow addressed Limping Deer, saying, "It is clear from what you tell us that the flaming arrows you saw in the sky meant that your people and mine were to meet. You have found us. Let us remain close together. Build your houses over there in the valley we spoke about. Let our children marry with one another. Together we will flourish. If raiders come to make war on us, we shall be strong and stand together. If you are short of corn, come and take some of ours. If our corn is not plentiful, you may give us a mouthful. We will share our medicine with you, and you with us. If we live together this way we shall have our own Mesa of Flowers." Limping Deer answered,

"What you say has power of meaning. We will discuss it with our people."

That night the Grey Fox People again talked about whether to continue their northward journey or to stay. One side of the argument was that they were still in the wilderness, that the flaming arrows told them to go north and that they should not stop until another sign came to them. The other side was that signs were good, but that there could not be a sign for everything — the Great Spirit intended men to use their judgment and make decisions of their own. The women and children were asleep, but the old ones and some of the young men as well sat debating the question far into the night.

When at last there was nothing more to be said one way or another, Yellow Corn spoke. He said: "We debate about two places, the Mesa of Flowers and the valley Long Arrow has offered us, but we have not seen either of them, so how can we know what we are talking about? Then let us continue our journey but go first to the valley to see it with our own eyes. When we know what it is like we can speak again, and if there is no agreement the old ones will meet in council and decide."

This is the way it was left, and when morning came Limping Deer and Badger Boy went to the village to let Long Arrow know what the people were going to do. In the afternoon the village held a dance for the Grey Fox People. The villagers gave out presents — melons, baskets, ears of corn, bits of coral and other things. The young people gathered in groups of their own, exchanging banter and jokes, and they thought such things as "That girl would make an attractive wife," or, "If that boy knows anything about work he would be a good husband." Late that night the Grey Fox People returned to their camp and slept. In the morning, long before the forehead of the sun was visible, they took up their loads and resumed their journey, this time travelling west.

It was only part of a day's running, but the people could not go any faster than the old ones could walk, so they did not arrive at the valley that day. Late in the afternoon of the next day Red Sky and Walking Bear, who had been sent ahead to scout, came with the news that the place they were looking for was only a short distance west. It was green with grass and trees and there was a running stream, just as Long Arrow had described it. The people hurried forward until they came to the rim of a shallow canyon, from where they could see the valley below, half of it already in shadow because of the setting sun. The scouts had already found a place to descend and they led the people down.

At the floor of the canyon it was now getting dark, so they camped. When the light returned in the morning, they stood silently for a while looking at things, and when they spoke, except for the children, their voices were muted. The land they saw sheltered between the cliffs of the canyon was fertile and green. They picked up their loads and crossed to the far canyon wall. There Limping Deer said: "My children, let us camp here where we are protected on the west side. Let the men explore everything so that we shall know how it is in this place." The young men took their bows and set out, some in one direction, some in another. Falling Snow went alone, following the stream to the lower end of the valley. He saw no sign whatever of people, though he discovered a badger hole and an abandoned coyote den. When he returned to the camp others also were coming back. Young Antelope was the last, for he had gone out running and travelled a long distance. Most of the young men agreed on what they had seen, saying, "It is a fine valley. Our corn will grow well here." Some had gone up the western cliff, and they said the clifftop would be a good place for a guardpost, for from the point directly above the encampment it was possible to see in all directions.

Badger Boy sat without saying anything. At last Limping Deer said to him: "My brother, there is something that distresses your heart. If you wish to speak we will listen." Badger Boy said: "Very well, hear what I see when I look around me. I see a valley with plenty of water. I see many cornfields and plentiful crops. I see people becoming accustomed to much of everything and not wanting to leave. I also see Serpent Spirit observing us, saying, 'Those people to whom I gave a way of life and a place to settle, they tired of the journey. They found a place in the wilderness with grass, and so they remained there instead of going on. The hearts of these people are not good. I will no longer guide them, and they will discover what they have thrown away.' This is what I see, and my heart feels sad."

The people were troubled to hear this from Badger Boy. But Yellow Corn spoke, saying, "My brother, we have stopped at many places, and now we merely stop at another. We promised to see what is here so that we should know what to do. I have not yet heard Crying Wolf, our caller, proclaim that a decision has been made. Later we will smoke and purify our thoughts. We will speak in harmony with one another and learn one another's minds. Only then can we say how it will be."

And so there was no more talk of going or staying until, at last, they sat around their night fires.

Then the old ones and all those who shared in the council gathered in one place and did what they would have done in a kiva. They purified themselves with a buzzard feather, chanted the song that told of their beginnings and their migrations, and harmonized their spirits with smoke. Each man had something to say about whether to go or to stay. Among the old ones, only Badger Boy said they must continue the northward journey. He said: "We people were meant for a hard land where others find life too difficult. In such a land strangers will not encroach on us, and raiding parties will not seek us out. Yes, the corn will grow well here and we will fill our storage bins with ease. Thus the people will not work hard anymore. They will forget where they came from and what the meaning of life is. They will entertain themselves with much gambling and with wives and husbands belonging to others. Children will grow up thinking, 'So this is the meaning of life.' Because food is plentiful, young ones will say to the old, 'You worn-out people, take care of yourselves, go and take what you want.' To strangers it will be said, 'We do not have to greet you with food, for there is plenty everywhere.' I cannot live in such a place, for such things have happened in the past and we should not forget them. Therefore I will not stay here. I and my people are looking for the Mesa of Flowers. That is why we began the journey. We will continue until we have reached the place the flaming arrows pointed out to us."

Yellow Corn responded, saying, "My brother, let us see things as they are. Yes, this valley has grass, it has a stream. But it is not a place where we will not have to work hard. Are we faithful to what the Serpent Spirit told us to do only if we have no moisture in the ground to make our corn and beans grow? Only if our crops are parched and the people go hungry? When we came into this world from below it was not said that we would have to die to be faithful. Will the Great Spirit punish us for feeding our children and taking care of our sick? You and I have lived many years, and some of our brothers who sit here with us are no longer hunters. They have travelled much in their lifetime. They have grown corn season after season and their fingers are gnarled. Now perhaps it is a time for them to rest. If the people settle here for a while and build strong houses, it does not have to be for as long as the sun shines. When we need to go on to another place a sign will tell us and we will know what to do. This is what is in my heart."

Badger Boy said: "My brother, I have known you since we were both young men. Your heart is good. But my heart tells me we should not remain in this place. Let us remember that the corn that was given to us in the beginning of things is not like other corn. It is meant to grow in land where other corn will not survive. Our corn is a messenger and a guide, it tells us where to live. If we go too far north where the summers are too short, the corn does not mature and we know that we have to turn back. If one looks at the roots of the corn that others grow, we see a few strands coming out at the bottom of the stalk. But our corn is meant to be planted deep in the sand, and its roots grow out one above the other to drink all the moisture from parched ground. It tells us what kind of country we must live in. The country meant for us is not here. Therefore I will not plant my corn seed in this place."

When the argument grew too warm, Limping Deer interceded, saying, "My brothers, my children, we have done much talking. Let us leave it for now. We will hold council again. Meanwhile let us remain here a few days more to give us time to see the issue clearly." And so the matter of whether to go or stay did not come to the ground but remained floating like a thistle seed in the wind.

On the following day, men whose families were short of meat went hunting, and Limping Deer arranged for Falling Snow to accompany Red Sky and Young Antelope. They went north in the direction of the running stream, and at the end of the canyon where the land spread out on both sides and turned color from green to brown they found deer tracks. Red Sky and Young Antelope followed the tracks, instructing Falling Snow to continue in the direction of the running water to see if there were signs of game farther on. The day was still young, and Falling Snow was eager to find a deer of his own. He looked at the ground for tracks and at the land around him for anything that moved. Once he discovered deer droppings, but they were old. He went on, determined to bring something back no matter how insignificant, a groundhog perhaps. In time the stream withered and disappeared into the earth. The sun had not yet reached the crest of the sky, so Falling Snow went farther into the unknown country, but there was no living thing to be seen except an occasional hawk soaring overhead. At last he knew he must not go any farther if he was to get back to the encampment by dark, and he sat in the shade of a large boulder to rest. His mind dreamed a little, thinking that he would soon have a wife and a house of his own. Would the people have reached the Mesa of Flowers by then, or would they still be travelling in the wilderness? Well, even if there was no village, still he would have a wife and the sky would be their roof.

He became alert. He did not actually see anything, but he sensed movement among the rocks. He raised himself silently to one knee, placed an arrow in his bow and waited. He heard nothing but the blood pulsing through his ears. At last, through the corner of his eye, he saw a slight movement, perhaps a lizard scurrying, or a bird. After that there was nothing to catch his attention until a human figure rose up from behind a pile of jagged stone and stood looking at him. At first the figure seemed to have no age. Then Falling Snow saw that it was a youth with red hunting paint obscuring the features of his face. Like Falling Snow, he held a hunting bow, but there was no arrow in it, and so Falling Snow put his weapon down, saying, "Ha'u." The stranger replied, "Ha'u." Neither of them spoke for a moment while they examined each other. The stranger was naked except for his face paint, a loincloth and simple anklets made of grass cord. His hair was long and hung in disarray over his shoulders and down his back.

Finally Falling Snow said: "I saw you move. I thought there was game there, what is why I raised my bow." The stranger answered, "I also thought you were something to hunt, that is why I remained quiet so long." Again they were silent, until the stranger said, "You have a good bow." Falling Snow answered, "Yellow Corn, one of our old ones, made it for me." The young man said, "I hunt here often, and never before have I met anyone." Falling Snow said: "My people have just arrived. We are staying back in the canyon." The young man said: "I did not know it. What people are you?" Falling Snow answered: "The Grey Fox People. We come from the south." The youth said again, still observing the way Falling Snow was dressed, "I did not know it." Falling Snow said: "I did not find any game. That is why I came this far. Is there anything here to hunt?" The youth answered: "Yes, sometimes there are desert deer, small ones, but they move with the seasons. Now there are not very many because they are going to the western hills where there is more grass. Not long ago there was rain and the grass grew up, but now it is gone. The deer have eaten it." After a pause he said: "The canyon where your people are camping, it is sacred to us and so we do not hunt in that place. Up above on the western cliff we have a shrine."

Falling Snow could not restrain his question, even though he had already surmised an answer. "What people are you?" The youth answered, "Yaya. We have a village a day's running to the north." Falling Snow's heart beat a little faster as he asked, "Yaya, is that the same as Yayatu and Yayaponcha?" The young man assented with a motion of his head, adding, "We ourselves say Yaya." Falling Snow waited for some sign that the Yaya would bewitch him, but he did not perceive anything. After a while he asked, "By what name do people know you?" And the Yaya answered, "Elk Horn."

Now the two of them were sitting together in the shade of the boulder. Little by little Falling Snow's fear of being bewitched fell away. Some of Elk Horn's words were strange to him, but most of his speech was familiar to the Grey Fox People. Elk Horn said: "Since we are both looking for game, let us hunt together. I know a spring where the deer sometimes go for water. We might find something there." Falling Snow looked at the sun before he answered, "I must begin to return to the canyon or the sky will be dark before I get there." Elk Horn said: "Do you go out only for one day when you hunt? Among our people we do not return until we have found game." Falling Snow said, "Among our people too. Let us hunt together."

So the two of them went to the spring known to Elk Horn, but they saw no deer there, only footprints and old droppings. By this time the sun was low in the sky. Elk Horn said, "There is a small cave over there where we can shelter." They went to the cave, and as the sky turned dark and Evening Star opened her eye they sat and ate. Falling Snow had only a little piki, but Elk Horn shared his dried meat.

He said: "Our village has two hunting dogs. Once we had four, but two of them were killed by bears. One belongs to my uncle, but he follows me sometimes. My uncle says: 'This dog, he is mine. No one else is to use him.' But if the dog follows me and catches the scent of game, can I help it?" They laughed. Falling Snow said: "In our village we have no dogs. Once we had some, but it is said they were killed by Tinneh hunters and eaten. If our village had dogs now it would make it easier to find game."

Elk Horn said: "There was a man in our village who wanted a dog, but he never found one. So he caught a coyote cub and raised it, thinking he could teach it to hunt. When he went out for game one day he took the coyote with him. The coyote put his nose to the ground and found a scent. The man followed him. The coyote went faster and faster, and the man was running to keep him in sight. All morning they were running and the man was getting tired. But he said, 'That coyote is on to something, I will keep going.' They went far. The coyote still had his nose to the ground. The man's bones ached and he began to slow down. At last he had to stop. The coyote went over a hill. That was the last he was seen, and the man had a long journey home without any game. Since then no one has tried to use a coyote for a hunting dog. Everyone remembers it. If a person insists on doing something foolish, people say, 'Never mind, he is hunting with a coyote.'"

When they were through speaking of coyotes, Elk Horn said, "Your cotton sash, was it woven by your mother or your grandmother?" Falling Snow said, "No, by my grandfather." Elk Horn laughed, saying: "Are you teasing me? Surely you meant to say your grandmother?" "No," Falling Snow said, "our women make pots and baskets but they do not weave." Elk Horn seemed astonished. He said, "You mean that the men do the weaving?" Falling Snow said: "Yes, I thought it was that way everywhere. I never heard that women weave." Elk Horn said, "It is natural for women to weave and spin cotton, just as it is natural for men to hunt." Falling Snow answered, "Well, among our people it is natural for men to spin and weave." He was not certain whether Elk Horn looked down on men who did such things. They went on discussing the ways in which the Yayatu and the Grey Fox differed, until sleep overtook them.

In the morning they retraced their steps to the rocks where they had met. There they parted, Elk Horn saying, "Let us hunt together again, cousin," and Falling Snow answering, "Yes, cousin, let us hunt together again." On the way back to the canyon Falling Snow saw movement at the foot of a low hill, and there he cornered a marmot and killed it. A little beyond the hill he discovered two turkeys and killed one of them. With this game he returned to the encampment. White Moccasin said: "Why did you not come back yesterday? Red Sky and Young Antelope returned. We worried." Limping Deer looked at him closely, and at the game he had brought. He said, "Where did you go and what did you see?" Falling Snow spoke of how he had parted from the two hunters. "When we parted they said nothing about meeting again. They said, 'Go that way, see what you can find.' I could not find anything, I went on. I came to a certain place and rested there, seeing that the sun was high." Until that moment he had not known whether he would mention Elk Horn, but now he passed over the encounter as if it had not happened. "And while I was resting I said, 'Among our people a hunter returns only when he has found game.' I went on. I came to a spring, and there were deer tracks there but no deer. I slept in a cave. This morning as I came toward the canyon I found the marmot and the turkey." Limping Deer said: "It is good. Young Antelope and Red Sky brought a small deer. Our families are fortunate." Young Antelope came to where they were talking. He said: "You are back. That is good. We thought perhaps you had been eaten by the Yayatu."

Falling Snow's heart was not in harmony. He should have told of his meeting with Elk Horn. But Elk Horn did not have the attributes that people associated with the Yayatu. Falling Snow had seen only a young hunter who shared his food. He thought: "If I say he was not an evil person they will think, 'A-heh! The boy does not know a witch when he sees one.' They will say Elk Horn was sent out merely to scout our camp. Yet my grandfather always says a person truly knows who a man is by looking into his eyes. I do not know about the other Yayatu, but Elk Horn is not a sorcerer. He is my friend." So he resolved not to say anything more about it for the time being.

However, he spoke to Limping Deer about weaving. He said, "My grandfather, I have heard that among some people only women weave, not men." Limping Deer answered, "Yes, my grandson, it is so." Falling Snow said, "Who, then, should be doing it, the men or the women?" Limping Deer smiled. He said: "Among those whose women do the weaving, it is a woman's affair. Among those whose men do the weaving, it is a man's affair."

Falling Snow would not leave the matter there. He said: "My grandfather, I have heard that it is natural for women to weave and for men to hunt. Is it true?" Limping Deer answered: "Let us look at the question closely. Among the Utaheh and the Tinneh it is the women who weave, because for them weaving is a thing of the household, like preparing food or bringing water from the spring. The woman is like the earth, all good things come from her. She feeds us, she warms us, she comforts us. She is the keeper of the home. But from the distant days of our ancient ancestors, our men have been the keepers of our ceremonies. It is the man who does what is necessary to communicate with Desert Spirit. It is he who makes the prayer feathers. It is he who performs the purification rituals. With our people, weaving is prayer. Weaving is the act of bringing together all the forces of life. Each thread is a supplication. When I made your waist sash for you, I wove prayers into it for your life to be long and worthwhile. If a man makes a blanket for his daughter, the threads between threads are prayers for her fertility and happiness. At the ends of the blanket where the weaving is loose, the openwork is a supplication for rain to penetrate and water our fields. So you see that a blanket is more than a blanket. It is made of cotton and it is made of ritual, and that is why among the Grey Fox People the men do the weaving." When Limping Deer became silent, Falling Snow said: "My grandfather, I did not know it. I also want to weave." And Limping Deer answered, "Yes, when your time comes you will weave."

It was the fourth night at the encampment. There was quiet tension, because on this night a decision would be made. Men were terse or altogether silent, and the women spoke in low voices to the children. When the eating was finished, Crying Wolf went from fire to fire calling the old ones to join a council at the far end of the camp. The Grey Fox elders and others who were heads of families went to the designated place and sat in a circle.

When they were all assembled, Limping Deer said, "My nephews, my children, let us purify ourselves so that we may speak in harmony." They smoked. Then Limping Deer said: "We have had time to think. We have considered everything. Sometimes we have argued with divided hearts about this matter. Yet surely the Grey Fox People can act together. We have seen that this is a good valley. If we continue to the north, winter will come before we arrive at the Mesa of Flowers. It will be hard on the children and the sick to be without shelters. Who knows if we will be able to find enough game to keep us alive? Will we have enough bear fat to treat our wounds and sores? It is said by some that we should not consider such things because we have been sent on our journey by Serpent Spirit. Yet what good will it do to starve and die on the way? Yes, we saw flaming arrows in the sky, but all they said to us was to go northward. We have come northward and we have found good cousins at Red Rocks Place. I have pondered much on what we ought to do. It seems to me that if this place was not intended for us we shall know it later on and continue our journey. Meanwhile, we have a place of good shelter and moist fields to plant. This is where my pondering has lead me, and I will speak no more. It is for you to choose."

Other old ones spoke and no one disagreed with Limping Deer until Badger Boy's turn came. He said: "My brothers, my nephews, I have heard you. My people and I have considered all the things you are saying. But when we left Bend-of-the-Water we followed a sign that pointed the way to the Mesa of Flowers. We knew then that somewhere in the wilderness we would meet other people, good or evil. We did not say, 'The first friendly valley we come to, we will settle there.' We said, 'We go out to find the Mesa of Flowers.' We know of other people who were not steadfast. They went one way and settled for a while, another way and settled for a while, and they did not flourish. Some of them even lost their own language and began to speak the tongues of strangers. They forgot their purpose, and so they were truly lost. They vanished and were never heard of again. This is not the way for us. Let us not forget who we are."

No one replied to Badger Boy, so he spoke again, saying, "Now I too have said everything. My words have come to an end. The council will not hear from me again. Tomorrow my family will leave. Whoever wishes to come with us, let them come. Whoever wishes to stay, let them stay." Badger Boy arose and left the gathering.

There was no more speaking in the council. The men arose and went to their fires. They spoke in low voices. There was sadness in the camp and a vague foreboding. When morning came, Badger Boy's party prepared to move out. There were ten persons in his family, and another family of seven joined them. Badger Boy waited for more, but none came. At last he gave the signal for them to begin, and as the people departed he turned to those who stood there to see them go, saying, "We shall learn now who are the true Grey Fox People." Badger Boy's followers went through the canyon along the stream, and after they passed over a small ridge they were seen no more.

Limping Deer said: "My children, what has happened is sad, for our brothers, sisters and friends have chosen to leave us. But do not be downhearted, because somewhere we will all meet again. Now we have work to do. Let us now make strong houses to protect us when winter comes." And so the people began, some saying, "I will build here," and others saying, "I will build there." Limping Deer said: "Let us be thoughtful about how we do things. Put your houses near the canyon wall and build in the manner of our old village. Where the great flat rock is, that will be our courtyard, and next to it we will build our kiva later on. On the edge of the cliff above, there we will have a guardpost."

The people began to search for flat stones for their walls. For some days housebuilding was everyone's preoccupation. Shalelike rock was pried out of the cliffside and, with the help of forehead straps, carried to the building sites. There women and children sorted out the pieces according to size. Wherever the houses abutted on one another, the families on each side shared the labor of the common wall. And while this was going on, some men went out in search of trees from which roof beams could be cut. The trees in the valley were too far from the camp, so the tree hunters went to the top of the cliff instead. There they cut their beams, trimmed them and threw them over the cliffside.

Falling Snow provided the timbers for the house that Limping Deer and White Moccasin were building. The trees he selected were some distance from the cliff's edge, and when he had dragged his timbers and thrown them over the side he was tired. He rested a while and ate a little piki. Before descending, he wandered a little to the north, and at a place where many large boulders formed a kind of mound he found the Yayatu shrine. He became troubled, remembering that he had not told Limping Deer about meeting Elk Horn. It became clear to him that the Yayatu now knew that the Grey Fox People were in the valley but the Grey Fox People knew nothing of the Yayatu. The Grey Fox People had been weakened by the departure of Badger Boy's party, and Falling Snow saw that his silence could be a danger to the village.

That night as they sat by their fire he said, "My grandfather," and Limping Deer answered, "My grandson." Falling Snow began haltingly. He said, "Advise me. When a thing is said of something we do not know, is it said truly?" Limping Deer looked closely at Falling Snow's face before speaking. He said, "My grandson, what are you thinking about?" Falling Snow said: "I am thinking of the Mesa of Flowers. Does such a place really exist? We have never seen it. No one has seen it, yet we speak of it. How do we know it is true?" Limping Deer meditated with his eyes closed, then he answered: "My grandson, in our hearts we feel that it is somewhere, just as our old ones spoke of it. Have we not heard from Long Arrow that other people have already found it? Therefore it must be there." Falling Snow said, "But Long Arrow himself did not see it."

Again Limping Deer meditated. He said: "No, he did not see it with his eyes, but his heart told him. What is true cannot always be seen with the eyes. Let us say we are hunting. The night falls, and we are in the wilderness. We sit at our fire and we see each other. But beyond the light of our fire there are other things. There is a hill, there is a mountain, there are clouds, there are trees, there are deer and antelope. We look at one another across our fire and you tell me there is nothing out there because nothing can be seen. We argue. You say, 'The mountain, the clouds, the trees and the animals were there when it was light, but now they must have gone away because they are invisible.' Experience teaches us not to think in this manner. There are true things seen and true things unseen. We speak of Desert Spirit, yet we do not see him. We speak of Earth Old Woman, yet few of us have met her.

"Let us approach the matter another way. The old ones tell us our first settlement after we emerged from the earth was at Red Cliff. Shall we say that none of us now alive ever saw Red Cliff and that, therefore, it never existed? Surely we know that somewhere, somewhere, our people had a village, the first village. Our hearts tell us so. And if we argue that it was not Red Cliff but Grey Cliff we are not getting anywhere. What is in the night is unseen. What is in the past is only dimly remembered. What is yet to come, we cannot see it but it is there. Perhaps in ancient days the Mesa of Flowers was not really there. Yet because so many believe it to be, by the force of their singing about it the Mesa of Flowers will one day appear to us."

Falling Snow said: "My grandfather, I hear what you say. The Mesa of Flowers I understand. But if we speak of something smaller, is it the same? Let us say we hear that the people of such-and-such a clan are good or evil. Because we have heard of it, is it therefore true?" And Limping Deer replied: "A-heh, so now we are talking about people. Whatever we hear of a man or a clan we put in our minds for another day. Let us say that a man is spoken ill of. Perhaps there is a good reason, or perhaps there are those who want to destroy him with words. Whatever is said, it rests on those who say it just as it rests on the person they condemn. How do we truly know what a person is or what is in his heart? We sit with him, smoking or not smoking. We look at one another. His eyes tell us something. His heart speaks through his eyes. His hands speak, his whole body speaks, even though his voice is silent. We sense that he is in harmony with himself. We know that he is not a carrier of evil. If a man has evil thoughts, his eyes reveal it. If this man lives in a distant place and we have never seen him, we cannot know for certain that what we have heard of him is truly so."

Falling Snow answered: "My grandfather, I hear you. Now I speak of the Yayatu. Can it be said truly of the Yayatu that they are evil people?" Limping Deer said: "Yes, it is a wise question. We have heard much about them and we have stored it away in our minds. That they may be evil, we suppose it to be so. Yet who among us has sat with them and known them face to face? We have only words about them to consider, and therefore we are wary so that they do not harm us. If those words that guide us are wrong, then we are not in balance with the world."

At last Falling Snow said what he had come to say. "My grandfather, I have sat with one of the Yayatu. I have hunted with him. My heart spoke well of him. His heart spoke well of me. He was not evil. He was not a sorcerer. If his hair were trimmed like mine, or if mine grew long like his, people would say, 'Elk Horn and Falling Snow are brothers.' He guided me to a spring. He took me to his cave to sleep. He shared his meat with me because I had only a little piki." And Falling Snow told everything he had withheld, not forgetting that the canyon was sacred to the Yayatu and that they had a shrine on the cliff above.

Limping Deer listened, his mind busy with the implications of what Falling Snow revealed to him. He said: "Now you have told me everything. It is good that you have spoken. What you tell me of your friend Elk Horn, I believe it. But if this canyon is sacred to the Yayatu it would have been better if we had known before we decided to remain here. Perhaps we have desecrated something they value. We do not know if they will be hostile. Yet let it be for now. We will find a way to deal with it." Limping Deer was silent for a moment, then he said: "My grandson, the safety of the Grey Fox People is not only in the hands of the old ones meeting in council. Every scout, every hunter is the eye and the ear of the village. If a person sees something or hears something he must make it known to others, or the village could perish." Falling Snow said, "My grandfather, I hear you."

After that, Limping Deer was preoccupied with thoughts of the Yayatu. The next morning he met with Yellow Corn and Yellow Bird. They sat within the unfinished walls of his house and smoked. Limping Deer told everything he had heard from Falling Snow, and they pondered the possible consequences of settling in the canyon. Limping Deer said: "Now that we have this matter in our hands, what shall we do with it? It is not good to merely wait. Let the three of us go to the Yayatu and smoke with their chief. If we do this, we will know how strong they are and how they feel about our being here. We may also learn something about what kind of people they are. It is not enough for us to say, 'We already know about the Yayatu, we have often heard of their bad ways.' What we have heard is only what we have heard. Perhaps we have heard nothing but the fear in other men's hearts. Let us learn truly. Falling Snow will be our scout and guide. Let us go early, before daylight comes."

Yellow Corn and Yellow Bird agreed, but Yellow Bird said: "We will not spread the news about where we are going. But if four of us go on this journey and none returns, how will the people know what has happened? Therefore, let us tell Crying Wolf, and if we do not come back he can announce to the people what has happened and they will understand that the Yayatu are dangerous." So they brought Crying Wolf into the meeting and explained everything to him.

Then they slept, and in the faint grey of morning they began walking northward along the bank of the stream. Falling Snow recalled details of his hunting trip as they went, pointing out landmarks and identifying them: "Here I parted from Red Sky and Young Antelope. . . . Here I saw deer tracks, but they were old. . . . Here I killed a turkey on my way home. . . ." And when, finally, he said, "Here among the boulders I met Elk Horn," they asked him, "Where is the Yayatu village?" He said: "I did not see it, because we went west looking for deer. But Elk Horn said it is one day's running to the north." Limping Deer said: "Good. Let us continue. Perhaps we can arrive the day after tomorrow." So they went on, and they camped that night in the shelter of a large standing rock that was all that remained of a crumbled butte. Yellow Corn had brought a fire bow, and so they had fire to keep them warm. They ate strips of dried meat, and after that they slept. The second day was like the first. They rested when the sun was high, then went on.That night they sheltered in a small cave, where flint chippings on the floor indicated that other men also had once sheltered there. On the third day they saw two hunters in the distance, but the hunters had seen them and disappeared from sight. In the late afternoon Yellow Bird saw a flash of light from a low butte, some moving object reflecting the rays of the sun. He said, "The Yayatu village is there." Limping Deer said: "Let us remain here. We will see how things are."

So they sat on the ground and waited as the sun slipped down behind the western horizon. As darkness began to cover the world, Yellow Corn said: "Let us make a fire. It will shine like an eye in the night. It will guide them to us. By the firelight we can see if they are hostile or peaceable." When their fire was burning they moved away and climbed into a dry wash. Soon they heard a soft sound, and again a soft sound, like feet on a trail. They heard a small stone rolling. Then several faces appeared in the firelight, two young men and an old one, and others were dimly visible behind them. "It is not a war party," Yellow Corn whispered, "they are not wearing paint or feathers." So he called out a greeting. Instantly the men drew back from the fire, and one of them replied, "Who are you, and why are you here?" Yellow Corn said: "We are Grey Fox People. Our bows are unstrung. We are here to speak with your chief and your men of knowledge." The words that came back were not all familiar, but they seemed to say, "Let us see you so that we may know whether you are friends." Yellow Corn went forward to the fire. After a moment he called out: "Let us all come. They will take us into the village." Limping Deer, Yellow Bird and Falling Snow climbed out of the wash and approached the fire. One of the Yayatu said, "That is all?" Yellow Corn held up four fingers, saying, "This many, no more." In single file, the torches lighting the way, they proceeded to the foot of the butte, and from there they climbed slowly up a worn trail marked by occasional chiseled stone steps. The Grey Fox old ones were not agile, and the torchbearers stopped occasionally to wait for them. When Limping Deer reached the top he said, breathing heavily, "The young man in me has gone away." The Grey Fox delegation entered the village. They could only dimly see the walls of the houses, but they sensed that people were on the roofs watching them. They were led to a kiva, and they waited un- til they heard a voice from below call: "Enter, whoever you are. Come down, sit with us and rest." They descended the ladder, Limping Deer first, followed by Yellow Corn, Yellow Bird, Falling Snow and, finally, the old one who had met them in the valley.

In the center of the kiva four men sat side by side in a line before a fire. Others sat on a stone curb along one of the walls. Of the four in the center, an aged one with white hair held a feathered staff in his lap. Another held a gourd rattle. All had bare chests and wore woven waistcloths and anklets made of shells and turquoise, and their hair hung down their shoulders. The aged one with white hair motioned for the Grey Fox People to sit down near the fire, and as they did so he looked intently into their faces. When his eyes came to Falling Snow he smiled and said something they did not understand. One of the men sitting at the wall brought a lighted pipe and they smoked. Falling Snow also smoked. When the tobacco was burned out, the white- haired one spoke, first using unfamiliar words, then repeating in language that was known to the Grey Fox: "You have come far. You are hungry." They answered, "Yes, we have come three days walking." A woman entered the kiva with melons, and they ate. The Yayatu watched silently. At last the white-haired village chief said: "You are welcome here. But what has brought you?" Limping Deer answered:

"My cousin, we came to sit with you and talk. In this way we will come to know one another." The Yaya chief said, "Yes, that is good."

Limping Deer said: "We are the Grey Fox People. Our home was in the south, and before that far to the east. We have made many villages since the journey of our ancestors began. Now we rest in the canyon that is said to be sacred to you. We are a people with unstrung bows. We seek to avoid conflict. We want nothing but a place to settle. If there is nothing but wilderness around us, we want peace with the wilderness. If we have other villages nearby, we want peace with those villages. Therefore we have come to talk about matters. I am called Limping Deer, and I speak for all of my people."

The Yaya chief said: "I hear you, Limping Deer. Let your other old ones also speak." So Yellow Corn said: "What Limping Deer told you comes from his heart. We want only harmony. When I was a young man I liked war. If we were in conflict, if raiders came to steal our women and corn, I fought fiercely. It seemed to me that fighting was manhood. Yet wisdom came. I know now that harmony is manhood. That is what my heart tells me. We are many people on the earth. The earth is our mother. Without the gifts she gives us none of us would survive. We must share the earth like cousins, even though we speak different tongues. If we cannot do that we must part. The Grey Fox People do not raid. They do not steal women. We live on the corn that our Earth Mother grants us. The corn that others grow, we do not want it. If we continue to stay in the canyon no one needs to fear us. If we have to defend ourselves from others, we will fight. But we want a peaceful village. If we have settled in a place you object to, we will go away. This is why we are here talking to you."

Yellow Bird then spoke briefly. It seemed to Yellow Corn and Limping Deer that his words were more cautious than theirs, and that he looked more into the fire than into the Yaya chief's eyes. When Yellow Bird was finished, the Yaya chief's face appeared troubled. He looked at Falling Snow, saying, "You also, young one. Have you no words?" Falling Snow could think of nothing to say, only: "I have no words. I came only to guide my grandfather." The Yaya chief said sternly: "Speak, young one. It is not good to come to a council and lose your tongue." This time Falling Snow answered: "I know a person named Elk Horn who lives in your village. He is my friend. We hunted together. We slept together in a cave. He shared his meat with me. He is my friend." Now the Yaya chief smiled, and he said to Falling Snow, "What you have said is good." After that he turned to address the old ones, emphasizing each thing he said by thudding his staff down on the kiva's stone floor. Sometimes he forgot to use words that were known to the Grey Fox People, but they comprehended the story he told.

"We Yaya people, we once were Utaheh. We come from far in the north where Winter Old Man lives. Our people also journeyed a long time. Often there was war. Often the people were hungry. We lived here, we lived there. Winter Spirit advised us, saying, 'Before the snow falls again, go where the geese go.' We followed in the trail of the geese. In time we arrived in this country, some days' running to the north of here. Things were not good. We were raided for our corn and meat. Women and children were taken from us. Little by little we became a people without enough women. Fewer and fewer children were born. So we went out, made war and took women. In this way we survived. But the fighting, there was too much of it and our young men diminished. The old men and the women had to defend the village. We said, 'In this country we cannot survive.' Again we followed the geese. In time we came to the canyon where you are living. At first we thought we would settle there, but one of our old ones had a vision. It instructed us to turn back, and for that reason we named the canyon Turn Back Place.

"We came to this butte and built our village here. It is good all around us. From the direction of your approach you could not see everything that we have. On the other side of the butte we have fields and water. Four springs are there, and they keep the fields moist. After we settled we did not have war anymore. So you see we are Utaheh but not really Utaheh. Now we are Yaya. We defend ourselves if we are attacked, but we do not go out to raid other people's corn and take their women. The canyon where you are staying is sacred to us because it was there that the vision instructed us what to do. The shrine on top of the cliff is where the vision was seen. A bear appeared to an old one. He took off his skin and became a man, who said, 'Keep a shrine for me here and I will watch over you in time of trouble.' And he pointed the way to this butte, which we call Star Place. We arrived in the evening, and as darkness fell a star shone brightly just over the edge of the butte wall, therefore we named the place after the star. About the canyon, I cannot say one thing or another. It is dear to us. The people will have to decide. Let us sleep with it. Perhaps the rising sun will bring an answer. I will let you know what the people say."

The Grey Fox People were taken to a house at the edge of the village. Before they slept they spoke in low voices about their talk with the Yaya village chief. Limping Deer thought that everything was going well, but Yellow Bird said: "I am not sure. There was a man sitting against the wall. He had white spots painted on his face. He resembled a dead spirit. Why was he there, painted this way, if all was well? I do not trust them. They are Yayatu. You speak of them as if they were ordinary people. Yet one thing we know of sorcerers is that they do not seem to be sorcerers." Limping Deer said: "If one does not look like a sorcerer, then, does that make him a sorcerer? I do not know what medicine the Yayatu may have. But as for their chief, my heart does not tell me that there is evil behind his words."

Yellow Bird answered: "We were told by our old people that witches do not have any character. Witches do not struggle between good and evil as other people do, because to them there is no difference. They do not perform wicked deeds merely because they want to depart from goodness. They perform evil because they are capable of doing it. As a coyote howls in the night because he must, so the man of two hearts uses his evil medicine because it is natural to him. Therefore if one looks into the eyes of a witch he sees nothing of wickedness, for the witch does not know he is evil. Whatever your heart may tell you about other men, it is useless in dealing with a sorcerer."

Limping Deer did not reply. Falling Snow spoke, saying, "My grandfather." Limping Deer answered, "My grandson." Falling Snow said, "My heart, also, says that the Yayatu are not bad people." His grandfather said, "That is good." But Yellow Bird said: "Let us not seek wisdom from boys. Before we leave this place we must test them." Neither Limping Deer nor Yellow Corn answered, and after a while they slept.

They were awakened in the morning by the sounds of voices and, in a nearby house, a mata grinding against a metate. When they ascended the ladder to the roof there was a young girl waiting for them there with a basket of food. They ate only a little, for the Grey Fox People began their days austerely. From the rooftop they could see a large part of the village, perhaps forty houses in all. It was much like other villages they had known, except that the walls were not as well made as some, and a number of houses had entries at the ground level rather than through the roof. They could see some of the fields on the far side of the butte, and smoke rising from pottery fires.

When Limping Deer thought the time was right they went again to the kiva, stamping on the roof to announce themselves. They heard the call, "Come in, come in," and descended the ladder. This time the chief was alone. They smoked, and then the chief addressed Limping Deer. "I, Running Buffalo, will speak to you of the canyon, Turn Back Place. The people debated far into the night until the Dog Star appeared overhead. We know you came here with peaceful hearts. The people approve your coming to discuss the canyon with us before building your houses. But some of them said: 'The Grey Fox People, before now we have never heard of them. Perhaps we will live to become cousins, perhaps we will live to become enemies. Who can say? When times are hard will they raid us for corn and beans? We do not know them.' Others said: 'The canyon means something to us. But have we not said many times that it would be good to have a peaceful village living nearby? Let the Grey Fox People hold our canyon in trust. If they do not harm us, and prove that they are true cousins by their actions, they can go on living in the canyon forever. Let them respect our shrine above the cliff, and acknowledge that we have left our footprints in the valley.' Our hearts tell us that you are good people, so it was decided that you should stay in the canyon and build your dwellings there.

"The argument was hard on both sides, but it came out well. Shall I tell you what moved the stone? We trust the hearts of the young. They have not yet found the wisdom of the old, but their hearts speak truly. It was the young one, Falling Snow, who touched us when he said, 'Elk Horn is my friend.' We also want friendship, and therefore we risk our fate for it. So go and tell your people what you have heard here in the kiva. We give them Turn Back Place in trust."

As they went up the ladder out of the kiva Yellow Bird drew back a little, saying, "Now I will test them." Limping Deer asked, "How will you do that?" Yellow Bird answered, "I will challenge Running Buffalo to move his finger in the air and make white marks on that peak in the west." Yellow Corn said sharply: "You are determined? Why do you have to be a corn worm destroying good maize? We came here not knowing what would happen, anxious for our lives, imagining that these people might kill us and throw us from the cliff. Now we have smoked together, eaten together and talked together. They have given us approval. We are in harmony. Why do you want to destroy everything?" Yellow Bird responded angrily, "I have come to a council with children."

They went down the steep trail to the flat land below without talking. Then, after a time, Yellow Bird spoke again, saying, "Your hearts do not understand what they hear. Those people are Yayatu. The words they speak reveal nothing. Perhaps Badger Boy spoke wisely when he said we should not remain in the canyon." Yellow Corn said: "If you do not find it good to stay, take your people and follow Badger Boy. But if you stay let us hear no more about making white marks on mountains." Limping Deer tried to cool their anger, saying: "How is it with us? Our new life is just beginning, and already we are barking like dogs. Let us put it away. If we have judged the Yayatu well, we will have harmony. If we have not judged well, we will know it in days to come. We have been hunting, we have caught game, so let us not go home saying that the deer is not to our liking."

When the Grey Fox delegation returned to the canyon the reason for their absence was revealed, and the people considered it a good augury that the Yayatu, as well as Long Arrow's village, had given their approval.

By the time the first winter winds blew across the valley many families had finished building their houses. Women and children now foraged for firewood and piñon nuts, or gathered white potting clay from a deposit at the southern end of the canyon. Slabs of sandstone found above the cliff were shaped into corn-grinding stones. At night, sitting at their fires, the men made arrows, smoothing the shafts by drawing them back and forth in grooved stones, and chipping flint and obsidian into piercing points. Meat that the hunters brought in was cut into strips, dried and hung away for the winter. In their spare time the men worked on their kiva, excavating and building walls, and slowly the form of the prayer house became visible.

Although meat was plentiful, the corn they had carried from the south was becoming scarce, and some families did not have enough to last them through the winter. It was proposed that the people should take barter goods to Red Rocks Place to exchange for corn. They had ample supplies of tobacco and salt, some of which could be used for trade. Women would make extra pots, and they could also make buckskin moccasins and leggings, and some families had turquoise and shells that they had brought from the south. So Young Antelope was sent to Red Rocks Place with a message for Long Arrow, saying that in sixteen days a Grey Fox trading party would arrive. When he returned, Young Antelope reported: "Long Arrow says, 'Let the Grey Fox People come. They are welcome. We will hold a Desert Spirit Dance. Also, let your unmarried young ones come. Perhaps they will find wives and husbands here.' "

In the days that followed, many families in the village were busy making their trade goods, and on the fifteenth morning they began to straggle east toward Red Rocks Place in small groups, carrying their loads in pack baskets in which they hoped to bring home corn. There were some who had little to trade, but they wanted to share the Red Rocks festivities and see the Desert Spirit Dance. It was the first time most of them had been on this trail since their arrival at the canyon. The fastest walkers reached Red Rocks Place while the sun still hung in the sky, but most came into view of the village only as the daylight faded. They camped that night around fires in the open, and to make the time pass more swiftly some of the men gambled with throwing sticks, the losers paying in tobacco or other items they had brought for barter. The older men were pressed by the children for stories, and Yellow Corn told tales of how humans acquired the knowledge of curing from the animals.

He said: "I myself learned the art of curing from my uncle, who passed his medicine on to me. So it is with others. They receive their knowledge from their uncles. But it was not always this way. In the past there were men who learned from coyotes, bears, wolves and snakes how to cure diseases and mend broken bones. Even today such things happen. A certain man of our own people—an old one called Bear Brother, who died long ago—when he was young he wanted to own the knowledge of curing. He used to study the skeletons and sinews of the animals he killed while hunting. He saw that though the bones of animals were different, yet in many ways they resembled the bones of humans, and that the forelegs of a deer were really arms. He once went hunting and killed a deer, and he sat contemplating the carcass, saying to himself, 'See how it is, this bone fits here and that one there.'

"While he sat thinking about such things a shadow fell across the dead deer. He turned his head and saw a large bear watching him. The bear spoke, saying, 'You are searching for the art of medicine.' And the boy answered, 'Yes, I am searching for it.' The bear said to him, 'Come with me, my people will teach you something.' He followed the bear to a cave. There the bear removed his bearskin and became a man. In the cave there was a hole like the entrance to a kiva. There was a ladder, and they went down. They were in a kiva. Many bear people were there. Their skins were hanging on the wall. The bear-man who had brought him said to the others, 'This boy, we must instruct him in the art of curing.'

"Other bear-men went out and returned with the carcass of the deer the boy had killed. They placed it on the floor and covered it with a sacred blanket. Then they gathered in a circle around the body and chanted their curing songs, sometimes putting their hands under the blanket and doing things that others could not see. The power of their singing entered the body of the deer. In time, after they had sung four curing songs, they removed the blanket. The deer was alive. He stood up. He removed his deerskin and became a man. He thanked the bear people for giving his life back to him. The boy remained in the kiva many days and the bear people taught him how to cure. When at last the teaching was finished, the bear-man who had found him put on his bearskin and became a bear again. He took the boy out of the kiva and guided him back to the place of their meeting. He said, 'Remember the bear people, for it is they who have given you your knowledge.' Then he went away and was not seen again.

"The boy returned to his village. He told his people: 'I have been to the kiva of the bear people. They have given me the secret of curing. From now on, this is my work. I will no longer hunt, for I have seen that the deer I killed, when he removed his skin, was a person not different from any of us.' After that the boy lived on and cured many people, and they gave him his new name, Bear Brother. That is the story as I heard it. I believe it to be true, for my father and my uncles pledged it to be true, and they never spoke to me falsely."

A young girl, granddaughter of Yellow Corn's sister, said, "Grandfather, are all the curers men? Were there no women?" Yellow Corn said: "Yes, my granddaughter, there have also been women who owned great medicine. The greatest of all curers is Spider Old Woman, our Earth Mother. It is told that people were living in a certain village after they came from the womb of the earth, and the village was attacked by a war party of gigantic monsters who wanted to take the women and the corn. The fighting was terrible, for the monsters shot arrows of death and wielded war axes so heavy that an ordinary person could not lift them. These gigantic monsters lived in the land before the people came. Whatever game they killed, they ate it without skinning or cleaning it. They did not build houses but slept in caves where, sometimes, we still find the bones of their victims. Their faces were not like ours. They had large protruding jaws like those of a wolf, and jutting eyes and long pointed teeth. For clothes they had only untanned animal skins which they tied around them."

Yellow Corn paused and looked into the fire as if he could see there the sight he was describing. After a moment he went on, saying, "Now, when these monsters attacked this certain village they made terror rise in the throats of the people. But the men said: 'If we flee we cannot escape. Therefore let us stand before them with brave hearts and give the women and children time to hide themselves.' The battle was very bloody and many warriors were killed. A few of the men who were still alive stood in a small group surrounded by the monsters. And when it seemed certain that the men would soon have to let the breath of life depart from their bodies, then the two Warrior Brothers appeared, those two brothers of whom we often speak, the grandsons of Spider Old Woman. In the form of children they were only naked boys racing in the grass after butterflies, but they had transformed themselves into warriors with terrible anger in their hearts. Their faces were painted black, with white lines around their eyes. They wore red battle collars around their necks and eagle feathers in their hair. Their legs were covered with buckskin, and they had tortoiseshell rattles on their calves. They wore armbands studded with jasper, and on their backs they had quivers full of flaming arrows. First they rained fire on the monsters, then they hurled lightning. They killed many of the enemy, and those that still lived scattered to the four directions.

"When the battlefield became still, the Warriors disappeared and Spider Old Woman came. She went among the dead humans, touching them and bringing life back into their bodies, until all who had gone out to defend the village breathed again. Had it not been for the Warrior Brothers, the giant monsters would still be the owners of this land. And had it not been for Spider Old Woman's knowledge of curing, humans would not be living here anymore."

When Yellow Corn concluded his story, Still Water, the snake priest, spoke, saying, "Yes, about Spider Old Woman it is true, I have heard about it from my uncle. But there were still others besides men who earned great knowledge. I can tell you something about this, but not everything, because some of it is secret to the Snake Brothers. This much I can say, that there was a certain village where our people lived long ago, but not yet back in the time of our coming from the earth. Deep beneath the village there was a large snake living in his kiva. He made life good for the people by causing rain to fall when the corn was thirsty. But these people did not understand the nature of things. If they saw a snake in their fields they killed it, and in this way many snakes died even though they did not mean harm to anyone. At last the large snake who lived in the kiva below the village could not stand it anymore. He came out of the ground into the plaza of the village where people had gathered for a dance. Because of his great size they were frightened and cowered against the houses.

"The snake said: 'I will take one of you down with me to my home in the earth and teach him respect for the snake people. Which one of you is it to be?' But no one answered. Out of fear they kept silent. Again the snake asked, but no one replied to him until a young girl called Gathering Flowers came forward. She said, 'I will go down with you.' Her parents held her by the arms, saying that she could not go. But the girl was persistent, she said she would accompany the snake to his kiva. Other people stood in her way to prevent her. The snake said: 'Very well, I will wait four days. If no one comes by then I will destroy your fields and houses and drive you away from this country.' He reentered his hole. The people said, 'Let us cover the hole so that he cannot come back into the village.' They brought heavy stones and covered the hole, saying, 'Now we have made ourselves secure,' and they sought to forget the matter. On the fourth day they said: 'He cannot come again. Now it is forgotten.'

"But when they finished speaking the earth began to rumble and the walls of the houses broke and fell. The pile of stones they had placed over the hole rolled away. The snake appeared in the plaza again, this time larger and fiercer than before. He said, 'Now it is time for me to destroy everything.' Gathering Flowers called out, 'No, I am coming with you.' She ran forward, and this time the people did not stand in her way. She put her arms around the snake, and he took her below the ground into his kiva. There, as you must know, he removed his skin and took on the appearance of a man. He said: 'Do not be afraid. I will teach you things the people need to learn. First, as you see, snakes are cousins to humans, so they should not be killed or abused. It is the snakes in the fields who come to tell me when people need rain. Therefore they should be respected and honored. The second thing is that we have the gift of curing. Because you have been willing to come with me I will give you knowledge that other humans do not have. I will teach you the art of counteracting snakebites, of mending broken bones, and of using grasses and roots to drive away fever.'

"The girl remained in the kiva many days and the people thought that she was dead. However, one day the snake brought her to the surface again. She spoke to the people, urging them to respect the snakes they found in the fields. They did as she said, knowing for the first time that the snakes gave them rain. Afterwards she became a medicine woman, and when people were sick they asked for her help. In time she had a kiva of her own. Other villages sent for her. She was known everywhere. She lived long and grew old, and a time came when it seemed that she would soon die. One day when people came to her kiva they discovered that she was not there. They saw her footprints leading out of the village and they followed them. The tracks led to a large snake hole, and there they ended. It seems that Gathering Flowers had entered the hole and gone below into the snake's kiva. The people never saw her again. At the place where her footprints ended, the people built a shrine to the snake who sent them rain and who had given Gathering Flowers the knowledge of curing. After that the people often brought prayer feathers and left them at the shrine, and some brought flowers as a way of remembering the girl who had saved the village from total destruction. It was from Gathering Flowers that people learned to respect our snake brothers. I have told this story the way it was told to me," Still Water said, "and if I have not told it well, let him correct me who can."

The Grey Fox People discussed the powerful medicine of curers far into the night. At last, when they looked into the sky and saw that the Suitor had chased the Three Maidens halfway to the edge of things, they slept.

In the morning they entered Red Rocks Place with their trading goods. In front of some of the houses were piles of beans or corn, meaning that these things were available to the visitors. Many village women had carried baskets of corn to the edge of the chief's kiva and waited there. An atmosphere of festival pervaded the settlement. Trading went on all morning, and by the time the sun was overhead there was nothing left to trade. The Grey Fox and Red Rocks people already had made friends with one another. The women sat in small groups talking, sometimes exchanging pots as gestures of good feeling. In the game court there was gambling among the men. They threw sticks to win each other's moccasins or wristbands. Sometimes if a man lost all such things he would offer his hair so as not to be left out of the playing, and if he lost his hair the winner would cut it off with a knife while others laughed and cheered.

The young unmarried people found one another and stood against the house walls, sometimes talking solemnly, sometime bantering. Boys of the two villages played stick ball on a stretch of flat ground. Others wandered through alleyways among the houses, and all through the day women appeared on the roofs to offer Grey Fox people gifts of food. In the late afternoon masked spirit dancers came from the kiva and raced through the village brandishing whips and clubs, and admonishing people to eat well, dance well, procreate well and remember that mankind did not create itself but was given the medicine of life. After that the masked figures gathered in the village court and performed the Desert Spirit Dance.

That night Grey Fox visitors lodged with Red Rocks families, and when morning came they began the journey home carrying heavy loads of corn and beans. Two men who had lost their hair at gambling were subjected to endless jokes. There was an air of well-being, and the trail seemed shorter than it was before. When at last they came to the eastern cliff of their canyon they could see their village nestled securely on the far side, and it made their hearts glad.

In the weeks that followed, the sun shone brightly but there was a chill in the air. People said that Winter Old Man, who lived somewhere in the northern mountains, was sending cold winds to put the earth to sleep. Women sealed up chinks in the walls of their houses with clay, and men dragged dead trees to the edge of the western cliff and threw them down to provide reserves of firewood. And when these things were done, people helped to finish the kiva walls and make a roof of timbers covered with sand and earth.

One morning a scout from the guardpost above the village came running to the kiva to report that a group of strangers had arrived on the eastern cliff. How many there were he could not tell for certain, perhaps ten or more. The old ones asked numerous questions. What did they look like? How many were of fighting age? Was it a war party? Were there women among them? But the scout could not answer, for the eastern cliff was far away and the strangers could scarcely be seen at all. So Still Water, who was war chief, instructed that they be kept under observation from the guard post. The strangers camped on the eastern cliff where the trail descended into the canyon and showed no signs of moving one way or another. So Young Antelope and Red Sky were sent to ask them who they were and what they wanted.

The report they brought back was that the new arrivals were southern people who spoke an unfamiliar language, and it was unclear whether they planned to stay where they were camping or go elsewhere. When several more days had passed, another messenger was sent inviting them to come and speak with the Grey Fox leaders. The next morning one man came down from the cliff, and he was taken to see Limping Deer, Yellow Corn and Still Water in the kiva. When they had smoked, Limping Deer said: "We see you have travelled far. Why have you come?" The man replied in a tongue that was difficult to understand. He used gestures and hand signs as he spoke, thus making his meanings clear. He said: "We travel. Now winter comes. We must have a place to rest." Yellow Corn answered, also using hand signs: "We do not know you people. We do not understand your tongue. We do not know the place you come from. We do not know anything about you." The stranger said: "We call ourselves Bean People. I am the clan elder. I am known as Grey Badger. We come from the south, where the sand blows into large hills. Our journey has been long. Five times we have watched the moon die and be born again. The people are tired. A baby is sick. We will stay a while on the cliff and grow strong again. We will hunt for meat. In the spring we will go away." Yellow Corn said: "Yes, one must hunt to live, but we do not have so much game here. We too are looking for our winter meat. As we are short of corn, we need even more game. We do not know if there is enough game for all."

Grey Badger said: "We will not eat your meat. If your people go out two days' running to find deer, we will go four. If you hunt to a distance of three days' running, we will go six. If we hunt in your hunting grounds you may throw us away, that is our pledge." Yellow Corn answered: "That is good. Still, we do not know you." Grey Badger said: "I have seen your village. You have many strong young men. You have many bows and lances. Our people, we are only twelve including the children, with two mature men and two growing boys. How can we harm you if we remain on the cliff until the sun grows warm again?" Yellow Corn, Limping Deer and Still Water discussed it for a while, and finally Yellow Corn said to Grey Badger: "Rest for a while where you are camped. We will think about it. We will wait for a sign to tell us what to do. If you have such a sign to show us, if you have medicine, bring it. Then we will know how it is."

Grey Badger departed and returned to his camp. And that same day the Grey Fox People saw smoke rising from the top of the cliff. The next day also there was smoke, and the people wondered about it. They decided that scouts should go up and find out what was happening. So that night Red Sky, Young Antelope and Falling Snow went up the cliffside and approached the camp in the darkness. They smelled smoke and saw the glow of fire. They went as close as they could without being discovered and saw that the fire was in the form of a wide ring, the hollow center of which was smooth sand. A man sitting nearby occasionally got up to feed the fire with dry wood. The Grey Fox scouts crouched for a long while watching from the darkness, but there was nothing else to be seen. And finally, at a signal from Red Cloud, they returned to the village and reported to those waiting for them in the kiva. The next day smoke was still rising from the cliff top, and that night a faint red glow could be seen at the same place. The fire continued to burn day after day. The scouts were sent out again to see what was happening, and this time when they returned Red Sky said: "The large ring of fire is still there, and the embers are deep. Now things seem to be growing in the sand. That is all we could see." When the Grey Fox people heard this they wondered, and some grew anxious.

As the sun rose on the sixteenth day the Bean People were seen coming down the cliffside. They walked across the canyon floor in a line, each person carrying something in his hands. A small red and white dog trotted at their heels. With Yellow Corn, Limping Deer and Yellow Bird in front, the Grey Fox People went to the edge of the village to meet them. Grey Badger was first in the line of Bean People. He held a live bean plant in his hands, and he placed it on the ground at Limping Deer's feet. As each man, woman or child arrived he laid another living bean plant on the earth. Grey Badger said: "Have you ever before seen living bean plants at this time of the year? This is the proof that we are truly the Bean People." Then Grey Badger took off the soft deerskin covering of a flat stone which he held up for the Grey Fox People to see, turning it from one side to the other. On one side were incised human figures and signs signifying rainfall, but part of the stone had been broken off and a piece of the picture was missing. On the other side there were signs for corn and beans, but that picture also was not complete. Grey Badger rewrapped the stone and placed it in his knapsack. Speaking slowly and using many hand signs he said: "This is the tablet by which we know ourselves. Once there were many of us, but we parted ways, half going toward the rising sun, half toward the setting sun. This was in the time of our grandfathers. Those who went toward the rising sun we call the Morning Branch, and those who went toward the setting sun we call the Evening Branch. When the two branches parted it was said that in time they would come together again. Those of the Morning Branch, who went eastward, carried one portion of the Bean People's tablet, the same that I have showed to you. Those of the Evening Branch carried the other portion of the tablet. It was said that when our people meet again they will know each other by fitting the broken tablet together."

Grey Badger paused, looking closely at the Grey Fox old ones to see if they comprehended. Yellow Corn, with a movement of his head, indicated, "We understand." Grey Badger continued: "In the east, which is where my own people come from, life was hard. Sometimes our crops did not grow well and we suffered. Raiding tribes made war on us and stole some of our women. From many we became few. Then the Sun Spirit made known to us that we should go west and find the Evening Branch. Yet we did not know exactly where to find them. It was said by some that the Evening Branch settled where the land ends and the great water begins. Others did not agree. They said that when the western Bean People reached the great water, Endless Water Spirit put a rainbow down for them to walk on and they crossed over to another land. About these things we ourselves cannot say what is true, only that we are following the other part of our clan wherever it is. That is where we are going. But we are tired. If we rest here for the winter we will not be a burden on you. When spring comes we will not remain any longer. For now, our people want to bring something worthwhile to your village. We have very little. But this dog is a hunter. His nature is good. We give him to you. Someday after we have gone away from your canyon we will find another one. Take him to remind you that we did not come empty-handed."

The Grey Fox old ones moved away and conferred. They agreed that the Bean People could stay, but that they should move down from the cliffside and build their shelters near the village. Limping Deer addressed Grey Badger, saying, "It is decided now. The people want you to stay. We will show you where to put your houses. We will talk again to know each other better. For now, come into the village and eat with us."

While he was speaking, White Moccasin stood not far behind, and when he was finished she said to him: "They have given us their only dog. Let us give their sick baby a curing ceremony." Limping Deer said, "Yes, it will be done." They took the woman with the sick child to the kiva, and there Yellow Corn made a curing ritual. The baby was laid in the center of the room, and four of the Grey Fox elders sat around it in a circle, positioned to represent the four directions. They sang curing songs, and Yellow Corn sprinkled sacred meal. He drew designs in the meal scattered on the ground, each design representing a malignant force, and one by one, corresponding to the words of the songs, he brushed the designs away with a parrot feather. The ceremony was long. Finally, when they had sung a prayer to Desert Spirit, it was over. The baby was handed back to its mother, and she departed.

That night after the Bean People had gone back to their camp Falling Snow asked Limping Deer, "Old grandfather, how did they grow beans in the sand without the summer sun?" And Limping Deer answered: "Do not say that they did not have the summer sun. For does not fire come from the sun? Fire is known as the Child of Sun. They planted their seeds and made a fire around them and kept it going day and night. The warmth made the beans grow even if it was not the growing season. There are some who know how to grow corn with fire also. These things were learned from Death Old Man who owned the earth before people arrived. Death Old Man lived alone in a certain place, we do not know where, and because the sun did not yet move across the sky he built a great circle of fire around his fields, and within that circle he grew his corn. It was from him that people received the knowledge. But first of all he gave this secret to the Fire Clan which is also known as the Death Clan, and they claim him as their guardian. The Fire Clan passed this knowledge on to other clans, so that all people know fire and what it can do. But it was not merely fire that caused the beans to grow up there on the cliff. It also required good hearts, good medicine and good songs. Without good hearts the Bean People could not have caused the beans to sprout. It was for this that we thought well of them and agreed to let them stay."

Falling Snow said: "Old grandfather, I understand about the fire. But you say that Death Old Man owned the world. How can that be? For the world is full of living things. Can the living be ruled by the dead?" Limping Deer pondered a while before answering: "My grandson, Death Old Man is not dead, but a living spirit, for death lives within all creatures. We say he ruled this land before the people came from below because he alone was living in it. In the underworld death was not known to people. When Death Old Man gave the Fire Clan fire they were still below, and he said to them: 'If you come to the land above where I live, I will protect you, because I have chosen you as my own clan. But there is one condition. Consider it carefully. If the people come up they will find a world better than the one where they now live. With the knowledge of fire they can perform great deeds. Yet in the world I rule life does not go on forever. A person is born, grows old, dies. This you should know.' What Death Old Man told the Fire People down below is true. Like all other creatures in the land, people are born and they die. There is no escape from it. Thus Death Old Man rules now as he ruled in the beginning. His living spirit is within all of us."

Falling Snow puzzled long into the night about whether a poorer life down below might not be preferable to a better life up above with Death Old Man waiting on the trail. And the next night, again, he pressed Limping Deer to justify the choice that people made in accepting Death Old Man's conditions. Limping Deer said: "My grandson, the choice was made long ago. Yet think of what it would be like if men and women did not die. The world would be full of ancient ones crippled by their years. They could not hunt, they could not defend the village, they could not even carry water from the spring. Do not forget that when we speak of death it is only the stalk that becomes useless. The breath within a person lives on." Falling Snow said: "Yes, I understand. But why, then, do people cry when a person dies?" Limping Deer smiled. He said, "Because they are only people and cannot help it."

The people had now replenished their corn somewhat by trading at Red Rocks Place, but there was still much hunting to do to see them through the winter. Every day men went out for game, and frequently they were gone for many days. There were casualties sometimes. One hunter killed a bear, but he was mauled before the bear died. His shoulder flesh was torn and he could no longer bend a bow. Yellow Corn made a bear grease poultice to cover his wound, but though the flesh healed, the man could no longer hunt. Another man fell from a high place while pursuing a deer, breaking bones in his leg. Yellow Corn set the broken bones and splinted them.

But there were some things that could not be healed. One day Young Antelope returned from the hunt carrying two bows instead of one, and Red Sky, who had gone out with him, did not return at all. Young Antelope entered the village and laid Red Sky's bow at the entrance of the kiva. The people asked: "Where is Red Sky? Has something happened?"

Young Antelope waited until Limping Deer and other old men arrived. Then he began, speaking in a solemn voice. "We were together. We followed tracks. We did not see anything that moved. We camped two nights without fire. We ate a little dried meat. The third morning we saw a small mountain. We said, 'Let us try there. Perhaps we will find a bear's cave.' When we arrived at the mountain we saw the tracks of several deer. We followed. We saw two deer standing but they ran along the base of the mountain. We could not catch up with them. Red Sky said, 'They will circle the mountain. Follow them and I will go round the other way.' We separated. Red Sky went one way, I the other. We said to each other, 'We will meet on the far side.' It was not a great mountain, not more than a morning's run around it. When I arrived at the far side Red Sky was not there. I waited. When night came I built a fire to guide him, but he did not come. I sat, not sleeping. I listened to the sounds of the night. I watched the stars in the sky.

"When the Dog Star was above me," Young Antelope continued, "I heard Desert Spirit calling with the voice of an owl, warning of danger. I extinguished the fire. In the darkness I could not do anything. I waited. When the moon rose there was light and I went seeking Red Sky. I walked a long time. Then I saw fire walking ahead of me like a glowing ember. I knew it to be the breath of Death Old Man. When I stopped, the fire stood still. It began to approach me. I thought, 'Death Old Man seeks me.' I turned back, walking quickly until I no longer saw the breath of Death Old Man. I rested among the rocks, not sleeping. The eye of morning opened. I ate a little piki and went again searching for Red Sky. At a certain place among the rocks I found him lying, already dead, pierced by these two arrows." Young Antelope placed the two arrows at the kiva entrance with the bow. "I could not carry him home. I placed his body in a cleft among the rocks and covered it with stones. Then I returned to the village without hunting anymore."

Already there was wailing in Red Sky's house. Outside the kiva the men passed the two arrows back and forth, examining the flint points and the shafts. One of them said, "The points are of brown flint, they do not come from this country." Another said, "The shafts have a red painted ring near the feathers. It is a mark we do not know." They speculated on what might have happened. It seemed to them that whoever killed Red Sky was also pursuing the two deer. Probably there was more than one of these hunters, perhaps two or three, otherwise there would have been only a single arrow. Seeing Red Sky following the game they wanted, they killed him. The Grey Fox men could not think of any other possibility. But who were these hostile hunters? Perhaps the markings on the arrows would tell. It was suggested that one of the arrows be sent to Red Rocks Place and the other to the Yayatu village to see if the people there could recognize them. But Yellow Bird protested, saying: "What if the arrows belong to the Yayatu? Our messenger will be killed."

So they did not send an arrow to the Yayatu, only to Red Rocks Place. When the messenger returned from there he said: "The people there believe the arrow is Utaheh or Tinneh. Though they have not seen any Utaheh for many seasons, they believe the Utaheh paint their shafts this way." Yellow Bird said: "Yes, Utaheh. Are the Yayatu not Utaheh by their own admission?" Yellow Corn answered: "They did not admit anything, We did not press them, asking about their ancestors. They said it straightforwardly, 'Once we were Utaheh, but we are not Utaheh anymore.' " Yellow Bird said: "It does not matter. It is the arrows that concern us. Perhaps they still make their arrows the way their grandfathers taught them. Let us see one of their arrows, then we will know." It was agreed that they would try to obtain a Yayatu arrow. Also, to make the village more secure, they would build another guardpost at the north end of the eastern cliff and keep two scouts there to warn them if raiders approached from that direction.

A time came when Limping Deer's house grew short of meat, but Limping Deer was too old now to go many days' hunting. So Falling Snow prepared to go alone to find game. But Limping Deer said: "My grandson, there are dangers out there that we did not know before. Therefore, do not go alone, go with Young Antelope or Walking Bear." However, Young Antelope and Walking Bear were already hunting, and when, after several days, they had not yet returned, Falling Snow said he would go alone and perhaps meet them. His grandmother said: "My grandson, do not go by yourself. Who knows whether there are Utaheh waiting, or even Breather of Fire? Our meat will last a while. Perhaps we can catch rabbits in the valley." He answered: "My grandmother, do not be anxious. I may not have to go far. I may find a deer only a day's running from the village, or even closer, and then I will return quickly." Limping Deer said: "Well, then, I will go also. Our deer may be waiting for us by the knoll with the piñon trees."

But the next morning Limping Deer could not get up from his blanket because of the pain in his back. He said to Falling Snow, "Let us wait another day." But the next day, also, Limping Deer could not get up. Falling Snow said: "Now I will go. I will try not to go far. I will surely find something." So Limping Deer said reluctantly: "Yes, it is good. If you meet any of our people hunting out there, join them. Take care. If you shoot a bear, do not approach him while he is still alive. A bear will save his last strength to strike at a hunter." Falling Snow said, "Yes, I will be cautious." Limping Deer said: "There are other things to know. If you see strangers, avoid them. If you see a campfire, avoid it. The arrows that killed Red Sky were not shot by animals but by men. If you see the glowing breath of Death Old Man do not follow it but turn away. Listen for the call of the owl, it will warn you of danger. Listen to Coyote barking at night, for there is knowledge in Coyote. Save some of your arrows for your return journey, for you may need them." Falling Snow said, "My grandfather, I hear you." White Moccasin put food in his knapsack and water in his water bag, saying, "May you come home safely." Then Falling Snow departed.

He went the way he knew best, north along the stream till he was out of the canyon. After that he could have gone one way or another, but he kept to the trail he had once followed with Red Sky and Young Antelope, saying to himself, "Perhaps Young Antelope and Walking Bear came this way." After a while he branched off toward the Yayatu settlement. He was well beyond the dunes before he saw any game tracks. He judged the tracks to be old because they had been drifted over by sand. In time he arrived at the place of rocks where he had first met Elk Horn. There was no one there, and so he went on to the spring. He found animal tracks at the water's edge, but no human signs, so he went next to the cave where he and Elk Horn had slept. He ate some of the corn pudding White Moccasin had prepared for him, thinking, "Well, now, have I come out to find meat for my old grandfather and grandmother? Or have I come out to find Elk Horn?" And he resolved to begin early in the morning to hunt down a deer no matter where it led him.

He slept, and in the faint light of early morning as he was about to leave the cave he heard a faint fragment of a human voice disturbing the silence of the wilderness. He stood at the cave entrance, his eyes searching, and at last he saw movement in the distance, two hunters approaching leisurely. Falling Snow ran quickly to a hill of broken rocks, stepping from stone to stone so as to leave no tracks, and squeezed into a cleft from which the cave opening was visible. Soon he heard their voices, but they spoke in a strange tongue. When they appeared at the cave entrance he saw that one of them carried a small antelope over his shoulders. Their hair was long, hanging down their backs in braids, and they wore buckskin leggings. They did not resemble the Yayatu. After placing their antelope in back of the cave they rested, drank a little water, and departed.

When they were gone, Falling Snow made his way cautiously back toward the east, keeping high ground between him and the strangers. When he felt safe he began to run, loping at the gait he had learned from Red Sky and Young Antelope, until the cave was far behind. Once more his eyes scanned the broken terrain for deer. Two hawks soared above him and he thought, "They too are searching for game. Everyone searches for something to eat. The deer I am after is looking for grass. Is life nothing but searching for food?"

He came to a stretch of smooth blue rock cleared of sand by the wind, and he saw markings in it resembling great bird tracks. He paused to ponder on them. Then he saw a depression in the rock in the form of a giant human foot, perfectly formed with the heel, the toes and the arch clearly visible. He thought, "I have seen something to be remembered, but I do not know its meaning." He left the blue rock behind and went running toward the east. And when the sun was high in the sky he saw two hunters ahead of him. It was evident that they had seen him also, for they stood without moving, waiting for him to approach. Now he went forward slowly, and when the distance between them was small he saw that they were Yayatu, and a moment later he recognized Elk Horn. They greated one another. Elk Horn said, "I see you, Falling Snow." And Falling Snow answered, "I see you, Elk Horn." They met and sat on the ground to talk. Elk Horn said: "My friend is Crooked Pine. We have been hunting, but there is no game here." Falling Snow said: "I too have been hunting since yesterday. I have not seen any living game."

They talked about many things, and at last Falling Snow said: "I did not see any living game, but I saw a dead antelope carried on a man's back." Elk Horn answered: "A-heh! Is it a riddle you are asking?" Falling Snow said: "I did not mean a riddle. I saw two hunters. They were not Yayatu or Grey Fox. They carried the antelope and put it in your cave. Their hair hung in braids and they spoke a strange tongue." Elk Horn said, "Why, they must have been Utaheh." But Crooked Pine said, "From the braids I think they were Tinneh." Falling Snow said: "Never before have I seen Utaheh or Tinneh. What kind of people are they?" Elk Horn said: "About the Tinneh I do not know anything, though my father sometimes speaks of them. An old woman in our village comes from the Tinneh. She was captured in war when she was a girl. The Utaheh, I think they are just ordinary people. Our old ones say we Yayatu were once Utaheh before we branched off and became what we are. Yet we are not really Utaheh now. We do not speak the same language anymore." Falling Snow said: "My friend Red Sky was pierced with arrows while he was hunting. People say it could have been the Utaheh that did it." Crooked Pine said: "Yes, I have heard such things about the Utaheh. They come and go in secret. They are hard to see. Sometimes they raid the villages." Elk Horn added: "Also they are strong in medicine. My grandfather spoke of it. He said his grandfather wore many medicine bags on his chest to guard him from arrows in battle."

Falling Snow's mind was still on the arrows that killed Red Sky. He said, "If an arrow is lost and it is found by another person, can it be surely said who made it?" Elk Horn answered: "Yes, arrows are different from one another. We Yaya, our arrows are different from those of the Utaheh. They are shorter and do not have the same markings. Those of the Cactus Eaters are short like ours but they make points differently. Our points are of black flint, while theirs are brown. The black flint is sharper, so we do not have to draw so hard on the bowstring."

In time, when he could no longer restrain the question, Falling Snow asked, "Who are the people who mark their shafts with a red band?" Elk Horn and Crooked Pine answered together, saying, "They are the Utaheh." Falling Snow said: "I am speaking of the arrows that killed Red Sky. We went to Red Rocks Place to see how they marked their arrows. There was no red band." Crooked Pine said: "At Red Rocks every clan uses a different marking. That is what is said in my village." Falling Snow said, "We did not know it." Elk Horn said: "You are troubled. You want to know the marking used by the Yaya people. We are friends, let us exchange arrows. I will put yours on my wall. You do the same, so your people can see it. Then they will understand that we are peaceful."

They exchanged arrows, and Falling Snow saw that Elk Horn's arrow shaft had no paint markings on it. He became lighthearted, saying, "Some of our old men think the Yayatu are sorcerers." Elk Horn and Crooked Pine laughed. Elk Horn said: "Do you remember when your people came to ask Running Buffalo if they could make their village in the canyon? Our old ones had a great argument. Wolf Child was against the Grey Fox People. He said they had the look of sorcerers because of the way they cut their hair."

Now it was Falling Snow's turn to laugh. Elk Horn said: "We have powerful medicine makers among the Yaya. One old man in my grandfather's time could turn the points of enemy lances soft like boiled cornmeal. Another one has medicine to hold back the sand from drifting across planted fields. My grandmother knows how to cure fevers with roots. Medicine, yes, we have it. But I do not know any sorcerers. My uncle once told of a family of sorcerers who lived somewhere, perhaps they were Tinneh or Cactus Eaters. They performed evil acts and caused people to fall sick and die. One night the father of this family went out of his house when he thought the village was asleep. But some men saw him from the roof of the kiva and they followed him. He went to the place where the dead were buried, and there he took on the form of a living skeleton with fire coming from the sockets of his eyes. He made witchcraft among the graves, and in the morning the people discovered that a child had died during the night. So they sent this family of sorcerers into the wilderness and warned them, 'Do not come back or we will have to kill you.'"

Falling Snow said, "We have an old one who calls the Yayatu People-of-the-White-Marks. He says all the Yayatu can make white marks on a far-off mountain by pointing their fingers." Elk Horn and Crooked Pine opened their mouths in astonishment, then rolled on the ground laughing. Elk Horn arose and solemnly pointed toward a hill, shouting, "Ka ka ka!" Falling Snow and Crooked Pine jumped to their feet, pointing at one landmark and another that rose from the valley floor and shouting, "Ka ka ka!" In their fantasy, white marks appeared everywhere. And when they had painted the landscape white they fell to the ground laughing again.

Falling Snow told, in time, of the flat blue rock where he had seen the imprint of a gigantic foot. Crooked Pine said: "Ah, so you have seen it. I also passed that place and spoke of it to my uncle. He said it is a footprint left by Corn Man." Falling Snow had not heard of Corn Man, so Crooked Pine continued: "Corn Man was one of the giants who lived in this country before people came. His body was like an enormous ear of corn. People did not know about corn in those days, they ate only roots and grass. Corn Man tried to drive the people away, but the two warrior gods came and killed him with lightning arrows. Corn Man fell on the ground and burst, and from his body there flowed corn seeds. The people planted the seeds and corn grew from the ground. Since then everyone has had corn."

They passed much time with talking, until Elk Horn said: "The sun moves, but we have found no meat. Let us hunt together." So they hunted, but that day they killed nothing except a desert turkey. The next day Falling Snow wounded a large deer, but the animal kept running, and he had to pursue it a long distance before he finally caught it and killed it. Elk Horn and Crooked Pine also killed a deer, but it was small. Because Falling Snow could not carry his heavy kill all the way home, they traded deer. Falling Snow's return to the canyon was slow and his back was bent. He slept that night in the open. Coyotes, smelling the meat, approached in the darkness and barked to one another. Falling Snow arrived at the canyon the next day. He placed the deer on the ground in front of Limping Deer's house. His grandmother cried, and Limping Deer said to her, "Do not cry any more, Falling Snow is now a man."

After he had eaten and slept, Falling Snow went to sit by the blanket where Limping Deer was lying. He said, "My grandfather," and Limping Deer answered, "My grandson." Falling Snow said: "Now we will know what to think about the Yayatu. My friend Elk Horn gave me one of his arrows." He took the arrow from his arrow case and gave it to Limping Deer, who examined it carefully. Limping Deer said, "No, it is not the same as those that killed Red Sky." Falling Snow said: "There is something more. Elk Horn and Crooked Pine say that in Red Rocks Place every clan has its own markings. How many markings do we know?" Limping Deer said, "My grandson, they showed us only one." He brooded then and became silent.

For some days Limping Deer did not pass on the news that Falling Snow had brought. He considered going to Red Rocks Place to talk with Long Arrow, but his body told him that it could not make the journey. Yellow Corn came one morning to treat Limping Deer's sickness. He sat next to the blanket with his eyes closed. When he opened them it was as though he were returning from a distant secret place. He took a feather from his medicine pouch and traced the bones of Limping Deer's body with it, chanting a curing song. He blew pipe smoke over Limping Deer, rubbed his joints with bear grease, and sprinkled sacred meal. Before Yellow Corn departed, Limping Deer gave him the news brought by Falling Snow. Yellow Corn said: "Now we know what we did not know before. It was not the Yayatu. It probably was the Utaheh. Yet we have not yet seen all the Red Rocks arrows. If we ask Long Arrow about it now he could turn his heart against us. We must proceed slowly and keep a straight trail. In time we will know the answer." When he left Limping Deer's house he met in the kiva with Crying Wolf, Yellow Bird and Still Water and informed them about what he had learned. They agreed that there was nothing to do but wait.

The dog that the Bean People had given to the village proved to be a good hunter. He belonged to no one and to everyone, and hunted with whomever he chose. Because he was their only dog, the Grey Fox People treated him almost as though he were a human child. Every family gave him cracked bones and he wandered at will through the village.

He ran with the children when they played stick ball and hunted rabbits with them. Sometimes, when there were no hunters to accompany, he went out foraging by himself. If he was gone a day or two at a time people did not worry because they knew he would return. Because his color was red on white they gave him the name Painted One.

It happened one morning that Painted One was not to be seen anywhere in the village, and people said he had probably gone out alone to find game. Or perhaps he was out talking to the coyotes, because a certain story said that dogs sometimes reported to the coyotes to let them know how things were going in the affairs of humans. Four days passed and Painted One did not return. Four more days passed, and after that still more days. People began to say that perhaps Painted One had left them to go back to the dogs' kiva somewhere, or possibly he had been killed by a cougar. At first the children did not accept such explanations, and every day they went to the edge of the village to call him, but after a while they stopped expecting him to return.

One afternoon two hunters came to the kiva with information about Painted One. One of them said: "Grandfathers and uncles, we went east toward Red Rocks Place to find game. There we found some turkeys and a groundhog. We killed as much as we could carry and began our way home. We came to a rocky place and saw the body of Painted One. It had been lying many days. Crows and coyotes had gnawed at it. How he came to die, this was the cause." He handed Yellow Corn an arrow, saying: "We found it still piercing him. He died from the bow of a dog hunter." The old ones examined the arrow, acknowledging that they recognized the marking on the shaft, a band of red paint. Yellow Bird said: "Now, can we keep putting this matter aside any longer? We will have to go to Red Rocks and see what Long Arrow has to say." And so it was agreed to, and Yellow Corn, Crying Wolf and Still Water were selected to make the journey.

Early in the morning while the sky was still grey they set out, and they arrived at Red Rocks Place the next day. They met with Long Arrow in the kiva. They called one another brothers and smoked. Long Arrow wanted to know why Limping Deer had not come. They answered that he was sick and barely able to descend into his own kiva. After a while Long Arrow said: "I see your hearts are troubled. Tell me what it is so that I can share it."

Yellow Corn spoke for the delegation, saying: "My brother, we are glad that you consider us close in spirit. We do not forget that you accepted us out of the wilderness and encouraged us to settle in the canyon. We have always felt welcome in your village. No Grey Fox person has ever felt anything but friendship for you. If there are any persons among you who resent us, I have not heard of it. Our people believe the canyon is a place where we will flourish because of your friendship. Yet there have been strange events that we cannot explain. When our son Red Sky was killed we brought an arrow to you, asking if you recognized it. You said it was Utaheh and you showed us your own arrow, which was different. We understood then that the arrows that killed Red Sky belonged to strangers. We were comforted that the arrows had nothing to do with Red Rocks Place. We have seen the arrow of the Yayatu, and they also have no red bands.

"Be gentle in your feelings for us that we come to you again on this matter. But we have heard that each of your clans, the Blue Fox, the Arrow, the Antelope and the Coyote, each of them makes arrows in its own style. You showed us one arrow, that of the Blue Fox Clan. Where are the others? We have not seen them. We wanted to forget everything and leave the burden on the Utaheh. But the Bean People gave us a dog. The children loved him and called him Painted One. He went out of the village and did not come back. Two of our hunters found Pained One halfway between your village and ours, killed by an arrow with a red band marking. Now, if the Utaheh are dog hunters I do not know, and we have never heard that Red Rocks people hate dogs. What disturbs us most is that the arrow that killed Painted One and the arrows that killed Red Sky are the same. A dog, we can live without one as we did before. But we cannot live in harmony with things without knowing what is true and what is not true. If we have wronged you and your people by coming with our questions, we will be sorry for the hurt you feel, but we will be glad that the matter is settled. Show us the arrows of the other clans so that we can go home with comfort in our hearts."

Long Arrow remained silent until the sounds of Yellow Corn's words had settled like dust on the kiva floor. When he spoke, his own words were even softer than Yellow Corn's. He said: "My brothers, let us see the truth of things. In this village we are four clans, but there are a few persons who came to us from other clans or who had no clan at all. The Coyote Clan, when they were wandering, took sons and daughters of different peoples and married them to their own sons and daughters. And so it is that there are several of the Cactus Clan, the Red Hawk Clan and the Ground Lizard Clan, but they are dying out and there are really only four main clans. The arrows we make are much the same, though sometimes a man puts his clan mark on the shaft. Thus if an arrow is lost and a stranger finds it he will recognize it and say, 'Ah, this must be the hunting ground of such and such a clan,' and go away so as not to cause trouble. Let us look at the arrows then, and judge what they say to us." He called through the kiva opening for someone to get arrows from each of the clan leaders. When the arrows were brought, Long Arrow put one at random on the ground by the fire. "This one," he said, "is marked by a forked line, meaning the horns of an antelope, and belongs to the Antelope Clan. Here is another with no marks at all on the shaft, but it has bluebird feathers, the mark of the Blue Fox Clan. Here is the one belonging to the Arrow Clan, this small sharp mark representing a flint point. And this fourth arrow belongs to the Coyote, with no marks on the shaft whatever. Now you have seen them. There are no red bands like those of the Utaheh."

Yellow Corn said: "My brother, you have made our eyes see what is real. We will rest a little now, for we are not young men anymore, then we will go back to the canyon and make known what you have told us. You have received us well at all times. We want to receive you in our village. We invite all the people of Red Rocks Place. We will hold a Desert Spirit dance. The young ones will play stick ball and run races. The old ones like us will smoke and find harmony. We will talk of many things that have not yet been disclosed between us. In this way we will be closer and understand each other better. Sixteen days from today we will stand on the cliff and watch for your arrival." Long Arrow answered: "Yes, that will be good. We will meet before Winter Old Man blows his snow on us. Our crier will announce it. Many people will come."

When they returned to the canyon, Yellow Corn, Still Water and Crying Wolf went to Limping Deer's house and told him of their meeting with Long Arrow. Limping Deer said: "Well, now, our hearts can be in harmony with Red Rocks Place, for we know that no one there is responsible for our troubles. Yet we still have the Utaheh to think about, because it is clear that they are watching us. If they are willing to kill hunters and dogs who are not hostile to them, they will not stop at anything to get what they want. We must stay alert. The young men must make arrows and repair their lances, and the guards on the cliff must be watchful." The others said, "Yes, these things must be done."

Afterwards Crying Wolf went through the village announcing that the Red Rocks people would be coming for a visit, and that there would be festivities. At the end of his announcement he said: "Our grandfathers have told us that when strangers come to the village they should be fed as if they were our brothers, sisters and children. This is the way of our people. Let it be that way." So the Grey Fox People prepared themselves. Young men went hunting for extra meat, and the young women ground corn, though in some houses there was little corn to spare. Boys who were good runners practiced for the races, running every day to the end of the canyon and back. The Desert Spirit dancers met every night in the kiva to sing their chants and make their masks and costumes ready. Some of them sewed new moccasins, made dance rattles and painted armbands.

The time for the festivities had not yet arrived when guards on the cliff called out that people were approaching from the north. In the village the young men put on their leather war jackets, and scouts were sent out to see if the people who were coming were hostile or peaceful. When the scouts returned they called out: "Loosen your bows. It is only an old man, two grandmothers and a child who are coming." People went to the edge of the village to meet them, and when the travellers arrived it was discovered that they were Grey Fox relatives, kin of Badger Boy who had gone out with him to find Mesa of Flowers. The man was Laughing Crow, Badger Boy's brother. The women were Butterfly Cloud, Badger Boy's older sister, and Green Corn, whose husband had died on the long journey from the south. The child was White Star, Green Corn's grandson. The people asked many questions, but Laughing Crow said nothing until they took him to the kiva. There he sat with the old ones and said: "We four are all that remain. Badger Boy is gone, the others are gone. My brothers, give us shelter." Yellow Corn answered: "Yes, shelter is yours. You do not need to ask for it. We are all the same people. But tell us what happened."

"The travelling was hard," Laughing Crow said. "We did not have enough corn. We hunted, but game was not easy to find. We went far. We came to a place where there was a high cave in the side of a cliff. We built shelters there, thinking to rest and hunt. One morning I took my bow and set out to find a deer. Green Corn, Butterfly Cloud and White Star went to dig for roots. When the sun had moved a little I heard battle calls and the crying of women. I returned cautiously. All was silent in the cave. The enemy was no longer there. Our old ones were lying dead, and the young women and children were gone. Who the raiders were, I cannot tell you. I did not see them. Apachu, perhaps, or Utaheh, or Kwikapa, how can I tell you if I did not see them? All I saw was the death they left behind." He recited the names of those who died and those who had been captured, and when he was finished he fell silent.

They pressed him for more details and he said: "Butterfly Cloud, Green Corn and White Star returned from digging roots. We buried the dead and covered them with stones. After that we said: 'Why should we go on to Mesa of Flowers? We are a broken family.' We stayed in the cave. There was nothing left for us. I myself did not care any longer that I was alive. I waited for Death Old Man, watching in the night for his breath, but he did not come. Butterfly Cloud and Green Corn, it was the same with them. We made no fire. We ate a little parched corn. On the third night after the raid I slept and dreamed that my mother spoke to me. She said: 'It is not yet time for you to die. The boy White Star is still young. Take him back to the village in the canyon so that the people can take care of him.' That is why we returned. We old ones are tired. The skin is worn from our feet. The boy is sick and he does not speak anymore. Give us a place to put our blankets."

They found places for the old ones to live in, and White Star was taken to Limping Deer's house. White Moccasin fed him, but he did not respond when she spoke to him. It was as if he did not know that anyone was there. White Moccasin led him to a blanket and left him to sleep, but he would not close his eyes. He lay looking at the roof beams, and when Falling Snow tried to speak with him White Moccasin said: "Let him rest. His thoughts are still in the wilderness."

In the kiva the men discussed the return of the small remnant of Badger Boy's party. Flowing Spring said: "It happened this way because Badger Boy broke with us and threw us away. The signs meant for us to stay here in the canyon. Badger Boy said that things would be too good for us, yet he wanted more. He wanted everything, so he went looking for Mesa of Flowers. One day we shall surely see that place, but Badger Boy was impatient and would not wait." Still Water agreed, saying: "Yes, what happened is a sign. If we are still to go on from here, the time will come when we know it. We have to go on living in the canyon. Perhaps other people will come this way. Perhaps our village will thrive, and in time we may build one house on top of another. We will build another kiva and hold many rituals for Desert Spirit, Corn Spirit, Water Spirit and Serpent Spirit and assure the fertility of our fields. Other clans will hear of it and come to join us." Crying Wolf said: "Who knows? It may happen. Yet for now the enemy are still out there somewhere. Our guard posts alone cannot protect us. We must prepare ourselves in case we are attacked. Still Water, you are war chief. You must take the responsibility. Tell us what to do and we will do it."

Still Water answered: "Yes, let us prepare. Because we are a peaceful people does not mean that we should hold our throats out to the enemy. Let us see to our weapons as we sit by our fires at night. Send the children out to find flint for our points. And when we have worked the flint let us stud our warclubs with the chips. Let us make many arrow shafts and smooth them. Let us renew the hide on our shields, and let the women make leather chest armor for the men. Now, let us say all these things have been done. There are other things. Our boys must become swift and enduring runners. If the girls wish to run, let them run also. Every day they will run from one end of the canyon to the other, as some do now in preparation for the festivities. They must practice scaling the cliffs, jumping from one rock to another until their bodies are hard. And so, if the enemy threatens us, any boy or girl can go to Red Rocks Place to ask for help, or to the Yayatu. But that is not all. Let us strengthen the walls of our houses, and let us build a new wall at the narrow place where the trail enters the village. We must draw up our ladders at night so that if the enemy enters by stealth in the darkness we can fight him from the rooftops. Let the children gather stones of the right size and we will store them on the roofs for our slings. Yet if the enemy comes by stealth through the mouth of the canyon in the dark of night, how shall we know before it is too late? So let us build a guardpost out there, and if there is danger our guards can light a fire."

When it was Yellow Bird's turn to speak, he said: "Yes, what Still Water says is good. These things should be done. Yet there is the matter of the Yayatu. Some of you say, 'Pay no attention to the Yayatu, there is nothing wrong with them.' Ask Long Arrow. He knows them. He understands what they are capable of doing. We have heard much about the arrows with the red bands. We have seen the arrows of the Red Rocks clans. We have even seen an arrow of the Yayatu. We say the arrows to fear are those of the Utaheh. Yes, the Utaheh are dangerous, and so are other raiders. But is it not possible for anyone to paint a red band on the shaft of an arrow? Let us say a man wants to do an evil thing. He wants to kill a hunter. Can he not paint his red bands and then do his evil work? Running Buffalo calls us his brothers, but how do we know what is in his heart? We do not know because it is his secret. What we know for certain is that the Yayatu have a bad reputation. What enemy attacks the Yayatu in their village? No one. People know the magic that they can perform. They avoid the Yayatu.

"As for the Utaheh, who knows for certain that they are out there? A boy says he has seen two Utaheh hunters. Perhaps they were Utaheh, perhaps they were not. But the Yayatu, are they not also Utaheh? Utaheh is their language. They say, 'We turned away from the Utaheh.' But the Utaheh have not raided them. Their village is safe because they are brothers to the Utaheh. Let us not go to sleep in a bear's den. Let Still Water take the responsibility. He is our war leader. Let him draw a line to divide our hunting grounds from those of the Yayatu. Send a messenger to Running Buffalo, saying, 'Do not cross over the line we have made from one peak to another. If we cross it the danger is ours. If you cross it the danger is yours. We will stay apart.' Only this way can our village be safe."

Then Yellow Corn spoke, saying, "Yellow Bird, you are a brave man. When we were young I saw you in battle. When your arrows were gone you went forward with your lance and your battle-ax. When your lance was broken you took a lance from the hands of an enemy warrior. Yet now you fear something. What is it you fear? Not a man, not a war party, but a story. Something is told by one person to another, and by that person to still another. But who of us now living has seen the Yayatu do anything wrong? If it is true that they can point to a distant cliff and make it turn white, then how are we safe with a line across the hunting grounds? Look around you. Have the Yayatu painted our cliffs? Have they painted the butte at Red Rocks Place? It is pointless to speak evil words about the Yayatu unless you know something you have not told us. How is it to be? If an old man dies when he has lived out his life, shall we say the Yayatu practiced sorcery? If the rain does not come, will we say it is because of the Yayatu? If the winter is cold, will we say it is the Yayatu? Badger Boy's party was far away when it was attacked. It could have been the Utaheh or the Apachu or the Tinneh or the Kwikapa, who knows who it was? But not the Yayatu. Or did they sit on their blankets and fly through the air to reach that place? We cannot live without seeing the truth of things. Let us defend ourselves when it is necessary. But let us be temperate, or we will lose the ability to distinguish good from evil."

Yellow Bird answered grimly: "Very well. I gave you something to think about, but you would not consider it. I will say no more. One cannot reason with a stone. Whatever is not done about the Yayatu while there is still time, the responsibility falls on those who refuse to do something. I was with you when you decided to stay here and build a village, and I will remain, even though we are sleeping in a bear's den. But remember my words. Put them away in a safe place. Perhaps, someday, they will speak to you again."

At last Limping Deer interceded. He said: "My brothers, my children, let us not go on disputing. Who knows what is waiting for us? Who knows what is to come? Let us remember to ask ourselves the questions: 'Who are we? Where do we come from? Where are we going? Why are we here?' We come from the earth, our mother, that is how we were born into the world. We came with nothing. Water Spirit gave us the gift of rain. Corn Spirit gave us our food. Desert Spirit gave us our knowledge of the wilderness. Serpent Spirit gave us something to look for and a reason for all we do. We have lived in many places, we have had many migrations, we have fought battles to preserve our people.

"Now we sit in our kiva in a canyon whose name we never heard before we arrived. We take warmth from our fire. We discuss the meaning of life. When we were in our last village we could not foresee anything, only that there would be a journey. What we see now is only where we are and where we have been. Today, sitting here, we are like the body of a tadpole. Its tail thins off into the past. The tail is the story of where we have been and where we came from, and what has been told to us by our grandfathers and grandmothers. The body is here and the tail is there; but tomorrow and the days of our grandchildren, we cannot see them at all because they are invisible. In time to come our grandchildren will sit like this, and we will be the tail of the tadpole. Let us give them a good story to remember. We must remain in balance with everything around us, and in harmony among ourselves. Otherwise we will disappear in the wilderness. We speak of this journey and that journey, but all of life is one great journey in which we seek goodness and try to leave dissension and evil behind. We have made our homes here, and the canyon is a place where we can rest and consider the landmarks of the journey.

"From now on," Limping Deer said, "let us call our village Refuge Place. When a stranger asks us who we are we can say, 'Our village is Refuge Place and we are Grey Fox People.' Let us go on living our journey, let us not break apart. Let us draw no lines across the land, for such lines leave scars on the earth. Let us trust what we see in a person's eyes and what we hear from his heart. Yellow Bird's words come from his heart when he speaks of dangers. Yellow Corn's words, also, when he speaks differently. We say what we believe, and that is good. But the future, we do not know it even though our journey will yet pass through it. Let us remain good brothers in all things. In the spring the valley will be full of sunflowers and our fields will be sprouting with corn. That is all I can tell you of the future. I have said everything I know."

In Limping Deer's house, White Star remained silent and indifferent to the comings and goings of people, and he would not eat unless White Moccasin put something into his mouth. Falling Snow sometimes tried to get him to speak, but the boy would not answer. White Moccasin would say: "Let him rest. He needs time. He saw the face of Death Old Man and it is still in his eyes." And when he had heard this from White Moccasin several times, Falling Snow asked her, "Is Death Old Man's face so ugly to look at?" White Moccasin answered: "Yes, it is terrifying. He has white spots on his skin, which are the marks of an ancient fire, and his teeth protrude like the teeth of a skull. Let the old men tell you about it. They discuss such things in the kiva. They can tell you more than I can."

That night as Limping Deer sat by the fire repairing his lance, Falling Snow asked again about Death Old Man. "Our grandfathers saw him," Limping Deer said, "and there are some men still alive who have seen him. Perhaps White Star also looked on his face. Death Old Man has no hair, because it was burned off in the fiery place where he was thrown. His skin is covered with white and red scars. He wears a bloody cape of rabbit skins. He smells of carrion. His eyes are deep in their sockets. To hide his terrifying face he sometimes wears a mask with the face of a young man, and feathers on his head to replace his lost hair. When he was thrown into the fiery place he swallowed fire, and ever since then a flame comes from his mouth when he breathes."

Falling Snow asked, "What was this fiery place, and why was he thrown there?" Limping Deer answered: "It happened long ago, after our people came out of the belly of the earth. In those days the giants and other monsters were still here. As we know, Death Old Man owned the land, and he told the people that if they were going to remain here they must pay something to him. They asked, 'What must we pay?' And he said, 'When the time comes, a person must die.' They said: 'How is this? We have just been given life. Are we now supposed to die just because Death Old Man demands it?' They protested against Death Old Man and they resolved to destroy him, but they did not know how to do it. One time they came to a certain mountain that rumbled and threw out great clouds of smoke. Men went to the top of the mountain and saw that it was hollow, and that down below the earth was boiling like water and throwing stones into the air. People said: 'Here is the place to dispose of Death Old Man. Let us throw him here, then he will never return to claim our lives.'

"Now, in those days Death Old Man was not terrible to see. He looked like an ordinary person. He would come smiling and speak gently, saying, 'You, old one, come with me on a walk.' The old one would go, leaving his body behind. Because the people had decided what to do they were on guard against Death Old Man's coming. And when he arrived smiling at the house of an ailing old woman they seized him, dragged him to the smoking mountain and threw him in. They looked below and saw Death Old Man sink under the boiling earth. They said, 'Now we are finished with death.' But as they watched, Death Old Man came out of the boiling earth and climbed upward. When he reached the top they saw that the fire had burned off his hair and his skin, and that flames came from his mouth. They fled back to their village, gathered their belongings and went on a long journey and built a new village. But Death Old Man followed them wherever they went. And so it has been ever since. Wherever people go, death follows them."

That night Falling Snow lay awake a long time pondering on the nature and mystery of death. He wondered what it would be like when his body ceased to live, when it could no longer grasp a bow or climb a trail or go running across the valley. And when at last he slept he saw Death Old Man climbing out of the fire, his skin burned away and flames coming from his mouth. Falling Snow dreamed that he was in a footrace with Death Old Man, and that the old man was coming after him relentlessly. The following day while he was gathering winter firewood he realized that there were still more questions to ask his grandfather. He said to Limping Deer: "My grandfather, it is said that when people die they go to live in a certain place. How can that be? For one who has died is placed in the ground and covered with stones, and he does not emerge again."

Limping Deer answered: "It is one of the great mysteries that it should be this way. But it is truly said that the body that is placed under the stones is merely the covering, and the part that goes elsewhere to live is the breath of life. When the breath of life leaves the body, it goes to a village in the west that we who are alive cannot see, and there it lives on among others of its kind. A living person could walk through that village without knowing it is there, as one walks through the wind or the mist, unless he had the gift of medicine to give him the power of sight. Whether a living person ever went to the place of the dead and returned, who can say? We have been told it cannot happen. But it is different with the spirit that is contained by the body. A spirit may go and return.

"I will tell you now of something that occurred in my village when I was a boy. That village was the one we lived in before we moved to Bend-of-the-Water. At that time my uncle, Flowering Gourd, was still a young man. He fell ill. He slept several days without awakening. Then he stopped breathing. He lay as if ready for the burial ritual. Our curer was named Tall Chief. He came and saw Flowering Gourd's body lying on the blanket. He sat there for a while. Then he said: 'Flowering Gourd is not alive. But neither is he dead. It is only that his breath of life has taken a journey.' So Tall Chief did not go away, but sat there sounding his rattle and chanting a medicine song all through the night. The song he sang was to urge Flowering Gourd's breath of life to return. When the sunglow of the morning came, Flowering Gourd began to breathe again. He opened his eyes and said, 'I must wash and purify myself.' He went outside and they brought him hot water. He poured the water on his body and washed himself with yucca suds. He burned his old clothes and put on a new waistcloth and new leggings. After that he entered the house again and ate. Tall Chief asked him why it was necessary to purify himself, and Flowering Gourd answered, 'Because that is what one must do when he returns from the place of the dead.' Tall Chief asked him, 'You went there, to that place?'

"Flowering Gourd answered, 'Yes, I went there. I was lying here on my blanket, and it seemed that I died. I heard someone speaking to me. I opened my eyes. Someone was standing beside me. It was Little Elk, who had been killed by a bear while hunting. He called to me. Then he turned and went up the ladder out of my room and I followed. As I went up,' Flowering Gourd said, 'I looked back and saw myself lying on my blanket as if I were dead. Little Elk took my hand, saying, "I want to show you where I live." We walked to the edge of the cliff. I said, "We cannot go any farther." He laughed, saying, "For us there is no falling." He put his kilt on the ground and we stood on it. It floated away and came to the earth in a dark place,' Flowering Gourd said. 'There was a trail. Where the trail forked, Death Old Man was standing there. He had two faces, one in front and one behind. The face in front was handsome, as if he were a young man. Then he turned his head and I saw his other face, covered with scars and dripping blood. He laughed at me. Little Elk led me away and said, "Death Old Man looks down one trail with his gentle face, down the other with his terrifying face. One trail is for persons who have done good deeds in their lives, the other for those who are to be punished. A person who has done evil, or who has not been generous, or who has injured innocent people thirsts forever without being allowed to drink, and he pleads endlessly for water. Water is given to him and he places it to his lips, but it blows away like fog." '

"Flowering Gourd then told Tall Chief: 'Little Elk led me to the village where he lived. It looked like our own village. Women were grinding corn. Men were caring for their fields. Children were playing stick ball. In one field I saw Standing Corn, who was our chief until he died. In another I saw Sleeping Owl, who was our crier chief. In a certain house, I saw my father and mother, and I also saw my grandfather descending into his kiva. I wanted to speak with them, but Little Elk said: "No, it is useless. They cannot see you or hear you. Only when your time comes and you arrive here like others who have died will they know you. That is the way it is. Now we have to return, because your body still lies in your house and it is growing cold." Little Elk brought me back to my house, saying, "Go quickly before it is too late." I entered. I saw my body lying on the blanket. I saw Tall Chief sitting there with his rattle. I lay down and entered my body. That is all.' "

Limping Deer paused, reflecting on the story, then he continued: "What Flowering Gourd told the people, I myself did not see it. But I was one of those who saw his still body on the blanket, and I saw that his breath of life returned to him. What he said about the place of the dead, we believe it to be true because it corresponds with what our old ones taught us. So let us not suppose that one dies and becomes nothing. Let us consider the place from which we come when we are born. We cannot see that place, but does this mean it is not there? It surely is there, for we must come from somewhere. And where we go when our bodies are dead, we do not see it, yet surely it is there." Falling Snow's eyes were fixed on the fading embers in the fireplace. He thought: "So that is our journey, from what is unknown to what is unknown. One comes from the mist and departs into the mist. In the mist is the secret of everything."

Two days before the scheduled festival another wandering family arrived on the eastern cliff and descended into the canyon. The group crossed the valley but did not enter the village. They sat on the ground waiting for someone to come and acknowledge their presence. Because Limping Deer found it difficult to climb the ladders of his house, Yellow Corn went out in his place, accompanied by several other old ones. There were ten persons in the strangers' party, two men and the rest of them women and children. Their faces were dark and creased by the sun, and Yellow Corn saw by the manner of their dress that they must have come from a distant place. Their hair was long. The men wore armbands of woven grass, and the women had strings of shells around their necks. Yellow Corn said, "Where are you people going and why are you here?" But the answer was in a tongue that the Grey Fox People did not know. So Yellow Corn sat on the ground with the older of the two men and they made hand signs to one another. The stranger cupped his hand and put it to his mouth, meaning his people were thirsty, so Yellow Corn sent for a jar of water. The man closed his hand against his chest, then extended his arm forward several times, meaning great distances and long journeys. He held his hands out palms down, lowered them a little and drew them toward his chest, meaning his people were tired. He held a closed hand forward and brought it to the ground, meaning his people would rest in this place. They conversed this way, watching one another's lips and eyes, and although some of their meanings were not clear, Yellow Corn understood enough to be able to go to the kiva and report.

"They are one family," he said. "They have been living alone in the wilderness many seasons. They come from the north somewhere and call themselves The People, though others have given them the name Earth House People. They are looking for a branch of their family which came this way five summers ago heading for the Western River. Now they are tired and want to rest here for the winter. Their language is not known to me, but it certainly is not Utaheh or Tinneh. Two of the women and one of the children are sick. The old man says they must find shelter now or the sick ones may die. He says, 'Allow us to build one earth house, maybe two, on the edge of the village, or perhaps on the small mound a little beyond.' He says, 'We had a little buffalo meat when we started, now we have nothing. Let us hunt for a deer now and then. That is all we want. When the grass begins to grow again we will leave.' "

The council discussed what should be done. Someone said: "This is a Grey Fox settlement. First we have the Bean People coming, then the

Earth House People. It is too much. We do not know them. Let them go on to the next canyon." Another said, "Yes, let them go on. Is there too much game here? Do we have more meat than we need? It is we who built the village and cleaned the spring and lined it with stones. After all this are we required to share with people who make their houses out of dirt?" But others argued differently. A man said: "If they settle on the small mound how will it hurt us? The people are sick. Shall we throw them away? They are hungry. Shall we tell them to eat snow when winter comes?" When all had spoken, Yellow Corn said: "If they stay, how will it make our life unbearable? The village will be one family stronger. And how do we know that they do not possess some power of medicine that would benefit everyone?" Yellow Corn's argument prevailed, and it was decided that he should find out what medicine the Earth House People owned. If it was good they could build on the mound and remain for the winter.

When Yellow Corn returned to the place where the strangers were waiting they were sitting exactly as he had left them. Again he spoke with their leader. Yellow Corn made the sign for medicine by holding the back of his hand against his forehead. He said the village wanted to know what powers the Earth House People could contribute. The stranger took a small leather bag out of a basket and placed a cloth on the ground. From the bag he took small animal figures carved from stone, bone and horn, and he placed them carefully on the cloth. Each of the figures was decorated with feathers or shells. Pointing first at one figure and then another, the man conveyed through hand signs that the Earth House People had been given the knowledge of animals and animal ways, and they had a spiritual tie with elk, deer, bear and other creatures. In times of scarce game their medicine was of great value. When they killed game they had special prayers to give the animals to take with them to their spiritual dwelling land. At last the man replaced the figures in their leather bag and sat waiting. Yellow Corn said: "Yes, it is agreed. Take the small mound over there, build your house. Another time we will sit together and talk of other things."

So the Earth House people went to the mound and began to make their house. Already in the village the people were calling the site Earth House Mound.

The day of the festival arrived. Scarcely had the sun come up over the eastern cliff when the scouts at the guard post called out that visitors were arriving from Red Rocks Place. As the arrivals entered the village they were greeted with words of welcome from the rooftops.

Children were given rolls of colored piki bread, and the older people were invited to sit on the stone curbs that surrounded the kiva, from which came the sound of the Desert Spirit dancers chanting purifying prayers. And when many people had gathered in the central court a clown dancer emerged from the kiva, naked except for designs painted on his skin to resemble clothes. He had a bulbous red nose made from a gourd, and his hair was plaited over basketwork so that it stood straight up. He pranced through the court pompously making ludicrous and sometimes indecorous gestures, shaking his rattle in the faces of the spectators. He lay down and snored. Then he jumped to his feet and became a hunter, shooting tiny arrows from a bow scarcely large enough to see. He pursued an imaginary animal around a corner, and soon came running back with a bear clown pursuing him. They disappeared around the far end of the court. The old people smiled, and the children laughed gleefully. A moment later the bear clown returned chewing on the hunter's bow. Now the old ones joined the laughter. As the bear clown left the court he stopped to urinate on the chewed-up bow, and received cheers from the spectators.

Later the Desert Spirit dancers came from the kiva, their bodies painted and their faces masked. They wore headdresses made of many kinds of feathers, and shell leg bands that made musical sounds. The dancers arranged themselves in a line facing the east. They moved forward and back as they sang, calling on Desert Spirit for his friendship and help during the coming cold of winter. When they finished their first song they returned to the kiva and prayed, and then the clown dancer came again, this time imitating women grinding corn and cleaning deerskins. Four times the Desert Spirit dancers came from the kiva and performed chants. Then women came from all the houses bringing food for the visitors, and there were games at the edge of the village. Children played stick ball and there were footraces between the young men of the two villages. The racers ran to a distant piñon tree, circled it and returned, a Red Rocks runner against a Grey Fox runner, while men sat gambling on the outcome of each race. They bet such things as armbands, bear claws, bits of turquoise and coral, and buckskin leggings.

When the footraces came to an end there was an arrow-shooting contest. A basketry tray was suspended from the branch of a cottonwood tree and weighted at the bottom with a stone. The cord was twisted until it was tight, then released, and as the tray spun around, the contestants shot arrows at it, some scoring hits but most missing.

Late in the afternoon as the light began to fade, the men went to retrieve their arrows and the game was over. The Red Rocks visitors were invited into Grey Fox houses for the night, though some slept on the roofs or in the kiva. Long Arrow and Limping Deer sat together and exchanged thoughts about the coming winter, corn, game and ceremonies. When at last Limping Deer's house slept it was almost time for the sun to rise. The Red Rocks people left early in the day, asking Grey Fox People to come to their winter festival. They crossed the valley and went up the eastern cliff, while workaday calm returned to the village.

In the afternoon of that day Yellow Corn came with a serious face to talk with Limping Deer, saying, "There is something for us to consider." Limping Deer answered: "Tell me, Yellow Corn. I see that it is not good." Yellow Corn said: "Today the children went to the cottonwood tree where the arrow-shooting contest took place. They searched for arrows that were lost and broken shafts from which they could remove the flint points. Here and there they found something." He paused, and Limping Deer said: "Yes, it was a thing to be done. Perhaps the points can be used again." Yellow Corn went on: "They found some good shafts and they found some points. Walking Bear's daughter was there. She found an arrow. She gave it to Walking Bear. He brought it to me." Yellow Corn placed the arrow on the ground before Limping Deer. Limping Deer looked at it closely. He said, "It is marked with a red band." Yellow Corn put down another arrow, saying, "This is one of the arrows that killed Red Sky." Limping Deer held the two arrows side by side and brought them close to his eyes to see them clearly. He said, "Yes, they are the same."

They sat silently for a while, neither of them wishing to speak. At last Limping Deer said, "My heart is sore, for I know truly that Long Arrow is a good brother." Yellow Corn answered: "Yes, I know it. But the arrow was shot by one of his people. Perhaps it is only a single man who marks his arrow this way. I thought about it before coming here. I thought: 'Perhaps the arrows that killed Red Sky and the dog really came from the Utaheh. Perhaps the man who painted this shaft merely copies something he has heard about. Why should I disturb Limping Deer? It will only make his heart heavy.' Yet I thought again, 'Whatever the truth is we must find it out, otherwise our two villages cannot trust each other anymore.' So I brought the matter to you. Let us think with care about it. We cannot hide from it." Limping Deer answered, "Yes, your words are good."

Several days later Limping Deer sent Falling Snow to ask Yellow Corn to come to his house. When Yellow Corn arrived, the two men smoked to bring their thoughts in harmony, and afterwards Limping Deer said: "The bands of the arrows gnaw at me. I must go to Long Arrow and ask him to deal with this thing. If it is not done our villages cannot live together." Yellow Corn said: "Yes, if it is not done soon it may be too late. But as for you, your health is not good. The cold winds are already blowing. Remain here, and I will go and speak for you." Limping Deer said: "No, it is for me to speak. I will go." Yellow Corn answered: "My brother, you now have difficulty with the ladders. How can you make this journey? If you go, will you return?" And Limping Deer said: "Tonight I will make prayer feathers for Desert Spirit and the grey fox who gave us our name. Let us begin early in the morning, with Yellow Bird and Flowing Spring. I will not let the breath of life go out of me before we see Long Arrow. This is the way it must be done."

When morning came, Falling Snow and White Moccasin helped Limping Deer out of the house. Yellow Corn, Flowing Spring and Yellow Bird were waiting for him and they began the journey. They went slowly across the valley, and when they arrived at the foot of the eastern cliff Yellow Corn said to Limping Deer: "To climb this trail is not easy for any of us. We are not young men anymore. But for you it is a big thing. Turn back to the village. I will speak for you, and Yellow Bird and Flowing Spring will speak eloquently for themselves." Limping Deer's answer was to begin the climb. He had to stop frequently to rest, but he continued on to the top, where he said, "As you can see, Grey Fox led me safely." They resumed walking, and though they went slowly, Limping Deer sometimes said, "As you see, I am going along well."

The following day they arrived at Red Rocks Place, and the four Grey Fox old ones went into Long Arrow's kiva and smoked with him. When the time came to talk, Limping Deer said: "My brother, many times I wanted to sit here with you. Now I have come because there is something for all of us to ponder on. The matter of the arrows has not gone away, and it disturbs the world around us. We want only balance and harmony, but they elude us. What you told us about your four clans and their arrows, we believed it. We know that you told us what was in your heart. And so we made a Desert Spirit ceremony for you. Your people came and we fed them, just as you have fed us. There were games. Arrows were shot at the twirling basket tray. When your people departed, our children picked up the lost and broken arrows for their points. This arrow was found by Walking Bear's child. And here are the arrows that killed Red Sky and our hunting dog." He laid the arrows side by side on the ground. "Now, my brother, how can we go on without something being done? The maker of the arrows is one of your sons, for all the Red Rocks people are your children. We do not tell a father how to deal with his children. You alone must decide how to do it. It is in your hands. When you have dealt with it, let us know. We want everything to be the way it was in the beginning. We want to share our lives with you. We want it said everywhere that we are twin villages, each one part of a whole."

Long Arrow answered: "My brother, your words are like hot embers. I had thought everything was in harmony. What you tell me now will take time to consider. You have matched the arrows, that is true. Yet to me the markings are still Utaheh. Red Sky could have been killed by Utaheh. I do not believe he could have been killed by any of my people. But you give me a red band and say it was found at the place of the contest. If one of our young men shot this arrow I cannot explain it. I have never heard that a Red Rocks hunter makes such marks, just as you yourself have never heard of a Grey Fox hunter making such marks. What can I tell you? I will pursue the matter. I will look for the maker of the red banded arrow shaft. Let us imagine that I find him and that he acknowledges himself to be the one who made it, but he says, 'My father, I shot such an arrow at the Grey Fox contest, but of Red Sky's death and the killing of the dog I don't know anything.' How then will I be able to make things right?"

Yellow Bird answered, saying: "If you find him, that is the end of the story. If he shot the arrow at our contest you will not need to know any more. The four arrows are identical. He could not choose any one of them and say, 'I made this one only.'"

Long Arrow looked at Yellow Bird reproachfully. He said: "My brother, you press me too hard. I need more room. There are two things to consider. The arrow is one, and the truth told by a man's heart is the other. For you it is only the arrow that counts. But I am the father of the village and I must listen to what a man says. I will follow the trail wherever it goes. If I find the person I will do something. I will let you know. I cannot say any more."

Limping Deer and his party returned to Refuge Place, but the journey was slow because Limping Deer often had to rest. He found it difficult to descend into the canyon. When he arrived at his house he had to be helped to climb to the roof and go down to his living quarters, and he went at once to his blanket, where, after that, he spent most of his days and nights. Sometimes he asked White Moccasin if there had been any word from Long Arrow, but she had nothing to tell him. One evening he said: "I have heard Desert Spirit speaking with the voice of the owl. Now I will go into the kiva."

So they took him to the kiva and prepared a blanket for him near the fireplace. Each day after that White Moccasin brought him food, though he ate little, and every night Falling Snow brought firewood and kept the fire going. Yellow Corn and Still Water came often to sit near Limping Deer and talk with him, and he sometimes asked them, also, if Long Arrow had sent any message. The answer was always the same, that there was no word from Red Rocks Place.

When Yellow Corn arrived at the kiva one day he saw that life was leaving Limping Deer, and he sent for other old ones to come. They sat singing sacred songs that gave the history of the Grey Fox People from the time they emerged from the earth. They sang of the first village and the second village and all the villages that followed, and of the signs that had told them where to go. By the time the song spoke of Refuge Place, Limping Deer was dead.

At the rim of the western cliff, above the place where the canyon floor merged with the wilderness, they found a cleft in the rock, and Limping Deer, wrapped in his ceremonial blanket, was carried there. They placed him in a sitting position facing eastward toward the spot where the sun rose in the spring. Next to him they set bowls of food, and a kiva pipe to bring him into harmony with things. When everything had been done and all was in order they closed the rocky cleft with stones and returned to the village. Falling Snow could not accustom himself to the silence that blanketed his house. White Moccasin made pots, ground meal and did all the things she had done formerly, but she did not often speak, and sometimes she sat on the roof and looked across the canyon, though her eyes did not seem to see anything that was there.

For many days after Limping Deer's death the Grey Fox People had no village leader. The old ones debated the question of a new chief night after night. They discussed one man's gifts, then another's. Yellow Bird had conversed with Desert Spirit; Still Water had brotherhood with the snakes; Yellow Corn had the knowledge of curing fevers and mending broken bones; Flowing Spring had once had a vision of the underworld out of which the people had been born. But they could not clearly see which gifts outweighed all others, and so they did not come to a decision.

The days grew colder and the nights longer. There was much hunting now because game was scarce. A hunter might spend six or seven days roaming the hunting grounds before killing a deer, and there were some who returned without anything. So it was suggested that the Earth House People might now show what their medicine could accomplish, and the matter was put to Small Buffalo, who was head of the family. He came to the kiva with his bag of sacred animal figures and set them out on a cloth. He sprinkled cornmeal on them and chanted songs invoking their spirits for help. He promised that every animal killed would receive a prayer feather to take with him on his journey to the sky. The ceremony lasted until late in the night. When Small Buffalo saw a certain star through the opening of the kiva he brought the ritual to an end.

Ten hunters went out the following day, and when they returned, four had deer and the rest came with turkeys, marmots or other small game. In the kiva the medicine of the Earth House People was praised. Yet soon, once again, game became hard to find, and the hunters had to go far beyond their old hunting grounds.

In the kiva the old ones debated what could be done, and they considered reviving some ancient ceremonies that had not been performed for many years. But Flowing Spring dismissed it, saying, "How can they be performed? The old men who conducted these ceremonies are dead, and their knowledge was taken with them. What is wrong is that we have no village leader. We are not in good order. A village without a chief is a body without a head. If we ourselves are not in balance, how can we be in harmony with the land? If we stay as we are the land will reject us." So once more they took up the matter of the leadership. In the end they decided that because Yellow Corn was related to Limping Deer on his mother's side, and because he understood the meaning of balance and harmony, he should be given the responsibility if he could evoke a sign.

Yellow Corn said: "I will take the responsibility. I will look for the sign." And on the third night after the decision Yellow Corn went into the kiva with the kiva brotherhood and prepared himself to seek a vision. They smoked, purified their hearts of dissension and bad memories, sprinkled sacred meal and sang sacred songs. Crying Wolf sat at the top of the ladder watching the stars, and when he announced that the Suitor had reached a certain place over the western cliff, Yellow Corn arose and put on his ceremonial waistcloth and moccasins. He painted his chest with white marks and made lines of red and black under his eyes. He arranged his hair and tied it back, cresting it with a bluebird feather. Then they chanted again until Crying Wolf announced that the first glow of the sun had appeared.

Yellow Corn left the kiva and went up the cliff trail behind the village. He walked westward across the flat tableland, putting thoughts out of his mind and letting himself merge into the singleness of the land around him. He went where there were no trails. He lost the sense of being Yellow Corn, as if he had no identity. He came to a cluster of piñon trees but did not pause. He came to a mound of broken rock but went on. In his mind there formed a picture of the place he was seeking. At last he came to a point of land at the edge of a small canyon, and there he found a large pothole in the smooth surface of the rock. Without hesitating he stepped into it and lay down among some small pottery shards that littered the bottom. He closed his eyes and chanted a purifying song.

He felt the warmth of the sun on his body, then shadow as the sun dipped into the west. Night came, and with it the cold wind. When he opened his eyes he saw bright stars looking down, and he saw the winter moon move across the sky. He did not know if he slept. Morning came and he heard the call of a crow and coyotes barking. In time the sounds of the living world merged into a low humming that enveloped him like a blanket. The rock bed on which he was lying became soft. At last Yellow Corn felt himself going out of the pit, leaving his body behind. Now he was standing before a large boulder whose edges had been rounded by eternal wind and rain. The boulder spoke to him, saying, "You are here," and he answered, "Yes, grandfather, I am here." He perceived that the surface of the boulder was only a soft covering of what was within, like a buckskin garment. And as he watched, the buckskin garment fell away and Ancient One, grandfather of all grandfathers, stood there in the form of a man. On his arms were bands dangling with bear and wildcat claws. His loin girdle was made of animal skin, and his moccasins were of woven grass. His hair hung long and straight over his shoulders, and across his face from cheekbone to cheekbone were two painted lines.

Ancient One said: "I have been waiting for you. Follow me." He descended into the ground through a small crack in the rock, and Yellow Corn followed. They were in an enormous kiva as large as a village, and many people were there, some sitting, some performing tasks.

Ancient One said: "Here we live. Now you understand that even hard substance has life within it. Now let us smoke." They sat on the ground and Tobacco Man brought them a lighted pipe. The smoke that they blew from their mouths went upward and formed clouds that drifted eastward toward Refuge Place. Ancient One said: "Because there is harmony here between what is old and what is new, the clouds bring rain to your people. Let us speak of the way things are in the world. My grandchildren are scattered everywhere, going and coming in the wilderness, not knowing what they doing. They build one village here, another there, and the earth is covered with the debris of their pottery. As for you Grey Fox People, you have not yet been able to put away dissension from your lives. And so, in time, you will have to journey again. You have been named Yellow Corn by your mother's family, but I am giving you a secret name now. It is a medicine name and will make your heart strong. I call you Stone Opener, because you have perceived that there is life within things that seem lifeless. This is the true nature of the world."

Yellow Corn wanted to know more. He wanted to ask about the journey, but the kiva and everything in it faded away and he saw that he was lying again in the pothole. He lay for a while reflecting on what he had seen, then he arose and began his return to Refuge Place. He was weak and his lips were parched, and he found the walking difficult. When he arrived at the western cliff he stopped briefly at the guard post for water before descending to the village. He went directly to the kiva and there he was soon joined by others of the kiva brotherhood.

They asked him if a vision had come, and after that they pressed him for details. He said: "In my vision I met with Ancient One. He had a blanket of stone. I sat with him in his kiva, and there were many ancestors gathered there." After a pause he told his story from the beginning, and as he finished, someone asked, "My brother, are you certain that you did not merely dream?" He answered: "No, there was no dreaming. I perceived it just as I perceive us sitting together now. It did not flow through me like the mist. I can tell you each thing I saw."

He closed his eyes to recapture the scene. "In the great kiva there are many persons. Next to the wall women are sewing buckskin with bone needles. They wear grass sandals and have nothing of woven cotton, only the skins of animals. At another place men are making flint points, and beyond them there are old ones carving prayer sticks and fastening eagledown to the ends. There are pegs on the wall from which hang snakeskins, deerskins, bearskins and the skins of antelope.

These are the skins the people wear when they go to the outer world in their animal forms. In the center of the kiva sits a man wearing buffalo horns. He writes the mysteries of history with colored sand, and the colors of the sand are black, yellow, red and white. I see Ancient One's face clearly. It has black lines across the bridge of his nose from one cheekbone to the other. On his jaw a mole is growing. His eyes are deep and I cannot see to the bottom of them. Hanging from his belt is a knapsack made of a bear's foot, the claws still on it. His voice, I hear it. If he were to speak in the darkness I would recognize him. Ancient One gave me a secret medicine name. All this I experienced truly. He spoke of another thing that troubles me. He said that the Grey Fox People have not finished their migration, though he did not say when we would travel again or where we would go. Now, there was more that I saw and heard, but is not this enough?"

Most of the men indicated with motions of their heads that it was indeed enough, but Yellow Bird persisted, asking questions that might reveal whether Yellow Corn had merely dreamed or had invented part of his story. At last Yellow Corn said: "My brothers, you want me to be responsible for the Grey Fox People. I did not ask to become chief. The responsibility you want me to take is like carrying a load of heavy stones up the side of a steep dune, and there is no rest from it until death comes. If you doubt me in any way, there are other men who are qualified to lead, and if you select one of them I will acknowledge him as father of the village. I will tell you one thing more, and after that I will be silent. When Ancient One and I smoked in the great kiva, the smoke went up and formed clouds in the sky, and these clouds floated toward Refuge Place. Ancient One said, 'The clouds bring rain to your people.' If no rain came to the canyon while I was away, then what I saw was meaningless. Yet if rain fell it is surely something to think about. Now I will go to my house to eat and sleep. It is not in my hands anymore."

In the silence that followed, Still Water said: "My brother, there is nothing more to discuss. The rain came and fell on the canyon." Crying Wolf arose and went to the kiva roof, where he called for the village to assemble. The people came from their houses, and whoever could crowd into the kiva did so. Still Water then said that henceforth Yellow Corn would be the chief of the Grey Fox village and take responsibility for the people's welfare.

The first snow fell that night and people said, "Winter Old Man lays his blanket down." In the morning the valley was white and the air was crisp and still. Children went out to play snow games. They made paths in the snow and chased one another pretending to be rabbits and coyotes. Women and girls filled their jars with snow and took them inside, sparing them a trip to the spring, and men saw to their firewood.

White Moccasin said to Falling Snow: "This is your day. On a day like this you were born at Bend-of-the-Water." Falling Snow answered in a serious tone, "And you, my grandmother, when you were born were there white moccasins falling from the sky?" White Moccasin was still considering whether Falling Snow's joke was disrespectful when White Star began to laugh. It was the first laughter that had come from his mouth since his return from the north. He became exuberant and climbed the ladder to the roof where he stood shouting, "The moccasins are falling, the moccasins are falling!" White Moccasin said, "I think life will go well for him now."

Falling Snow was still inside smoothing arrow shafts when someone called down to him: "Two persons have arrived. They are Yayatu. They are waiting for you at the edge of the village." Falling Snow went out quickly. He found Elk Horn and a girl standing there, blankets over their shoulders. He called out, "I see you, Elk Horn," and Elk Horn answered, "I see you, Falling Snow." Falling Snow said, "Do not stand here, let us go to my grandmother's house." Elk Horn and the girl followed him. When they were inside, Elk Horn said: "This is Buffalo Girl. We have left our village. We cannot return there." Falling Snow said to White Moccasin: "This is my cousin, Elk Horn. We hunt together. The girl's name, you have heard it."

Elk Horn said: "We wanted to be together, but her family wanted her to marry Sleeping Wolf. He has children but no wife. He spoke for Buffalo Girl. Her family said they would consider it. I myself went to her family. I said, 'I, Elk Horn, want your daughter.' They said: 'You, Elk Horn, you have not yet been initiated in the kiva. Therefore you are not yet a man ready to come asking for a wife.' Buffalo Girl spoke, saying, 'My father, my mother, I will wait until he is initiated.' They said: 'It is time for you to marry. Sleeping Wolf is a good hunter. His corn grows well. Do not throw away something good.' And they said to me: 'Elk Horn, let it go. When your time comes you will have a wife.' I said to them: 'Father and mother of Buffalo Girl, be my father and mother as well. I also am a good hunter. And are there no men among us who have not been initiated before getting wives?' I argued. At last they said: 'Elk Horn, it is done. There is nothing to talk about. Do not come any more asking for Buffalo Girl.' So when it was dark the two of us left the village. The wind was cold. We said, 'Where can we go in this wilderness?' And I thought: 'My friend Falling Snow is a good cousin. He will help us.' "

Falling Snow said, "Yes, stay in our village." White Moccasin smiled at the young people. She said: "Such things cannot be decided instantly. But for now, sit by the fire and eat." She gave them food, and for a while they did not speak. Then Falling Snow said: "I will take them to Yellow Corn. He will decide." He led them to the kiva and found Yellow Corn there. He said, "My grandfather," and Yellow Corn answered, "My grandson." Falling Snow said, "There is something to speak about, a serious matter." Yellow Corn said: "Very well, my children, but let us do things properly. One is supposed to smoke before talking of serious things." He lighted a pipe and puffed on it. He passed it to Falling Snow, who, in turn, passed it to Elk Horn. Elk Horn gave it to Buffalo Girl. She held the pipe uncertainly. Yellow Corn held back his smile, saying: "Yes, you also must smoke. If you do not smoke we will not know if your feelings toward us are good." So the girl puffed a little and coughed. Yellow Corn said: "Yes, that is enough. Our tobacco is strong." He put the pipe away and said to Falling Snow: "Now let us speak of things. Why are we gathered here?" Falling Snow said, "My grandfather, the meaning is this," and he told how Elk Horn and Buffalo Girl were forced to leave the Yayatu village. Elk Horn also spoke, elaborating on his conversation with Buffalo Girl's parents and on Sleeping Wolf's claim.

When he knew everything that Elk Horn could tell him, Yellow Corn said: "It is a serious matter. You, Buffalo Girl, your family has a grievance because you did not go the way they wanted you to go. You, Elk Horn, Sleeping Wolf has a grievance against you, for he was allowed to believe he would get Buffalo Girl as his wife. Buffalo Girl's clan was deprived of a chance to increase. And the village will resent everything, saying, 'We were to have a wedding celebration, but now there will not be one.' So we can see how it is back there."

Yellow Corn picked up his pipe with his right hand and transferred it to his left hand, indicating that he would now look at the problem from another side. He said: "Suppose we allowed you to stay in Refuge Place. Your people could be angry with us. They could say that we meddled in their affair. It could cause hard feelings. However, if two young people run away into the wilderness together it can be taken as a sign that the old ones were too obstinate and that they were looking for a solution that was not in balance. Perhaps now they will reflect on the situation and grow tired of being angry. They may look at the snow blowing across the land and say, 'Our daughter Buffalo Girl and our son Elk Horn, let us pray that they are safe out there in the wilderness.' They may say, 'Is it so easy to forget what it was like to be young?' "

Yellow Corn shifted the pipe back to his right hand, saying: "Yet it may not be like that. They may say, 'Those young people do not understand the order of things. They do not know that a village is held together like a person's body, with bones and sinews. They reject the knowledge of the old. Bring them back so that they can be corrected.' How the people are speaking of you back in your village I do not know. However, now you are here. We will find you a place to lay your blanket. Rest awhile. In time we will hear from Running Buffalo and then we will know how the matter lies."

That night in the kiva Yellow Corn informed the Grey Fox elders about the matter. Some of them were amused. They said: "Is this something for the council to debate? It is nothing, only a boy and a girl who ran away from one place to another. What is the harm? It doesn't matter about Running Buffalo. He is wise in the ways of the world. Let them stay and be done with it."

But Yellow Bird saw it differently. He said: "Well, now, are we finally allowing Yayatu to live in the village? Let us pause a moment before deciding. Who knows if the young man's story is true? Who knows whether or not they were sent here for a purpose? In a few days he will know how much corn is stored in every house, how many young women we have. He will know how many lances and bows are in the village, how strong the guard posts are, and how many men are out hunting. Then one night he slips away and takes his knowledge to Running Buffalo. I do not truly know what is in the boy's heart or in Running Buffalo's heart. You, also, do not know anything for certain. Suppose we agree to let them stay, and then, if no harm comes to us you will say, 'Yellow Bird was foolish.' Very well. But suppose they stay and the Yayatu come and sack our village. It will not help us then if people say, 'Yellow Bird's words were wise.' "

Yellow Corn refrained from speaking, because he had the responsibility of bringing harmony. It was Flowing Spring who answered Yellow Bird, saying: "Here we are, a substantial village. We have a chief, a war chief, a crier chief. We have a snake priest, a curer and others with strong medicine. We have brave young men, we have many lances and bows. We accept Bean People and Earth House People. Two children who run away to be with each other, are we supposed to fear them?" The old ones laughed, all except Yellow Bird. Yellow Corn continued: "As for the Yayatu, why should we be worried about them? What have they done?

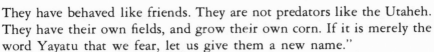

They have behaved like friends. They are not predators like the Utaheh. They have their own fields, and grow their own corn. If it is merely the word Yayatu that we fear, let us give them a new name."

Yellow Bird was angry. He said: "Flowing Spring asks whether we fear this and that, mocking my concern for the village. When have I been lacking in courage? When I was younger was I not always in the front of the fighting when we were attacked? Must I show you my scars? Must I bring out my shield on which I marked the number of enemies that I killed? But we are not young warriors now. We are the elders, the caretakers of the people. That is why we are here discussing this matter. We look at the corn ear with care. If it is rotten on one side we throw it away so that it will not spoil the good ears. If you are not willing to look at the rotten side, why do we bother to speak at all?"

At last Yellow Corn held out his hand, palm down, and brought it to the ground, meaning, "Let it rest here." He said: "Let us not speak angrily to one another. We all sit in the same kiva. We have not even finished plastering its walls. We have not even lived here a full year. We have not yet planted our first corn. Let us not be like a snake swallowing its own tail. We will let Running Buffalo know that the young people are here. Meanwhile, let us reflect peacefully on things." He sent for Young Antelope, who was preparing to go north to hunt. He said: "When you are out there, visit the Yayatu village and give this message to Running Buffalo. Tell him that the Grey Fox People greet him and want him to know that Elk Horn and Buffalo girl are with us. Tell him we are allowing them to stay, not knowing what else can be done. We do not want to offend the Yayatu people in any manner, and therefore we want to know what Running Buffalo says about these things."

The next day Young Antelope went north, and when he returned six days later he told Yellow Corn: "My father, I went to the Yayatu and I spoke to Running Buffalo as I was instructed. His answer was this: 'Tell Yellow Corn all is well between us. There are some in our village who are not happy that the young ones ran away. Now it is done, and it cannot be helped. It is not the first time that such things have happened. If there is anything to be done now it is up to Sleeping Wolf. If he asks me I will counsel him. Meanwhile, let our villages rest in harmony.' These are the words of Running Buffalo." And it seemed for the moment that there was nothing more to worry about. Elk Horn and Buffalo Girl were allowed to live in a house that had been begun and left unfinished, until such time as Elk Horn could build for himself.

However, the affair was not so simply resolved. One day Sleeping

Wolf arrived in the village, and he went and sat at the wall of the kiva. He would not move, and to those who questioned him he said, "I will speak only to the chief." Yellow Corn came and said, "Let us go inside the kiva and talk." But Sleeping Wolf replied: "No, I have nothing to whisper under the ground. I will speak openly so that everyone can hear. I came to get Buffalo Girl. Give her to me and I will go." Yellow Corn said: "I did not bring the girl here. She is not mine. How can I give her to you?" Sleeping Wolf said: "You are wrong. You have a part in it. Elk Horn brought her and the village said, 'It is good.' Is it your right to hide something that is not yours? Bring her out. I will take her away and it will be finished." Yellow Corn answered, "The affair belongs to her family and her family is not here." Sleeping Wolf said: "Her family agreed to it. They said, 'You, Sleeping Wolf, can have our daughter.' Then Elk Horn stole her out of the village when everyone was sleeping. If someone steals something from the village at night, does it then belong to him or to the person from whom it was taken?" By this time people had gathered, and they stood witnessing the argument. Yellow Corn said: "If you will not come into the kiva, then let us go to my house. We will eat something and talk in harmony." Sleeping Wolf answered: "Food, I cannot swallow it and I do not accept it. I will not go into your house. I will stay here until you give me what I came to claim. Bring Buffalo Girl and then you will not hear my voice anymore. If this is not done, I am ready to kill Elk Horn." Yellow Bird intruded on the discussion, saying: "Well, you see what the Yayatu business comes to. Send them both back, the boy and the girl. In a few days they have already brought dissension to the village."

At this moment Elk Horn appeared with a lance in his hand and stood confronting Sleeping Wolf. Sleeping Wolf said to him: "Bring Buffalo Girl. I will take her back." Elk Horn answered: "It is useless. She came with me because she did not want to be a wife in your house." Sleeping Wolf said: "I did not come all this way in the snow to hear you say, 'Go away.' I will leave only when matters are made right. If there is no other way I will kill you." It seemed as if Sleeping Wolf was about to raise his lance, and Yellow Corn stepped between the two young men, saying: "No, things are not settled this way in our village. Put your lances down. We will talk together in the kiva, and we will not come out until we find a solution." So at last Sleeping Wolf laid down his lance and Elk Horn did the same. They went into the kiva with Yellow Corn, followed by two other old ones.

It was a long while before they emerged, and when they did so Yellow Corn announced: "It is settled. Sleeping Wolf says that if Buffalo Girl freely ran away with Elk Horn and if she does not want to come back, then he does not want her for his wife. He will leave her here. But Elk Horn acknowledges that he owes indemnity to Sleeping Wolf. Since he has nothing now to give, he pledges to pay certain things to Sleeping Wolf by the time the snow falls again next winter. He will pay four blankets, four baskets of corn and a string of turquoise or coral. As a sign that he has received justice Sleeping Wolf will take some of Elk Horn's hair and hang it in his house. Elk Horn may retrieve it when he has paid what he owes." Sleeping Wolf took out his flint knife and cut a handful of hair from one side of Elk Horn's head. He tied it together and placed it in his bearskin knapsack. He then picked up his lance and went out of the village without looking back. People looked at Elk Horn's hair, long on one side and shorn on the other, and they began to laugh. He departed from the courtyard not knowing whether to be gratified that Sleeping Wolf had been disposed of or to be ashamed that his hair had been taken.

A few days later, Long Arrow arrived from Red Rocks Place with two elders of his Blue Fox Clan, and with Yellow Corn and Still Water they entered the kiva. Yellow Corn lighted a pipe and they smoked. When the tobacco was consumed Yellow Corn said: "My brother, we are glad that you have come. We do not ask any questions because we know you have a purpose." And Long Arrow answered: "Yes, I want to speak of things that have disturbed our villages. When you came to Red Rocks with the question of the arrows I heard you. What you told me weighed on my spirit. The thing I had to find out was not easy. I could not simply call out, 'Has someone here slain a man and a hunting dog belonging to Refuge Place?' I had to walk slowly, observe much and say little. At last I found a man of a certain clan who marked his arrows with a red band. He made this mark because that was what his father had taught him. He was here at your festival and he shot at the spinning basket. You found his arrow. In the secrecy of my kiva I asked him, 'Tell me with a single heart, was it you who killed Red Sky and the dog?' And he answered: 'With a single heart I tell you, my father, I did not do it. It was surely a stranger who did it, because I am not the one.'

"Now this man, he is one of my children. Every person in the village is my child. How would you deal with your child in a situation like this? He spoke to me with a single heart, saying, 'I did not do it.' If a person speaks to you truly you know it from his eyes. Yet there are hard feelings between our villages because of what happened. The trust we had for one another was disturbed. If I did nothing your people would say: 'Long Arrow protects the one who shot the arrows. He is not our friend after all.' So I acted with a heavy heart. I made him leave the village. I gave him blankets, I gave him food for his journey. I do not know where he went. He took his people and left us, walking out into the open land. Will he ever arrive somewhere at a safe destination? I do not know. My heart was heavy for sending him away. But I did all this thinking that now our villages could live in harmony as before." Yellow Corn replied: "My brother, you have given us the gift of harmony. I will tell my people that the affair of the arrows is finished. Because of what you have done, our people and yours may live as a single village in two parts."

But Long Arrow was not finished. He said: "My brother, there is still something else to tell. It is not good. Six days ago one of our young men was hunting. He met a young woman from your village who was gathering roots in the snow. He said to her, 'Why do you look for roots when the snow has covered them?' She answered, 'I dig roots for a special thing I am making.' He asked, 'What kind of thing?' She said, 'Something other people do not know how to prepare, a lotion to use after returning from the place of the dead.' He laughed, thinking that she was joking with him. They talked together. After a while the young woman proposed that they should lie together in a nearby cave. The woman attracted him much, but he said: 'This thing, I would like to do it but I cannot, because in two days I am going to be initiated into the kiva society in my village. Until then I cannot lie with a woman.' She said: 'In Refuge Place this is not done. It is a silly thing.' He answered: 'Among my people it is done this way. If I were to lie with you something evil would happen.'

"She became angry with him. She said, 'If you refuse, something surely will not go well.' He answered: 'Do not be angry. Afterwards it will be different.' She said, 'Afterwards it will be too late.' She turned away toward Refuge Place, and when she reached a certain ridge she paused to look at him. Then she was not there anymore. It was as if she had become air. The young man thought, 'This young woman must be a witch.' He hunted, he returned to Red Rocks Place. He told his uncle what had happened. His uncle said: 'My nephew, you acted wisely. The woman was without doubt a witch.' " Long Arrow paused, preparing to tell what was yet to come.

"Two days later the kiva initiation took place. Four young men were in the kiva with the old ones. They were singing and making prayer feathers, and while they were engaged in these sacred duties two main roof timbers broke, and the stones and earth that covered the roof fell in. All but two of those who were there perished, four young men and five old men. Some of our important rituals perished also, because there is no one to carry them on. We dug the dead out and buried them. For two days and two nights we have sat discussing the catastrophe. And now, as you came to me about the arrows, I come to you to find the sorcerer in your village who caused this terrible thing to happen."

Yellow Corn and Still Water were greatly troubled by Long Arrow's certainty that there was a sorcerer in Refuge Place. Still Water said: "Once in the time of my father the Grey Fox People found a sorcerer among them, but in our own time we have never heard of one. This young woman you speak of, can you point her out?" Long Arrow said, "How can I, who have never seen her, say what she looks like?" And Yellow Corn replied, "Where, then, can we begin such a search?" Long Arrow said: "My brother, it is a heavy responsibility. I cannot tell you any more. The woman said she came from Refuge Place, and she returned to Refuge Place. So here is where she lives. The harm she has done to my village is great. My people cannot forgive it. As you held me to account for the arrows, so they hold you to account for the witchcraft that destroyed our kiva and those who were in it. As to the arrows, you can see that I left nothing undone to restore good feelings between us. Now it is you who must do something." Yellow Corn answered: "My brother, you must give us time. We will discuss it in council, and we shall go wherever the trail leads us. For now, let us say no more. You must eat and rest." And when the three old ones from Red Rocks Place had eaten and rested they departed from the village.

After Long Arrow's departure, Yellow Corn and Still Water discussed the situation for a long while, and at last they sent word out that there would be a council. When everyone was gathered, Yellow Corn repeated the story told by Long Arrow. Everyone was incredulous that a sorcerer might be living in Refuge Place. Some said without hesitation that Long Arrow was wrong in believing such a thing. One man argued: "Was it not said that the woman disappeared as though she were merely air? So how can it be said that she came here?" Another argued: "Do not forget that the young man only had the woman's word that she belonged to this village. If she was truly a sorcerer, perhaps she lied to cause trouble between our villages." And still another said: "Nevertheless, she was seen not far from Refuge Place. What other villages are there to consider?"

Then Yellow Bird spoke. He said: "Now we can see where we have been going. I warned you many times about the Yayatu. You said, 'The Yayatu mean us well.' Then you took in two young Yayatu, saying, 'What harm can it do?' Now we have a sorcerer. Are not all Yayatu sorcerers? And the girl that Elk Horn brought, is she not a Yaya? You know it, but you say, 'We do not learn through the ears but through the eyes.' I spoke before. I spoke strongly. You said to yourselves, 'Yellow Bird barks like a coyote.' Now you know what is true. Only the Yayatu have the power to do what was done to the kiva at Red Rocks Place. It is already too late to send Elk Horn and Buffalo Girl home. They have done their work. They must be killed. Only that way can we be finished with them and restore harmony with Long Arrow."

Flowing Spring said to Yellow Bird: "My brother, what you say must be considered. Yet I for one do not know truly that what happened to the Red Rocks kiva was the work of a sorcerer. So let us walk slowly. It is said that the man and the woman met six days ago. Let us find out where Buffalo Girl was on that day. Also, it has always been said that there is a way to identify people who have sorcerer's hearts." Others asked, "What way is that?" Flowing Spring answered: "I will not say it, or you will believe that I invented it while I talked. Let some other old one answer." Crying Wolf said: "Flowing Spring's words are true. We were told by our grandfathers that a sorcerer always has a small blue spot on the tip of his nose and another on the tip of his tongue. Is this not known to everyone?" Flowing Spring said, "As Crying Wolf describes it, that is the way my own grandfather told it to me." Still Water said: "Then the matter is simple. Send for the two Yayatu. Let us look for the spots."

So they sent for Elk Horn and Buffalo Girl, and when the young people arrived the old ones examined their noses and their tongues. But there were no blue spots. The old ones asked where Buffalo Girl had been on the day that the witch appeared, and it became clear that she had been in the village all the time. So they sent Elk Horn and Buffalo Girl away, saying, "It could not have been they who performed the sorcery." But Yellow Bird would not be stilled. He said: "Does not a sorcerer lie? And did your grandfathers forget to tell you that a sorcerer can be in two places at once? Perhaps Buffalo Girl was indeed in the village, but her shadow could have gone out in the snow to dig roots for a medicine to be used after one returns from the place of the dead. Who goes to the land of the dead and returns? Not ordinary people. As for the blue spots, let us consider. If the Yayatu can bring a dead person back to life and make white marks on distant rocks, is it hard for them to make a blue spot disappear? Only if we kill the two Yayatu will we be rid of them forever and bring back trust with Red Rocks Place."

"Killing first and thinking later is easy," Yellow Corn said. "We have heard many things here, but I heard no one say, 'Perhaps the beams of the kiva broke because they were old and rotten.' " "Yes," Crying Wolf said, "it could have been that way. Yet I myself have never before heard of a kiva collapsing. And for the roof to fall at the moment the ceremony was taking place, someone must have caused it." Another old one said, "Perhaps it was the weight of the snow." But in the end the council decided that the timing of the catastrophe must have involved an evil one, yet they did not know how to begin the search. As they left the kiva, Yellow Bird said: "You recognize a mountain only when it falls on you. Things are not going well for the Grey Fox People, and it is because their old ones meet in council and stir words around in a pot."

News of the tragic event at Red Rocks Place spread quickly. Women talked of it in the plaza, and hunters looked about them in the wilderness with heightened alertness. There was much recalling of tales about sorcerers and their evil works. Some began to observe strange manners and peculiar behavior on the part of one person or another. Casual conversations sometimes alluded to the fact that this person or that had not been seen in the village for days. Outwardly everything went on as before, but distrust had come to Refuge Place.

Urged by Falling Snow and White Star, White Moccasin one night told them a story of two girls at Badger Spring. "There was Cloud Child and there was Blue Sand Girl, and they were friends. They often went to the spring together for water, and when they were not working they sat and talked about the things girls talk about. They fixed each other's hair and wove the same patterns into their baskets. There was a certain young man in the village, and both girls wanted him for a husband. The young man often stopped to talk to them. As time passed, it seemed to Cloud Child that the young man favored Blue Sand Girl, and her heart grew sick with envy. She could not bear it any more, and she decided she would have to do something. Now, Cloud Child had a heart that beat two ways, which is to say she was a sorcerer, and she contrived to dispose of Blue Sand Girl. One morning when they were at the spring together she showed Blue Sand Girl a small hoop that she had woven. It had many brilliant colors, and when it was spun in the air it glowed like sunlight. Cloud Child said: 'With this hoop we can play a game. I will throw it to you, spinning it in the air, and you will catch it. Then you will return it to me the same way.' So they began to play, and when Blue Sand Girl caught the hoop she turned into a coyote. Cloud Child laughed. She took her hoop and went home.

"Blue Sand Girl tried to take up her water jug, but she could not do it because now she was a coyote. She tried to return to the village but the dogs drove her away. For many days she lurked at the edge of the village, but at last she realized that she could not enter. She went away crying, thinking that she would never see her father and mother again. In time she came to a certain house in the wilderness. She was hungry, but she was afraid to approach. Two young boys came playing stick ball. They saw the coyote and captured it. They said, 'Let us give it to grandmother.' They tied the coyote's legs and carried it into the house. Now, this house in the wilderness belonged to Spider Old Woman. When she saw the coyote she said: "My grandchildren, what you have brought me is not truly a coyote. It is a girl who has been transformed.' And she began at once to do what was necessary to restore the girl to her true nature.

"She placed the coyote in a large pot of boiling water and covered it with a beautiful woven wedding shawl. After a time, she took the coyote from the boiling water. She hooked the claws of a cactus into the coyote's skin and twisted until the skin split and came off, and there was Blue Sand Girl in her human form. Spider Old Woman said, 'Girl, what happened to you?' When she heard Blue Sand Girl's story, she said, 'Very well I will see that you get back to your people.' She called four spirit beings to come from a certain western mountain. They arrived. One was Squash Spirit, and he wore a mask resembling a squash; one was Lizard Spirit, and his mask was that of a lizard; one was Sun Spirit, and his mask resembled the rays of the sun; one was Moon Spirit, and his mask was round like the full moon. She instructed the four spirit beings what to do, and she gave the girl a small cup, telling her how to use it. Then the four masked spirits took the girl to the edge of the village. There the spirit beings began to dance and sing, and all the people came out to see what was going on.

"Blue Sand Girl's parents also came, and they exclaimed, 'Oh, our daughter has come home alive!' When Cloud Child saw her she thought Blue Sand Girl would denounce her. But Blue Sand Girl said to her: 'Oh, thank you for turning me into a coyote! Being a coyote, I went into a coyote's cave. There I found this beautiful cup. When it is filled, the water gives off beautiful colors. And when I drink the water, spirit beings come from a western mountain and provide me with everything.' She handed the cup to Cloud Child. Cloud Child immediately filled it with water. The water gave off colors like those of the rainbow, and she drank some of it. Instantly she turned into a bullsnake, which crawled away into the rocks and disappeared. The four spirit dancers departed. Blue Sand Girl told the people everything that had happened to her. They understood that Blue Sand Girl was not a sorcerer, and that it was Spider Old Woman who had transformed Cloud Child into a snake. They understood it to be just. That is the story of the girl sorcerer of Badger Spring."

Falling Snow asked, "My grandmother, is this something that truly happened?" White Moccasin answered: "My grandson, I was not there. The way I have told it is the way it was told to me. My grandmother, who owned this story, spoke of it as something that had been witnessed by living people."

In other houses also the old ones were recalling such tales. Children looked at this person and that person in the village, wondering who might be the sorcerer who had destroyed the Red Rocks kiva. Among the older people there was a growing feeling that once again the Grey Fox People had failed to find a place of harmony where all things were in balance. They wondered if any of the newcomers to the village had brought this evil with them. And even while they were preoccupied by these anxieties, game began to disappear once more from the hunting grounds.

Hunters had to travel farther and farther to find deer. Those who went north passed far beyond the Yaya village. Those who went westward came within view of a mountain they had never known was there. The people ate sparsely, conserving what they had, waiting for their hunters to return. The Earth House elder carried out rituals with his animal carvings, and in the kiva the Grey Fox old ones made prayer feathers. Everything was done that they knew how to do, but there was hardly any game to be found. People began to link their hardships with the presence of a sorcerer in the village. They wondered if the sorcerer could be found, and some turned their minds again to their unfinished migration, thinking, "Must we move again? Will we die here because we did not fulfill what was told to us about going to Mesa of Flowers?" But they did not know the answer.

One morning before the sun was high a man from the Yaya village came running to Refuge Place. When he arrived at the central courtyard he asked urgently to speak with Yellow Corn, and he was allowed to descend into the kiva. He said, "My uncle, Running Buffalo sent me." He handed Yellow Corn a prayer feather, saying, "Running Buffalo made this prayer feather for you, and he asks for your help." Yellow Corn took the prayer feather. He asked, "How can I help him?"

The man said: "I have been two days running. The snow was bad, otherwise I would have arrived sooner. Three days ago a large party of raiders attacked us. We believe they are Tinneh, or maybe Tinneh and Utaheh together. The hunting is bad and so they are trying to take corn. They fought their way into the village and took corn from several houses. We resisted them and drove them away, but they returned again. The second time they entered as far as the kiva and took more corn before they fell back. We killed some of them. Four Yayatu were killed in the fighting and some others have bad wounds. Now the enemy are camped out on the plain east of our fields. They are staying. We need help. Running Buffalo asked me to tell you this, and he wants to know if you will send some of your young men. What has happened since I left I cannot tell you. Possibly the raiders already have attacked again, or maybe they will not come until they have consumed the corn they captured. Running Buffalo said to tell you, 'One arm alone cannot bend a bow, but two working together can launch an arrow.' "

Yellow Corn immediately sent for Still Water, and he said to him: "You are war chief. You are the one to say what must be done." And when Still Water had heard everything, he said: "If the Tinneh and the Utaheh were camped in the canyon we would want help from the Yayatu or Long Arrow's people. There is not time enough to meditate. Let us see who is willing to go." So Crying Wolf announced the emergency throughout the village. Eight young men, including Elk Horn and Falling Snow volunteered to go to the assistance of the Yaya village. They put on war jackets and marked their faces with red and black paint, fastened meat bags to their belts and filled their arrow sleeves with arrows. With their bows on their backs and lances in their hands, they set out running, slowing down when they came to deep snow, then running again when the way was clear. When darkness fell they huddled in the shelter of overhanging rocks to rest and keep warm, but after a while the rising moon and the whiteness of the snow-covered ground gave them light by which to travel. They arrived at the Yaya village in two days. The raiders were still camped out on the plain, where smoke could be seen rising in thin columns from several fires. In the village the people had erected a barricade of logs and brush across the main entrance trail, and now they were piling more logs to block the alleyways between houses.

For two more days nothing happened. On the third day an enemy truce party of three men approached the village, stopping well beyond arrow range. One of them held up a bow with a loosened string, meaning they did not come to fight but to talk. Running Buffalo and two others went out to meet them. The spokesman of the raiders said: "My cousins, we do not want to fight you. You are courageous people. As for us, we are hungry. All we want is corn. Give us some corn and we will not fight any more." Running Buffalo said: "From your speech I know you to be Utaheh. We here are distant cousins of the Utaheh. Our grandfathers broke off from you because you did not know how to behave. Now, again, you do not know how to behave. Why do you come to loot us as if you were hunters and we were some kind of game? We came and settled here, we worked, we grew corn. You people did not grow anything. You said: 'Why should we grow something? We can always take it from somebody else.' Now, after making war on us, you come with loosened bows and say, 'Give us some corn.' "

The spokesman for the raiders said: "We did not know that you are related to us. You are housebuilders, so we did not know. We saw from your old fields that you harvested corn. The winter has been hard on us. The women and children are hungry. Therefore we do what we have to." Running Buffalo answered: "We do not have much corn, only enough to last us till the weather turns warm. Already you have taken some of it. Now you want more. We cannot give you any. I am sorry for your women and children. But if we give up corn our own women and children will be hungry. We have nothing for you here. If you try to come back we will drive you off again. The first time you surprised us, but now we are ready." The raiders' truce party turned silently and went back to their encampment.

The Yayatu decided that if the enemy should choose to come back it would be best to meet them before they reached the village. Running Buffalo called his men together and instructed them this way. They would divide into two parties. One party would hide in a deep wash, the other would hide itself among the broken rocks. One party would meet the enemy head on, and the second would come from behind. "Search for the leader," Running Buffalo said. "Single him out. If you kill him the others will be like a body without a head. If a second leader emerges, kill him also. Move around so that one of our war parties always stands between the enemy and the village, and our other party can enfold them from behind. Those of us who remain in the village will stand with our bows on the rooftops."

For several days nothing happened. Then a sentry on top of the butte lighted a fire, meaning that the raiders were coming again. So the two war parties went out and hid themselves, one in the deep wash and the other in the rocks. Those in the wash were all Yayatu, and those in the

rocks were Yayatu and Grey Fox. When the enemy arrived at the cornfields, the Yayatu in the wash came out and met them with a shower of
arrows. The enemy also shot arrows and they drove the Yayatu back, but
the second party emerged from the rocks and attacked from behind. The
enemy were confused. They hesitated. Then they fought at close quarters
with lances and battle-axes. Little by little the defenders of the village
were pressed backward, until the enemy leader was struck by an arrow.
After that the Utaheh and the Tinneh turned away and went back to
their encampment, leaving four dead behind. The Yayatu found three of
their own dead and carried them back to the village. Running Buffalo
praised his young men, but in his heart he acknowledged, "We are bleed-
ing to death." Among the Grey Fox young men some were wounded or
bruised, but none had died.

The next day there were no fires to be seen at the place where the
Utaheh and the Tinneh had been camping, and the next day it was the
same. So the Yayatu said, "Well, now, the Utaheh and the Tinneh have
learned something and have gone away." The Grey Fox young men prepared to return to Refuge Place. Running Buffalo said to them: "Because
you came when we needed you, our villages are tied together. This is the
way it will be as long as the sun rises in the sky, as long as corn grows out
of the earth, as long as people inhabit the land." On the journey southward the young men recalled events of the battle and embellished them.
Falling Snow also had something to tell. But once while they were resting he said to Elk Horn: "When we were fighting it was easy to see who
was Yayatu, Utaheh, Tinneh or Grey Fox. But the ones who were dead,
they all looked the same." Elk Horn answered, "Yes, it seemed that way
to me also." Shortly after they crossed the sand dune the Grey Fox young
men found a deer caught in a deep snow drift. They killed it and brought
it back to Refuge Place.

Four days later a large group of Yayatu came straggling to the village.
There were three men leading, and the rest were women and children.
Yellow Corn and other old ones went out to meet them. One of the men
said: "The Utaheh and the Tinneh came back. We fought to prevent
them, but they were too numerous for us. They entered the village, they
fought us to the rooftops. They took young women. They took all the
corn they could carry. They took some children also. We killed a number
of the enemy. We ourselves lost many men. When we left, the fighting
was still going on at one end of the village. Running Buffalo instructed
us to bring these women and children here. He said we would find safety
for them in our old canyon. So we came."

The Grey Fox old ones conferred. They were troubled. Still Water said: "Yes, safety we can give you. But things are not good here. We have little corn left, and it will not last us very long. The game has gone away. Our people are growing thin. How will we all survive together?"

The Yaya spokesman said: "We are not asking for food. We will find our own meat. We only want a place to rest for a while, until we hear from Running Buffalo."

Yellow Bird said: "Why did you have to choose this place? Surely there is some other place to camp."

The Yaya answered: "My brother, we want to stay in the shadow of your village where the women and children will be safe for a while. We know this canyon. We came here before the Grey Fox People came. We have a shrine up there on the cliff. You know my words are true."

And Yellow Corn said: "Yes, your words are true. We were given this canyon in trust by Running Buffalo. There is a place near the cliff that is protected from the wind. Take your people over there. Build some fires. Make yourself some shelters. Our people will bring you something to eat."

So the Yayatu went to the wall of the cliff and began gathering dead wood and brush to construct shelters, while in the kiva the Grey Fox leaders discussed the disaster that had fallen on Running Buffalo's people. Yellow Bird refused to go into the kiva, saying to Still Water, "Why do you let them remain here? They are like blackbirds. One comes and a crowd follows. Soon we will be smothered by Yayatu."

But Still Water answered: "It is done already. There are women and children. What kind of people would turn them away?"

The next morning another party of Yaya women and children arrived, and late in the day Yaya men began to straggle in. By the following day there were nearly forty in the camp, but Running Buffalo was not among them. Another day went by, then two wounded Yaya men came in. They said, "We are the last." To the question, "Where is Running Buffalo?" they answered: "He is dead. He stood and fought in the village until everything was lost. He had an arrow in his leg and could not walk. So he went into the kiva and stood guard there with his lance. The enemy called out to him, saying, 'Come out, grandfather, and let us kill you.' He answered, 'Come down, you evil Utaheh and Tinneh, and kill me here.' They went down, they killed him. So now we are like an arrow without a point. We cannot pierce anything."

In the Yaya camp the people made more lean-to shelters and covered them with leaves and earth to keep the cold wind from passing through. A party of men went out in an urgent quest for meat, and a second party was formed to go back to their village to try to retrieve some corn if any still remained in the storage rooms. Among the refugees in the camp were Elk Horn's brother and sister and his grandmother, but no one could tell him anything about his parents. So he elected to go with the corn-gathering party, and Falling Snow said that he would go also. Elk Horn said, "No, it is not your trouble," but Falling Snow said, "Nevertheless I am going."

The corn retrieval party started out with the lope of long-distance hunters, but they were weary from their fighting and their flight from the Yaya village. Soon they were only walking. When they had left the canyon behind, they veered eastward on a trail that was not known to the Grey Fox hunters. Elk Horn explained that this was the trail the Yayatu once took when they departed from the canyon to their place of settlement. Late the second day they came within sight of the village. They sent two scouts forward, one to the top of the butte and the other into the village itself. The man who entered the village was the first to return. He said many of the houses had been destroyed by fire, and that burning rafters had been thrown into the kiva. A number of bodies were lying in the central courtyard. But the scout had entered some of the houses and found that corn still remained in the bins. The scout that had gone to the top of the butte returned with the news that the Utaheh and Tinneh were still camped out on the plain.

So the Yaya party went into the village, entering one house after another and bringing whatever corn they found to the open court. But while many of the bins were empty, the raiders had been haphazard in their looting and some bins were unmolested. They went also to the corn-parching pit and found some fire-dried ears there. Half of what they gathered they carried to a high cave in the butte. The rest they placed in large baskets salvaged from the houses. After that they took care of the bodies. Two of the dead were Tinneh. They carried them to a ravine and threw them in. There were six Yaya bodies, but Elk Horn did not find his father or mother. The men carried the Yaya dead to lower ground, laid them out and covered them with stones. When the last stone was placed on the first mound someone spoke, saying, "You, White Bear, my uncle, we will return when we can to give you a proper farewell. May your long trail be true." Each dead person was addressed in this manner. There were Red Lance, an old one; Crow Feather, an old one; Corn Silk, an old grandmother; Grey Rock, a warrior; Sitting Eagle, a warrior; and Snow

Peak, a boy warrior. When Snow Peak's mound was finished, a young man spoke, saying, "You, Snow Peak, my brother, you were courageous, for you died in the court where the main battle took place. You died without growing to manhood, but you stood before your house like a man, therefore you are a man. Strong heart, may Desert Spirit guide your way with sunlight."

After that the Yaya party began the journey back to Refuge Place with their loads of corn. They camped that night in a tiny glen nestled between two rock ridges. As they prepared to continue the next morning, one of the men called out, "Here come our dogs, Lean One and Black Tail." The dogs had been following their trail. They approached uncertainly, sniffing for the smell of meat, but there was nothing to give them. The men chewed a little parched corn, and then they were on the trail once more. When they finally reached the entrance to the canyon, people from the Yaya encampment came out to take the heavy baskets from their backs. In the village some of the Grey Fox women said, "They have more corn than we do." But others answered: "Why speak this way? What else do they have?"

That night in the kiva Yellow Bird said: "Never was it told to us in the past that we would get to be a mixed people. Now we are part Grey Fox, part Bean People, part Earth House People, and finally Yayatu. It is not good. Of the others there were only a few, but the Yayatu are enough to change the landscape. I will not speak to you of sorcerers among the Yayatu because you do not want to hear it. But we cannot have these people hanging on us. There is not enough game for us as it is. The Yayatu have rested. They have corn now. So let them take their corn and go elsewhere. Where did they come from in the beginning? Let them go back to that place. Otherwise we will all die of hunger. Badger Boy was right to leave this canyon. Desert Spirit rejects us here."

Flowing Spring said: "You, Yellow Bird, your heart is choked by thoughts of the Yayatu. If they were the sorcerers you claim them to be, could the Utaheh and the Tinneh have overcome them? They have asked us for nothing, only a corner of the canyon to rest in. They are in the shadow of a shrine built before we ever heard of this place. Brothers, let us be gentle. Let us see how it goes. Balance and harmony will come again. The game will return. As for Badger Boy, he feared that we would live too well and so he broke with us. As anyone can see, we are living a hard life. So are those other people of whom Yellow Bird has spoken. Even our enemies, the Utaheh and the Tinneh, are having a bitter winter. What is wrong is not the canyon but the way our hearts feel." Others also spoke, but when the council broke up there was disharmony over the Yayatu.

It was the Yayatu themselves who resolved the issue. Early the next morning three of them came to the kiva, one carrying a basket of corn, another leading a dog on a buckskin cord. Their spokesman said: "We know times are hard for you as they are for us. We do not want to sit on your back. Our people have met in council. We are going to follow the game to the big mountain in the west. If we go far enough we will surely find deer and mountain sheep out there. We will rest a few more days, then we will leave. We do not forget that your young men came to help us in our fight with the Tinneh and the Utaheh. We want to do something that you too may remember. We bring you some of the corn that we saved from our village. We also bring you one of our hunting dogs. She may help your village find meat. Soon she will have young ones, and you will have more hunting dogs. We have only one thing to ask you. We have two old women who are too weak to travel anymore. They would not live through the winter, and somewhere we would have to leave them behind in the wilderness. We want to leave these old ones with you, and a young girl to take care of them. We ask this as between brothers."

Yellow Corn answered: "The women and the girl, we will give them a place to live. We will make certain that they are safe and warm. They will have meat, corn, a share of whatever we have." The Yaya said, "One day our peoples will meet again, or our children will meet." Yellow Corn said, "Yes, let it be that way."

Four days later as the Yayatu were preparing to leave their encampment, Elk Horn came to the kiva leading two old women and a girl. When Yellow Corn came up from below, Elk Horn said: "My grandfather, these are the persons whom the Yayatu are leaving in our care. This woman standing here is my grandmother, Yellow Hair. This other old one is Butterfly Woman. And the girl, her name is White Blanket. She is my sister. They are not useless people. It is just that the winter journey would be too hard for them. We will all live together in one place. I will hunt for them. White Blanket and Buffalo Girl will grind corn and soften pelts. They will not burden the village." Yellow Corn answered: "My grandson, they are all welcome here. We will find shelter for them and see that they do not suffer in any way. I consider them to be a gift from my brother Running Buffalo. You, Elk Horn, hunt for them and bring them firewood. The responsibility that falls on you will guide you to virtuous ways."

By now most of the Yayatu had gone up the western cliff. First they went to their shrine, where they placed prayer feathers, and then they headed westward into the wilderness. The tension that had pervaded Refuge Place because of the presence of the Yayatu disappeared. There was a momentary calm, a feeling that all of their problems had been overcome. But then the people began to remember that their difficulties with Red Rocks Place had not been resolved, and once again their minds were filled with concern about the unknown sorcerer.

It was decided by the council that a message should be sent to Long Arrow. Flowing Spring volunteered to go. When he arrived at Red Rocks Place he sat with Long Arrow in his house and smoked. Long Arrow asked him, "My brother, why have you come?" And Flowing Spring answered, "Our hearts are heavy with remembering those who died in your kiva. But we still have not found any fault in ourselves for what happened. If there is a sorcerer in Refuge Place we have not found her. We have searched. We have sat in council late into the night thinking about the matter. We have named every name in the village and turned it over and over, but we cannot find anyone who might have had thoughts of harming your people. Yet we continue to search for an answer. Be patient with us. Yellow Corn gave me this message to bring: 'Long Arrow, my brother, consider my difficulty. What if, in fact, the sorcerer came from elsewhere and merely mentioned Refuge Place to stir anger between us? How then can I ever satisfy you that we are not at fault?' That is what Yellow Corn asked me to say to you."

Long Arrow sat silently with his eyes closed a long while before he answered. At last he said: "This is my response to Yellow Corn. Tell him: 'My brother, I never doubted your good heart. But my people are troubled. Many families lost sons and fathers in the kiva. Our kiva brotherhood is broken in half. The people want to know that the guilty one is punished. Otherwise, how can our villages live in trust with each other? Our people will not come to your dances. They will not trade their tobacco, corn and moccasins. Our hunters will avoid one another in the wilderness. If an enemy attacks Refuge Place, how will I get a war party together to help you? If a Grey Fox person comes hungry to our village, who will feed him? I have been just in the matter of the arrows, though Red Rocks was not truly at fault. You, my Grey Fox brother, I know your heart is troubled. But the responsibility is yours. I cannot tell you what to do. You must take a trail to one place or another.' Those are my words to Yellow Corn. May his guiding spirit show him which way to go."

Flowing Spring brought Long Arrow's answer back to Refuge Place. Discussions in the kiva began anew, but in the end they always seemed to come back to the place of starting, like a deer going around a hill. Finally a certain old one said: "We are standing at the edge of a high bluff with no way of getting across. Let us now consider how it was in the old days. Did they not have a sure test for discovering a sorcerer? It is said that when the people emerged from the belly of the earth there was a sorcerer among them, and they performed a ceremony to discover the evil one's identity. How it was done was this: A ball of sacred meal was prepared by the men strong in medicine. They prayed and sang to give the ball of meal strength. They did all the sacred things, and made prayer feathers. When all this was done they called the people together. The people sang sacred chants. When the ball of meal was strengthened by their singing, it was hurled into the air the same way the moon was lofted into the sky, and when it came down it fell on the head of the sorcerer. The sorcerer was a young woman. The people departed from the place of the ceremony, because they were in migration to their first village, but they left the sorcerer behind. In this way they expelled the evil that haunted them. You, Flowing Spring, know this to be true. You, Crying Wolf, know it to be true. Everyone who has ever sat with a wise uncle at his shoulder knows it to be true. Do you have any other solution?"

Some of the men in the council immediately made their agreement known, but Yellow Corn said: "Yes, you have proposed something to consider. But what if the sacred ball is thrown and the sorcerer is not here in Refuge Place at all?" Someone answered, "Why, then it will not fall on anyone." Flowing Spring asked, "If the sacred ball does not fall on anyone, how will it help us with Long Arrow?" Someone answered, "Surely Long Arrow will know then that the sorcerer does not live here." Yellow Corn said, "Long Arrow's people would not accept it as a just answer." They went on debating until the Warrior constellation was overhead, and by that time most of the council was in agreement that no other way was left to them. It was decided that the test would be carried out on the fourth day.

The next morning Crying Wolf stood on the kiva roof and made the announcement. After that he went through the village from house to house repeating the decision of the council. On the fourth day everyone was to gather at the wide flat rock at the northern edge of the village. No one was to stay away. No one was to hunt. Those who were too sick to walk were to be carried to the gathering. On the second day, and again on the third, Crying Wolf made the announcement from one end of the village to the other. It was whispered from house to house that the gathering would somehow discover at last the identity of the evil-hearted person living in Refuge Place. What would be done with him no one knew. He could be killed or driven out into the wilderness. Nothing like that had happened before in their lifetimes. The old ones were in the kiva night and day, praying, purifying themselves, making prayer feathers and other sacred things. On the night before the fourth morning the entire council and the kiva brotherhood were there. After chanting the song recalling the migrations of the people, they rested a while. They smoked.

Yellow Corn indicated with a motion of his hand that he wished to speak. When all was quiet he said: "My brothers, my nephews, we stand at the edge of a cliff. If we jump there is no returning. So let us consider once more where we are going. The thing we are about to do, never before except in the time of our ancient grandfathers has it been done. Do we have enough knowledge and understanding to repeat it? A ball of meal is only a ball of meal. It becomes sacred not because we call it sacred, but because we give it strength and force through our prayers. Unless our hearts are purified beyond any question, we cannot give the ball of meal the quality of true sacredness. If there is only one person among us whose heart is not true to what we are doing, the ball cannot receive the strength it needs to perform its task. It will be like an arrow without a feather to guide it. Let us look into ourselves. If there is anger against someone, if there is unwillingness to share, if we are willing to perform a cruelty, then, my brothers and nephews, we are not in harmony and we cannot give the ball of meal its sacred quality. If any one of us cannot sit here and say, 'All these men are truly my brothers,' then let us put the test aside and not go through with it. For what will happen if we go ahead no one can foresee. If the ball of meal does not speak wisely to us we will wound ourselves beyond healing. In ancient days when the people made the moon of buckskin and painted it yellow and lofted it into the sky at Spider Old Woman's direction, it was the force of their prayers and their true hearts that made it possible. Had one person among them been weak in the spirit of harmony and truth, the moon would have fallen back on the earth.

"This test that we are contemplating," Yellow Corn continued, "if you doubt it in any way, it cannot succeed, for the ball of meal will not have the power it needs, and it will only fall at random. And what if you then say, 'This person on whom the ball has fallen is a sorcerer, drive him out of the village,' how will you ever know that the true sorcerer does not remain behind? And how, then, will you ever be able to purify your hearts again? This test has the power to identify an evil one. It also has the power to create dissension and disharmony. How will we be able to exist without harmony? My brothers, my nephews, I do not doubt you. We have gone on long journeys together. Let us now act wisely and with true hearts. I believe we should put the test aside and find another way. Put it aside. I will speak no more."

The council meditated on Yellow Corn's words. When it seemed that no one else was ready to speak, Yellow Bird said: "I did not want to say anything, but you men are too silent. It was not I who proposed the test. You others spoke for it. I thought then, 'If I speak strongly to support it, some of you will laugh and say Yellow Bird flutters again.' So I listened. I heard no other proposal that was good. In the end I said I would agree to the test. Each of us agreed. We were in harmony. We did not doubt that our grandfathers knew what they were saying to us. We did not question one another's hearts. We wanted only to settle this matter so that it would not gnaw at us any longer. We wanted to throw evil out of our village. For three days we have been preparing ourselves. Now, on the night before the fourth day, Yellow Corn says to us: 'Put it away. Let us not do it.' He speaks thinking that perhaps we will not accept the outcome of the test. I will accept it. Is there anyone here who will not accept it? If Yellow Corn will not accept it, let him leave the village until the test is finished. Perhaps the ball of meal will fall on Elk Horn's wife, then we will know why Yellow Corn is reluctant. He will not be able to live with it because he is the one who brought the Yayatu into the village.

"It would have been better if Yellow Corn had stopped us at the beginning of the trail. Now it is too late. He brings dissension into the council. The Grey Fox cannot act on anything if they start on a trail and are pulled back. If the sorcerer is not found soon we will have to give up our village and go away. I would not have spoken if Yellow Corn had not spoken. Now the council must decide which trail it will follow. These are my last words on the matter."

Once more there was silence in the council, and Yellow Corn said: "My brothers, it is for you to say how it will be. I will go to my house to sleep. This way there will be no contention between Yellow Bird and myself. Your hearts will tell you what is true." Yellow Corn departed, and the old ones examined everything that had been said. In the end it was agreed that they would continue through the night with their chants and their purification, and that the next morning they would carry out the ritual.

As the forehead of the sun appeared over the eastern cliff and cast long shadows across the valley, the people began to gather. There was an air of tension and expectation. Someone noticed that the Earth House People were going about their affairs as usual. A messenger was sent to tell them that they also were involved. So they came and stood with the others, and the Bean People arrived as well. The village was empty. Still Water came carrying a bowl containing the sacred ball of meal, and Flowing Spring walked alongside sprinkling cornmeal in his path. Behind Still Water another old one carried a sacred kiva cloth. They set the bowl down in the middle of the flat rock and covered it with the cloth. The people were instructed to move as close as possible, allowing only enough room for those working at the ritual. There was the cloth-covered bowl in the center, and at each corner of the cloth stood a man with painted marks on his body. Around them in a ring were all the men who had participated in the council, and standing outside the ring, pressed tightly together, were all the other inhabitants of Refuge Place.

The ball of meal was taken from the bowl and placed on top of the cloth. The four men in the center grasped the cloth by its corners and stood waiting. There was chanting, and when the last sound of the chant died in the air there was a pause. Then came the signal, "Hai!" With a swift smooth motion the men holding the cloth lifted, tautened, and sent the ball of meal soaring upward. The eyes of the village followed its flight. The ball seemed to rest in the air for a moment, then it fell. There was a sudden turbulence in the crowd, and much pushing forward and backward, after that a stillness. The ball of meal had fallen on a woman named Flower Mountain. She looked from one face to another, not quite comprehending, and the Grey Fox People looked back at her in disbelief. No one said anything. Now that the ritual had been carried out, it seemed that even the men of the kiva fraternity did not know what to do. Slowly the people began to understand the full import of what had happened, for Flower Mountain was the oldest daughter of Yellow Bird.

The Grey Fox people went to their homes. The Earth House People went to their mound. The men of the kiva fraternity returned to the kiva, where they sat without smoking or speaking. Only Yellow Bird did not appear there. He went to his house and drew up his ladder. His family began preparations for a journey. So, too, in an adjacent house, did Flower Mountain and her family. Elsewhere, Yellow Bird's two sons and their families prepared. They laid out their dried meat to estimate how many days it would carry them. With the seed corn they had been saving for spring there was enough to feed them for fifteen or sixteen days, no more. They would have to do much hunting on the trail.

Yellow Corn sat brooding on the breakup of the village. He thought, "Perhaps Yellow Bird will come and we can discuss things." But Yellow Bird did not come. So at last when darkness began to fall, Yellow Corn went to Yellow Bird's house, where he found that the ladder had been drawn up. He approached the small window of the corn-grinding room and called through it: "Yellow Bird, my brother, let us sit and reflect on things. Let us find a solution that will not split the Grey Fox People in two."

Yellow Bird came to the corn-grinding room. He spoke in a tone that could not disguise his feeling of hurt and anger, saying, "My daughter is not a sorcerer. The test was false. Now we cannot stay here any longer. Badger Boy's words were wise. We never should have stayed in this canyon. Already we might have been at the Mesa of Flowers. But no, you and Limping Deer said, 'Here we rest.' You, Yellow Corn, I do not understand you. You refused to listen to cautions about the Yayatu. You made brotherhood with them and forgot brotherhood in your own village. It was you who caused the test to fail today. From your own mouth you said, 'If you doubt, if your heart is not clean, the ball of meal will not have the force to do what it is supposed to do.' It was you who doubted and deprived it of power. Everyone knows that Flower Mountain is not evil. But now, after this, we cannot live here anymore. The village is broken, but it was not my doing. It was yours. Tomorrow morning my people will leave. We will not call ourselves Grey Fox anymore. We will take a new name. Go to the kiva now and reflect on what you have done." And before Yellow Corn could answer, Yellow Bird hung a winnowing basket over the window and left the grinding room.

In the grey light of morning Yellow Bird's people gathered at the edge of the village with their baskets and all the other things they were taking with them. The ones who were remaining behind came out and stood nearby. Some who were staying wanted to go, and some who were going wanted to stay, for families were being broken apart. There were calls of, "May you be well guided on your trail." Soon, even before the sunglow came, Yellow Bird's party moved out in a long straggling line. Some of the people looked back as if perplexed by the shape of events. Yellow Bird walked in front, a rabbit-skin cape over his shoulders and a lance in his hand. He, for one, did not turn his head to look again on the village or the Grey Fox People.

In the village the people were subdued, as if they had been reprimanded by Desert Spirit, the Father of the Wilderness. The empty houses left by the departed families reproached them with silence. A water jar sat at the foot of Flower Mountain's ladder, and whoever saw it looked away. The people asked themselves questions. Could Flower Mountain, who gave colored piki to all the children on festival days, have caused the kiva at Red Rocks Place to collapse? A few did not doubt that it was true. But for everyone there was a foreboding that Refuge Place was falling apart.

In time, Yellow Corn journeyed to Red Rocks Place. He said to Long Arrow: "My brother, we have done what we promised to do. You asked us to find a sorcerer. We performed a ritual, and it placed the responsibility on a woman named Flower Mountain, the oldest daughter of Yellow Bird. So Yellow Bird took all his family away and we are a broken village. You asked us for something and we gave it. And now that it is over I will tell you what my heart feels. My heart tells me that Flower Mountain had nothing to do with sorcery. I do not believe that there was any sorcerer in Refuge Place. But we had a debt to pay to Red Rocks Place, so we carried out the ritual. Now we have paid too heavily. We have only a part of a village remaining. Our families have been torn apart. Yellow Bird rejected the name Grey Fox when he left, saying his people will take a new name. Whether they will go to the Mesa of Flowers I do not know. Whether they will survive I do not know. If I could have foreseen the outcome I would not have accepted your demand to find the sorcerer. What sorcerer? I do not know. I know only that we have become a small people. If an enemy comes we will not have the strength to resist. What has been done at your request binds us closer. Now let some of your young men bring their families to live in Refuge Place. They will help to defend us. In this way we will be able to survive."

Long Arrow answered: "Yes, my brother, we are bound even closer than before. But my people also are troubled these days. They have seen Utaheh in our hunting grounds. They wonder about the safety of the village. The Coyote Clan is demanding that we move our settlement to higher ground somewhere. In addition, the clans are arguing among themselves about their rights. So, as you can see, Red Rocks Place is having many difficulties. I do not know if anyone would be willing to go to Refuge Place. They are waiting for winter to pass so that they can plant, and they are impatient with everything. They constantly disagree with each other. Perhaps when the warm weather comes again it will harmonize us. Perhaps then there will be some families that will join you. If I find someone that is willing I will let you know." There the matter rested, and Yellow Corn returned home.

The days passed without any message from Long Arrow, and in time

Yellow Corn gave up expecting to hear anything. Refuge Place lived on. Hunters spent days at a time stalking game. Women and children foraged for firewood. Whenever they could, some families continued to work on houses that were not yet completed, or chinked up walls with snow. Yellow Corn also did these things, but he could not forget that Ancient One had spoken to him of further journeys for the Grey Fox People. He wondered whether Yellow Bird's departure might be a harbinger of the fulfillment of the prophecy.

Elk Horn's people were still lodged with several Grey Fox families, and whenever he was not hunting he was setting stones on his own slowly rising house walls. Good building stones were hard to find in the snow, and often they were frozen to the ground. Sometimes Falling Snow and White Star helped Elk Horn pry shale from the cliff, and afterward, returning home, they would pass the four empty houses left behind by Yellow Bird's people. He wondered why Elk Horn should have to build in the cold of winter while these other houses had no one living in them. One night he spoke to Yellow Corn about it, saying, "My grandfather, Elk Horn builds slowly, and his family is scattered through the village. Yet there are empty houses. Give him one of them to use until the winter is gone." Yellow Corn said: "My grandson, I have watched him carrying stones. But those houses do not belong to anyone living here. Only people of Yellow Bird's family can claim them. For now, they are ghost houses." Falling Snow asked: "Are there ghosts living there? I never heard anyone speak of it." Yellow Corn answered: "No, they do not speak of it. When they pass those houses they feel the presence of Yellow Bird and all his people. When they walk past Flower Mountain's water jar by the ladder they feel the spirit of Flower Mountain.

"Let me tell you of what happened to the Sagebrush Clan when they were going from one place to another. They found a village that had been abandoned by the Sand Clan, and they decided to stay in that place, for there were good fields and ample water. They took over the houses, thinking, 'How good Desert Spirit has been to us to guide us to this place.' They were content, forgetting that they had not themselves built the village. One night as the chief of the Sagebrush people was sitting at his fire a stranger entered and said to him, 'You are a visitor here?' The Sagebrush chief said: 'No, this is where I live. Perhaps it is you who are a visitor here.' The stranger said, 'Was it you who built the walls and placed the roof?' The Sagebrush chief said, 'No, this village was made by others who have gone away.' The stranger said: 'It was I who built the walls of this house. The village belongs to the Sand Clan. One day we will come back here, or our children will come back. This is our village. The fields out there are our fields. As long as we remember this village it remains ours, and we will not forget it because we call out its name in our prayers and ceremonies. Therefore you must take your people away.' When the chief of the Sagebrush Clan began to speak, the stranger disappeared without going up the ladder. The next night the stranger came again, and the third night again, until at last the Sagebrush Clan abandoned the village and went away.

"Now, even if some of our people took over Yellow Bird's houses and saw no one come in the night to send them away, still they would feel the presence of those who once lived there. So you see that I cannot give one of these houses to Elk Horn. Perhaps there are other ways to help him. Let us organize a rabbit hunt for all the young people, but instead of hunting rabbits they will hunt rocks. And whenever a boy brings in a rock, whatever girl wants to can give him piki or something else as a prize. In this way Elk Horn will have many rocks and can finish his walls."

And so it was that Crying Wolf went through the village one day announcing that there would be a hunt for stone rabbits. And when the hunting day came, the young people appeared with their throwing sticks and went through all the motions of encircling rabbits, but they threw their sticks at stones instead. Whoever hit a stone first was the killer. And when the stone was delivered at the place where Elk Horn was building, a girl would give a roll of piki as a prize. Buffalo Girl and White Blanket also gave out prizes, and there was humor throughout the village at all the antics of the hunters as they struggled with stones that tried to get away. From that day on, Elk Horn's work progressed rapidly, and a day came when he gathered Buffalo Girl, White Blanket, Yellow Hair and Butterfly Woman together and took them to their new house.

After that, Falling Snow went often to visit Elk Horn. Sitting together near the fire with Buffalo Girl and white Blanket they talked about hunting, or where the Yaya People had gone and how they might be surviving the winter. They spoke of Yellow Bird's people and wondered if they had gone in search of the Mesa of Flowers or had returned to the old Grey Fox village in the south. The young women did not do much talking at first, but after a while they were not so shy. Falling Snow found himself looking more and more at White Blanket as though she were the first young woman he had ever seen. Whatever she was talking about, even something commonplace such as softening a deerskin, it seemed to Falling Snow that she was saying something of uncommon value. Yellow Hair and Buffalo Woman, sitting on blankets in the shadows and working at small tasks, watched Falling Snow and White Blanket closely and nodded their heads as if they could perceive events yet to come.

Once when they were discussing great feats of hunting, Elk Horn said: "Listen to this tale of Cloud Breaker. He was a mighty hunter. He went out seeking meat, He came to a cave. He said, 'Surely there is a bear in this cave.' He called out, 'You, owner of the cave, come out and meet Cloud Breaker.' The bear was the grandfather of all bears. When he stood straight up he was twice as tall as a man. He heard Cloud Breaker and he came out of the cave. Cloud Breaker was astonished. Never had he seen so large a bear. The bear opened his mouth to seize Cloud Breaker. But Cloud Breaker's mind was swift. He knew that no arrow or lance could kill this bear. Seeing the bear's open mouth, he plunged his arm into it. His body also entered the bear's mouth, so that only his legs were visible. With his hand he grasped Bear Grandfather's tailbone, and he pulled. Cloud Breaker was strong. He pulled mightily. He came out of the bear's mouth pulling. He pulled Bear Grandfather inside out. The bear's fur was no longer visible because it was inside. On the outside was meat. From inside came Bear Grandfather's muffled voice, saying, 'Cloud Breaker, you have confused me. I do not know where I am.' Then Bear Grandfather died, and Cloud Breaker carried him home. His people ate the meat first, and many days later they came to the pelt. They stretched it and scraped it, and after that Cloud Breaker covered his house with it. That is the story of Cloud Breaker. Does anyone know a hunter as great as he?"

Falling Snow said: "Yes, Cloud Breaker was someone worth remembering. But have you ever heard of Flying Elk? He was the swiftest of all hunters. One day when he went hunting he began to climb a mountain. A rockslide began to come down from above. Had you and I been there we would have been crushed under the falling stones. But Flying Elk leaped on the first rock as it arrived, and from there he leaped on the second rock that followed the first. From the second rock he leaped on the third, and from there he went to the fourth. He continued doing this as long as the rocks were falling, and when it was all over he was standing on top of a high hill created by the slide. After that, Flying Elk continued hunting. He crossed the mountain and came to a plain. There he saw a herd of antelope. He shot an arrow, but while it was in flight he saw that it was going to kill a small antelope. He did not want a small antelope. He wanted a large one. So he ran forward where his arrow was flying and turned it with his finger, aiming at the largest antelope in the herd. His arrow killed the large antelope. Flying Elk hung the antelope over his shoulder. He went on. He came to a river. He wanted to cross, but the current was swift and he could not swim with the antelope on his back. So he threw the antelope over the river, jumped into the water and swam to the far side. There he caught the antelope just as it arrived in the air. Many deeds of this kind were performed by Flying Elk. Is there any hunter to surpass him?"

Elk Horn said: "Yes, Flying Elk was a great hunter. But it is my hunter that you are trying to outdo, not White Blanket's. So why are you looking at her? She has not said anything about a hunter." The two old grandmothers laughed, and White Blanket quickly left her place near the fire and found something to busy her in the subdued light at the other end of the room.

Now, Yellow Corn had delegated to Falling Snow the task of keeping the kiva fire. It was Falling Snow's responsibility to stack firewood on the kiva roof so that the fire could be kept burning inside whenever rituals were being conducted or councils being held. Late one night when most of the village was already sleeping, Falling Snow was on the kiva roof carrying out these duties. Just as he was preparing to leave, three specks of light beyond the eastern edge of the village caught his eye. At first they seemed to be stationary, but soon he saw that they were moving. Sometimes they seemed to merge and become one, then they broke apart and became three again. Falling Snow decided that they were torches carried by persons on the trail to Refuge Place. So he went to notify Yellow Corn or Crying Wolf, but on the way he saw Walking Bear standing on the roof of his house, and he said, "Uncle, can you see the torches coming from the east?" Walking Bear could not see anything from the roof, and he came down and went with Falling Snow to the top of the kiva. He said: "Yes, now I see them. Who would be coming to the village like this in the dark? Go and inform Yellow Corn. I will tell Still Water in case the village is in danger."

Falling Snow ran to Yellow Corn's house and called out to him, "My grandfather, someone is coming from the east with torches." Yellow Corn came out with a blanket around his shoulders, and Falling Snow described what he had seen. So Yellow Corn went to the kiva, and Still Water arrived with Walking Bear. The four of them stood looking at the distant flickering spots of light. Walking Bear said, "Can it be Death Old Man?" And Still Water answered, "No, with Death Old Man there is a single flame." And Yellow Corn said: "They are persons of some kind who are coming. But ordinary persons do not enter a village this way in the night." Falling Snow and Walking Bear were sent to awaken the young men and have them assemble with their weapons, and soon the entire village was stirring. People stood on their rooftops to glimpse the approaching lights, and they speculated on the meaning of the mystery.

The young men went to the bottom of the trail with their weapons, uncertain of what they would have to do. The torches were close now. They disappeared as they went behind a mound of rocks, and when they reappeared again the Grey Fox warriors put arrows in their bows but did not shoot, for what they saw was mysterious and awesome. The torches were carried by three masked figures of a kind not known in Refuge Place. The first figure wore a white kilt striped with green, and he had a buckskin cape around his shoulders. His mask was green, with an elongated single eye stretching across his forehead, and was topped by a great thatch of long hair. In his free hand he held a rattle which sounded as he walked. The second figure wore a kilt of pure white. His mask was black with red eyes, and it was surmounted by a headdress of turkey feathers. The third figure wore a wolflike mask with enormous white eyes. His kilt was striped with red, and he had red bands on his arms, which were painted black. Each of the figures wore a tortoiseshell rattle on the back of one leg. Those who guarded the trail fell back and moved aside to let the masked figures pass.

In the village court, the masked ones began to sing, stamping on the ground rhythmically to make their tortoiseshells sound. Some of the Grey Fox People expressed resentment that these strangers had invaded them in the depth of night, but most sensed the presence of a mystery and watched in silence. The men of the kiva brotherhood listened intently to the singing, knowing that it was there they would find an explanation. The words of the chant were in another tongue and had no meaning for the young, but the old ones who were experienced in languages comprehended something. The song seemed to say that at a distant place called Snow Mountain there were beings called kachinas who helped humans by interceding with the earth and sky spirits. They could bring rain clouds to help the corn, and hurry the spring and hold back the winter. But humans must respect them and recognize their role in the world. If the Grey Fox People accepted the kachinas they must hold ritual dances of welcome and departure. The song said that the kachinas would help the people to keep in balance with the land around them and guide their children into virtuous trails. They would help to drive evil out of the village. "It is for the people of Refuge Place to decide if they want us," the dancers sang. And when they concluded their song they walked silently out of the village. Their torchlights diminished into three specks of light in the distance and finally disappeared.

There was excited conversation in the village after the masked figures left. Fires were refueled in the houses, and though it was still night there were daylight sounds all around. The old ones went into the kiva to discuss the mysterious event. They asked many questions. Why did the masked figures come to Refuge Place? What did they want? Who were the kachinas? Some said, "These mysterious persons acted as if they themselves were kachinas, but of course they were only men with masks." Others answered, "How can you say so surely that they were nothing but men?" And one old man said, "If the Sun Spirit himself came and danced in the court there are those who would say he is merely a person with a covered face." Flowing Spring said: "Whatever we call them, men or spirits, they say that the kachinas have the power to help us. Let us not dispute about things that are not important. If the kachinas demonstrate their goodwill and their ability to help us, we can respect them and recognize them." It was almost daylight when the old ones came out of the kiva, and when they did so they observed that another mystery had taken place. For before the kachina dancers had arrived, the night had been cold, while now, as the dawn came, there was warmth in the air. And when the sun had risen into the sky the land basked in summer sunlight. Here and there a flower blossom could be seen poking through the snow. The Grey Fox People were awed. They said to one another, "It must have been the kachinas who did this." The old ones did not commit themselves, for they still had much to discuss about these things.

As they went about their daytime tasks, the Grey Fox People continued to talk about the mysterious visitors. Some were skeptical and asked what the visitors wanted from Refuge Place. Others said that the kachinas were obviously men, and that they should never have been allowed to come into the village without being identified. Yet there was a certain awe for the medicine the visitors had demonstrated by bringing warmth to the canyon. Falling Snow and Walking Bear decided that they would track the kachinas to see where they had gone. They followed the trail across the valley, watching for footprints in the snow. At the far side of the canyon the footprints disappeared among the rocks, and it seemed that the kachinas had gone up the cliff in the direction of Red Rocks Place. Falling Snow and Walking Bear turned back, and on their return Walking Bear found a red buckskin armband. He said: "Now we see that they stopped here and removed their dance costumes. In the darkness they lost this armband. If they were truly spirit beings, why should they have to do this? Let us tell the old ones about it." So when they came to the village they reported what they had discovered.

That night, and many nights thereafter, the old ones went on discussing the affair, and the red armband, lying on the ground before them, was part of their evidence. Again and again they analyzed the event in all its details. On the fourth morning after the visit of the kachina dancers, winter returned to the canyon valley. And because four was a sacred number, the old ones accepted this fact as an element to be considered. No matter how often they concluded that the visitors were men from Red Rocks Place, they always came back to the reality that four days of summer had descended on them in the middle of winter, and they did not doubt that the medicine of the kachina dancers was responsible for it. At last they decided that a group of old ones led by Yellow Corn would go to Red Rocks Place for an explanation.

So once again Yellow Corn, along with Crying Wolf, Burning Tree and Standing Rock, made the journey and met in the Red Rocks kiva, which by now had been repaired, with Long Arrow and several of his old men. They smoked and exchanged greetings, and then Long Arrow said: "My brothers, I do not need to ask why you are here. You want to know if some of our young men and their families will come to stay with you. I have spoken of it in council, and some of our young men were asked. But no one wants to go. They say: 'Red Rocks is a good village. Our relatives are here. Therefore we do not want to leave.' " Yellow Corn answered: "No, that is an old matter. We did not hear from you, and so we understood that no one would come. Today we want to speak of something new. We want to discuss something that happened in Refuge Place. It was night. The people were sleeping. Two of our young men came to awaken us, saying, 'A strange thing is happening. Three spots of light are approaching through the valley.' We came out. We waited. In time, three men in masks arrived in the village. One wore a wolf mask. One wore a black mask with red eyes. One wore a green mask with a single eye. They danced. They sang, and their words seemed to say that they were kachinas from Snow Mountain in the west. They asked us to accept them as beings who would speak for us to Desert Spirit and Earth Spirit. They said they would be able to call rain clouds for us whenever we need them. After that, they departed. But they did not go toward Snow Mountain. They went eastward toward Red Rocks Place. Our people want to know about them. If they were sent from here, we want to know why this was done without preparing us with a message."

Long Arrow said: "My brothers, I expected you to come with these questions. The people of Red Rocks do not want to make life hard for you. They want to do something to help Refuge Place. They could not send you any families to replace those taken away by Yellow Bird, but they decided to share something with you. Our people have seen your festivals and rituals, and they have concluded that you do not have kachinas as we do. The leaders of the Kachina Brotherhood said they would share their kachina medicine, and therefore the three kachina masks were sent to you. Now, why it was done in this way I will tell you.

"In the time of our fathers," Long Arrow continued, "the kachinas were living there at Snow Mountain, and they were known to some villages and clans but not to others. Our fathers did not yet know of them. It is said that three kachinas came one night from Snow Mountain to tell us what they could do for us. They wore masks like those you saw. The people were sleeping. So the kachinas went to the dance court, and there they chanted the sacred song that you heard. But the people did not understand the purpose. They feared the kachinas and resented their intrusion. They took them to be enemies trying to disrupt the village, so they stoned them and drove them out. They pursued them with slings and bows. The kachinas disappeared in the darkness. The people said: 'Well, now, we have disposed of the intruders. We have done well. If we killed any of them in the darkness, that is good. If any of them survived he will tell his people and they will not come again.'

"The people talked this way, but that was not the end. When morning came there were no clouds in the sky. Yet before the sun was high there were small dark clouds on all sides where the sky meets the earth. Those clouds approached the village. Never before had the people seen clouds approaching from many directions at once. The clouds in the east were tinted with white, those in the north with black, those in the west with yellow, in the south with blue. They came together and met over the village, and then everything was in total darkness and rain began to fall. The rain fell angrily without stopping. Water ran through the village and into the houses. Roofs collapsed because of the weight of the water. The rocks and earth came loose and slid from the hills, washing across the fields and covering the corn. Four days the rain fell, and after that the clouds retreated. The sun reappeared, and the people saw that everything was destroyed. They understood then the power of the kachinas.

"The old ones made prayer feathers," Long Arrow went on, "and sent them with runners to Snow Mountain, asking the kachinas to cease being angry at them for their ignorance. The oldest man in the village had a vision, and in the vision a kachina spoke to him, saying: 'We will never come back to the village where we were mistreated. But we are not angry anymore, for the people were not aware of who we were. So we will help you. If you want the power of medicine that we offered you, let your wise ones create a Kachina Brotherhood. They will make masks and clothing in the manner of the kachinas. We will inform them what to do. We will show them the rituals. They will act for us. If everything is done faithfully, if the masks are made properly, if the men of the Kachina Brotherhood are of good heart, if they do each thing as it is supposed to be done, we will hear their supplications and send the rain clouds when they are needed. We stand halfway between humans and the great forces of nature. It is we who can speak directly to Desert Spirit, Earth Spirit and Sun Spirit and be heard.' After that the Kachina Brotherhood was established. It does the work of the kachinas, and because everything is done faithfully the kachinas of Snow Mountain send rain for our crops.

"It was our Kachina Brotherhood that sent the masked ones to Refuge Place. They wanted to give your village something. Although I am village chief, I do not have authority in such matters. It was they who did everything. This man at my side is Sleeping Hawk. He is chief of the Brotherhood. If I have not said everything the way it was explained to me, he will correct me. I have said everything I know."

When Long Arrow finished, Standing Rock said: "What you have told us, we understand it. You sent your three masks in the night just as the kachinas came to your people. You instructed us as you were instructed. We will consider everything and discuss it with other aged ones in our village. But there is still one more thing to know. When the masks departed from Refuge Place a summer warmth came down. We need to understand this."

Sleeping Hawk, chief ot the Kachina Brotherhood, said: "Before we sent our masks to you we spent four days and four nights praying for something special to happen so that you would truly know the power of the kachinas. You did not drive the masks from the village. That was good. The kachinas were pleased. They sent four days of warmth as a sign that they were pleased. However, you men of Refuge Place, do not think that everything is already accomplished. If you accept the kachinas there is still much to learn. There are many masks. Each of them has its own meaning. Every kachina has his own story and his own character. We invite you to send one of your wisest persons to be instructed by us. We will teach him everything. If his heart is good and his understanding is deep he will learn something here. After that your village will be able to call on the kachinas for help."

Yellow Corn answered, saying: "My brothers, we will tell our people everything. Among them are some who are asking, 'What does Red Rocks want from us that they sent their masks here?' I do not perceive that you are trading anything, only that you are willing to share something. I will tell the people what I perceive, and Standing Rock, Burning Tree and Crying Wolf will do the same. My heart tells me that I should accept now, for you are giving us a good gift. But we need time to meditate on the meaning of everything, and we have to consider that some things are not going well these days in Refuge Place. Some of our houses are ghost houses. Game is scarce. People's minds are disturbed and they are short-tempered with one another. So be patient with us, my brothers. We who sit here with you are grateful, and in time we will have an answer to give you."

The Grey Fox delegation was given food and a place to sleep, and the next morning they began their return journey. On the way, they spoke at great length of the kachinas, and their discussion made the journey seem swift. But when they arrived at Refuge Place they discovered that something was wrong in the village, and they heard the story from several persons speaking at the same time. Grey Badger of the Bean People had been caught with a deer he had killed in Grey Fox hunting territory. Two hunters had taken the deer away from him and brought it to the village. They had argued about the incident until all of Refuge Place was in turmoil. Seeing the way things were, Yellow Corn called for the council to meet. He ate a little, slept a little and then went to the kiva, which was already crowded. He looked around but he did not see any Bean People. He said: "Where is Grey Badger? Let him come and sit with us. Let him bring his brother to speak for him. Then we can begin." Some of the people protested, saying, "This is our village. This is our own kiva. The affair is clear. Grey Badger killed a deer that belonged to us. He does not deny it. Why do we need the Bean People here? Let us judge the matter for ourselves."

But Yellow Corn would not begin without Grey Badger and his brother, so Crying Wolf was sent to get them. When they arrived and descended the ladder, the Grey Fox people reluctantly made room for them at the front. Yellow Corn addressed himself to Grey Badger in these words: "My nephew, we have this difficulty to examine. Let us speak

openly so we can find the truth. When the Bean People came to us looking for shelter from the winter it was said that game was scarce in this
place. You said, 'We will not hunt in the Grey Fox hunting grounds. If
the Grey Fox go to a distance of three days' running to find their game,
we will go six.' We believed you. We accepted you. Now we hear that
you killed a deer not far from the canyon. What is it, then? How do we
explain it?"

Grey Badger said: "My uncle, your people did not say anything false,
but they did not say everything. I went out with my bow, because my
people needed something to eat. I passed through your hunting grounds,
for I pledged that we would not hunt there. I went far. I went four days
running. I went farther still. I found no game. I did not stop hunting.
At last I thought: 'I will die here if I stay any longer. Then what will
my people do?' So I returned without anything. I came again to your
hunting grounds. When I was only one day away from the canyon a
deer appeared. I thought: 'It is a time of hunger. Can I throw a deer
away? Perhaps the Grey Fox people will let us have a share of it.' So I
followed the deer. I killed it. I was preparing to take it home when
your hunters came. They said: 'Why are you hunting here? This is not
your place for hunting.' I explained everything, but their ears were
deaf. They took the deer away. They abused me. I said it was their deer,
and all I wanted was a small portion of it. They heard nothing. I went
home without anything. I had no meat for the women and the
children. If this is not the way it happened let someone contradict me."
And Grey Badger's brother said, "Yes, Grey Badger told it to me this
way, and he has never told me anything that was false."

Yellow Corn asked the Grey Fox hunters for their side of it. The
eldest of them said: "We were going for game. We found him dressing
the deer not far from the canyon. We took it from him, saying, 'You have
killed our deer.' The Bean People do not know how to speak well. What
he said, we understood only a part of it. He became angry, so we became
angry. He tried to take the deer back, but we would not let him. That is
all."

Yellow Corn said: "You two who took the deer from Grey Badger,
why does it belong to you? Did you kill the deer?" They answered: "No,
we did not claim it for ourselves. We claimed it for the village." Yellow
Corn said: "If it belongs to the village it belongs to everyone. So it will
have to be cut into many small parts. Will one of those parts be enough
for a person to taste? How can a single deer be divided this way?" The
eldest hunter answered: "How can we allow him to have it? He will sit

in front of us eating a deer that belongs to us."

Flowing Spring spoke, saying: "He was walking, a deer passed him. Should he have let it go as if no one needed meat? If he had not killed it, how do we know that anyone would have ever seen it again?" The hunters answered: "Why, the deer would have been there somewhere. One of our hunters surely would have found it."

Many persons spoke, some of them angrily. At last Yellow Corn said: "If I am wrong, let my brothers in the council tell me. The Bean People promised to go beyond our hunting grounds for their game. Grey Badger went beyond. He hunted, he found nothing. He returned hungry. His people at home were hungry. He saw a deer. Now, all you people, let us say you were there in his place. You saw the deer. You said: 'No, I will not touch it. Let my people remain hungry.' You went home. How would you explain it to your women and children? Surely you would not do it that way. You would kill the deer. You would say to your friends who owned the hunting grounds, 'This deer, it is yours. But I killed it because the people need meat. It is your deer but I am the one that found it and I need something for my family. Because I bring this deer home, surely you will give me a small part of it.' This is what Grey Badger did. Have we forgotten the words of Snake Spirit already? He told us, 'Do not forget the old ones, the weak, and strangers. Care for them, for we are all younger brothers in this land.' Let us try to say now how to be just about the deer. There are many families but only one deer, and there is only one hunter who found the deer. Speak with open hearts. It is up to you."

There was a long debate in the kiva, but finally they came to a decision. Grey Badger would receive a hind quarter for his family. The rest would be divided into as many parts as there were old people and children, so that each of them would have a portion. The skin was allotted to Grey Badger's wife to make clothing, and the bones and marrow to whoever might need them. This was how the dispute was resolved, but there were still some in the village who silently nursed anger because the Bean People had taken a deer in the Grey Fox hunting grounds.

When the crowd had departed and only a few old ones remained in the kiva, Flowing Spring said: "It has often been told to us that too much corn and easy living would cause the people to forget the straight way of life. Yet it is the same with too little game, for it brings dissension and anger. Too much and too little, they are brothers. Let us strive to keep the village in balance until Winter Old Man goes to sleep. Then we will plant and find a good trail once more." Burning Tree asked, "Yes, but what if the people get so hungry that they cannot refrain from eating their seed corn?" And Flowing Spring answered, "Why, then the Grey Fox children will disappear in the wilderness and leave only the ruins of their walls behind."

The winter lived on. The people hunted and gathered firewood. There was much discussion of the kachinas and the benefits they might bring, and at last it was agreed that they should be accepted. The responsibility was given to Burning Tree to go to Red Rocks Place, live there until planting time, and learn whatever the Kachina Brotherhood could teach him. When he returned, it would be his responsibility to apply his knowledge in Refuge Place. And so, one morning, Burning Tree took his food bag, put a blanket around his shoulders to shield him from the cold wind, and began his journey to Red Rocks. In the days that followed in Refuge Place there was a restless waiting for the spring. Men who knew the sky watched as the stars gradually moved northward. Little by little the cold became less bitter, and people said hopefully that the winter would soon be gone.

Then when it seemed at last that warm sunlight and spring air were about to flood over the land, another snow fell and covered everything, so that hunters could not travel and firewood could not be found. The snow fell for three days, and when it ended the world was white. Some Grey Fox People were discouraged, saying, "Why are we here? This is a land of perpetual winter." While the snow was deep on the ground, the Bean People made a ceremony. They built a circle of fire and planted beans in sand in the center. The snow near the fire melted away, the beans sprouted, and some flowers also came out of the ground. It was a good omen and people said, "The medicine of the Bean People will help us." And suddenly, as if Winter Old Man had fallen asleep, warm air entered the canyon. The snow turned to water and ran in rivulets into the stream. Game began to appear in the hunting grounds once more. The men cleared stones from the fields where they intended to plant, and women searched for clay for their potmaking. Laughter was heard on the rooftops, and young men became suitors.

Falling Snow had decided that he wanted White Blanket for his wife. When he was not hunting or preparing his field he went often to Elk Horn's house and talked to her through the window of the corn-grinding room. Sometimes they met in hidden places outside the village and learned of each other's bodies. The two old grandmothers in Elk Horn's house pretended to be angry about it, but when they were alone they laughed and reminded themselves of how it had been when they were young and sought after by suitors. Elk Horn confronted Falling Snow one day, saying: "What are you waiting for? You keep the stones rolling under our feet. Do not wait until you are an old man. Someone else will get her." Falling Snow said, "Who are you to instruct me?" Elk Horn said, "I am her brother." Falling Snow said: "Then instruct White Blanket, do not instruct me. Why should I want her, anyway? She still does not know how to speak Grey Fox language very well. Can she make pots? If so, I have never seen her do it. If I want to touch her I have to chase her. Do I need a wife like that?" They laughed, and as always when something preposterous was said, they pointed their fingers at the cliffs, shouting, "Ka ka ka!"

Seeing that something was about to happen, Elk Horn became concerned about where he would get corn for the corn-grinding marriage ceremony. A girl had to bring ground meal to the young man's family, and in Elk Horn's house there was little corn to be ground. He thought about the corn that his people had cached in the cave near the deserted Yayatu village. He wondered if he had a right to it, and so he went to Crying Wolf one day and spoke of the matter. He said: "My uncle, Falling Snow wants my sister, but in my house there is nothing to grind. My people put some of their corn in a cave before they went away. May I take a small share of it?"

Crying Wolf pondered on the hidden corn, and finally he said: "My nephew, it is difficult to say. Among our people it is one thing, among others it is something else. There are those who will take corn wherever they find it, saying only, 'It is something to eat.' But we are not like that. We say that if people go away from their village and leave corn behind, it is their corn and no one should touch it. The village is theirs as long as there is a sun and moon in the sky. Perhaps one day they will return from wherever they have gone and rebuild their houses and plant again in their fields. Still, the corn in the cave came from many houses, and surely some of it belonged to your family. Did you not help to cultivate the field? White Blanket's grandmother has a right to something. I will make you a prayer feather to leave in the cave. It will explain things to the people if they ever come back." So Crying Wolf made the prayer feather for him and Elk Horn made his expedition to the Yayatu cave. When he returned he brought forty ears of corn and gave them to his grandmother to care for.

There was a rabbit hunt in honor of the marriage of Falling Snow and White Blanket. The young people went out with their throwing sticks, and whenever a boy killed a rabbit a girl ran to him and ransomed it for her family with a piece of cornbread or piki. Falling Snow killed one rabbit, and White Blanket exchanged cornbread for it. The next day Yellow Hair sent White Blanket to the corn-grinding room and gave her the corn Elk Horn had provided. White Blanket ground until all the corn had been turned into meal, then she brought it to White Moccasin who used it to prepare a wedding feast. There remained only the head-washing ritual. The hair of the two young people was washed with yucca suds, and the ceremony was finished. The first night they slept in White Moccasin's house, and after that in the house of Elk Horn's people. Within a few days, Falling Snow and White Blanket began work on a house of their own.

It was while Falling Snow and Elk Horn were looking for building stones along the base of the cliff wall that they discovered a shallow cave whose entrance had been closed with rocks. They pried out an opening and went inside, finding there the skeleton of a man and numerous skins that had been shed by snakes. When they returned to the village they told Still Water about it, because he was the authority on all matters having to do with snakes. The following morning they guided him to the cave. He entered and sat close to where the skeleton was lying. He touched the fingerbones of the skeleton. He touched the dried snakeskins. He remained there until evening, meditating and allowing the cave to speak to him. That night in the kiva he spoke of what he had learned.

"The cave told me about many things. The one whose bones lie there was a snake person. I heard his story. He was a young man, living in a village far from here. He went hunting, and he came to a place where many snakes were crawling. He held a lance in his hand, but he said, 'These snakes, why should I kill any of them? Have they harmed me?' He did not molest them. He camped and made a fire. While he was sitting there in the night, the snakes came close to warm themselves. They looked at him to discern his intentions. He was not afraid. He did not drive them away. At last one of the snakes spoke, saying to him, 'Why is it that you do not try to injure us, but allow us to share your fire?' He said: 'What have you done to me that I should hurt you? If you stay by my fire, does that take warmth away from me? You are my elder brothers. You were here in this world before people came. So share my fire and some of my food as well.'

"Morning came. The snakes were still there. One of the snakes said to him, 'Follow us. We have something to show you.' He followed them, and at a certain place they descended into the ground through an opening in the rocks. The hunter went down also. They were inside a kiva. The snakes took off their skins and hung them on pegs. They were not snakes anymore, but people. They sat and smoked with the hunter, and the one who was the uncle of all the others said, 'We are impressed with you. Most hunters do not respect us as you do. We have something to give you. What we give is the knowledge of healing snakebites. Sometimes when we are threatened we bite people to protect ourselves, but we do not mean to harm them. So we are going to give you the medicine for curing these bites.' The young man stayed with the snake people for four days, and they taught him many things. When he was ready to go back to his village the snake uncle said, 'Now you are one of us. Remember what we have given to you. You possess strong power for curing. May you live long and do many good deeds. Yet all things that live have only a few seasons. When it is time for you to die, come back to us. We will send someone to lead you to the proper place.'

"The young man returned to his people. He became a healer. If a child was stung by a snake, the young man cured him. He taught the women of his village to make buckskin leggings to protect themselves from snakes when they went to the spring for water. He taught the people to be gentle to snakes and not fear them. A time came when he grew old and knew that the time of his dying was drawing near. One morning he met a snake in his field. The snake said, 'My brother, I have been sent to get you.' He followed the snake. Where they were going, he did not know. They travelled many days. They came to the cave. The snake said to him, 'We come to this place to shed our skins. Wait here. Be patient. Here you will shed your outer form. After that we will be together.' The old man stayed there, and in time he shed his outer form. That is why we find these things in the cave, the skins and the skeleton. This is what was told to me. It was said that we should take prayer feathers there and disturb nothing. It was said that we should recall in our ceremonies that snakes are our older brothers. That is all I heard."

Word of Still Water's revelations went through the village, and people reflected on them at night in their houses. They readily accepted that snakes were their elder brothers and did not mean to injure them, because this had been told to them long ago by Serpent Spirit. Yet they were awed that the events described by Still Water had taken place so close to where the village was standing. As for Falling Snow, he was perplexed, and one night after he had brought wood into the kiva he said to Yellow Corn: "My grandfather, how can a cave speak to a person? Elk Horn and I were there. The cave did not speak to us."

Yellow Corn answered: "My grandson, a cave can speak. A tree can speak. A mountain can speak. A cloud can speak. But everyone cannot hear them. You and Elk Horn were like full jars of water. There was no room for anything else to come in. When Still Water went into the cave he emptied everything from his mind. What he saw with his eyes faded away. What he heard with his ears became silent. His thoughts, he put them out of reach. Thus he made room to comprehend whatever the cave had to say to him."

Falling Snow said, "My grandfather, did he hear voices like yours and mine?" And Yellow Corn answered: "No, it was not the same kind of hearing. What he heard was the spirit of a voice speaking to the spirit of a person. When a person hears such a voice he knows that he has been spoken to. He understands what is said. He perceives it and grasps it. He knows it to be true. In this way a man sometimes comes to know what he could not learn in any other way. When I was a child I thought that trees were only trees, and mountains only mountains. But one day when I was out gathering firewood I lay in the grass and looked at the sky. I watched a large white cloud floating above me. How it came to be I cannot tell you, but suddenly my heart was happy. I said to myself: 'Before I was born I was not anything. When I die I will not be here. But now, in this moment, here I am. The grass, the trees, the water in the stream, they are all my brothers. It is a fine thing.' In this way the cloud revealed something to me that I had never understood before. So now I say that the cloud spoke to me. But was it the cloud? That is only a manner of describing it. When Still Water said that the cave spoke to him, it was a way of saying that something had been revealed to him there."

Falling Snow said: "My grandfather, I want things to speak to me also. I would like to have visions. I want to understand things that people cannot tell me." Yellow Corn replied: "Visions do not come to everyone. There are old men who have sought all their lives for visions without finding one. Yet all of us can be spoken to. A man approaches a hill. The hill speaks to him, saying, 'On the far side a deer stands.' He goes around. The deer is there and he kills it. A man is at war. He goes quietly among the rocks. He hears no sound. Yet the rocks speak to him, saying, 'Just beyond the tree over there the enemy are lurking.' He goes to a high place and looks down. The enemy are visible beyond the tree. A man goes out of his house in the morning and looks at the sky. Nothing is different. But the sky speaks, saying, 'A strong wind comes.' The man looks around. He sees nothing blowing, but he knows what he did not know before. He covers the entrance to his house. The wind comes, a great wind that scatters everything and blows sand into the houses that are not well covered. Anything we can see has the power to speak to us. But there are many who cannot hear as well as Still Water does."

The time was approaching when the earth would be warm enough for corn to be planted, but there were some families in Refuge Place that had no seed, having eaten all their corn during the winter. Already several men had gone on an expedition to Bend-of-the-Water to get some of the corn that had been left in the storage rooms there, but it was a long journey and they had not yet returned. Elk Horn went again to the Yayatu cave and brought more corn from there for his own family's needs.

It was Burning Tree, returning from Red Rocks Place after sixteen days with the Kachina Brotherhood, who reported that Long Arrow's village had corn that it would be willing to barter. Falling Snow and Walking Bear decided to go there together to obtain seed corn. They gathered trade items from their own houses, and borrowed more from relatives who had anything to spare, until at last they had an assort-ment to take on their expedition — baked pots, leggings and moccasins, flint knives and points, several strings of coral and a small amount of tobacco and salt. Together with White Moccasin and Soft Rain, Walk-ing Bear's wife, they went up the eastern cliff and began the journey to Red Rocks Place. They stopped frequently to put their baskets on the ground and rest. By nightfall they were within sight of the red butte for which Long Arrow's village was named. They slept in the shelter of a small grove of piñon trees, and when they arose in the morning they went forward again without stopping.

The sun rose sluggishly and cast a yellow light. Walking Bear took note of it, saying, "Father Sun is not well." A little later he added, "It is not a good sign." Soft Rain laughed. She said: "Why speak of signs? We have almost arrived." But Walking Bear was gloomy. He sensed that things were not right, and his eyes searched the butte for the thin columns of smoke that should be coming from pottery fires. When they were close enough to see the outlines of the house walls, Walking Bear put his load down, saying: "It is not the way it should be. Some-thing is wrong up there." They stood looking at the village. Falling Snow said: "There are no sounds. The people are asleep." Walking Bear said: "Also, the dogs are not barking. No one calls from the guard post. Nothing is moving. There is only one sound that rises, the sound of emptiness."

They walked a little and stopped again. Walking Bear went on alone, moving slowly, keeping behind rocks whenever he could. When he reached the edge of the village he listened for the sounds of people, but he heard nothing. He entered the village, sensing only the echoes of living things. He saw pots and grinding stones scattered about, and a broken forehead carrying strap in front of a house. He went to the kiva and peered into the opening. He could see nothing, but he smelled the ashes of a fire that had died days before. Without looking further, he returned to where the others were waiting. He said: "The people are not here. There is no one to speak to. The rooms are empty. The kiva is lifeless." They pondered a while. Soft Rain said, "Perhaps they have gone somewhere for a visit." And White Blanket suggested, "Perhaps they are merely hiding." But Walking Bear answered: "No, the village is a stalk from which the breath of life has departed. The people took their belongings with them, and what they could not carry they left lying on the ground."

Now the four of them went together into the village, trying to understand the nature of the disaster that had come to it. They went from house to house, mounting ladders and looking into the entrances from the roofs. There was nothing to be seen except the debris of departure. When they had gone halfway through the villages they did not look anymore, certain that life had gone out of Red Rocks Place. It was then that they heard a voice coming from one of the houses.

They entered and saw an old man sitting there with a blanket wrapped around him. They said, "Father, what has happened to the people?" He answered in a cracked voice, "They have been eaten up by the wilderness." They asked if there had been raiders and he answered: "No, it was worse than the Utaheh. It was the Desert Demon." Falling Snow said, "Father, we do not understand you." The old man said: "Have you people never heard of the Desert Demon? She rules over all the animals. She is terrible to see, worse than Death Old Man. She came. She drove everyone away." Falling Snow said, "We do not know anything about Desert Demon." The old man said: "Yes, the people were in great fear. The Desert Demon would not let us alone. We prayed in the kiva. We offered prayer feathers. But she was relentless. She would not go away. She said, 'Do not try to stay here or I will destroy your houses. Do not try to plant here or I will destroy your corn. I will dry up the springs and make the village sterile.' She gave a terrible cry, 'A-neh!' The people could not stand it. They went away."

Falling Snow said, "Father, tell us from the beginning so that we can understand everything." The old man closed his eyes as he spoke, saying, "It happened in the night. People were asleep, all except a man who was tending the kiva. He saw a moving spark of fire in the distance, like the breath of Death Old Man. He called out from the kiva roof that a spark of fire was coming. The people came out of their houses and saw Desert Demon enter the village. Flames came out of her mouth, and she carried grinding stones in her hands. She sat on the roof of the kiva and ground the stones together without any corn between them. She sang words we could not understand, 'tutaheh, tutaheh,' like that. The people were afraid. When she finished with the singing she said: 'You people have been killing animals in my country! You do not belong here! Go away!'

"She departed. That night a man died. They buried him. Desert Demon came again the next night, and again she ground her stones without any corn between them. She went away. A woman died. They buried her. Desert Demon came the third night. A child died. They buried her. On the fourth night Desert Demon came once more. A man died. They buried him. The people said, 'We cannot stay here any longer.' They took what they could carry. They went away quickly into the desert."

Walking Bear asked, "But you, father, why are you here?" The old man answered, "I am old. I have had too many journeys. I do not want any more. The people said, 'Old man, let us get ready to go.' I said, 'No, I will stay in my house. Let Desert Demon be angry, I do not care. I will die soon anyway. I do not want any more of this going from one place to another in the wilderness.' The people journeyed toward the Eastern River. The Desert Demon followed them, crying, 'A-neh!' That is all."

After a while Walking Bear said, "We brought things to trade for corn, but now there is no one to trade with." The old man said, "I am still here. I am Red Rocks Place now. Whatever you have to trade, bring it and leave it on my roof. The corn, take whatever you can carry." Walking Bear said: "My father, that is good. Yet it is not good for you to stay here alone. Come back with us to Refuge Place." The old man spoke impatiently, saying, "No, this is my village. I do not need anything. When I am ready to die I will go out and find a place to lie down. Meanwhile I will stay. You young people still have a long journey before you arrive at the place where I am now. Take your corn and go back to Refuge Place and continue living."

So they went out and brought all of their trade goods and left them on the roof. After that they filled their baskets with corn from the bins in the houses. But Falling Snow was still uncertain. He said: "The old one is very old. Perhaps it did not happen the way he remembers it. Perhaps there were raiders. If the people have not gone far, perhaps they are waiting for a safe time to return. Therefore is it right to take the corn?" Walking Bear answered: "You heard the old man say, 'I am Red Rocks Place now.' If there was no single person here to give us permission we could not take the corn. But the old one is here. He said, 'Take it, as much as you can carry.' " Falling Snow said, "Perhaps the old man does not understand things. Maybe he was dreaming." Walking Bear answered: "Look around you and see the way things have been scattered. The people were in haste, they were running from something. But there is no sign of a raid. No, it is as he said, an evil spirit drove them out." Falling Snow asked, "Have you ever before heard of Desert Demon?" Walking Bear said, "No, until now I never heard of her." White Blanket said, "Whatever it was that drove the people out, the old one should not be left here alone." Falling Snow said: "Yes, but he does not listen to us. When we arrive at Refuge Place we will tell Yellow Corn and the others about it. They will know what to do." White Blanket said, "No, first let us try him again."

Walking Bear and Falling Snow went again to the old man's house and descended into his room. He was singing in a language they did not know. In one hand he held a sacred rattle, in the other a sacred stick decorated with beads and feathers. They spoke, saying, "Grandfather, let us take you to Refuge Place so that you can tell our people your story." But he did not seem to hear them. His eyes were closed. He went on singing. Walking Bear said: "There is no use. This is what he wants." They went out of the house, took up their baskets of corn and began their return journey to Refuge Place.

As soon as they reached home late the next day, Falling Snow went at once to the kiva to talk to Yellow Corn. He said: "We have brought corn from Red Rocks Place. But the village is abandoned. Everyone has gone away except one old man. He said the people were driven out by Desert Demon." Yellow Corn heard the story, but he could not accept that Red Rocks Place had been abandoned, and he made Falling Snow tell his story again. Finally he asked about the kiva, and Falling Snow said, "It was dark inside and there was nothing alive down there." Yellow Corn asked no more questions, but immediately sent for the men of the council. The old ones sat into the night discussing the disaster that had fallen on Long Arrow's village.

Only a few of them had heard of Desert Demon, so Standing Rock said: "My people knew of Desert Demon, but they called her by another name, Fire Spitter Old Woman. My uncle told it to me this way, that before she became Fire Spitter Old Woman she was the daughter of a certain village chief far in the south. She was ready for marriage, and there were several young men who wanted her but she rejected them all. It was observed by her brother that she went often to the spring for water and that she was gone from the village a long time, even though the spring was not far away. He became suspicious and followed her one day. She did not go to the spring where other young women got their water, but to a secluded pool. She arrived there, she slapped the water four times with the palm of her hand and a large water snake came out. The girl and the water snake embraced. The brother was very astonished and ran home to tell his parents what he had seen. They became very worried about what they heard. Early the next morning the boy guided his father to the pool. At first there was nothing unusual to be seen, but the boy slapped the water four times as he had seen his sister do, and instantly the water snake emerged. Then the father shot the snake with an arrow and it fell lifeless back into the water.

"Now, when they returned to their house and told the girl what they had done, she lost her reason. She said that the water snake was the chief and protector of all the animals in the region of the pool. She ran from the house with her family in pursuit, but they could not catch her. She came to the pool, leaped into it and disappeared. She descended into the water snake's kiva and remained there. As her snake lover was dead, she took over the chieftainship of the animals and became their protector. She grew old and fearsome in appearance. Flames came out of her mouth when she talked. She acquired great powers of sorcery and medicine. From time to time she came from her kiva below the water to drive humans out of the country where she lived. That is what my uncle told me of Fire Spitter Old Woman. But I have never seen her. I tell you only what was told to me." They asked Standing Rock if he knew the meaning of the words tutaheh and a-neh, but he knew nothing of them.

Although they had identified Desert Demon, still there was mystery about the events that had taken place at Red Rocks, and much foreboding about what they might portend for the Grey Fox People. Burning Tree had not yet spoken in the council, but now he said: "I myself do not understand everything. But I am a Kachina Brother.

Of all the members of the Kachina Brotherhood, I am the only one left. Who else understands the secrets and responsibilities that can bring the kachinas to assist us? I will have to go to Red Rocks Place and gather the masks and other paraphernalia of the Brotherhood, unless they have already been taken away. I will take two young men with me, and when I am there I will speak to the old man who refused to leave. Perhaps there is something more for us to learn."

Burning Tree asked Falling Snow and Young Antelope to go with him, and they agreed. The next morning they set out for Red Rocks Place, and when they arrived on the following day Burning Tree at once lighted a torch and descended into the kiva, the young men following. It seemed as if nothing had been disturbed. On the walls were the deerskin costumes used for the deer dance. On the hearth were cold ashes from the last fire, and lying nearby were a pouch of tobacco and a pipe. At one side of the kiva was an altar with a bowl, carved wooden figures and some prayer feathers. At the far side of the kiva, covered with a blanket, they found five kachina masks.

Burning Tree said: "These are what we have come for. Let us take them out, and I will purify the kiva of any evil that may have entered." Falling Snow and Young Antelope carried the masks to the kiva roof, from where they heard Burning Tree chanting inside. He was a long time singing and doing things that they could not see. When he came out he said, "Now let us cover the entrance." They covered the opening with pieces of cottonwood that had been stacked up for fuel, and on top of the wood they placed small brush and stones. Burning Tree wrapped the masks in the blanket from the kiva. Then he said, "Now take me to the house of the old man who remained behind."

Falling Snow led him to the house on the far side of the village. They heard the old man singing. Burning Tree went to the roof and called down, "My brother, let me come and speak with you." The answer came, "Yes, enter and speak with me." Burning Tree went down. The old man was sitting with a blanket around him. On the hearth the ashes were cold. Burning Tree took the old man's fire drill and made a fire. Then he sat down, saying: "I know you, Sun Caller. Do you know me? I am the person from Refuge Place who was taken into the Kachina Brotherhood. I have come to protect the masks." The old man answered, "Yes, I know you, Burning Tree." Burning Tree said, "The two young men to whom you spoke brought us your story. But they are young. They do not perceive what was behind your words. Was it truly Desert Demon that caused the village to be deserted?" And the old man replied, "Who knows anything about Desert Demon?" Burning Tree said, "My brother, tell me what happened."

Sun Caller said: "What happened? Dissension and anger came into the village. They danced across the roofs of the houses. They danced on top of the kiva." He fell silent, and for a long time he said no more. Burning Tree took some piki from his knapsack and handed it to Sun Caller. The old man ate a little and put the rest aside. He said: "It was the Coyote people who caused the trouble. Since the beginning, this village was under the Blue Fox Clan. But the Coyotes said that they should lead because they are related to the Firewood Clan which claims Death Old Man as a relative. Long Arrow said to them, 'True, you are related to the Firewood Clan, but you are only the Coyote Clan. So why should you lead?' Then the Arrow Clan gave their support to the Coyote people, and the Antelope Clan supported the Blue Fox Clan. The village was divided. If there was a ritual led by Blue Fox people, the Coyotes would not participate. The Kachina Brotherhood broke in two. Half the village would not speak to the other half. We could not all meet in the kiva anymore. The Coyotes continued to demand that they should lead.

"Long Arrow spoke strong words to them," Sun Caller went on. "He said: 'Dissension is like the rain that falls from the sky. Once it begins it cannot stop until it reaches the earth. Until now everything has been in balance here, but today there is no harmony. You claim the leadership? How is it, then, that you did not mention it when we accepted you out of the desert? You are destroying everything. If you cannot live without leading, lead your people elsewhere and have a village of your own.' The Coyotes answered him, 'No, gather your Blue Foxes together and take them away.' Long Arrow answered, 'You are the ones who are discontented. It is you who must leave.'

"The Coyotes were angry. They gathered everything they could carry, and the Arrow people also gathered their things, and they went out cursing the village. The Antelope people were distressed. They did not want to go with the Coyote Clan, but the village had been cursed, so they took their things and went in a different direction. There remained only the Blue Fox. One house out of four had living people in it. The rest were ghost houses. One day after the Antelope Clan left, Long Arrow said to the Blue Fox people: 'Let us also depart. There has been too much evil in this village. We must go away and leave the memory of dissension behind.' The people looked around them. They said, 'Yes, this is a ghost village. We are ready to go.' So they took whatever they could carry and departed. The village became silent. Now I have told you everything."

Burning Tree said: "I have not heard you speak of Desert Demon. When the young men spoke with you before, you told them that Desert Demon had driven the people away." Sun Caller answered, "Who can say that she did not?" Burning Tree said, "But one thing or the other happened. Which was it?" Sun Caller replied: "Desert Demon is a spirit of wild anger and destruction. Were we not broken by such a spirit? She has fire in her mouth, like Death Old Man. Is not the village a dead remnant from which life has gone out? The kachinas sit on their western mountain looking at this gopher hill that we called Red Rocks Place. They see small people running in all directions. Surely they are saying: 'What is this? How can it be explained? It must be that Desert Demon has driven them out.' If one person goes mad we say he has been given the gift of seeing what we cannot see. If a whole village goes mad we can say it is the doing of Desert Demon."

Burning Tree persisted. He said: "My brother, I understand you. Yet in your story to the young men you spoke of the death of four persons, one each night. What is the meaning of this?" The old man answered, "Why, the four who died were the four clans, the Coyote, the Arrow, the Antelope and the Blue Fox." Burning Tree said: "Yes, now we understand each other. It is an unfortunate thing. Our village also has been wounded, but it still has strong life in it. We will grow stronger. The corn you have provided will give us more corn. The people will learn to keep evil away. But you, my brother, do not remain here by yourself. Come back to Refuge Place with us. We will listen to you in the kiva. You can teach us things that we do not know. You can reveal to us ceremonies and medicine that we do not have. Let us not waste the brotherhood that our two villages made together. Because of us, Long Arrow sent a family into exile. Because of your people a piece of our village broke off and departed. Both of our villages sacrificed something to make our brotherhood durable. You are all that is left of Red Rocks Place. Come back with us. Sit in our councils. Help us to deal with things."

The old man listened and considered. At last he said: "I have heard you. I thought to stay here until the end. But your words spoke to my heart. I will go to Refuge Place and live on for a while. In this way the experience of our people will not be thrown away."

So Sun Caller came back with Burning Tree, Falling Snow and Young Antelope, and they brought with them the kachina masks. Yellow Corn welcomed Sun Caller, He said: "We will find you a place to live. There are empty houses here that were left by Yellow Bird's people, but they are ghost houses." Sun Caller answered, "Why should I, who will soon leave my own ghost behind, fear the ghosts of others? Give me one of the houses. I will not claim it for my own. I will be Yellow Bird's guest. I will make a prayer feather for him, and his ghost will understand. Yellow Bird, I know him. He is a bow that refuses to bend, but he will not begrudge me shelter. However, ladders are for the young, so I will make a door in the wall." Yellow Corn pondered on it. At last he said: "Yes, live in Yellow Bird's house then. As for the kiva, use it freely whenever you want to make prayer feathers or discuss matters with us. You will smoke with us in council. You will teach us things that we do not know." So it was that Sun Caller came to stay in Refuge Place.

One night, a few days after their journey to Red Rocks, Burning Tree sent for Falling Snow and Young Antelope to meet with him. He said: "My nephews, you are the ones who helped save the masks, and because of this a responsibility comes to you. When the Kachina Brotherhood sent its three masked dancers to us, it did so at the prompting of the kachinas themselves. This I now believe to be true. It was the beginning of a web, and each strand is woven to the first and the web becomes larger. I went to Red Rocks and became a strand, then the three of us went to retrieve the masks and became more strands. It is a story with great meaning for the future.

"We Grey Fox are the only ones remaining in this country. A gift was given to us and we must preserve it. In Refuge Place we will carry out our own kachina rituals and encourage the rain to come. I will be your mentor uncle and teach you the ways of the kachinas. I will sit at your shoulders and give you the proper songs. I will teach you the dances. I will teach you the meaning of each design on the masks. Together we will perform ceremonies for the village when the time comes. If you agree, then we will remain quiet about it in public and do our work in the solitude of the kiva. You must learn, you must rehearse, you must practice the songs, you must do everything without fault. You must put fresh color on the masks when the old paint fades, thus renewing their force. You must be dedicated. When we are learning things or praying, do not say, 'The Suitor passes overhead, I am finished for the present.' If we sit together throughout the night doing our work, it is to merit the good opinion of the kachinas and to further the welfare of the village. Only in this way can our Kachina Society be a force in putting us in balance with the clouds and the land. If you do not want the responsibility, tell me now and I will look for others." Falling Snow replied, "My uncle, I want the responsibility." Young Antelope said, "I also want the responsibility."

So the two young men became neophytes in the Kachina Fraternity, and night by night they learned more of the mysteries so that when the time was right they could do something to assure rain for the corn.

Warmth had come to the earth in the canyon. The people made their fields some distance from the western cliff so that the corn would not be shaded in the late afternoon. The men who had gone on the expedition to Bend-of-the-Water returned with seed and with the news that their old village had not been molested. They had rested there for a day, and marked on the rock walls that they had come for corn and departed again to the north. They also reported that they had sighted a small group of people following them at a distance, and so it was no surprise when, a little later, a Bear Clan family arrived and asked permission to stay at Refuge Place long enough to grow some corn. Now the spring had come, the people were in an optimistic mood and there was no objection. They designated a part of the canyon valley where the newcomers might plant something.

That night the grandfather of the family was invited to the kiva to tell of his journey. The old ones smoked together, and then he began, saying, "My people are of the Bear Clan. With other clans we emerged from the underworld by climbing through the center of a giant reed. Those who came with us from below were the Fire People, to whom Death Old Man had given the knowledge of fire. Though they were his relatives, they refused to lead the people to their destination. So my clan said, 'Very well, then we shall lead, and for that reason we will henceforth rate first among the clans.' Some groups followed us, but the Fire Clan and others went in different directions.

"The Fire Clan already had a name," the man said, "because Death Old Man had given them fire, but our group was not yet called the Bear Clan. How we received our name was this: We were on our journey and we came upon the carcass of a bear. Our old ones said: 'This is a sign given to us. We will call ourselves the Bear Clan.' Other groups that followed us also found the dead bear, and they took their names at the same place. One group made forehead straps from the bear's skin, and they called themselves the Strap Clan. Another group saw grease in the cavity of the bear's skull, and they called themselves the Grease Cavity Clan. Another group saw a bluebird eating fragments of meat from the bones, and they called themselves the Bluebird Clan. Another saw a gopher hole beneath the carcass, and they called themselves the Gopher Clan. Another saw a spider web spun across the bones, and they called themselves the Spider Clan. The last group to come that way saw a spruce tree growing through the bones of the bear, and they named themselves the Spruce Clan. Because it was the bear from which they took their names, all of these clans consider themselves to be related.

"But there were many journeys, and some of the clans broke up, part going one way and part another, so people from the same clan were separated. Yet it was prophesied that some day we will all come together again at a certain place. My family is a small piece of the Bear Clan, and now we are looking for our people. We hear that some of them are living up there in the north somewhere, and that is why we are travelling in this direction. We were living at a place near the Eastern River in a village of mixed clans. But the land dried up, so the village was abandoned. The Eagle People went looking for their clan relatives. The Juniper People went looking for their clan relatives. Everyone departed.

"We have had a hard journey. We rested for the winter in a cave. We hunted, we survived. Many things happened to us after we left our eastern village. At first there were five Bear Clan families. When winter approached we could not agree on what to do, so some went one way, some another, each family by itself. But before we separated something unusual happened. We saw a village in the distance where pottery fires sent up stems of smoke. We said, 'Let us approach the village and greet the people who live there.' Then we said, 'Perhaps it is better to go cautiously until we find out who these people are.' So we made our camp and rested. We thought, 'Perhaps one of their hunters will come this way and we can ask questions without risking our safety.' We ate a little meat. We put down our blankets. Then a child called out, 'Someone is coming.' It was not yet dark. We saw an old woman coming from the direction of the village. She arrived at our camp. She said, 'May I enter?' We said, 'Yes, old woman, come in, sit with us.' She sat down. She did not speak. We asked her, 'Grandmother, are you from the village over there?' She said, 'I am from one village and another.' We said, 'Grandmother, is it good to travel alone like this?' She laughed, saying, 'Why should I fear anything?' We said, 'Can an old woman hunt if she is hungry?' She said, 'Well, I am not a hunter. Perhaps there is something for me to eat in your pots.' We said,

'Yes, here is something for you.' We did not have much but we gave her something. She ate without speaking for a long while.

"At last she said, 'Who are you people and where are you going?' We said: 'We are Bear People. We are going to find our relatives.' She said: 'That is good. Follow the star that does not move.' We said: 'Yes, we are doing that. But Grandmother, what is the name of the village from which you were coming?' She said, 'It is called Gamblers' Village.' We said, 'It is a strange name.' She said: 'It is because the people there are perpetually gambling. It is a place to avoid.' We said, 'Grandmother, we also know gambling.' She answered: 'Yes, but those people do not know anything else. In their kiva no one makes prayer feathers. They throw gambling sticks instead. When they hunt they gamble to see who owns the game they kill. They gamble to see who takes the corn in the fields. They gamble for each other's clothing and pots. When there is nothing else, they gamble for each other's wives or children.'

"We said: 'Grandmother, are there really such people as this? We have never heard of them.' She said: 'I was on a journey from one place to another, and I saw you camping here. So I came to warn you. Turn your trail a little to the west and pass around this place.' We asked, 'Are these people Tinneh or Utaheh?' She said: 'No, they are a kind of their own. They have forgotten the meaning of life. Their old ones were good people who sought the help of Sun Spirit and Earth Spirit, but now these men and women have forgotten everything. They believe only in chance. They do not seek harmony, only new gambling games. If strangers pass, they come at once to gamble with them and take everything away. If they win something they gamble for it among themselves in the kiva. The man who leads the village won his chieftainship by gambling.'

"We asked, 'Grandmother, do you have a name?' She answered, 'My name is Dew Catcher.' We said to her, 'That is a fine name.' She said, 'Well, now I have warned you,' and she prepared to depart, but we said: 'Old woman, do not go away in the darkness. You will get lost.' She laughed, saying, 'Well, then, give me a blanket for the night.' We gave her a blanket, we slept. When daylight came she was not there anymore. In the dust next to her blanket she had marked a sign meaning for us to go west. We said: 'She is a strange old woman. She wants us to go west. But our journey is north, therefore let us go northward.'

"We continued on our trail. We travelled until the sun was overhead. Then we saw a large party of men coming toward us. They carried bows and lances, but they did not want to fight. Their hearts seemed happy. They said, 'Let us gamble for something.' We answered, 'We are tired from walking and we have nothing to gamble. We are going to a certain place and cannot stop.' They said, 'Surely you need meat for your meat bags, or corn? We have plenty.' We said, 'Yes, we need food, but we have good hunters.' They said: 'We see the things you are wearing. We see coral. We see blankets. Let us gamble for something.' We said: 'You people have much and we have only what we can carry. We cannot spare anything.'

"They threw some lances and bows in a pile, saying, 'Put something down. We will throw sticks for a while, then you can continue on your way.' The gamblers were many, and we were only a few. So we put down some leggings, moccasins and other small things. We threw sticks. They won everything. They put down more things, saying, 'Let us try shooting arrows.' We did not want it, but they grew angry. We put down some things, only a few, saying, 'That is all we have left.' They put a piece of cactus on a stone. They said, 'Whoever hits the cactus wins everything.' Three of our young men tried. The cactus was too far away, they could not hit it. Three of the gamblers tried. Two of them missed, but one hit the cactus. They took everything.

"Then they said to us, 'Let our young men race against each other.' We said, 'No, already you have taken too much. What we have left we cannot spare.' They said: 'Some of your women have coral strings around their necks. Some of your men have armbands. You have plenty of arrows. Put them down. We will put down whatever we have already won from you. If your runner wins, you will take everything. If our runner wins, we will take everything.' We chose Parrot Feather to run for us, and they chose one of their young men. The runners set out. They had to go to a certain mound far away, circle it and return. At first they were together, but after they circled the mound Parrot Feather was in the lead. Halfway back he was still ahead. The gamblers became angry. They took knives in their hands and said they would kill Parrot Feather if he won. We picked up our lances. We knew we would have to have strong hearts and die.

"But something happened. A black cloud moved across the sun. It became dark. A bolt of lightning struck some high rocks nearby. The lightning came again. Four times it came. Balls of ice began to fall from the sky. The air was full of fury. The gamblers hesitated, then they turned and fled, leaving behind all the things they had won from us. The cloud that had covered the sun moved on. We took up our belongings and continued our journey. On our way, we saw the old woman, Dew Catcher, sitting on a rock. She got up and went away without speaking."

The Grey Fox old ones listened intently to the story, and when it was finished one of them said: "My cousin, it is a strange story. But surely you knew who the old woman was?" The Bear Clan grandfather said: "Yes, we did not know at first, but now we think we know. She said her name was Dew Catcher. What is a dew catcher? It is the spider's web that gathers drops of dew in the morning. It is the sign of Spider Old Woman. When she warned us, we listened with only one ear. We did not recognize her then, and we went ahead obstinately. When everything became difficult for us and it seemed as if we would have to die, she sent the lightning and frightened the gamblers away. Even when we saw her the second time we did not recognize her. Only afterward did we begin to grasp it all."

Now there were numerous clans in Refuge Place—the Grey Fox, the Bean Clan, the Yayatu (though whether they were exactly a clan was not clear), the Earth House People, the Blue Fox and the Bear Clan. The Bean Clan had intended to resume its journey with the coming of spring, but Grey Badger went to Yellow Corn one morning and said: "When we arrived we promised to stay only through the winter. But now we have friends in the village. We have made ceremonies together. We would like to stay for a while and plant corn. If you tell us we must go, we will go. If we stay we will help the village to flourish. We will do everything according to the Grey Fox way. We have learned to speak your language. Give us a field for our corn. We will earn it." Yellow Corn brought the matter to the council. No one objected, and so the Bean People stayed on and planted. The Earth House People also asked to stay, and again the council agreed. There was a growing feeling of well-being. Even though Refuge Place had been wounded by the departure of Badger Boy and Yellow Bird and their followers, people sensed that the village was growing strong again. Some of the old ones searched among their recollections for a prophecy to explain why other fragments of clans were converging on Refuge Place to join with the Grey Fox People.

The corn was planted, and in the days that followed, children were sent out early in the morning to protect the germinating seeds from birds, gophers and field rats. They made buzzers on long strings which they whirled in the air to frighten away crows. The field rats had a gift for knowing where the seeds were hidden in the freshly worked earth, and unless they were deterred they could destroy many hills in a single day. The children poked sticks into the burrows and killed the field rats when they came out, using rabbit-hunt sticks or slings. Yet often when a stick was poked into one hole the rats would come out another and escape. But because this was the first time corn had been planted in the canyon valley the field rats had not yet come in large numbers, and so not many hills had to be replanted.

Some of the children asked their fathers, "Why is it that the field rats have two entrances to their houses while we have only one?" And their fathers answered, "That is the way it is with rats." The children persisted, saying, "With rats, if the enemy comes in one door, the rats go out the other." Their fathers acknowledged that it was so, and the children asked: "Why is it that people do not have two entrances to their houses? Then if the Utaheh were to come in one way we could go out the other." Their fathers said, "Why, we will not let the Utaheh enter, we will drive them away." What the children said about the dwellings of the rats lingered in the minds of their fathers, and they spoke of it jestingly in the kiva. But when they were through making jokes some of them agreed that it was something to think about whenever they might build houses again.

The canyon valley became green and full of flowers. In the fields, beans and squash were planted among the corn hills, but it was the growing cornstalks that dominated the people's thoughts. It was almost as if each hill of stalks were the navel of a universe. The men went early each day to cultivate and weed. In the kiva there were continual prayers for the corn to grow and mature. Prayer feathers were made at night and placed in the fields by day as supplications to Desert Spirit. Hunters no longer had to go far to find game, and the people felt that once more their world was in balance.

Burning Tree, Young Antelope and Falling Snow spent many of their nights in the kiva preparing for the first appearance of the village kachina dances. Burning Tree sought perfection. When the young men sang he listened with total absorption, and if he heard an untrue note he would say: "Let us do it again, the trail is not yet clear. You go forward but you do not turn at the right place. Let us not get lost." He would sing for them, and afterwards they would sing again. He would say: "Let us remember that this prayer must find its way to the mountain where the kachinas have their dwellings. If we do not sing well our words will not have the strength to get there." They rehearsed until their eyes became heavy with fatigue.

Burning Tree taught them the dances and the meaning of the masks. He strove to make them understand what they were trying to achieve, saying, "Let us remember that we are only men, that it is not we who speak to the clouds, for the clouds do not hear us. We speak to the kachinas, saying, 'The masks we wear are yours. Let your medicine enter them. Let your medicine appeal to the clouds to bring rain for our fields, which are the breast of the earth.' We must make our ritual perfect in every way so that the kachinas know we are sincere. We must give to our singing all the power of our hearts so that the kachinas will hear us.' "

After discussing things at length with Yellow Corn, Burning Tree sent for White Star, Badger Boy's grandchild, and Elk Horn, and he designated them as kachina apprentices. They were not yet taught any of the deeper secrets of the Kachina Brotherhood, but they were given specific duties to carry out during the ceremonies such as helping the dancers put on their costumes and carrying paraphernalia from one place to another.

A day was set for the first appearance of the masks, and Crying Wolf announced it to the village from the top of the kiva. After that he went to other rooftops and repeated the announcement that the masks would come at a certain time and that the people should be present to receive them. In the afternoon of the designated day the dancers and their assistants carried their paraphernalia to a hidden place in the valley. As darkness fell, they dressed and put on their masks, lighted torches, and began to run toward the village. They stopped first at a small pool among the rocks, and Burning Tree sprinkled sacred cornmeal there. Then they resumed running to the village along the same trail that the kachina brothers from Red Rocks had used. On top of the kiva, Crying Wolf called out their progress, saying, "They arrive at the pool. They arrive at the fork in the trail. Now they are coming upwards. They enter the village. They pass the first house. They approach the court." As the three runners came into the court their torches cast a flickering light that made the masks resemble monstrous living faces. And having passed through the court, the three runners descended into the kiva where they removed their masks and began to sing their prayers. The sound of the singing emerged from the kiva opening and was heard throughout the village.

That night they chanted, rested, chanted, rested. And when the Dog Star showed itself at a certain place, Burning Tree said: "The sun prepares to show his head above the eastern cliff. We too will come out."

They put on their masks once more and emerged from the kiva. They danced in the court, stamping their feet to sound the tortoiseshell rattles they wore on the calves of their legs. All the village was there to watch them from the roofs of the surrounding houses. When they were tired the dancers entered the kiva to rest, then they came out and danced again. It was late when they finished the last of the chants. Then, instead of entering the kiva again, they departed running along the same trail that had brought them. They went to the hidden place in the valley where they had begun. There they rested and removed their costumes. When night came they returned to their homes.

People watched the sky the next morning but they saw no clouds. The second and third days it was the same. But on the fourth day the clouds gathered, coming from the west. In the afternoon the rain fell and the corn in the canyon was refreshed.

The father of the Earth House People came one day to see Burning Tree. They smoked, and afterwards Burning Tree asked, "Why have you come?" His visitor replied: "I saw the rain-calling ceremony. I saw the faces of your kachinas. They are not known to my people, but we respect them. They hear, they send rain. Yet among the faces I saw, one that I know was not there. If I say I did not know the faces of your kachinas, that does not mean that our people do not know anything, for we also have strong spirits to help our corn grow. There is one whom we call Earth House Old Man. It was he who taught our people to build our houses in a certain way. It was he who brought us the gift of corn. That was long ago in the time of our grandfathers. From what I have seen of your kachinas, I now believe that Earth House Old Man is one of them. He also should have a mask and participate in the ceremonies."

Burning Tree said: "Indeed, the kachinas are truly numerous. Speak more about Earth House Old Man." And the Earth House father said: "When our grandfathers were in the wilderness, things were not as they are now. We built our houses of broken branches covered with brush. We had corn, but it was not truly corn. It was more like grass with clumps of seeds on the end. Each stem had only a single clump of grains, no more. So the people did not have enough to eat through the winter. One year the winter came early. The people were cold. They burned much firewood. Bitter winds blew from the north. Heavy snow fell and kept falling. Many grew lean with hunger. Some died.

"The chief sat in his house wondering what he could do for the village. And one night while his thoughts were going this way a person with a mask over his face entered the house. The chief was surprised. He said: 'Sit down. Share my fire. Eat with me.' There was only a small piece of meat. The chief gave it to him, saying, 'Eat, we have plenty more.' The person with the mask ate. When he was finished he said: 'You and your people are suffering. But it does not have to be this way. I will show you how to build a house that will turn back the cold. It will keep the people warm.' He took some twigs and made the frame of a house. He mixed earth with water and made mud, and he plastered the walls and roof of the twig house with it. He said, 'Henceforth make your houses like this.' He said, 'Your corn is not good. It does not feed you well. Do not depend on it anymore. Instead, plant the corn I am giving you now. It will grow deep roots. It will produce large ears.' He put a bag of corn before the chief. He went away. Planting time came, and the people planted their new seed. When the corn matured there were three large ears on every stalk. In the fall we built earth houses, as we have been doing ever since. Earth House Old Man was not seen again, but he watches over us and sends rain when we need it."

Burning Tree said, "That is good." And the Earth House father continued: "Your people have been good to us. Now we are ready to share Earth House Old Man with you. I will make the mask, just as our grandfathers described it. Let Earth House Old Man show his face among the other kachinas you already own." Burning Tree said, "Yes, it is something to think about." The matter was left there, and for some time thereafter Burning Tree considered whether Earth House Old Man could be regarded as a kachina. In the end, the spirit of the Earth House People was accepted. The Earth House father made the mask, and when the proper day came he danced with it in the village court.

Just at the time when the corn ears were beginning to fill out, news came to the village that a small band of Utaheh had arrived somewhat north of the canyon and was camped there. There was a flurry of anxiety as people asked one another what the Utaheh were doing there. Were they merely resting on a journey, or were they waiting for the Grey Fox corn to mature? Scouts were sent out to maintain a vigil on the encampment. The first day they sent back word that the Utaheh party consisted of no more than four or five families, and that they seemed to be busy with peaceable activities. On the fourth day the scouts sent word that another group of several families had joined the first. And a few days after that, still another band arrived. By now there were forty or fifty men in the camp, and the anxiety of the Grey Fox

People grew more acute. There was a feeling of foreboding in the village, and people began to wonder whether their corn planting had been in vain.

There were numerous discussions in the kiva about what ought to be done. Some of the men urged immediate preparation for war, and some counselled caution, but there was no agreement about the meaning of the sudden arrival of the Utaheh. Yellow Corn called on Still Water, as war chief, to give his views. Still Water said: "We are not yet at war, so I cannot speak as leader of the warriors. I will speak merely as a kiva brother. If the Utaheh are going somewhere, eventually they will depart. But we cannot wait forever to find out what their intentions are. If they mean us no good, we must be prepared. We can begin to fortify the village so that we can defend it. But we cannot build walls around the fields. If they want our corn, they will wait until they see us bringing in the ears, then they will attack. One party will strike at the village, and while we are fighting here other Utaheh will be taking the corn from the growing stalks. So if we decide to wait for them to come, let us plan to meet them at the mouth of the canyon and hold them there. But we do not have to wait. We can attack them at the encampment, and if we surprise them they will scatter and pull away. Yet if they have it in their minds that they want our corn they will regroup and return. It is for the council to say what we will do."

The council went on debating the possibilities. Then Yellow Corn spoke. He said: "We have looked at the stone from all sides, but we have not turned it over to see the bottom. We do not know that the Utaheh intend to pillage us. We assume it to be so, but we cannot confirm it. If we have to defend ourselves we will do so. But first we can try the way of peace. I will go to their camp. I will speak with them. Still Water and Burning Tree will stand with me and verify everything that is said. We will take Elk Horn along to translate for us. We will take ten warriors to stand behind us."

It was agreed that Yellow Corn should go, so he and his party went out toward where the Utaheh were camped beyond the mouth of the canyon. They stopped before they reached the encampment, the three elders in front and the armed warriors behind, and there they waited until the Utaheh saw them and sent out a delegation to meet them. Yellow Corn said: "My cousins, we do not know who you are, or whether you are peaceful or hostile. Where you people are resting is the doorway to our hunting grounds. You come, you sit, but you do not say anything to us about what your reasons are for being here. We do not want to misjudge you, so we have come to hear what you have to say."

One of the Utaheh began to speak, but the Grey Fox People did not understand all of his words, so Yellow Corn motioned to Elk Horn to come forward and translate whatever could not be understood. The Utaheh spokesman said: "My cousins, as you see, we are a peaceful people. We do not want any trouble with you. When we saw that you had a village in the canyon we stopped here and did not come any closer. The reason we are here is this: Two years ago we were travelling. We did not have enough corn. We were eating only the seeds of kwakwi grass. Where we were, game was scarce. We agreed to break up into small groups and go in different directions. This summer we were to meet here. Some of our families have already arrived. Others are coming but they have not yet appeared. If you are thinking that we plan bad things for your village, put it out of your mind. We have corn, we have dried meat, we do not need anything."

Yellow Corn said, "My cousin, are you the leader of these people?" The man answered: "No, we have no chief here. We are merely a few small families and clans that have joined together." Yellow Corn asked, "Who then can speak with the voice of all?" The man answered, "No one speaks with the voice of all except a council of families." Yellow Corn said: "I cannot speak with a council. Who knows what the heart of a council is? Cousin, I want to talk to the oldest grandfather in your camp." So the Utaheh spokesman went back to the encampment and returned with an aged one who had to walk slowly. Yellow Corn sat down. The old man sat down facing him. His front teeth were gone and one of his eyes was dead, but with his good eye he peered sharply into Yellow Corn's face. Yellow Corn said: "My brother, our languages are not the same, but you have heard many tongues in your lifetime. Do you understand me?" The old man made a sign with his hand meaning that he understood. Yellow Corn continued: "Let us speak together as two old ones who have lived long lives. We belong to the fraternity of age. We have seen many born and many die. We understand as the young cannot that harmony is the secret of life. Therefore we can speak together with open hearts. My people who live in the canyon are concerned. They want to know why you Utaheh have assembled in this place. Many bad things have happened here because of raiding bands that passed this way. We want to know your intentions. This is our first summer here. In the winter we had much suffering. Now we are going to gather a little corn. We cannot lose it. We will defend it. So tell me how it is with your people. What are they going to do?"

For a while the old man sat thinking. Then he smoothed the dust on the ground with his hand and began to make marks in it with a stick. He said: "We once were many families, now only a few. Where the others are I do not know. Since we were created we have moved one way and another in search of game. When game is scarce our families go different ways so that we are not all pursuing the same buffalo or the same deer. Then, when we can, we come together again. We stay together as long as possible. We enjoy one another. We dance together. We sing together. We call on the Spirit of the World, thanking him for his help. When the time comes, we part once more. Now we are coming together, all except those who have lost the way. We are not here to steal your corn. We have our own corn, for which we traded with the Tinneh. We have meat in our meat bags. After a while we will go away, for we are not housebuilders like you. Your people make villages out of stone as if life were forever. We Utaheh follow the game and the rivers. Wherever there are some trees and flowers growing, it is home for us. We do not waste time making stone houses, thinking, 'These walls will keep death away.' We are here for a while, that is all. This is why you find the Utaheh here and there, scattered about. They are tasting life. Now, let your people have no worry about us. We will not bring them any bad luck. We only want to see our relatives again and find out who has been born and who has died. After that we will go, family by family, wherever the Spirit of the World guides us."

Yellow Corn's eyes were on the marks the old man had been making in the dust. He said: "My brother, I hear you. But what is your stick saying? I do not understand it." The old man answered, "Why, it marks things down as they truly happened, so that I do not forget what is real and what is unreal. This mark indicates the day I was born. This mark recalls the time we were broken and scattered by enemies. Here is the trail we took from the north when life was too hard there. Here is the river we came to where people called Tewas were living. Here is the trail we took when the Tewas tried to subdue and enslave us. This mark remembers how we found some Water Clan people wandering without anything to eat, and how we took them in and made them Utaheh. Here the Tinneh attacked us and we drove them back. This mark tells of the appearance of the Tall Warriors who saved us from the Tewas. The reason I make these marks is that I wish to speak truly. They remind me of the things that really happened, so that I cannot dream and say what is false."

Yellow Corn answered: "My brother, I have heard everything. But the Tall Warriors you mention, can they be the same ones whom our people know?" And the old man answered: "How can I say what your people know? There was a battle with the Tewas. We were outnumbered. It seemed to us that we would all die. Then the two Tall Warriors appeared on the battlefield. They came between us and the Tewas. They shot smoking arrows, and the enemy ran away. When the fighting was over we could not find the Tall Warriors. They were gone." And Yellow Corn said: "Yes, they are the same that we know. Since they defended you, you must be good people. I know now that you do not have bad intentions against our village. Still, our people have not sat here with you as I have. They will not understand what I understand. So I ask you, as one old one to another, to help me persuade them. Take your families away from the entrance to the canyon. Move your camp a little farther to the north. Then my people will know that you are peaceful." The old man answered, "Yes, it can be done." Yellow Corn handed his bow to the old man, saying, "This bow, I have had it for many years. Take it. Whenever you see it you will remember that we sat here and talked. Here we trusted each other, two old ones who met in the wilderness." The old man took from around his neck a string of stone beads and gave them to Yellow Corn. He said: "They are old. They are weathered like my face. I received them from my uncle when I was a young man. Take them, and you also will remember our sitting here. You will remember that what I pledged was true."

Then Yellow Corn and the old man parted. The next day it was reported by the Grey Fox scouts that the Utaheh were breaking camp and going northward. By nightfall the encampment was deserted, and once more the Grey Fox People felt that everything was in balance.

Now the days seemed to pass swiftly. Soon the corn was being harvested and stored away in the houses. The kiva society began to prepare for a harvest dance, and green cornstalks were brought from the fields to decorate the village. One morning a woman standing on her roof looked across the valley and saw something move on a small rise of ground. She called to another woman nearby, saying, "On that mound over there I see a deer or some other animal." The other woman shaded her eyes with her hand and gazed across the valley. After a while she said, "Yes, there is something there, but I think it is a person."

Others turned their eyes toward the mound and wondered what a person was doing there. Two boys went running to investigate. When they returned they said a strange-appearing man was sitting there singing and scraping a notched stick. A young man went into the valley to see for himself. He went beyond where the boys had stopped. When he came back he would not speak to the people on the roofs about what he had seen. Instead, he descended into the kiva, where preparations for the dance were going on, and said: "The old one has a beard on his face. His hair is long. On his head he wears a cap made of a coiled basket, and on his back is a cape made of rabbit skins. What he sings, I cannot understand it. I do not know what kind of a man he is." Some of the men in the kiva went up to the roof, but they could not see anything from there and so they came down again. Someone asked: "Where did he come from? How did he get there without being noticed?" But no one could answer these questions. Someone else said, "If he has hair on his face and a cap made of a basket he must come from a far-off place, because we do not see such things here."

Sun Caller spoke, saying, "I have seen this man before. I do not know his name. I do not know the name of his people. But once, shortly before the breakup of the clans, he came to Red Rocks Place. He sat on the roof of the kiva, singing and playing his scraping stick. The people tried to talk to him, but he understood nothing. Several times he came to the village in the evening and sang this way. After that he went away and disappeared." Someone asked, "What kind of people can he come from that they let the hairs of their faces grow this way?" Sun Caller answered, "How can we say anything about these people if we do not know them?" Another man said: "Since you have seen him several times in Red Rocks Place, perhaps you are the one to go to the mound and find out what he wants. Speak with him, ask how he arrived in the valley without being noticed, ask what he is singing about. We do not like it that he arrives yet does not come to the village to announce himself. He must have evil things in mind."

Sun Caller said, "No, I do not think he has an evil purpose. It is only that he perceives what ordinary men do not perceive. Perhaps when he came to Red Rocks Place he wanted to warn us about the breakup of the clans. The evil that came afterward was not his doing. The people brought it on themselves."

Again Sun Caller was urged to talk to the stranger, so at last he left the kiva and went out to the mound where the man was singing. Sun Caller greeted him, but the man did not answer or turn his eyes from where they were fixed on a distant place. Sun Caller sat down, but the old man did not notice that anyone was there. In time Sun Caller arose and returned to the kiva. He said, "I was there. I spoke to him but he did not answer. He merely went on singing and playing his scraping stick. He was looking at something that I could not see. So I sat with him and listened. I heard his song, then I came back to the village."

They asked Sun Caller, "What were the words of his song?" Sun Caller hesitated. He said: "His language is unknown to me. So how can I tell you what he was singing?" But there was something in his manner suggesting that he was holding back, and they pressed him. He said: "If I tell you what I heard, how will you believe me? If you like the words you will say, 'Yes, Sun Caller grasped it.' If you do not like the words you will say, 'Sun Caller takes us for fools, he understood nothing but pretends to be wise.' So why should I say anything?" Yellow Corn answered: "My brother, we are not here to judge you, for we all know you have a true heart. The village needs knowledge. If you learned something out there, tell us." Sun Caller said, "Yes, I heard the man's song. His words were in a strange tongue, but it was clear that he was singing a death chant. Shall we leave it there?"

Yellow Corn said: "We do not speak now of language but of meaning. A person may say nothing and still we understand him. The wind has no language, yet it may speak to us. We do not know what the sky is made of, yet we often hear it. Therefore, tell us what your heart knows of the old man's death chant." At last Sun Caller replied: "Very well. In the song, the old man says he has come to the mound to die and be buried. As to the other things the song speaks of, I cannot explain them. He sang this way:

'Here I die, meeting the spirit of things.
Here I will be buried, yet my hand remains out.
Here, though I sing no more, the counting will take place.
And from here can be heard much crying in the village.'

If any of you sitting here know the full meaning of this song, tell me. As for me, I know only what I heard, and I cannot tell you any more."

The old ones meditated on the mystery, and they asked each other to explain what the song was trying to say by such phrases as "my hand remains out" and "the counting will take place." They wanted to know why crying would be heard in the village. The discussion continued late into the night without any answers. And at last, when they were beginning to feel weary, one of them said: "It is often said that when a trail is lost a man should go back to the place where he started and find a new trail. Therefore let us go back. Let us make a new start. At the beginning of the trail Sun Caller said, 'His language is unknown to me, the stranger spoke words I could not understand.' Yet Sun Caller gave us words. Let us ask ourselves again how Sun Caller could give us words if he did not understand them. Let us say he comprehended something but not everything. Perhaps the words he gave us were just a little different from what he heard. If the song did not say, 'my hand remains out,' but, rather, 'my hand does not hold anything,' then we are debating the wrong thing. How can we be sure we know what we are talking about?"

Sun Caller replied sharply, saying: "I did not want to tell you what I heard, knowing that someone would say, 'How could Sun Caller repeat the song if he did not know the language?' I said, 'It was only a death song, let us leave it there.' But you people urged me, saying, 'We want to know everything that you know.' So I spoke, and now you want to reject what you heard. Very well, let us go back to the beginning of the trail and start again in a direction that will have a better ending. I have just now returned from the mound. This is what happened. The old man was singing something and playing his notched stick. He did not speak to me. His song, I understood none of it. I waited, I learned nothing. I came back. Let us leave the matter there. There is nothing to argue about, and now we can go to our blankets and sleep." Thereupon Sun Caller arose and went out of the kiva. Yellow Corn said: "It is an injustice to Sun Caller. If a person hears something that we do not hear, how can it be said that he did not hear it? It is late. Let us also go to our blankets. Tomorrow we will discuss it again."

The next day the old man was seen still seated on the mound in the valley, and some children who had crept close in the tall grass reported that he continued to sing and scrape his notched stick. Once again the Grey Fox men went into the kiva to go on with their discussion, and when it was his turn to speak, Still Water said: "If we go along the same trail as yesterday we can only end up in dissension. Other clans wandering in the wilderness may know things we do not know. Should we not find out if the Bear Clan knows something of the bearded people?"

So they sent for Stretching Bear, the grandfather of the Bear Clan family, and when he arrived and heard their questions he said: "I myself have never seen these people, but our old ones told us many things. It is said that in the beginning we emerged from a deep canyon far to the west of here, and that we migrated first in one direction and then another. When we were still travelling toward the setting sun we met a tribe of people with light skins, and the men all had hair on their faces. They told us to turn back, for in front of us lay the endless water that no humans could ever cross. They said, 'Your direction is elsewhere. Go south, go east, and in time you will go beyond several large rivers. We ourselves have been to the great water, but we have received signs that tell us the long trail that we must follow will take us into the country of the rising sun.' They said, 'On a certain day we are going to meet again in a faraway place, and when you see us coming you will know that we are bringing the force of harmony with us. Yet many generations may pass before that time, and perhaps it is only the children of our grandchildren who will meet. They may not recognize one another. Therefore let us break the shaft of this lance in half. We will carry the part with the flint point and you will carry the part with the feathered emblem. When our people meet again they will fit the two parts together so that they become one, and then it will be known for certain that the time of harmony has arrived.'

"This is what the bearded lightskins told us, and so it was done. The lance was broken and each party took one piece. But all this happened long ago, and the piece that was given to us rotted away through the years until there was nothing left of it. Still, we keep looking for the people with the light skins and the beards, even though we no longer have the piece of the broken lance. It has been told to us that they will come from the east, and for this reason we have always buried our chiefs facing eastward, so that they would be able to see the lightskins coming."

When Stretching Bear had finished, Sun Caller said: "Yes, my brother, it is truly told. I also have heard that the lightskins would bring us harmony from the east. But the man who sits out there on the mound has a dark skin resembling old buffalo leather. He is not the person your people have been waiting for."

One of the younger men said: "Was it not always told to us that when people first came into this world there were bearded giants and sorcerers here? This man does not even disguise his beard by plucking out the hairs. I say he must be a divided heart person. The song he is singing is undoubtedly sorcery against the village. Let us tell him to go away. If he does not go away, then let us kill him." Burning Tree answered: "The man is singing a death song. He sits on the mound waiting to die. Let him die his own way, and speak no more of killing. We have learned something from the kachinas. Have we already forgotten what happened when the people of a certain village drove the kachinas out? Perhaps a kachina guided the old man here." Someone said: "Yes, Burning Tree is right. Yet what is the meaning of the song? What does it mean that his hand remains out and that the counting will take place?" The council fell silent then, for they had gone full circle and were back at the beginning.

Yellow Corn said: "We do not have any answers. Let us wait. Let us not do anything harmful. Perhaps the man is not seeing this ordinary world around us. Perhaps he sees things as they truly are, the spirit of things. If we do not understand what he is saying it could be that we are blind to what he knows. If he comes from somewhere with a message for us, if a kachina has sent him, then he wishes good things for Refuge Place. Even if this is not so, is he a monster? He is an old man. Perhaps he is hungry and thirsty. Has anyone said that we should send him food? Has anyone said that we should send him water? I did not hear it. Now that we have harvested our corn have we forgotten how hard life can be? Let us send something to the old man to comfort him." There were some in the council who did not agree with Yellow Corn, but they did not speak out. So a certain woman was asked to take a bowl of corn pudding to the mound, but though she willingly provided the food she was afraid to carry it. Other women also refused.

In the end it was Falling Snow who went out with the bowl in one hand and a jug of water in the other. He found the old man still sitting on the mound, though he was no longer singing. He was busy pulling stones and sand toward his body and piling them over his legs. Falling Snow put the bowl and jug down, saying: "Grandfather, here is something to eat and drink. Take it. The village wishes you well." For a moment the old man stopped what he was doing and looked into Falling Snow's face. He spoke a few words that Falling Snow did not understand. Then, once more, he was busy covering his legs with stones and sand.

Falling Snow returned to the kiva and told what he had seen. Some of the men wondered what it meant and asked what the old man could be doing. But Still Water said: "Why, it is just as Sun Caller described it. The old man was singing a death song, and now he is gathering together a blanket of stones and sand. He is alone and he is making his own grave."

No one approached the mound again that day, and on the following morning no one on the rooftops could see anything happening. So Sun Caller and Still Water went out together. They came to the mound. There were no sounds. Where the old man had been sitting there was now a shallow bank of stones and sand covering his body, and the hand that had placed the last stone was protruding upward out of the grave. Sun Caller and Still Water placed a few more stones on the grave, but remembering the words of the song they did not cover the protruding hand, leaving it just as it was, pointing upward. After that they returned to the village and reported what they had found.

That night in the kiva other things were talked about, but again and again the men came back to the subject of the old man and his grave. Already they were referring to the place as Hand Mound. They were relieved that the riddle of the hand had been answered, but now they were saying: "Is there not something else? The song said, 'Here the counting will take place.' It also said there will be much crying in the village. What is the meaning of it?" The next morning a hunter passing across the valley stopped at the mound to look at the grave. What he saw perturbed him and he went quickly to find Yellow Corn. He said, "My father, I was there at Hand Mound. The grave remains the way it was, but the hand has done something. In the beginning there were four fingers pointed upward. Now the first finger is bent down as if the hand were counting." Yellow Corn said, "We will not worry about anything. Fingers sometimes curl that way in death." But afterward Yellow Corn went to the grave and saw that the first finger was indeed bent down. By nightfall word had gone around Refuge Place that the hand was counting, and people wondered what it signified.

The next day Still Water and Sun Caller went again to the mound, and they observed that not one but two fingers were now turned down. They understood that something was in motion that could not be stopped, and they asked each other questions that they knew could not be answered, for only the passage of time would reveal the meaning of what was happening. On the third day they went again to see the grave, and there was deep foreboding as they noted that three fingers were folded down and only a single finger remained pointing upward. In the kiva they reported that the counting was still taking place. That night the old ones pondered on the mystery almost until sunrise, and they also made prayer feathers to take to the mound to hold off evil forces.

When daylight of the fourth day came, a group of four went to the old man's grave carrying the prayer feathers. When they arrived they saw that someone had come in the darkness and covered the protruding hand with soil as if to smother the counting. One of them thought that since the hand could no longer be seen there was nothing more to be concerned about, but Yellow Corn said: "We must uncover the hand. Whatever is there will not go away because we refuse to look at it. It is too late to turn away." Other old ones agreed. They brushed away the soil that covered the hand, and what they expected was there. The fourth finger was turned down and the hand was closed. So they planted their prayer feathers at the grave and returned silently to Refuge Place.

In the village there was waiting. People moved about as if performing their work and tried to speak casually to one another, but anxiety was in every house. The sun rose higher in the sky and pleasant breezes flowed through the valley. The voices of birds could be heard, and the stream continued to flow. When the sun began to slide down in the west, people began to feel better. They said: "Nothing at all is happening. It is a day like any other day."

Then without warning there was a low rumble like distant thunder from the direction of the setting sun. It grew louder and moved swiftly toward Refuge Place. The earth trembled, and the rumbling passed across the canyon and receded toward the east. It seemed as if the air stopped moving, and there were no bird calls to be heard. Everything was silent. People looked into the sky in surprise, as if to find an explanation there. Even before they had a chance to speak, the distant rumble began again in the west and raced toward the canyon. It became a roar, and the ground shook violently. Trees whipped back and forth, shaken by an invisible hand, and stones fell from the walls of the houses. As the tremor moved across the valley another one followed. The village shook and walls crumbled. Unheard in the maelstrom of sound, the kiva roof collapsed, falling on the old ones who were inside. Still another tremor came, and the people went running toward the open fields, all except a few who huddled at the canyon wall. And now the edge of the western cliff split off and a great avalanche of rocks poured down into the village. A cloud of dust rose into the air and hovered over Refuge Place.

In the fields the people stood dazed and silent, trying to comprehend the dimensions of the disaster. They began to look about them for the sight of relatives and friends. There were frightened calls and the sound of crying children. People began to run back to the village, not yet accepting what they knew they would find there. The houses that had stood nearest to the cliff and the people who had sought sanctuary at the canyon wall were invisble under a great pile of broken rock. In other houses they found aged ones who had not been able to run away, some unhurt, others dead. There were bodies in the dance court near the kiva, and from the kiva itself they heard voices, meaning that living persons were inside. Darkness came and they lighted torches. Throughout the night the searchers went here and there calling out names and poking in the rubble of fallen walls. When at last the sun rose over the eastern cliff they knew that some of the Grey Fox People would not be seen again. They pried two timbers from the collapsed kiva roof and brought out Yellow Corn and Still Water, who were unhurt. Afterwards they brought out the bodies of Crying Wolf and Sun Caller and laid them with the other dead.

That day the people of Refuge Place buried eight bodies in the valley. And when this was done, Yellow Corn and a council of elders decided that after the people had salvaged whatever they could from the ruins they should make a camp in the valley. So once again they slept under the open sky as they had done on their migration from Bend-of-the-Water, and they seemed to understand that Refuge Place was only a point of passage on the long journey that was not yet finished. The dead who had been buried in the valley were Crying Wolf, the village crier; Sun Caller, the old one from Red Rocks Place; Standing Rock, another old one; Yellow Dog, one of the Bean People; Mockingbird Singing, Flowing Spring's eldest daughter; Butterfly Woman, the old Yaya woman who lived in Elk Horn's house; and two of Yellow Corn's grandchildren. Those who had been covered by the rockslide, four in all, were Sunflower Blossom, a hunchbacked woman; Spotted Antelope, Walking Bear's younger brother; Warm Wind, one of Badger Boy's nieces who had remained behind when he departed; and Floating Leaf, Red Sky's mother.

For several days people scavenged among the village ruins for pots, baskets, grinding stones, weapons and food. They brought corn to the camp from the houses that had not been buried by the avalanche, and when that had been done they looked on Refuge Place as a ghost village and avoided it. Sitting around the council fire at night, the men discussed the implications of the disaster. Some of them were certain that the bearded one who had died on the mound was responsible for everything, but others felt that the old man had merely foreseen the event and had tried to warn them. They argued about whether the rockslide into the village had been chance without meaning.

Still Water said: "Could it truly have been chance? Let us consider how it was. There was cliff to the north of us, all the way to the mouth of the canyon. Did any of it break and fall? There was cliff to the south, all the way to the throat of the canyon. Did any of it come down? And the western cliff across the valley, did any of it break off? No, only here above the village did the rocks come down. So let us stop speaking of chance as if we saw something happen that had no meaning for us. If we say it was chance, then we will not learn anything from it."

Burning Tree said: "My brother, there is wisdom in what you say. Let us look to the meaning of it. Was it punishment, then? What have we done to deserve it? When Badger Boy left us he said life would be too good here and we would begin to think we had created ourselves. Perhaps in time we might have begun to think this way. Yet we grew only enough corn to feed ourselves. We did not become arrogant. We carried out our ceremonies. In the kiva we purified ourselves and made prayer feathers. We did not forget where we came from. So how did we merit punishment?"

Then Yellow Corn spoke, and he was troubled. He said: "When we stopped here we were on a journey to a place whose name had been told to us. We stayed because the people were tired. This is something we have done many times. There was no evil in it. Yet perhaps we forgot that we were only resting here and began to think of Refuge Place as our destination. Other people came to us out of the desert. Perhaps we thought that if the Bean People and the Earth House People and the Bear Clan came to this place it must be the navel of the world. We did not say to one another, 'We will not go any farther,' but perhaps we said to ourselves, 'Why should we hurry to go on?' Perhaps we built our houses as if they should stand forever. Perhaps Serpent Spirit heard our thoughts." Yellow Corn was silent for a moment, then he said, "The answer we are looking for, does it not lie in our chant that tells the story of our people?" He sang,

"We built our houses at Red Cliff.
We lived there until Serpent Spirit spoke to us.
Serpent Spirit said go forward to the Mesa of Flowers.
We departed from Red Cliff not knowing which way to go.
We settled again at Cottonwood Spring.
How long we lived at Cottonwood Spring is not known,
For we forgot Serpent Spirit's advice.
Then the earth trembled and the cliffs fell. . . ."

168

When Yellow Corn finished singing no one spoke. They understood everything. And so the Grey Fox People prepared themselves for what was to come. The women ground corn and processed it into food that could be carried on a long journey. They made new carrying baskets and forehead straps. The men hunted for meat and dried it. They made new arrow shafts and points. And while doing all these things they watched the sky for some signal that would guide them on their way.

The Bean People did not wait for a sign. Grey Badger came to Yellow Corn, saying: "Your people were good to us. They gave us shelter when we could not walk anymore. Now we are going to look for the Evening Branch of our clan. I do not know if we will find them, but if we do our clan will be reunited again, and we will be finished with our travels. We will not be just a small band lost in the wilderness. You people are our friends now. We would like you to have something so that you will remember us. Here is a buckskin pouch containing twelve beans, one for each of us with whom you shared the valley. Put it away. Some day you will look at it again. I will not forget that my brother Yellow Dog is buried out there with your own people. When our grandchildren tell our story the Grey Fox People will come alive in their hearts." The next morning the small band of Bean Clan people departed. They went out of the mouth of the canyon, because the cliff could no longer be scaled, and after that they turned westward and were not seen any more.

A few days later the Earth House People also announced that they were leaving. Like the Bean Clan they were going west, but only as far as the Western River where their relatives were said to be living. The Earth House leader gave Yellow Corn a figure of a deer carved from horn, decorated with feathers and small bits of coral. It was to assure that the Grey Fox People would have good luck in their hunting. The Bear Clan family had not decided yet what to do. They said they would remain for a while in the camp until they knew which way the Grey Fox were going.

Among the Grey Fox there were some who maintained that there was no need to wait for a sign, for only the year before they had seen the flaming arrows in the sky, and it was clear in any case that they were supposed to find the Mesa of Flowers. But there were others who maintained that a sign would surely come, and that it would be foolish to go out as Badger Boy's people did with nothing to guide them. So they continued to wait for a sign. And one night when the moon inclined toward the west the people saw that it had a wide ring of light around it. Some thought it was the sign they were awaiting, but most said no, they had never heard that a ring of moonlight could direct them. Two days later, in midafternoon, there was a shower in the canyon, and when the rain ended a complete rainbow encircled the sun. That night Walking Bear told the council he believed that the rings around the sun and moon were signs, one confirming the other. "The moon speaks to us," he said, "and the sun speaks to us also, each in the same way. How can we doubt what we see in the sky?" Still Water, who was wise in matters concerning snakes, said: "It was told by my uncle that the circle around the moon is the image of Serpent Spirit holding his tail in his mouth, and that the complete rainbow is Serpent Spirit dressed in his festival clothes. Let us agree that Serpent Spirit manifests himself this way. But a circle cannot give us a direction, for it encloses all directions. Therefore these rings in the sky do not tell us anything about our journey."

Flowing Spring took a different position, saying: "We agree that Serpent Spirit is seen as a circle around the moon or a rainbow around the sun. But it was Serpent Spirit who sent us out to find the Mesa of Flowers. By showing his image in the sky, is he not saying, 'Do not hesitate. Leave your ruins behind'? Now, when we saw the ring of light in the night sky the moon was moving toward the west, and when we saw the circle rainbow the sun also was in the west. Therefore, has not Serpent Spirit given us a direction?" The debate went on, and when the time came for them to go to their blankets it seemed that they were divided down the middle, half believing one thing and half another thing.

Yellow Corn was deeply troubled by the way things were going, for he saw that the people were of two minds about the coming journey. So he sought out Flowing Spring privately and said to him: "My brother, something is happening. Things are not good. Is it not enough that our village is destroyed? If we old ones struggle against one another about directions it will end badly. We must remain united or the Grey Fox Clan will fall apart. It will disappear in the desert and never be heard of again. Let us look at what has happened to us since we arrived in this canyon. First Badger Boy's people broke with us and went out by themselves. They were slaughtered by the enemy. Then Yellow Bird's people departed. Other clans joined us, they too are gone. The falling cliff took twelve lives. We are a diminished people now. Dissension will destroy us. We have spoken much about the circle around the moon and the rainbow around the sun. Does not the circle signify wholeness? That is the message of the sun circle and the moon circle. It tells us to remain whole. Ever since our journey began in the time of our grandfathers it was said that we would go to the Mesa of Flowers. We know it to be in the north. Let us not now be turned aside."

And Flowing Spring replied: "My brother, it is true that the Mesa of Flowers is in the north. But many times we have had to turn one way or another because of a mountain or a river. Who knows why, now, we are told to go west? The answer will become apparent in time. Perhaps there is something we still have to see or learn. Perhaps we are not quite prepared, for our journey is not merely from one place to another but from one level of knowledge to another. No one ever promised that you and I would set foot on the Mesa of Flowers. Limping Deer died on the way. Others died on the way. But one day the Grey Fox people will arrive there. That is all that I know. If we must now go westward, then let us go that way. Later we may have to go south again, or east, who can say? We will do what we must."

But Yellow Corn could not agree. He said: "When we were at Bend-of-the-Water we saw the flaming arrows going northward. Had we not arrived at Long Arrow's village we would still have gone northward. And now that we have wintered here and grown our corn, north is still our direction. The rings in the sky did not tell us otherwise. They said only, 'Remain whole.' Therefore let us remain whole." Flowing Spring said: "My brother, let us remain whole, as you say. But you yourself have been waiting for a sign. If the flaming arrows we saw at Bend-of-the-Water told us everything we need to know, then why are you now waiting for something more?"

And Yellow Corn answered: "The people are uncertain about things. The destruction of the village was too much for them. Some of them are saying to themselves, 'How has Desert Spirit been good to us? How has Serpent Spirit been good to us? They have thrown a cliff on us and made us homeless. Why should we listen to them? Is the Mesa of Flowers worth it?' So let us wait a little. The signs that were given to us at Bend-of-the-Water will be reaffirmed."

Flowing Spring said: "Yes, surely we should wait a little. But what if the sign you are waiting for does not show itself? The people cannot spend the winter in this place. We must go from somewhere to somewhere."

To which Yellow Corn replied only: "My brother, we must go somewhere, but not just anywhere. Between the two of us there must be harmony and understanding or the Grey Fox Clan will be broken and scattered."

Flowing Spring said: "We have been friends since we were children. May we both see the spirit of things truly." And there, for the moment, the matter rested.

One evening Burning Tree sent for Falling Snow and Young Antelope. They met in a sheltered place near the throat of the canyon, and Burning Tree said: "When we depart from this place we must take the kachina masks with us. I have left them where they are in the ruined kiva to protect them from the rain. It seems that our journey will begin soon, so let us prepare. Tomorrow we will retrieve the masks and wrap them in dry grass and buckskin." So the next day Burning Tree, Young Antelope and Falling Snow returned to the ruins and descended into the broken kiva. They brought out the masks, wrapped them and tied them with buckskin thongs. And as they were about to leave the village they saw a grey fox watching them from the crest of the stone pile that had fallen from the cliff. Burning Tree said, "Grey Fox Grandfather still is with us. It is good." They carried the masks back to the camp, set them under an overhanging rock and covered them with a blanket.

The sign that Yellow Corn was waiting for had not come. The old ones met at a council fire and Flowing Spring said: "We cannot wait any longer. The people are ready to go. They do not want to sit here anymore looking at their destroyed houses by the cliff wall. Let us begin. We will go west. There are villages out there near the Western River, so it is said. In the mountains there are settlements of the Water Clan. If the winter comes before we have found what we are looking for, those people will give us a resting place." Still Water said: "My brother, you are like an arrow escaping from the bow before it is aimed. We cannot go without the sign." Flowing Spring said: "The sign, we saw it twice, once around the moon and once around the sun. It tells us to go westward. My family is ready. We will leave in the morning. Let us all leave together and bring our uncertainty to an end." Burning Tree said, "Wait a little, there is no need for such haste." And Still Water said, "No, it is not to the west that the Mesa of Flowers is to be found."

Other old ones spoke also, and there was dissent between them. Words became sharp and they were not speaking together as brothers. Yellow Corn said: "We cannot go to our blankets to sleep until it is settled. We are at the place where the river forks. Now we have to choose which way it will be. You, Flowing Spring, are forcing us to it. Therefore I say I will remain here until the proper sign gives us a direction. I will wait as long as I must, even if winter comes. And if there is no sign by then I will go back into the village and rebuild my house. How many others are willing to follow my example I cannot tell you. But whoever now goes west following the circles will never be able to forget that he turned his back on what was prophesied for us."

Burning Tree said to Flowing Spring: "My brother, you see how it is. Do not decide anything now. By tomorrow we may have learned something more that will help us." But Flowing Spring answered: "My heart is not happy. I did not come to the council to contend with anyone. But the rings of light spoke to me. I listened and I understood, therefore I cannot stay here any longer. To you the circles around the sun and moon may have spoken differently. I do not challenge what you understood. You are my brothers. Do not challenge what I understood. I have never heard it said that a sign conveys different things to different persons, yet perhaps it is so, because in this world mysteries are piled on mysteries. Can it be that some of us are meant to go west and that others are meant to go north or to stay behind as Yellow Corn says he will do? I do not know. In time we will understand everything, or maybe we will not understand everything. Perhaps it is only our grandchildren who will be able to look back and understand what is now happening to the Grey Fox People." The other old ones were sad to hear Flowing Spring speak this way, and they did not want to talk anymore. They arose from the council fire and went to their blankets to sleep.

And so, when the sun began to show its forehead over the eastern cliff, Flowing Spring and his family, Walking Bear and his family, and two other families took up their carrying baskets and went north out of the canyon. At the place where the Bean Clan and the Earth House People had turned to the west, they also turned to the west. Those who remained in the camp listened to the silence of the valley, wondering about the fate of the Grey Fox People. Of all those who had come from Bend-of-the-Water, only a handful were left. There were Yellow Corn and his wife, Gentle Mist; Still Water and his wife, Cotton Flower; Burning Tree and his wife, Floating Leaves; White Moccasin, Falling Snow's grandmother; Falling Snow and his wife, White Blanket; Elk Horn and his wife, Buffalo Girl; Yellow Hair, Elk Horn's grandmother; Young Antelope and his family; and White Star, the young boy who had survived the enemy attack against Badger Boy's people.

Yellow Corn reflected for a long time on the turn that events had taken. He wondered if it was the purpose of the Spirit of the World to send the Grey Fox in different directions, or whether it was the lack of harmony among people that was the cause of things. And it came to him that human destiny was a game between two forces. On one side was the spirit of order, goodness and purpose. On the other were the imperfections, whims and limited understanding of humans. The two forces were endlessly at play with each other as if they were throwing gambling sticks or running footraces. Yellow Corn saw that it could not go on this way. If men were to survive they would have to struggle harder to perceive the spirit of the world as it truly was and not be satisfied with the outer husks of things. They would have to blend themselves into the invisible forces out of which rivers, buttes and mountains were made.

His eyes moved across the half-deserted camp, and he saw that his people were sad and uncertain. So he put away his reflections and called the people together. He said: "My children, let us not doubt it, the sign will come. In the meantime, let us put our hearts and thoughts in order. Our brothers and sisters who have gone ahead, they will not disappear forever. We will go one way and they will go another, and a day will come when we will all reach the Mesa of Flowers. There we will put our experiences together and add them to the history of the people. For now, however, we are only a small band. At Bend-of-the-Water we took the name Grey Fox, and sometimes we called ourselves a clan, but we were not yet a clan.

"From now on we are the Grey Fox Clan, and if children are born to our women they will be Grey Fox no matter where they are. Whoever is a Grey Fox cannot marry with a Grey Fox. The Blue Fox was Long Arrow's clan and we affiliated with them, so our children must not marry with the Blue Fox Clan. The world is full of clans, and so no young man or woman will go without a wife or a husband. If one of our young men should take a Bear Clan woman and she wants to stay with her people, then he also will go to live with them. But if she chooses to come with us, she is welcome. Her children, however, will belong to the Bear Clan. If a Bear Clan man takes one of our young women, he will live with us unless his wife wants to go away, and all of their children will belong to the Grey Fox Clan. In this way our people will flourish, just as other clans do. In time there will be Grey Fox people living in many villages. For now, let us do whatever needs to be done to prepare for our journey. Let our carrying baskets be heavy with food to sustain us."

When he had finished talking to the people, Yellow Corn went to a smooth rock near the village, and with his flint point he engraved the head of a fox and a concentric spiral, meaning that the Grey Fox Clan had arrived and rested at Refuge Place. Then he engraved clouds and corn, indicating that they had stayed throughout a growing season, and after that three smaller unwinding spirals, meaning three departures from the canyon. He contemplated the marks he had made, conscious of how little they told. Whatever else there was to tell of the history of the Grey Fox Clan would have to be engraved in the minds of the people.

Three nights later the sign that he had been waiting for came. There was a spectacular shower of meteorites in the north, and the following morning the people took up their loads and went out of the canyon. They crossed the high dune, and in time they came to the rocks where Falling Snow and Elk Horn had met. Elk Horn, who was in front with the scouts, turned and called, "Ka ka ka!" And Falling Snow answered, "Ka ka ka!" Some of the people asked, "Are they talking Yaya language?" And someone answered: "It means nothing. They have been eating crazy weed."

On the fourth day of the journey, the scouts reported that a short distance ahead, on a wide knoll somewhat to the east, a large group of Utaheh were camping. The people halted to discuss what to do. Young Antelope and Falling Snow went ahead to inspect the encampment more closely. When they returned they said that there were many women and children there, and that the women were busy making baskets and softening skins. Yellow Corn and Still Water thought it might be the same party that had camped near the canyon and that it would be safe to go on. So they went forward and were passing to the west of the camp when they saw four men coming from the knoll. One of them was the old man with whom Yellow Corn had spoken some days before. The old man held a bow above his head, and Yellow Corn recognized it as the one he had given as a pledge of friendship. He took off the string of stone beads the old man had given him in exchange and held it out.

They approached each other and the old man said, "I see you, Grey Fox father." Yellow Corn answered, "I see you, grandfather of the Utaheh." The old man said, "So you are leaving the canyon?" Yellow Corn answered, "Yes, we are leaving it." The old man said: "There are not many of you. Have the others dispersed?" Yellow Corn said, "Yes, we are the last to go." The old man said: "We heard that your village was destroyed. Our hunters told us you were camped in the valley. I thought, 'My Grey Fox brother is having difficulties.' So I made a medicine arrow for you. I placed it in the ground and asked the Good Spirit for your safety." Yellow Corn said, "I am grateful." The old man said: "That same night I saw many arching stars fly through the sky. Then I knew that you would be safe." Yellow Corn said: "The flying stars spoke truly. We are safe."

One of the Utaheh held a small basket of corn, and the old man took it and gave it to Yellow Corn saying, "Mix this corn with your own. It will mean that our people and yours will be close." Yellow Corn answered, "Yes, I will do it." The old man said: "To the north where you seem to be going, there are some Coconino people out there. They are peaceful." Yellow Corn said: "That is good. But tell me, do you know of a place called Mesa of Flowers?" The old man said: "No, I never heard that name. Everyone has a different name for things. However, far beyond the Coconino is a mesa ledge with several villages. Their houses are of stone like yours." They parted then, Yellow Corn saying, "Your beads, I will keep them. May the Tall Warriors protect you." And the old man answered: "Your bow, I will keep it. May your trail be true."

The Grey Fox resumed their walking, and some of them did not comprehend how it happened that the Utaheh did not attack them. That night at the fire Falling Snow said to Yellow Corn: "My grandfather, how can we know about people? The Utaheh attacked Elk Horn's village, but today they behaved as good cousins." Yellow Corn answered: "My grandson, what do we mean when we say 'the Utaheh'? We mean many people who are related and speak the same language. What do we mean when we say 'the corn'? You go into your field and see many ears. Some are large and strong, they are good ears. But some are stunted and half grown. Most are blue, but others are speckled or yellow. Some have worms. Yet we call all of these ears 'corn.' It is like this with people as well. Some have split hearts, half good and half bad. Some have a heart for harmony. So it is with the Utaheh. So, also, it is with our own people.

"It has always been like this, even in the beginning when we were still inside the earth. We sometimes speak as if there was one world there from which we emerged into the world where we now find ourselves. Yet down there we went from one place to another in search of harmony and understanding. The first world was far below. People did not yet have human form. They did not yet understand good and evil. They did not care for others, only for themselves. Nevertheless, there were some who asked one another, 'Is this the meaning of life?' Because he heard this question being asked, Sun Spirit sent Earth Grandmother down to help them. She said: 'Sun Spirit wants to help you achieve understanding. I will take you to another world above this one, but you must leave everything evil behind.' She led them to a second world above the first. But some of the dissension and evil of the first world clung to them. Things were better in the second world, and the people were more like humans, but still there was much evil mixed with virtue. And so Earth Grandmother led them to a third world, and it was from that world that we emerged here. It was a long journey in search of understanding, and the journey we are on now is part of that journey that began down below. We have not learned everything. We are still seeking. We still have dissension and evil to contend with. So if there is evil as well as good among the Utaheh, it is like that with us also."

Still Water said: "A-heh! Yellow Corn has said everything. His words are true. When all of our people were living at the Eastern River there were some who were good and some who were bad. It was because of the bad ones that our grandfathers and grandmothers departed from that place. Have you never heard what happened at a certain village there called Shell Mound?" He waited until he heard calls of "No, we have not been told." Then he went on: "The people were living there at Shell Mound. They had strong houses and large fields. Their storage rooms were heaped with corn. Food was so plentiful that the men stopped working their fields.

"They said, 'There is nothing to work for. We have everything.' Instead of performing rituals in the kiva they went there to gamble. They brought women there. The women gambled with the men, and if they lost the wagers the men would take them and have pleasure with them as if they were wives and husbands. No one had respect for anyone. They forgot to take care of the old ones and the children. The chief of the village saw how things were going. He went from one house to another admonishing people for their wrongdoing, but they laughed at him. They said, 'Old man, come to the kiva and gamble with us, maybe you will win a young woman to lie with.' One night he could not find his wife in his house and he went to the kiva looking for her. He found her there having pleasure with the men, and he called out: 'Now how can this village live on anymore? There is nothing but evil here!'

"He went to another village some distance away. The people there had great powers of medicine. He said to them: 'My village is totally corrupted and there is no reason for it to go on living. I want you to destroy it and every living person who is there.' They asked, 'What will you give us?' He said, 'I give you all of our fields and our hunting grounds, our springs and all the things that grow on the land.' They asked: 'How is it to be done? By sickness, wind, hail or fire?' He said, 'Let it be fire.' They said: 'Very well. On the fourth day it will be done. But you yourself must be there.' He said, 'Yes, I will be there, for I do not want to live any longer.' He went home. He stayed in his house. And on the fourth morning a great brush fire came burning from the north, and the smoke that rose into the air was yellow. Another fire came rushing from the east, and the smoke above it was white. Another fire came from the south, and its smoke was red. And from the west came a fire whose smoke was blue. These four fires surrounded the village so that no one could get out. The chief stood on the roof of the kiva, saying, 'In this way our evils are consumed.' The fires met and destroyed everything.

"This is how Shell Mound disappeared, though they say that the burnt ruins can still be seen. But was evil destroyed? We cannot say that it was, for it lives on. Even the chief, who could not bear the sight of what he saw around him, piled evil on evil when he arranged for the destruction. He was the father of the village, and how can it be that even in anger a father will kill his own children? No, the evil was not burnt away, it merely took another form. It rose from the village as black smoke soaring into the sky, but black soot fell all over the land and contaminated it. Evil lived on, for it could not be destroyed by fire, only by good living and understanding. This is what we are looking for. This is the meaning of our journeys."

Falling Snow asked, "My grandfather, when we have arrived at the Mesa of Flowers, will evil be there also?" Still Water answered: "My grandson, who can say? How can we tell what lies in the future?"

In the days that followed, the Blue Fox Clan passed through country that did not reveal in any way that other people had been there before. So if they came to a certain rock or a formation that resembled something they gave it a name, and in this way they marked the sequences of their travelling. Two tall spires of stone they named the Warriors, after Spider Grandmother's grandsons. Another standing rock they named Corn Ear, for it looked like an ear of corn standing on end. As they approached a large butte one evening, a star was shining brightly above it, and so they called it Star Butte. The sun rose one morning over an eastern ridge, which they named Sunglow Mountain. And by the remembrance of these places they counted the days of the journey. Yellow Corn also kept count on a long string. Every night when they camped he added a knot to the string. Sometimes he tied a fragment of wood, or a bit of grass, or a colored stone into a knot to remind him that on that day something happened that ought to be remembered. Occasionally a deer was killed and the meat divided, and several times they had rabbit hunts, but now the old as well as the young had to go out with throwing sticks and no one received any prizes if a rabbit was caught.

Buffalo Girl spent several evenings making a cradleboard, weaving it out of strong grass, with Yellow Hair at her side instructing her. And several days after it was finished, while the people were on the trail, she had to stop because she was giving birth to a child. They found a sheltered place for her beneath an overhanging rock. Elk Horn and White Blanket gathered sand and spread it on the ground for her to lie on, and after that Yellow Hair took charge of everything.

The Grey Fox Clan camped nearby, and Falling Snow and Young Antelope went hunting for whatever game they might find. Although they discovered no game that day, they found a rock with inscribings on it and went back to tell the old ones. They guided Burning Tree to the place and he stood for a long while studying the record on the rock. Later, at the camp, he told the people: "The marks say that several clans passed this way going north. The Water Clan came first and stayed only briefly. Then the Sand Clan came, and they went on. Then the Rainbow Clan and the Lightning Clan, and after that the Frog Clan. They made their marks together, meaning that they are related. Other clans came afterwards and made their marks apart from the others. They were the Coyote, the Fire and the Wolf clans, and from the way their marks were made we know them to be related. All the marks were worn by the sun and the wind, and so we know that it was long ago that they came this way."

Buffalo Girl's child was born in the afternoon, and it was decided that the people would rest for a full day where they were. So they stayed around the fire late that night listening to the old ones talk and tell stories. Yellow Corn, Still Water and Burning Tree debated about whether the Grey Fox could consider themselves related to the Coyote and Wolf clans. Still Water believed that because the fox, the wolf and the coyote were cousins the clans that took their names must also be cousins. But Burning Tree said: "Does it follow? For the Bow Clan and the Juniper Clan also are said to be affiliated with the Coyote, yet the bow and the juniper do not run on four legs. And let us remember that the closest of all clans to the Coyotes is the Fire Clan, which claims Death Old Man as its sponsor. What do we have to do with Death Old Man?"

Yellow Corn said: "Let us also remember that the Bear Clan claims as its relatives the Strap Clan, the Bluebird Clan, the Gopher Clan and the Spider Clan. The names do not tell us anything. As for Death Old Man, he may be the sponsor of the Fire Clan, but the Fire People die just as others die. Death Old Man has something to do with all of us. Also, the Spider Clan claims Spider Grandmother for itself, but we all know that Spider Grandmother does not favor one more than another. What makes clans related is not their names but their experiences. We do not know what clan Yellow Bird now claims his people to be. If they call themselves Squash Clan or Moon Clan makes no difference, they are related to the Grey Fox forever. Let us look back at the way things were when our people were still at the Eastern River. I heard from my uncle that the Coyote Clan and the Fire Clan lived at that place in those days. I think that we must have some connection with those people. In time to come we may learn more about these things."

"Uncles," Young Antelope said, "can you tell us anything we do not already know about the Warriors?" Yellow Corn answered: "How do we know what you already know? They are sometimes boys playing stick ball, they are sometimes fierce warriors. Have we not heard from the Utaheh how the two brothers saved them from the Tewa?" Young Antelope said: "Yes, we have heard it. But surely there is more?" None of the old men was ready to say anything. It was White Moccasin, Falling Snow's grandmother, who spoke. She said: "Your uncles always think of the Warriors in battle. But if you want to hear about the Warriors as children, I can tell you what my mother told me when I was young." There were calls of "Yes, grandmother, we want to hear it."

White Moccasin began, saying: "What I am about to speak of, I was not there to see it, yet it was told to me truly and vouched for by the old ones. If you do not believe it, why, then, complain to those who first gave us this tale. The two small brothers that we call the Warriors, now that is their name only when they are fighting battles or destroying monsters. As children they are known as the Ball Players, for they spend much time playing stick ball and prefer it to everything else. At the time I am speaking of, they lived with Spider Grandmother in the wilderness some distance from the nearest village. Often they went hunting to keep Grandmother's house supplied with meat, and one day they killed a large bear. They said, 'Let us do something with this bear to amuse Grandmother.'

"So they skinned the bear and cut up the meat, but then they sewed the skin together again and stuffed it with dry grass so that it looked like a living bear. They set it on its feet and tied a cord around its neck. The other end of the cord they tied around the older boy's waist. The younger one went running toward Grandmother's house, calling, 'My brother is chased by a bear! My brother is chased by a bear!' Soon the older boy came running and dragging the stuffed bear behind him. When Grandmother saw that she cried out, 'Oh! My grandson is pursued by a bear!' Spider Grandmother had no bow, no arrows, no lance. But in the inner room of her house she kept lightning buried under the corn. So she quickly grasped the lightning and went after the bear that was chasing Older Brother. She threw the lightning—crack!—and it struck the bear. The bear was now lying on its back with its feet pointed upward. Spider Grandmother said to Older Brother, "Thanks that you are safe!' Both brothers were laughing, and then Spider Grandmother saw that the bear did not have any meat inside, only dry grass. She said: 'Oh, my grandchildren! Why do you tease your old grandmother this way?' They said, 'Grandmother, it is because we are lonesome for other people.' Spider Grandmother said: 'Yes, it is true. You do not have anyone to play with.'

"Grandmother thought about what might be done so that her grandsons would not be so lonesome. That night she said: 'Well, now, I have heard that there will be a festival tomorrow over there at the village. There will be dancing, and the dancers will throw corn ears and armbands and moccasins and other things to the crowd, and whoever catches these things may keep them. Clean yourselves up. Go to the village, spend the day there and enjoy the excitement.' The next morning the brothers made themselves clean and started out. They carried their playing sticks and their ball, and after a while they began playing their game. They hit the ball and followed it, hit it and followed it. Sometimes they were in the sand, sometimes in the water, sometimes in the mud. When they arrived at the village they were very dirty.

"The dance was already going on. The dancers threw moccasins to the crowd. The brothers tried to catch the moccasins, but the adults pushed them aside and caught the moccasins themselves. The brothers tried to catch the corn ears and armbands and other things that the dancers threw, but always they were pushed aside. They could not catch anything. When the dancing was finished, the people who lived in the houses brought out food to give to visitors from other villages, but whenever the brothers reached out their hands the people said: 'You dirty ones, where did you come from? We have never seen you before.' They would not give the brothers anything to eat.

"At last Older Brother said: 'Why are we lonesome for people? They are not good. Let us take something to show Grandmother that we were here, an ear of corn, an armband and a pair of moccasins, then we will leave.' They saw a pile of these things by the kiva, so the Ball Players quickly took one of each kind and began to run away. People saw them going and cried out, 'The dirty ones have taken some of the gifts!' They began to chase the brothers out of the village, throwing stones at them.

"When they were outside the village the people were still chasing them. Older Brother said, 'Let us not be abused anymore.' Younger Brother said, 'Yes, we have been abused enough.' They stopped running. They changed themselves into fierce warriors. They spat on the corn ear and threw it at the ones who were chasing them. They spat on the moccasins and threw them. They spat on the armband and threw it. And all those persons who had abused them were turned into stone. After that the brothers returned to Grandmother's house, and for a long time after that they did not yearn for the company of people. Now, that village where the dance took place disappeared long ago, but the ruined walls are still there, and a little bit east of the ruins still can be seen the stones into which those inhospitable people were transformed."

The next morning Elk Horn, Falling Snow and Young Antelope went out to look for deer. They were some distance north of the camp, walking across a low ridge, when they saw a party of eight Tinneh approaching. All of the Tinneh were men and all carried lances, and Young Antelope said, "I do not know if they are a war party, but they do not look peaceable. They are prepared for something. Let us go back and tell the people what we have seen." The hunters returned to the camp and reported to the old ones.

Yellow Corn looked around for a place where the Grey Fox might be invisible until the Tinneh had passed, but he saw nothing but a dry wash. He said, "Let us put the women and children over there in the wash and we will meet the Tinneh here." Burning Tree said: "Well, now, we will stand if we must, but how will we fare? They outnumber us and if they are out to prove their valor we will not be able to reason with them. Yes, hide the women and children in the wash. Yes, let us make our weapons ready. Yet maybe there is something we can do to turn the Tinneh aside. Let us try." He instructed Young Antelope and Falling Snow to unwrap the kachina masks. When this was done they carried the masks to a place north of the camp where some large boulders were standing. They set the masks on top of the boulders facing the direction from which the Tinneh were coming, and Young Antelope concealed himself in a cleft of rock from which he would be able to see everything. The others returned to the camp, hid the women and children in the wash and took up their weapons. They waited.

Young Antelope saw the Tinneh coming. They were laughing and talking loudly until they were close enough to see the masks. Then they stopped and talked in low voices. It seemed that they argued. One of the warriors raised his lance as if he were about to throw it at the nearest mask, but the others remonstrated with him and he put his lance down. They argued. They sat on the ground where they were, making no further approach to the masks, and talked for a long while. At last they arose and went westward. Young Antelope came back and said: "The masks turned them aside. They were afraid of the medicine and went to the west to pass around this place." Yellow Corn said: "It is good. The kachinas intervened for us. Now let us prepare so that we may leave here in the morning before the sun shows its forehead. The Tinneh may decide to come again from another direction." And so the next day while the sky was still grey, the people left their camp and continued their journey northward. Once again the kachina masks were in their buckskin wrappings, and Buffalo Girl carried her child on her back.

For many days thereafter there were no encounters with other people, and the knots that Yellow Corn put in his string were simple ones that did not mark any noteworthy events. The Grey Fox Clan drifted on, always to the north, but sometimes detouring around canyons or ranges of hills. There were many buttes now. Whenever one was left behind, another was visible ahead or to the east or west.

While they were resting one night in this country, Still Water told of how the buttes came to be formed. "In the beginning," he said, "when the people first came from the earth all the buttes were joined, and from the top of one a person could walk to the top of the next. The land surface was up there and not down here. The people were just beginning their journeys. They complained to Spider Grandmother, saying, 'Everything looks the same, there is no variety.' So Spider Grandmother called on the Warriors to create variety. You have already heard that the Warriors made the buttes and mountains. Yet how did they do it? They did not make something out of nothing. They scooped up flat land from one place and piled it in another. They took rock and sand from here where we are now resting and carried it to the west, and there they made the Western Mountains. They scooped yet more from here and took it eastward to make the Eastern Mountains. They took some to the north and some to the south, so that we have mountains in all those directions. What we now see as buttes are simply pieces of the original land that were left behind by the Warriors because they were in a hurry and did not have time to be neat. It is said that up there on the butte tops people have found the Warriors' footprints turned to stone."

On occasion, Grey Fox scouts would climb a butte to see what kind of land lay ahead. Usually there was nothing but more buttes, but one afternoon, in the red light of the setting sun, Young Antelope and Falling Snow saw the grey outline of a mesa on the northern horizons surmounted by pink clouds. Two days later the main party reached high ground from which the mesa was visible to everyone. People asked, "Is this where we are going?" But the old ones could not give them an answer. Yellow Corn said, "It seems that we will soon arrive in a new country, but we do not yet know what it is." From where they stood, the mesa was at least five or six days distant for a running man, ten or twelve for a group on a journey. Yellow Corn said, "Let us go forward patiently. In time everything will be known."

Four mornings later Young Antelope, who had been scouting ahead, came running with the news that he had seen a small settlement of three or four houses on high ground next to a deep wash. The Grey Fox People went ahead without stopping until they came within sight of the settlement. Then Yellow Corn and Still Water approached the houses, noting that no humans were visible, only a dog sitting on a roof. They called out, but there was no answer. They called again and an old woman appeared. Yellow Corn said, "Are the people at home?" The old woman said: "No, they are not here. They have gone to a festival at Ash Hill." Yellow Corn said: "We are strangers here. We do not know the land. Where is Ash Hill?" The old woman motioned to the north, saying, "Out there, around the point of the mesa." Yellow Corn asked, "May we rest a while where we are and take some water from your spring?" The old woman said: "Take it. I would give you something to eat, but I do not have enough for so many. Who are you, and why have you come?" Yellow Corn said, "We are travelling." The old woman said, "Where do you come from?" Yellow Corn said: "We are from Bend-of-the-Water. We lived also for one year at Refuge Place." The old woman said: "I do not know those places. They must be far away." Yellow Corn said: "Yes, they are far. Here where you are living, what do you call it?" The old woman said, "We call it Six Houses." Yellow Corn asked, "Who are the people who live here?" The old woman answered, "This is a Spider Clan settlement." Yellow Corn said, "And those people living at the edge of the mesa, who are they?"

The old woman laughed, saying: "Who are they? They are everyone. Sit down, sit down, I will tell you." Yellow Corn and Still Water sat on a stone ledge near the house, and the old woman said: "There are several villages on the mesa. Over there a little to the east is Bow Height, that is a village founded by the Bow Clan, and living with them are the Tobacco Clan, the Rabbit Clan, the Tadpole Clan and other clans. A little farther on, to the north, is the village called Yellow Cliff. There the people are the Coyote Clan, the Fire Clan and their affiliated clans. A little more to the west of that place, around the point, is Ash Hill, and the chief clans there are the Bear Clan and the Snake Clan, and many other clans are living with them also." The old woman paused a moment, then asked, "Who are you people?" Yellow Corn said, "We are Grey Fox Clan." She said: "Yes, I have heard of the Grey Fox. But there are none of them living in the villages."

Yellow Corn hesitated before asking his next question, then he said: "Does the mesa ahead have a name? We are looking for a place called Mesa of Flowers." The old woman said, "Why are you looking for a place with such a name?" Yellow Corn answered: "It was told to our grandfathers that we would come to that place. Therefore we have journeyed. We are still searching." The old woman said: "Many different clans have settled around here. They gave the mesa different names. Some called it Dark Mesa; some called it Finger Mesa because of the points that extend from the edge; some called it Antelope Mesa because there were antelope wandering on top; the Bow Clan called it Bow Mesa after themselves; and the Tinneh and Coconino gave it still other names. But the Bear Clan was the first to arrive there in the north where the village of Ash Hill stands, and they saw that in the spring the whole mesa was covered with flowers as far as a young man could run in several days, and therefore they called it the Mesa of Flowers."

Yellow Corn and Still Water had no more to ask. They were silent, pondering the significance of what they had learned. They arose to leave, but the old woman was not finished. She said: "Do you not want to know anything else? Let your people rest a while. Talking is good. I do not meet many people out here. I will tell you something about the villages. Bow Height is big. It has many kivas. It overlooks a wide valley that is beautiful to see. But the people there are not getting along with one another. Yellow Cliff also is a big village. It has people living at the foot of the cliff and on top of the cliff. But they and the Ash Hill people are not tolerant of one another. They have built a wall on top of the cliff, and when they are hunting or gathering firewood the wall is the boundary between them. That is not good. You Grey Fox ones, perhaps you should try somewhere else. To the west of here, several days' walking, there are more villages where things are going better." Yellow Corn and Still Water said: "Thank you, grandmother, that you want to help us. But it is the Mesa of Flowers that we are looking for." They departed from the house, leaving the old woman sitting there, and went back to where the main party was resting.

Yellow Corn said to the people: "Let us thank Desert Spirit for guiding us. The place that we were told to find, there it stands, the Mesa of Flowers. The Bear Clan, the Coyote Clan and the Bow Clan have large villages at many places along the rim. Somewhere among the villages we will surely find relatives." The people stood looking toward the mesa, unable to grasp that they had reached their prophesied destination. Someone said, "My father, it looks like any other mesa." And Yellow Corn answered: "We will see how it is. Every mesa has its own spirit. Let us now continue in our direction." So the people picked up their loads and went forward.

Before the afternoon was old they sighted another settlement on a rise of ground, and they met a hunter returning to it with a deer on his back. Still Water went forward and greeted him, saying, "Cousin, what is the name of this place?" The man answered: "We call it Piñon Mound. You people, where are you coming from?" Still Water said, "We are coming from the south." The man asked, "Are you going to Ash Hill?" Still Water said: "About that, we do not know. Perhaps we have relatives somewhere. As Bow Height is the closest, we will go there first." The man asked, "What clan are you?" Still Water said, "We are Grey Fox." The hunter said: I do not think you will be welcome at Bow Height. They have been having trouble there. There were Blue Fox people in the village and they were sent away. I think they went to Yellow Cliff to find shelter." Still Water said, "This settlement here, to whom does it belong?" The man said, "It belongs to Spider Clan people." Still Water said, "Oh, yes, we passed another of your settlements this morning." The man answered, "No, we do not have any settlements out there in that direction." Still Water said: "Yes, we passed it. It was a small place called Six Houses." The man seemed surprised. He said: "Six Houses? We used to have families living there, but several years ago it was abandoned. Some of those people are here at Piñon Mound, others are now living on the mesa." Still Water said: "The old woman did not mention it. She said only that the others had gone to Ash Hill for a festival." The man said: "Someone is living there now? I did not know it. I have passed it many times, and the sand seemed to be covering everything." Still Water said, "Only the old woman was there, we did not see any others." The man asked, "What did she look like?" And Still Water said, "She was a little bent but full of spirit, that is all." The man did not press the matter. He said, "Well, perhaps she came there out of the desert and did not have anywhere else to stay." Still Water said, "Perhaps that is the way it was."

After a moment, Still Water said, "My cousin, who is the village chief at Bow Height?" The man answered: "He is Broken Lance. If you go there, do not try to go into the village right away. Make your camp outside and send a messenger to say you have arrived. Perhaps he will come, perhaps he will send for you. Do not be too impatient." Still Water said, "Thanks, my cousin, that you have told me."

The Grey Fox People did not try to go any farther that day. They made camp within sight of Piñon Mound. They looked often at the mesa cliff in the north, wondering what meaning it held for them. In the morning they went a little to the west until they arrived at a spot from which they could see the outline of the houses of Bow Height. There, not far from a spring, they stopped and made some lean-tos for the old ones and the children. Yellow Corn, Still Water and Burning Tree discussed what should be done next, and it was agreed that Burning Tree would enter the village with a message for Broken Lance and then return.

So Burning Tree went into Bow Height. He had not been in so large a village before. It had several rows of houses, some of them two or three stories high. The first court he came to was a large one, and there were two kivas in it. Somewhat beyond, he saw another court, and there he saw the ladders of three more kivas protruding from the ground. A man approached him, saying, "You are a stranger here?" Burning Tree answered, "Yes, I am looking for the chief." The man said: "The chief is not here. He is away on an expedition. Over there is the Bow Clan kiva. Go there, they will tell you something."

Burning Tree went to one of the kivas in the second court. He stamped on the roof, and called out: "I have arrived. I want to see the Bow Clan chief." A voice from below said, "Come down, come down." Burning Tree descended the ladder. There were four men there, and one of them said, "Where do you come from?" Burning Tree said: "My people are out there camping. I came to speak with the village chief, but it is said he is not here. Therefore I came to your kiva." The man answered, "Who are you people and where do you come from?" Burning Tree answered: "We are Grey Fox. We come from the south." The man answered, "There are no Grey Fox here." Burning Tree said: "My cousin, we do not know if we have any relatives in this place. From the way you speak, I think you people may have come from the Eastern River. We also come from there, but we have lived in many villages since then. Now we are coming from Refuge Place. It was told to us that we would come to the Mesa of Flowers. Now we are here. Our leader is Yellow Corn. He wishes to speak with Broken Lance."

The other man said: "Broken Lance is away. Now it is the Bow Clan chief who speaks for the village." Burning Tree said, "My cousin, are you the clan chief?" And the man answered: "Yes, I am the one. What do you want with us?" Burning Tree took out his pipe and tobacco, saying, "Let us smoke together." The Bow Clan chief was abashed. He said: "Put your pipe away. We have pipes here." He lighted a pipe, puffed on it and passed it to Burning Tree. Burning Tree smoked. Then he said: "Now, what is to be said should be said by Yellow Corn. He is our father. He wants to sit with you and talk." The Bow Clan chief said: "We are busy now. We are preparing a ceremony." And Burning Tree said: "Yes, that is important. I see you have been making prayer feathers. I should not have intruded. Our people will stay out there. We will be patient. You will speak with us when you can. Whenever you wish, send a messenger. Yellow Corn will come."

He arose and departed from the kiva. When he arrived at where the Grey Fox people were waiting, he said to Yellow Corn and Still Water: "Now, I have seen something big. That village has many hundreds of families, and there are three courts there and seven kivas. Yet something does not go well. The village chief is away somewhere, and the Bow Clan chief is in charge. He is not cordial. He speaks as if we were Utaheh. I told him a little, but not everything. I told him it was you who should speak for us. I said we would wait. But he did not say anything to that." And Yellow Corn said: "My brother, you did well. There is nothing for us to do but wait. We shall see how it goes." So the people waited, but Yellow Corn would not let any of them go into the village. A day passed, and another day, but there was no message from the Bow Clan chief. On the fourth day someone approached the encampment. Burning Tree said, "Perhaps it is a messenger."

The man arrived, saying to the old ones, "Our kiva chief sent me to speak with you." Yellow Corn said, "Sit down, let us smoke." So they smoked, and the man said: "Our kiva chief cannot come, they are making a ceremony. He said I should tell you there is no room for any more people now in our village. Also, we had trouble here with the Blue Fox Clan and we had to send them away. Now we can not take any of their relatives, or the trouble will start again." Yellow Corn said: "We do not know the Blue Fox people you are talking about. We knew some Blue Fox in the south, but they were a different group. As for us, we are only a small clan. Some of our people were killed by the Utaheh. Some departed from us and went to the west. We are peaceful. We do not make trouble. We do not claim to be above any other clan. All we want is to live quietly. If the village should be in danger, we will take up our weapons and help to defend it. If our neighbors are hungry we will give them corn from our houses."

The Bow Clan spokesman said: "Well, now, do you have something that the village needs? Do you have a good ceremony to bring game or to make the corn grow?" Yellow Corn said: "Yes, we have some of these things. We also have kachinas." The man replied: "We also have kachinas, many of them. We do not have room for any more kachinas. Do you have a special guardian spirit who could help the village? Already the clans have brought us many such spirits. Thus we have Corn Grandfather, Bird Woman, Death Old Man and Hard Substances Old Woman. Are you related to Germination Spirit or to the Warriors? Do you have special knowledge of Sun Spirit or Moon Spirit? What do you have that could persuade us that we need you?"

Yellow Corn answered: "My cousin, we are merely people like most people. We have journeyed far from our beginnings, and now we are going to remain here at the Mesa of Flowers. Perhaps Bow Height is not the place for us. We do not understand the manners and ways of Bow Height. One of our old ones comes to your kiva to talk, but he is not welcomed. No one says, 'Sit, old man, rest a little, have something to eat.' No one says, 'Old one, let us smoke the smoke of harmony.' We said to ourselves, 'There must be trouble in the village, they are upset and suspicious, therefore let us make allowances.' The Bow Clan chief does not come himself to say, 'Do you need corn? Help yourself to water from that spring over there. Do your old ones need anything?' No, he does not come, neither does he send a message saying, 'Yellow Corn, the prayer feathers are made. Now come and let us speak together in my kiva.' But I see that it would have no value to sit in the kiva talking. For it seems that Bow Height will open its heart only to gods such as Germination Spirit and the Warriors. We Grey Fox are too small and simple a clan to live side by side with the deities. So tell your clan chief not to worry anymore about us. We will depart promptly in the morning."

They left at sunrise, going toward the northwest, and by early afternoon they were in sight of another large village nestled against the mesa wall. They presumed it to be Yellow Cliff, because the old woman had told them Ash Hill was on the other side of the point. They camped on a mound that had growing trees. Yellow Corn said: "My children, let us prepare to be patient. Make summer shelters here, go on living. We will be cautious. In time we will find out what kind of people are in this place. Then we will know what to do." They ate their evening meal, and afterward Yellow Corn said to Still Water and Burning Tree, "I have been thinking about the old woman at Six Houses." Still Water said, "I too have been thinking about her." Yellow Corn said, "The hunter said the settlement had been abandoned." Still Water said, "How would an old woman like that come out of the desert and settle by herself?" Burning Tree said, "It was a Spider Clan place." Yellow Corn said, "Is it not the Spider Clan that claims her for a relative?" Still Water and Burning Tree said, "Yes, it is so." They were silent for a while, then Yellow Corn said: "She seemed to warn us away from Bow Height, but we did not grasp it. She also said that feelings are not good between Ash Hill and Yellow Cliff." Still Water said: "Perhaps it is not serious trouble. Perhaps it will subside." Yellow Corn said, "Yes, we will see how things go."

Even from where the Grey Fox People camped it could be seen that Yellow Cliff was a large village. It spread over several knolls along the base of the mesa wall, and up above, on the edge of the cliff, were two large mounds covered with houses. A little to the east, on the flat ground running along a wash, were several small compounds of four or five houses each. Below the main village were a number of rectangular cornfields, each of them marked out with neat rows of stones. Although the Grey Fox camp was visible from the upper village, no one from Yellow Cliff approached it the first day except a small boy. But he stayed at a distance, and after a while he turned back to the village.

Falling Snow and Elk Horn decided to go around the point of the mesa to catch a view of Ash Hill. Before reaching the point they came to where a group of women were filling their jugs at a spring. One of the women said: "You young men have just arrived? Where are you coming from?" Falling Snow answered: "We are Grey Fox People. We are resting over there south of Yellow Cliff." The woman said, "And why are you over here?" Falling Snow said: "Why, we have heard of Ash Hill. People tell us it is a good village. We wanted to see what it looks like." The woman said, "Oh, yes, it is a good village, much better than those other villages in the west." Falling Snow said, "Is it permitted for strangers to enter?" The woman answered: "Yes, there is no harm in it. But where the trail enters the village by the first house, if you see a line of meal across your path, then do not go in. Wait there, perhaps a One Horn priest will come to question you."

Falling Snow and Elk Horn followed the trail around the point. It ascended until it reached the lower shelf of the mesa, and there in front of them was Ash Hill. There were numerous houses, and some of the buildings were two or three stories high. The entrances were in the front walls rather than in the roofs, and corn and peppers were hanging from almost all of the projecting roof beams. The smoke from numerous pottery fires hung in the air, drifting slowly across the crest of the mesa.

At the first house, a line of meal crossed the trail, so Falling Snow and Elk Horn stopped there. Soon an old man wearing a One Horn headdress and holding a lance came to meet them. He said: "You young men, are you from the western villages? Or from Yellow Cliff or Bow Height?" Falling Snow said: "Grandfather, we are from none of those places. We have just arrived and are resting out there in the valley." The One Horn priest said, "Who are you then, where do you come from and what are the names of your clans?" Falling Snow said: "Most of us are Grey Fox. My friend, Elk Horn, we adopted him from the Yayatu. His people were scattered by the Utaheh."

The old one looked at Elk Horn closely. He said: "A-heh! Your people are magicians?" Elk Horn answered: "Grandfather, there are those who believe this, but my people can do only what other people can do. We are not sorcerers." The old one said: "No, you do not look like a magician. But there is a Yaya village out there on the mesa top, and those people have great medicine." Turning to Falling Snow he said, "Why are the Grey Fox here?" Falling Snow answered: "My grandfather, we have been travelling from a southern village. It was told to us that we should come to the Mesa of Flowers." The old one said, "It is not proper that young men like you should enter the village before the old men have arrived to explain their presence." Falling Snow answered: "We regret it. We did not mean to offend anyone. We were simply walking to catch a sight of Ash Hill. We heard that it is a good village. From here we have seen a little, now we will go away."

The One Horn priest brought his staff down with a thud, saying, "Young men, you are here now, and it is I who say what to do. You are well-behaved. You stopped at the line of meal. You see it?" They said, "Yes, grandfather, we see it." He answered, "Now, how can you see what is not there?" He brushed the meal away with his foot, saying, "I, with my old eyes, see that there is no line there. You with young eyes, can you not see as well as I? Come in. Walk through the village. Go past the houses but do not approach the kivas. Then go away. Tell your Grey Fox old ones to come and be recognized." They answered, "Thank you, Grandfather," and entered Ash Hill. They wandered among the houses and through the courts. They greeted people and received greetings. After that they departed from the village and returned to the Grey Fox camp, where they told Yellow Corn everything that they had done and seen. Yellow Corn said: "It seems that they are good people in Ash Hill. In time, we will go there to speak with them."

On the third day after their arrival, a delegation of three elders came from Yellow Cliff. Yellow Corn, Still Water and Burning Tree went out to greet them, and the six of them sat together on the ground and smoked. Then one of the Yellow Cliff men said: "I am Great Pine, the father of the village. Why have you come?" Yellow Corn answered: "My cousin, since the time of our grandfathers we have been travelling. It was said to us then, and we have never forgotten, that our destination would be the Mesa of Flowers. Our last village was Refuge Place. It was destroyed by a falling cliff, and so we understood that we were to move on and complete our journey. This we have done. The Grey Fox is our emblem. We asked ourselves, 'Where are our relatives to be found?' We believe that we are related to the Blue Fox, the Wolf and the Coyote, for these creatures are similar in form and they can speak to one another. We stopped briefly at Bow Height, thinking it might be the place where we would find affiliated clans. But they did not receive us well there. They told us the Blue Fox Clan had been expelled from that village, and that they did not want us. So we knew it was not the place that Serpent Spirit had designated. Therefore we approached Yellow Cliff, knowing that it is a Coyote Clan village. We said, 'We will wait to see if our Coyote cousins approve of us.' We are glad you are here. We can speak heart to heart."

Great Pine answered, saying, "Yes, we also think that the Coyote and Grey Fox may be cousins. Is this all there is of the Grey Fox Clan?" Yellow Corn said: "No, there were more before we came to our last village. We have been broken twice. One party went out and was killed by the Utaheh. Another party followed a sign westward. Where they are now we do not know. But we are the ones who survived to reach the Mesa of Flowers." Great Pine said: "We also had numerous trials before we reached this place. Yet now we flourish. We have many clans, including the Fire Clan, which is our close relative, and the Yellow Fox, the Piñon, and the Yellow Bird people. We are in harmony here. There are no sorcerers. At first we built below the cliff, for there is a good spring coming out of the cliff wall. Then we built a guard post on top. When there were too many houses below, the people went above, so now we have an upper village and a lower village. Some people came to us from the Eastern River. Also, some of the Bow Clan from Bow Height grew discontented there, and they came here and built their houses just below where you see the fields."

Still Water said, "It was told to us that in Bow Height things are not going well, and that their chief is away on an expedition." Great Pine said: "Yes, it is not good over there in that village. There are many people from Kawaika who came in a large group, and ever since then there has been trouble of one kind or another. But the real trouble is in the Bow Clan itself. They wanted to get rid of Broken Lance, the village chief. In the kiva they persuaded him that he should take prayer feathers and a bowl of sacred meal to a certain spring in the west near the Great Canyon. So at last he went on the expedition. He departed at corn-planting time, and he has not yet returned. The Bow Clan people over there say mouth to ear that he was killed by the Paiutes or the Coconino, but they pretend to be waiting for him to come back. At their winter ceremony they will select another person of the Bow Clan to be chief. They expelled the Blue Fox Clan from Bow Height because the Blue Fox accused them of sending Broken Lance out to die. Therefore, no relatives of the Blue Fox are welcome there."

Yellow Corn said: "My brother, how would you advise us? We see that there are small groups of houses here and there outside of Yellow Cliff. Can we consider building a settlement for ourselves somewhere? Or should we look for a place on the cliff?" Great Pine said: "Let us not hurry things. I do not know how the village will decide. Over there to the east, the fields belong to the Fire Clan. From that grove of cottonwoods on both sides of the wash, that is the land of the Coyote Clan. To the west are the fields of the Yellow Fox and the Wolf. Up above on the top of the mesa are fields belonging to various clans. But up there we are in conflict with Ash Hill. They say the land was given to them by Death Old Man when the Bear Clan first arrived here, and even though they are not using it they do not want our people to have it. Out here, where you are resting now, there is land. But it is not up to me to tell you to stay or go away. I will bring the matter up in the kiva. The old ones will discuss it. We will let you know if they decide anything." Yellow Corn said, "My brother, thanks that you will consider it."

Several days passed without any word from Great Pine. Then there was a lone visitor from Ash Hill. He carried a lance, though now he did not wear the One Horn headdress. He said brusquely, "Where are the two young men who could not see if there was a line of meal or not?" Falling Snow came forward, saying, "Yes, Grandfather." The old man said, "One is not two. Where is the magician?" Falling Snow answered, "Elk Horn has gone hunting, Grandfather." The old man tamped his lance on the ground. He said: "Well, then, we will do without him. Announce me to the father of this pack of grey foxes." Falling Snow guided him to Yellow Corn. He said, "My grandfather, this is the One Horn priest who guards the trail to Ash Hill." Yellow Corn said, "My cousin, thanks that you have come." The man said: "You are the leader here? I have been standing at the gate three days. Why have you not appeared?" Yellow Corn said, "I did not hear that the father of the village invited us." The One Horn priest said, "When you are invited, then what is there for me to do at the gate?" Yellow Corn asked, "You are the guard of the village?" The One Horn priest answered: "Yes, that is what I do. The strangers arrive, I draw a line of sacred meal across the path, and there they must stop. If they are good people I allow them to enter. If they are bad I send them away." Yellow Corn said, "My cousin, how can you tell if people are good or bad merely by standing at the line?" The One Horn priest answered: "Why, if they stop and do not cross until I have questioned them, they are respectful. If they ignore the sacred meal, they are disrespectful. In the village everyone respects the One Horn priest. If I say, 'Do not go into the kiva,' they do not go. If the old ones are meditating in the kiva and people outside are boisterous I tell them, 'Be quiet,' and they are quiet." Yellow Corn said, "My cousin, let us sit and smoke."

They sat on the ground and smoked. After a while the old man said: "Once I was a young One Horn priest. Now I am an old One Horn priest." Yellow Corn said: "I understand. Once I too was young. Now I am not young anymore." The old man said, "When I was young I was a great runner. The young people do not know it. They say, 'There goes old Lame Badger, see how he hobbles.' They do not understand that a young person is merely an old one who has not yet arrived." Yellow Corn asked, "My cousin, who is your village chief, and are the people doing well?" The One Horn priest said: "The chief is Standing Bear, my half brother. But he is Bear Clan and I am Snake Clan. The Bear Clan is on top in Ash Hill. But we Snake Clan people are very strong in ceremonies. We hold the village together. We do not have very many Fire or Coyote people. They are always making trouble, that is why we do not care much for Yellow Cliff. Ash Hill was first. We came when Death Old Man was still living by the big rock up on top of the mesa. Later the Yellow Cliff people came. Where they settled, that was land Death Old Man gave the Bear Clan." Yellow Corn asked, "Your Snake Clan people, where did they come from?" And the old man replied, gesturing toward the north: "Out there, far away. We brought the Snake Ceremony. Before we came, the people here did not have the Snake Ceremony. So we are a very important clan." He was silent for a while, then he said: "You, father of the Grey Fox Clan, come to the village early in the morning. I will make a line of meal and I will be standing there. When you come to the line, stop and do not cross, and I will ask you what you want." Yellow Corn said, "My cousin, I will be there."

After Lame Badger, the One Horn priest, had departed, Still Water said: "Perhaps you had better not go. The old man's mind has been touched by the Great Spirit." But Yellow Corn said: "Who knows? Perhaps, through him, something is speaking to us. I will go. There will be no harm in it. If he should prove to be our only friend in Ash Hill, then at least we will have one friend there. After all, it is in Yellow Cliff that we hope to settle."

And so the next day Yellow Corn went to Ash Hill. He passed the spring where the women were drawing water and ascended to the lower shelf around the point of the mesa. Where the trail entered the village, Lame Badger was standing there with his lance in his hand and wearing his One Horn headdress. As Yellow Corn approached he saw the line of sacred meal across the path, and there he stopped, asking, "May a peaceful one enter here?" Lame Badger said: "Who are you and where do you come from? And what have you ever done in the world to show that you are peaceful?" Yellow Corn answered: "I am Yellow Corn, father of the Grey Fox Clan. We have made a long journey and now we are resting below in the valley. We do not raid other people, we only defend ourselves if we are attacked. We have never taken anything that belongs to others. When strangers come and are hungry, we feed them. We cherish the young and respect the old." Lame Badger said: "A-heh! What you say is good." He obliterated the line of meal with his foot and said: "Come in, come in. Do not stand out there, enter the village."

Yellow Corn entered. Lame Badger walked ahead of him, gesturing with his lance toward the various features of Ash Hill. "Those houses there belong to the Bear Clan. Over there are the houses of the Snake Clan. Over there, the Horn and Flute clans. Over there, the Reed Clan. The Reed Clan people say they were the first people here, but nobody believes them. They say they were created by the Warriors and didn't come from the lower world. They say the Warriors made them at a spring not far from here. The Reed Clan chief bothers Standing Bear all the time. He tweaks Standing Bear's ear and tells him everybody knows that the Reed Clan arrived first, but Standing Bear says, 'Go and weed your corn.' Over there is where the Squash Clan lives. This is a big village. The Utaheh don't bother us the way they do some of the other villages. They know we have strong medicine. Over there is the chief kiva. The next one is the One Horn kiva. Now you have seen enough. You are taking up my time. So follow me, I will take you to Standing Bear's house."

Yellow Corn said: "My cousin, perhaps that is not the way it should be done. I will wait for him at the chief kiva." He went to the kiva and sat on the stone steps that led to the roof. Lame Badger disappeared toward the Bear Clan houses, and after a while Standing Bear came to where Yellow Corn was waiting. Yellow Corn said: "My cousin, I would not have come in this manner if it had been left to me. I would have waited below, but Lame Badger insisted that I should cross his line this morning." Standing Bear answered: "Yes, he is using up much meal with his lines. Let us descend." They went into the kiva. While they smoked, Standing Bear kept his eyes closed, concentrating his thoughts on the character of the stranger who had just arrived.

At last he said: "I know why you are here and who you are, for Lame Badger had told me everything. So I do not ask you anything. My cousin, do not think that Lame Badger is a village clown. The Great Spirit has given him a gift. Though other men may ponder the meaning of mysteries, Lame Badger understands them instantly. He sees what is right and what is wrong. He perceives at once who is good and who is evil. Last night he came to my house and said, 'I have found a good one for you.' This morning he came and said, 'I have brought the good one here.' "

Yellow Corn answered, "Thanks, that you believe what he told you." Standing Bear asked, "You are the father of the Grey Fox?" Yellow Corn said: "Yes. Once we were more numerous, and at Refuge Place I was the village chief. Now we have no village of our own, and I am the journey chief. If we are permitted to settle here at the Mesa of Flowers, then I will be merely the chief keeper of our history." Standing Bear said: "My cousin, may you keep the history well. We have many histories here. But there are some who have no histories at all. We have one family at Ash Hill that spoke a strange language when it came. Now it speaks our language but remembers nothing of its past, only that it came from a distant place where the sun sets over the great water. What can a clan amount to if it has no history?" Yellow Corn replied, "Yes, my cousin, what you say is said truly."

Standing Bear said, "We hear that you want to join Yellow Cliff." Yellow Corn answered: "We have spoken to them, but we do not know anything for certain. We stopped at Bow Height, but they did not welcome us, so we thought of Yellow Cliff where many Coyote people are living. If the Coyotes regard us as relatives they will let us know. Meanwhile we are resting out there for a while. Perhaps we will have to build houses in the valley somewhere, or on the mesa top." Standing Bear said: "We also have Coyotes living here, but only a few. They departed from Yellow Cliff because of a quarrel. Ash Hill is a peaceful village, except when we need to defend ourselves. If Yellow Cliff does not welcome you, come back, we will speak of it." Yellow Corn answered, "Thanks, my cousin."

Standing Bear went to the top of the kiva ladder and called for someone to bring food. Soon a woman came bringing two bowls, and the two men ate together. Standing Bear seemed to brood, and at last Yellow Corn asked, "Have I said anything to displease my cousin?" Standing Bear answered: "It is another matter that troubles me, something between Yellow Cliff and ourselves. For a long while we were good friends, then things began to happen. Great Pine, who is father of Yellow Cliff, he is a good man. We often speak together. But the troubles come from below. The people sometimes do not act well toward one another. Yellow Corn, I see what kind of a man you are. We will smoke together again. Perhaps some time I can tell you how things are in these villages." Yellow Corn answered, "Yes, may we sit together many times." He arose, left the kiva and returned to the Grey Fox camp.

Two days passed without any visitors coming from Ash Hill or Yellow Cliff. The old ones had counselled the Grey Fox People to be patient, and everyone was doing something as if they were living in a real village. Falling Snow, Elk Horn and Young Antelope had gone hunting. Yellow Corn's wife Gentle Mist was softening a deer hide. White Blanket and Yellow Hair were out in the valley looking for roots. Still Water was making a new set of moccasins for himself. Sometimes the people looked toward Yellow Cliff and felt uneasy at the thought of living in so large a settlement of strangers. Gentle Mist said to Yellow Corn: "For as long as I can remember we have come and gone as we ourselves decided. In Yellow Cliff it will be different. You and Still Water and Burning Tree, maybe they will not even let you in the kivas." And Yellow Corn answered: "I do not know how it will be. But this is the Mesa of Flowers. It is here that we were told to come."

In the afternoon of the third day, Lame Badger came again to the encampment. This time he was wearing his One Horn headdress. With the point of his lance he marked a line on the ground, then another, and kept on marking until he had made a large square. He sat in the center and said to Yellow Corn, "Stamp, now, on the roof of my kiva and ask permission to enter." Yellow Corn stamped his foot, saying, "My cousin, I have just arrived." Lame Badger answered, "Come in, come in, do not stand there on the roof." Yellow Corn entered the kiva. Lame Badger said, "Let us sit together and smoke." Yellow Corn sat down facing Lame Badger, who was lighting his pipe. Lame Badger said, "Why have you come?" Yellow Corn replied, "I have come so that my cousin and I may speak of things that matter."

They smoked, and when the tobacco was consumed Lame Badger said: "I am going to tell you how my people arrived from Black Mountain in the north. We had been journeying in the wilderness a long time. We were tired. At last we saw before us the Mesa of Flowers. We said: 'Now, here we are going to bring our journey to an end. There is a village up there on Ash Hill. There we will live.' The people in the village were the Bear Clan. Up on the very top of the mesa, right out at the point, Death Old Man was still living. It was he who originally owned all the land here. He was going to give it to the Fire Clan people, that was his plan. But the Fire Clan was lost somewhere, and when the Bear Clan arrived Death Old Man said, 'You people arrived first, so take the land.' He gave them Ash Hill and the fields on all sides. He himself went to the top of the mesa and lived there. From up above he could see in all directions, people coming and going in the valley. Death Old Man saw our Snake Clan approaching. When he saw we were not his relatives, the Fire Clan, he became angry. He went down to Ash Hill and told the Bear Clan leaders: 'Out there in the valley the Snake Clan is coming. Tell them to stop where they are and go elsewhere.' The Bear Clan leader said: 'Old man, you have entrusted the land around here to us, but it belongs to you. You are the one to go down and stop those people.'

"So Death Old Man descended into the valley and made himself look fierce and terrible, the way he was when he emerged from the deep pit of fire. His skin was covered with fire scars. He was splattered with blood. His rabbitskin cape was full of bloodstains. His lips were scarred and twisted, so that his teeth were revealed. There was no hair on his head. He gave the cry of the wolf and went running toward the Snake Clan people. As he breathed, jets of fire came from his mouth. When the people saw him they were overcome with fear. Some ran away. Some fell unconscious on the ground. But he who led the Snake Clan did not fall down or run away. He stood facing Death Old Man, saying, 'Why do you threaten us? What harm have we done?' And Death Old Man said to him: 'You do not know me? You do not fear me?' The Snake Clan leader said: 'Yes, who does not know you? But why should I be afraid? Like everyone who lives, you have a good face as well as a bad face. Also, we Snake people have powerful medicine.

We are not wild dogs roaming the desert. We have something worth-while.' Death Old Man said, 'Very well, we will see what you have.'

"He went behind a large rock and transformed his appearance so that he seemed to be an ordinary man. He returned. He said, 'I am ready.' The Snake Clan chief instructed his people. They prepared a ceremony. They put on their dancing kilts. They put eagle, parrot and bluebird feathers in their hair. They painted their bodies. They danced the ceremony they had brought with them from Black Mountain. Now the snakes began to come in from all directions. Blacksnakes, bullsnakes, rattlesnakes and all other kinds that live in this country. The snakes crawled among the dancers. The dancers picked them up. Sometimes they held them in their mouths, brushing them with feathers to soothe them. Clouds appeared in the sky where there had not been any clouds before. Rain fell.

"And when Death Old Man saw what the Snake Clan people could do, he said: 'Now, you Snake Clan people, I see that you truly bring something. When I first saw you coming I did not recognize you. I am glad that you have arrived. Your chief did not fear me, and you have great medicine. Therefore, rest here a while, and after that you may enter Ash Hill.' Death Old Man returned to the village and said, 'Make the Snake Clan dear to your hearts. They are worthwhile.' Then Death Old Man went back to his place on top of the mesa and stayed there. The Snake Clan entered Ash Hill. There we remain."

Yellow Corn said, "Thanks that you have told me. The Snake Clan is something to remember." Lame Badger said, "If Death Old Man should come down to tell you to go away, say that you are Lame Badger's friend." Yellow Corn answered: "Yes, I will do it. But is he still living up there on top of the mesa?" Lame Badger said: "Who knows where he lives now? He gave all his land to the Bear Clan. The Bear Clan gave some of it to the Snake Clan and the Horn Clan and the Flute Clan and other clans that are living here. He did not have any land left to grow his corn. He went away somewhere where people are not planting in his fields. But sometimes he comes back, and in the night we can see the fire of his breath up there where his house used to be." Yellow Corn said, "You have seen it?"

"I have seen it. I have seen Death Old Man himself. One year there was not enough rain. I saw him breathing in the night and I went to the top of the mesa. He was sitting there by a tall rock near the point. I said, 'You, Death Old Man, the way you are breathing you will set the grass on fire and the village will be destroyed.' He said, 'I cannot help it, that is the way I breathe.' I said, 'Then you must go away until the grass is green again.' He went away, he did not return until the spring when everything was green." Yellow Corn said, "That was good, that he went away." Lame Badger said: "Once, when I was young, the kachinas sent a grass fire to us. Over in that western village that they call Round Rock, the people remember it. Behind Round Rock there was another village. The people there were not very good. They did not respect the old ones. Sometimes they tormented them. Also, they were not good to the women. The kachinas did not like it. They set the grass on fire out there at Snow Mountain where they live. They made the wind blow, and the fire approached Round Rock. On the fourth day the fire was near the villages. The chief at Round Rock saw that everything was being destroyed. He went to the house of Spider Old Woman, which was not very far away. He said, 'A great grass fire is coming. Our village will be burned away.' Spider Old Woman said, 'Do not worry, I will not let your village die.' She went to a certain spot south of Round Rock. She stuck an arrow into the ground. Some distance away she placed another arrow. Then she made a spider web between the two arrows, and she moistened it with water. The fire arrived. It could not pass the spider web, and so it went around the village. It arrived at the village of the evil people. The fire consumed everything." Yellow Corn said, "Thanks, that Earth Grandmother saved Round Rock."

Lame Badger said: "Did not Spider Old Woman make a mistake? When the bad village was destroyed, all the old people living there were also destroyed. They did not do anything to deserve it." Yellow Corn said, "Perhaps Earth Grandmother had her own reason." Lame Badger said: "No, she thought only about her spider web. Have you never seen how spiders are? If you tear their webs they can think of nothing but building them up again. Old people are like that. They think of one thing and cannot remember anything else. Why was it that Grandmother did not remember the good people who were living in that bad village? I do not forgive her. She should have saved the old ones. I told her this. I scolded her." Yellow Corn asked, "You have spoken with Earth Grandmother?" Lame Badger said: "I went to her shrine up there on the mesa. I said, 'Old woman, next time do not let your thoughts get scrambled. There are some good people in every village.' I said this, and she could not think of anything to reply."

After a moment, Lame Badger said: "I hear footsteps approaching Ash Hill. People are coming. I must go and meet them as they enter."

He arose and went away, leaning on his lance as he crossed the rocky ground.

One morning Great Pine and a delegation of old ones came from Yellow Cliff. Yellow Corn greeted them. Along with Still Water and Burning Tree, they all sat on the ground and smoked. Then Great Pine said: "My cousin, we have sat in the kiva discussing things. Our wise ones have debated whether the Grey Fox and the Coyote are related. They have concluded that it is so. Therefore, they say, if you Grey Fox can bring us something that we do not have here already, you can settle at Yellow Cliff. Do you have something we need?"

Yellow Corn pondered. He said: "It was the same question they asked us at Bow Height. They wanted to know if we were sponsored by a spirit like Corn Grandfather or Bird Woman. If Serpent Spirit is our sponsor I cannot say, but it was he who instructed our ancestors to look for the Mesa of Flowers. Now that we have found it, it is certain that he has been guiding us all these years. From him we learned that it is good to be gentle and not seek war. To be gentle and not seek war, is not that good medicine? That is what we bring. Also, I carry a figure made of horn, given to us by the Earth House People, which helps us to find game. There is one thing more. The people of Red Rocks gave us knowledge of the kachinas. Red Rocks Place exists no more, but we bring their masks, which are sacred to us. We have learned the attributes of these masks, and our Kachina Society knows the rituals."

Great Pine said: "May we see the masks? Then we will know what we are dealing with." So Burning Tree arose and brought the masks in their buckskin coverings. He unwrapped them, set them out in a row, and sat down again without saying anything. The old ones from Yellow Cliff talked among themselves, and after a while Great Pine said: "Thanks, that you have showed them to us. We do not own kachinas such as these. We will take the news back with us and discuss everything again." Great Pine and the other old ones returned to Yellow Cliff.

Numerous days passed after that without any further word from Great Pine. The people said: "Now the summer is gone. Soon Winter Old Man will be sending cold winds. If we wait any longer our lives will become difficult." Some thought they ought to begin building houses in the valley. Others said to Yellow Corn, "Let us see whether Ash Hill will have us." Yellow Corn, Still Water and Burning Tree talked about it when they were alone. Yellow Corn said: "I do not think they mean to offend us. I believe they are still arguing about it in the kiva." But Burning Tree replied: "Perhaps they have had time enough to decide one way or another. At Bow Height they did not behave well. They rejected us without even discussing things. But they did not keep us waiting, and we knew that they did not want us. Here we do not know anything. They speak to us with respect, they argue among themselves in safe kivas, and we sit here in the valley. It is time for us to do something. We also must decide. Let us either see what the Ash Hill people are willing to do or start making winter houses for ourselves out here." Still Water said: "We selected Yellow Cliff because the Coyote and Grey Fox Clans are related. But we did not come here to find relatives. Let us see how it is at Ash Hill." In the end it was agreed that Yellow Corn would go again to speak with Standing Bear.

He went to Ash Hill by the trail that passed the spring, and when he arrived at the entrance to the village, Lame Badger was there with his One Horn headdress and lance, and a line of fresh meal was marked across the path. Lame Badger said sharply: "Stand at the line! Who are you and where do you come from? If you are from Bow Height, do not enter, for the Bow Clan has murdered its chief. If you are from Round Rock, go away, because the Round Rock people cheat at gambling." Yellow Corn answered, "I am from the Grey Fox who are resting below." Lame Badger said: "I have never heard that the grey fox is good for anything but its tail. Have you done anything good in the world?" Yellow Corn answered: "When the old ones are sick we take care of them. When hungry strangers come, we feed them."

Lame Badger kicked away the line of meal saying: "Enter, enter, there is nothing in the way. Why have you been so long in coming? There is much to be said mouth to ear." Yellow Corn answered, "My good cousin, we must speak together often, but this time I have to talk to Standing Bear." Lame Badger said: "He is in the chief kiva. I will take you," and he conducted Yellow Corn through the village. He stamped on the kiva roof, calling out, "The chief of the great Grey Fox Clan has arrived." From below came White Bear's answer, "Come in, come in." As Yellow Corn stepped on the kiva ladder, Lame Badger said: "Speak slowly so he will know what you are talking about. Old ones like him, their minds wander."

Yellow Corn descended. He and Standing Bear greeted each other, then they sat to smoke and talk. Yellow Corn said: "My cousin, we do not know if Yellow Cliff will receive us. Soon the weather will be changing and we will need a place to build our houses. We could go elsewhere, but we want to stay at the Mesa of Flowers." Standing Bear said: "We old ones here have already discussed it. We have room for a few more houses on the edge of the village. You chose Yellow Cliff because you believe the Grey Fox and Coyote clans are related. That also was discussed by our people. We do not think the Coyote and Grey Fox are related. That is why the people here would be willing to take you in. If you were truly affiliated with the Coyote, our people would not want you. Many times we have had trouble with the Coyote and Fire clans. They insist that Death Old Man did not actually give the land to the Bear Clan, but merely lent it until the Fire Clan should arrive. When those people came here we did not object to their building houses and growing corn. But up on top of the mesa they are using our land as if Death Old Man had not given the Bear Clan anything. Great Pine tries to control them. He does not want any trouble with us. I try to soothe the people here, saying: 'Let us not get angry. They are not taking anything we need for ourselves. There is plenty of land for all.' Sometimes Great Pine and I meet. We speak together like brothers. You see how it is. We do not want any more Coyotes or Fire Clan people in Ash HIll. We ourselves do not think you are related to the Coyotes. That is why, if your people want it, you can build your houses here." Yellow Corn answered: "That is good. Thanks, that you offer it to us. I will tell the people so they can consider it."

Standing Bear said: "You have just arrived here. Perhaps you are thinking, 'This Standing Bear old man talks too much to a stranger about unpleasant affairs in the village. I speak this way because my heart tells me I can trust you. There is another affair that makes our lives difficult now. One day, a while before you Grey Fox People arrived, we had a festival here in Ash Hill. Young men came from Yellow Cliff to look at the unmarried girls. There was a young man named Lone Peak. He saw one of our girls, Many Flowers, and he wanted her. He asked, 'Who is she?' People said, 'Many Flowers, the daughter of the village crier.' That night he went to her house and tried to talk with her through the small window of the grinding room. But she was not disposed to speak with him. He was persistent. Finally she left the grinding room, so he returned to Yellow Cliff.

"The next day he came again, looking for her and trying to speak with her, but she avoided him. He sometimes waited for her at the spring down below. He pursued her. This girl, he could not live without her. Yet she did not care anything for him. He tried to get her to go out on the mesa with him, but she did not want it. Again, many times, he came to her grinding-room window. He put presents through the window, she pushed them back. When she was tired of seeing him at the window she hung a winnowing basket over it. All this we know because of witnesses. The girls in the village made jokes about Lone Peak. He was the son of Yellow Cliff's village crier, and the girls sang a song that said, 'The crier will speak to the crier, but the crier's daughter will not speak to the crier's son.'

"Now, one night it was very late, and the girl was in the grinding room working. Her mother and father were in another room preparing to sleep. Her mother called to Many Flowers, saying it was too late to go on working. Many Flowers did not answer. Her mother said: 'Why, I have not been hearing the sound of the grinding stones. What can the girl be doing?' She went to the grinding room. There she found Many Flowers lying on top of her grinding stones with an arrow in her back. The mother called out to the father and the girl's brother, saying, 'Hurry, someone has killed Many Flowers!' The family wept. The village was aroused. Everyone came and stood outside the house. They asked one another: 'Who could have done this evil thing? Who could kill an innocent girl, shooting her in the back?'

"The parents of the girl were broken. They could not say anything or do anything. But the girl's brother, Red Wing, took the arrow that had killed her and examined it by the fire. He said, 'This arrow comes from Yellow Cliff. It is someone over there who has committed this terrible crime.' He wanted to go immediately to Yellow Cliff and kill Lone Peak. We restrained him. We said, 'That is not the way. We are a peaceful people.' I myself went to Yellow Cliff to talk to Great Pine. I showed him the arrow. He was sorrowful. He said, 'Do you know who shot the arrow?' I said: 'Yes, everyone in Ash Hill knows. It was Lone Peak, the son of your village crier.' He said, 'Is it known for certain that he was the one?' I answered: 'Yes, for certain. He pursued the girl day after day. She rejected him. Therefore he revenged himself by shooting at her through the grinding-room window.'

"So together we went to see the crier chief. When he heard everything he said: 'No, my son could not have done it. On that day he was in Bow Height with friends.' We said, 'On that evening he was seen in Ash Hill, therefore he could not have been at Bow Height.' The crier chief answered, 'No, on that day he was at Bow Height.' He would not do anything. He would not consider anything. Great Pine said: 'I myself would do something about it, but the crier chief insists Lone Peak was at Bow Height. Let it rest for now, I will get at the truth of it. Then we will know what to do.' So I returned home. Great Pine is a just and peaceful man. If he can find someone over there to say Lone Peak did not go to Bow Height, then he will let me know. But I have heard nothing. Our own crier chief stands on his roof and calls out, 'My daughter was killed by a person from Yellow Cliff.' His son, Red Wing, goes around saying nothing, but his eyes say he is ready to do something. Therefore you can see how it is between our villages." Yellow Corn said, "It is a sorrowful thing."

That evening Yellow Corn told the Grey Fox People that they had been invited to come to Ash Hill. But they were hesitant, thinking it would be better to go where an affiliated clan was living. Still Water said: "Yes, it is true that our relatives are in Yellow Cliff, but they have not yet invited us to join them. They keep turning the matter over from one side to the other without being able to decide anything. Let us give them a little more time. Then if they still do not know their minds we will go to Ash Hill."

So the Grey Fox people agreed to wait four more days. On the third night they began putting their belongings in their carrying baskets. The following morning, just after sunrise, they saw Great Pine approaching their camp with two other men, one of whom carried an object wrapped in a white ceremonial blanket.

Yellow Corn, Still Water and Burning Tree greeted them. They sat together and smoked, after which Yellow Corn said: "My cousins, we have been waiting for you. As you can see, we have been preparing to leave. Have you something to tell us?" Great Pine answered: "These two persons who accompany me are Twisted Spruce, who heads the Fire Clan in our village, and Grey Coyote, who heads the Coyote Clan. These clans are paramount in Yellow Cliff. Last night the three of us did not sleep. We were in the kiva until daybreak discussing which way to go. We have been seeking a sign that would help us decide. When the sun was rising we were about to leave the kiva and go to our homes. Twisted Spruce said, 'Stop a moment.' We stopped. He said: 'When we went the second time to see the Grey Fox Clan they showed us their kachina masks. We thought that the masks were strange to us. Yet something lingers in my mind. One of those masks has something familiar in its appearance.' Twisted Spruce went to where we keep our masks and brought one of them out. We have it with us. Now we want to see your masks again."

Burning Tree arose and took the Grey Fox masks from their buckskin coverings. He laid them on the ground in a line. Twisted Spruce went forward and touched the green mask with the thatch of long hair and the single eye. "This is the one," he said, "put the others away." When Burning Tree had put the others back in their buckskin coverings, Twisted Spruce took out his mask and laid it next to the one remaining on the ground. Whereas one was green, the other was blue. One had a crest of hair, the other had a pelt of bearskin on top. Otherwise the two masks were as brothers. Grey Coyote looked from mask to mask, back and forth, and at last he said: "What Twisted Spruce said, it is true. I am satisfied." Great Pine said: "I also am satisfied. The two masks are merely different faces of the same kachina. Thus we are sharing something important. Your kachina is ours, and ours is yours. Before we came we agreed that if the masks matched one another it would be a sign that all is well. Therefore, it is done. Enter Yellow Cliff, you Grey Fox People, and settle there. We will give you a place to build your houses. Later we will designate your fields."

Yellow Corn said: "My brothers, thanks that you have recognized us. We will live in harmony in Yellow Cliff. We will help to defend it. It will be our village as if we were born there."

Great Pine answered: "That is good. Remember only that the Coyote Clan is first in the village, and that the Fire Clan is its closest relative. Even though we are first, we listen to wise words from whomever they come. If a woman or a child speaks, we listen. It was a child's words that gave our village its name. Our grandfathers were travelling. They camped out here where you Grey Fox are now. And while they were wondering where they would build their houses, a little girl said, 'Let us live over there by the yellow cliff.' The people looked, but they did not see any yellow cliff, only this grey one. The girl repeated her words. The people said, 'Perhaps she sees something truly, perhaps the spirit of the cliff is yellow.' They came and stood on those high knolls. They saw it was a good place for a village. They saw there was a good spring flowing out of the cliffside. So they remained here. They built the village and called it Yellow Cliff. I tell you this so you will know that we listen. If you have something good to tell us, speak. If we have something good to tell you, we will speak. Now we will go back to Yellow Cliff. You people come when you are ready."

The three old ones from Yellow Cliff departed. Yellow Corn said to the Grey Fox People, "Now we have truly arrived at the Mesa of Flowers."

So, at last, the Grey Fox Clan entered Yellow Cliff. They passed through the large dance court and wove their way among the houses, carrying all their possessions. People greeted them from the rooftops.

Before the Grey Fox procession reached the highest ground, where the chief's house was located, they were met by Grey Coyote, who took them to the western edge of the village. He said, "Here you may build," and then he left them. From where they were standing they could see far to the south, from where they had come, and to the southeast they could see that part of the mesa where the Bow Clan village was located. Yellow Corn said: "My children, now that we have come, let us not waste our time. Let us begin making our houses. Plan them well, build them well, for at this place we will remain as long as there is a Grey Fox Clan. Choose your stones carefully, and set them on solid foundations, for now we are here at the place that our grandfathers and our fathers were trying to find. Let us begin."

Still Water also spoke, saying, "Now, when we were back there at Refuge Place the children went out to hunt rats in the cornfields. They said to us, 'The rats have two doors to their houses, so that if an enemy enters by one they depart by the other.' They asked us, 'Why is it that people are not as clever at rats?' In this village many houses have an entrance in the roof and an entrance in the side of the wall. Our children foresaw it, that we would build our houses a new way. As we heard, the Coyote Clan listens to the good words of their children. We also can listen to good words of our children. How you build your houses, that is up to you. But my house will have an entrance through the wall." And some of the other Grey Fox replied, "We also will have entrances through the walls." They began to build. The children helped to gather the stones, and the young men took their axes and went looking for good timbers for their roofs. Yellow Corn wandered among large boulders on the western side of the village, and when he found one that was right he inscribed on it that the Grey Fox Clan had arrived after a long journey from the southland. After that, he also gathered stones.

The days passed, and as their homes took shape the Grey Fox People began to have a sense of well-being they had not felt since they departed from Bend-of-the-Water. They came to know many persons in Yellow Cliff. Old ones talked with old ones, and the young with the young. White Blanket and Buffalo Girl met with other women at the spring below the cliff where everyone came to fill their water jars. Falling Snow, Elk Horn and Young Antelope went to the dance court every evening to speak with the other young men of the village. Some of the women living nearby brought bowls of food to Yellow Hair. The only concern the Grey Fox People had was whether they would have enough corn to carry them through the winter. And so they set to work making moccasins, leggings, armbands and other things to trade. Yellow Corn, Still Water and Burning Tree set up looms in their unfinished houses so they could weave whenever there was any time to spare.

One morning they heard calls from the village that a new group of strangers was camping in the valley. Great Pine sent out a scout to see where they were coming from and what kind of people they were. When the scout returned, he went first to report to Great Pine and then he came to Yellow Corn, saying, "The ones who are down in the valley claim you as their relatives. They say they are Grey Fox." Hearing this, all the Grey Fox went running out of Yellow Cliff toward the camp, the young in front and the old behind. When they were halfway there they began shouting greetings, and the people in the camp also came running. Those who had just arrived were Flowing Spring and everyone who had gone westward with him. There were calls of recognition. People were laughing. Flowing Spring came forward to meet Yellow Corn, Still Water and Burning Tree, saying, "My brothers, I see you." They said, "Our brother, you are here, we are glad."

Yellow Corn said to Flowing Spring: "We thought Desert had swallowed you all. Thanks, that the Spirit showed you the trail!" Flowing Spring said: "We went westward when we left you. The people were not too happy. They were thinking, 'We should have stayed in the canyon with our brothers and sisters. How will we ever see them again?' We were out there camping one night, then we saw your sign, a shower of flaming stars going across the northern sky. We said: 'Yellow Corn was right. Now we will go north again until we find the other half of our clan.' So that is what we have been doing. We arrived at a village called Round Rock. They said you were not there, but that you might be here in one of these eastern villages. We travelled safely. We have arrived." Yellow Corn answered, "Desert Spirit has been truly good to us." The Grey Fox people spent all morning in the valley laughing and exchanging news. Yellow Corn, Burning Tree and Still Water explained how they had been accepted by Yellow Cliff. Yellow Corn said: "Well, now I will speak with Great Pine and the clan chiefs again. They are reasonable men, though they struggle to make decisions. Remain where you are until you hear from us."

Yellow Corn met with Great Pine in the chief kiva. He explained about his Grey Fox relatives who were camping down below. He said: "When you gave us permission to enter Yellow Cliff there were only a small number of us. Now the other half of our people have arrived. We did not expect to see them. We thought they were following signs westward, and that our clan had been broken. But now they have arrived. We ourselves came straight to the Mesa of Flowers, like the cord that binds two ends of a bow. They went in an arc, like the bend of the bow itself, and they arrived here looking for us. Now we are together again and our clan is whole. All of our people have completed the journey that was assigned to us. As I pledged before, I pledge again. We want only harmony with others." Great Pine answered: "I hear you, Yellow Corn. But I must bring this matter to the council. They will debate it. When Grey Coyote and Twisted Spruce assented before, they agreed that a certain number of Grey Fox People would not unbalance the village. Now that there are more of you they will have to consider it again."

So Flowing Spring's party camped in the valley, awaiting the decision. When two days passed and he had heard nothing, Yellow Corn went again to see Great Pine, but the Yellow Cliff chief said there was no news. "The Coyote and Fire clans are discussing it," he said. "We will let you know on the fourth day. This is the way it is with us. You think we are avoiding something, that we do not want to dispose of the problem. But we want to prevent any possible friction. If we were to say yes, and then there were some dissension between us, someone would say, 'I told you to hesitate and to look at all sides of the matter before you allowed the Grey Fox People to come in.' Then there would be dissension within the clans. Therefore, among ourselves we must first say everything that is to be said, and whatever is said wrongly, we dispose of it. Be patient, soon we will have something to tell you."

Two days later, Great Pine, Grey Coyote and Twisted Spruce came to where Yellow Corn was working on his walls. They said: "We have debated everything. Let your relatives come in. There is room enough for your houses here. But if you have more relatives coming from somewhere, we cannot accept them. We have to keep the clans in balance." And now, like arrows flying from their bows, women and children were running out to Flowing Spring's camp shouting, "Come in, come in! Everything is arranged!" So Flowing Spring's party entered the village and went to where the Grey Fox Clan was building and set down their loads. Once again the Grey Fox Clan was whole.

That night everyone gathered around a fire and exchanged news about their journeys. Flowing Spring took out a knotted string, and feeling the knots one by one he related what had happened to his group after leaving Refuge Place. "We went from butte to butte. We came to an abandoned Water Clan village, and the writing on the rocks said that they were going westward toward some high peaks that could be seen from that place. We met a Sand Clan family in the desert who said the mountains were called Snow Peaks, and that they were the home of the kachinas. They also said that there was a river ahead of us, but we never reached it because we saw the shooting stars in the northern sky and changed our direction. We passed some old Bear Clan ruins. We came to a large cave in the side of a hill. We thought, 'We can camp in this cave for the night.' But that cave was not an ordinary cave. There was a deep hole in the center of the floor, like the opening through which the people came from the underworld. Even with our torches we could not see the bottom the hole. We called into it. Our voices went down and down and were swallowed in the depths. At the back of the cave we discovered an altar. A bowl was sitting there. It had prayer feathers in it. Marked on the bowl was the figure of Growth Grandfather. By this, we understood that the hole was the entrance to Growth Grandfather's kiva."

Children asked, "Did you see Growth Grandfather?" And Flowing Spring said: "No, he was deep below, in the fourth kiva. It is said that few humans have ever descended there. One must pass through three other kivas before arriving at the kiva where Growth Old Man lives. In the first kiva are foxes, coyotes and wolves. In the second are bears. In the third, cougars are living. And below that is a great kiva as large as a village. Here Growth Grandfather lives. In the winter he sleeps. In the spring he awakens and makes the medicine that causes all life to become fertile.

"We did not stay there at that hill because it was too sacred. We put prayer feathers in the bowl and departed. We continued northward, walking, resting, walking, resting. In time we came to a high mesa. We arrived at a village called Round Rock and asked for news of our relatives, but the people said: 'There is no Grey Fox Clan here. Try those other villages to the east.' We went eastward and came to two more villages. They also said, 'Go eastward.' That same afternoon we saw smoke from pottery fires, thus we knew that there was a village here. We arrived out there in the valley, and there you discovered us." When Flowing Spring was finished it was late. The people went to their blankets and slept.

Early the next day the Grey Fox people heard Black Cloud, the crier chief of Yellow Cliff, making an announcement from the top of one of the kivas, but they were too far away to understand what he was saying. So Falling Snow and Elk Horn went to the center of the village, where they learned that in eight days kachina runners would be coming from Ash Hill to race against the young men of Yellow Cliff. Already some of the young men were making plans to train for the event. In the afternoon they went out running into the valley. The following day there were more of them. They ran alone or in groups toward a small butte in the south. When they arrived at the butte they rested, then returned running to the village. Some climbed up the steps of the cliff and practiced on top of the mesa.

Young Antelope said to Falling Snow and Elk Horn: "You two are fleet runners. Go down and train with the others. Show them how fleet the Grey Fox can be." They said, "Yes, we would like to do it, but our houses need building." He said: "The houses will not go away. Train in the morning when the sun rises. Harden your sinews. In the afternoon you can work on your walls. Do not be afraid of the kachina racers. They are just young men. Perhpas you can win something from them." They said: "You, Young Antelope, are a fine distance runner. If you train with us, we will train." Young Antelope said, "Well, then, let us run together, the three of us."

So every day after that the three of them went running toward the southern butte. One morning they overtook a young man who was running alone. They said, "Run with us," and the four of them went together to the butte, where they sat down and rested. The young man said, "You Grey Fox know how to run." Young Antelope answered: "Yes, we were born running. That is how we are able to catch the girls." The young man said: "Last year kachina racers came here from Round Rock. I trained to harden my sinews, but I did not win. This year I want to win something. Formerly my running companion was Lone Peak, but now he is away so I run by myself." Young Antelope asked, "Is he not the son of the crier chief?" The young man answered: "Yes, he is the one. He wanted to marry a girl from Ash Hill, but she rejected him. So Black Cloud sent him to Round Rock to stay with our relatives who are living there, thinking he would find a wife in that village. But they do not give him much time to look at the girls. He arrived one day, and the next day they took him on an expedition to get salt from Salt Canyon. He is a good runner. If he were here he would surely win something."

Young Antelope asked, "The girl in Ash Hill who rejected him, was she the daughter of the crier chief over there?" The young man said,

"Yes, her name was Many Flowers. Someone killed her. Over there they are saying that Lone Peak did it, but he did not do it." Young Antelope said, "They are saying it was a Yellow Cliff arrow." The young man replied: "There are many young men in Yellow Cliff, so why do they say it was Lone Peak? That day he was not there at all, he was at Bow Height. But they complained to Black Cloud that Lone Peak was responsible. Black Cloud did not want any trouble about it. That is why he sent Lone Peak to Round Rock." Young Antelope said, "We also have had affairs like this." After a while they resumed their running and returned to the village.

Four days before the kachina races, Lame Badger, the One Horn priest, came to Yellow Cliff wearing his horn headdress and using his lance as a staff. He went to the chief kiva, stamped on it and called out, "Where is Yellow Corn, the father of the great Grey Fox Clan, living?" A voice from below answered, "Out there on the western slope." Lame Badger went to the edge of the village, where he found Yellow Corn working on his house. He said: "How is it that you have not come? I have been standing at the line, but you did not appear." Yellow Corn answered: "My good brother, it is just that I have not yet finished my walls. I have to work hard to be an example to my people." Lame Badger said, "Work goes on forever, but men grow old and disappear, so they must speak to one another when they can."

He marked out a large square in the dust with his lance and said, "Enter my kiva, let us blend our thoughts." Yellow Corn entered the square and the two men sat down and smoked. Lame Badger said: "The bear scratches bark from the tree. Ashes fall on the cliff." Yellow Corn answered, "My brother, I do not understand your meaning." Lame Badger said, "This is what is sorrowful, that men do not understand what is clearly spoken." Yellow Corn said, "It is because you hide your meaning behind your words." Lame Badger said: "No, I do not hide it, I speak of it. To hide something a person remains silent, or if he cannot remain silent he puts his mouth to a crack in the rock and whispers his words there." Yellow Corn said, "I will ponder on what you have told me."

Lame Badger said, "Has Bold Fox arrived yet in your village?" Yellow Corn answered, "I do not know him." Lame Badger said: "He is our crier chief. I saw him coming on the lower trail. He has become a great singer. In the kiva his voice was always faint. His lips moved, but feeble sounds came out of his mouth. Now pain has made his voice strong. Ever since his daughter died he has been singing, going through

Ash Hill from one end to the other. People say that Sun Spirit reached down and touched him. He sings only one song, as if it were the breath of the world." Yellow Corn asked, "What is his song?" Lame Badger answered, "Why, you will hear it and then you will know." After a moment he said: "Lone Peak was not at Bow Height, but at Ash Hill. He crossed my line of meal when he arrived. He departed by another trail on top of the mesa."

Lame Badger's thoughts seemed to change. He said: "When I was a young man I ran in many kachina races. Once I ran against Hair Cutter Kachina, but I did not win, so he cut off my hair. It is not good to race against Hair Cutter. For me it does not make any difference anymore. I do not run, I drag my feet." Yellow Corn said, "You walk well, my brother." Lame Badger said, "My inner breath runs, my stalk hobbles." Yellow Corn said, "Only a person who dies in his youth does not hobble a little." Lame Badger said: "When I was trying to catch a wife, my feet were swift. I chased many rabbits for her, and she gave me piki in exchange. I was very fond of piki. She was my piki giver until she was kidnapped by sorcerers. She went to the spring for water. She disappeared. Only her jar was standing there. I went everywhere looking. I found her dead in a cave. That is where the sorcerers had taken her. Coyotes were barking up above on the hill. They were the evil ones, wearing their coyote skins. After that I had two more wives, but they were not piki givers." Yellow Corn said, "Life is a long journey on a crooked trail." Lame Badger suddenly stood up, saying: "That is all. I have no more time to listen. I hear feet approaching my line of meal." He departed, taking the path to Ash Hill.

Hardly had he gone when the people heard singing in the dance court. Soon the sound shifted to another place, moving among the houses. Then it came closer, and the Grey Fox saw a man approaching. He was singing and shaking a gourd rattle. At first they did not hear his words well, but when he arrived, walking slowly, they heard him sing, " 'Yellow Cliff killed me at my grinding stones. It was Lone Peak's arrow.' That is what Many Flowers says from her grave." The man turned into another part of the village, singing his song over and over again. He came to Black Cloud's house. He stood there singing until Black Cloud came out. Black Cloud was angry. He ordered Bold Fox to go away. Bold Fox did not listen. He went on singing. Black Cloud shouted at him: "My son had nothing to do with it! He was at Bow Height! Do not come here stirring dissension!" Bold Fox did not stop. Many people gathered in front of Black Cloud's house. Black Cloud struck Bold Fox several times with a stick. Finally Bold Fox resumed walking through the village, a crowd following him. He stood on the chief kiva singing. After that he went to another kiva and sang. When he had sung there, he departed from Yellow Cliff, taking the valley trail back to Ash Hill. Black Cloud closed himself up in his house. Yellow Cliff became peaceful again.

That night Yellow Corn told of Lame Badger's visit. He said: "His mind is not snarled. It is only that he speaks in riddles." Burning Tree asked, "What was the riddle?" Yellow Corn answered: "He said, 'The bear scratches bark from the tree. Ashes fall on the cliff.'" Burning Tree pondered a moment, then he said: "It is not so difficult. The bear is Standing Bear. The tree is Great Pine. The ashes are Ash Hill. The cliff is Yellow Cliff." Still Water said: "Now, what you say persuades me. Yet if that is the answer, the answer itself is a riddle. What is its meaning?" Burning Tree replied: "I cannot tell you. But it seems to prophesy. Let us watch things carefully, perhaps we will learn the meaning." Still Water said, "Perhaps it is merely something out of the past that confuses him." Yellow Corn said: "Lame Badger does not ramble. Sometimes he speaks as if he has nothing to say, but his words are like bits of turquoise hidden in the sand. If you do not grasp his meanings quickly they are hard to find. He said something else, 'It is not good to run against Hair Cutter Kachina.'" Still Water said, "I think he meant to say that Hair Cutter is their fastest runner, that we should not bet against him." "Yes," Yellow Corn said, "perhaps that was his message."

The appearance of Ash Hill's crier chief in Yellow Cliff and his accusation against Lone Peak troubled Great Pine. The Yellow Cliff chief met in his kiva with Grey Coyote and Twisted Spruce to discuss the event. He said: "Things have gone too far. Bold Fox stands in front of Black Cloud's house and sings that Many Flowers calls from her grave for vengeance. We can not let this matter go the way it is going. There are some who say Lone Peak was in Bow Height when the killing took place, but there are others who whisper that he was not there. We have had difficulties with Ash Hill in the past but we have been able to live with them. Now things are getting worse, and who can say where they will lead? Let us speak with Black Cloud. He does not want to acknowledge anything. Last night some young men from Ash Hill stood on the cliff above with slings and hurled stones down on our houses. I would go to my friend Standing Bear and complain, but what would he say? Only: 'A few stones? How does that compare with the death of our crier chief's daughter?' Unless Black Cloud does something to smooth matters over, our difficulties will grow." Grey Coyote said: "What can he do? He cannot bring Many Flowers back to life." But Twisted Spruce said, "He can acknowledge that this sad thing happened and offer Bold Fox presents as an indemnity." Grey Coyote said: "I know him. He will not do it. He believes his son was at Bow Height." Great Pine said: "Perhaps he does. But I have talked to people living in that village, and they say no one saw Lone Peak there. Black Cloud says he sent his son to Round Rock to look for a wife, yet he was very hurried about it. I think we must talk to him and persuade him to do something."

So they sent for Black Cloud, and when he arrived Great Pine said to him: "My brother, things are not good between us and Ash Hill. The killing of Many Flowers was a bad thing. We fear it is leading somewhere that we do not want to go. We believe you should go to see Bold Fox and talk to him as one father to another. Make him see that none of us now living in Yellow Cliff is responsible. We know that you sent Lone Peak away to keep him safe. Let him stay at Round Rock. But you yourself must do something. Black Cloud looks to you for redress. Speak with him. Tell him of your regrets. Show him that you had no part in the affair. Bring him something of worth as a token."

Black Cloud answered, saying: "Sorrow that old man surely has. Yet I know that Lone Peak did not kill his daughter. Because Bold Fox puts my son's name in his song, must I therefore give him presents?" Great Pine said: "It is not he alone who has mentioned your son's name. When Bold Fox sang in front of your house you struck him with a stick. Will you now go around striking everyone who speaks of Lone Peak? The matter no longer concerns you alone. It concerns all of us. If Bold Fox is not soothed, one thing will lead to another. It is only you who can do what is necessary. If you are not willing to do anything, then bring Lone Peak back from Round Rock to speak for himself." They talked this way far into the night.

When at last the sky became light, Black Cloud agreed to go to Ash Hill. He went to his house and gathered some objects of value. He took two blankets that he himself had woven. He took the bridal shawl that he had woven for his daughter, Glistening Shell. He prepared a bowl of meal and set prayer feathers in it. He took some sacred tobacco that had been brought from the Eastern River. And he carried all these things to Bold Fox's house.

Bold Fox was sitting on a blanket near the fireplace. His son, Red

Wing, sat in the shadows by the wall. Red Wing said: "Do not wait for him to speak. He will not say anything. His voice comes only when he sings. And what he sings, you do not want to hear it." When Black Cloud began to speak, Bold Fox turned to look into his face. Black Cloud said: "My brother, your daughter's death hurts my heart. You came to Yellow Cliff and accused my son. That also hurt my heart, for I believe my son did not do anything except to seek your daughter as his wife. Had she agreed, my son would now be living with you in your house. You would be looking on him as your own son. I sent Lone Peak away so that no more blood would run. I do not know if he will ever return to Yellow Cliff. If your heart says you must pursue him, even though he did not do anything, why, then you must pursue him to Round Rock or wherever he goes. I came to tell you what my own heart says. When you sang in front of my house I was blinded by suffering. Therefore I picked up a stick and struck you. You did not deserve it. Take my bow and strike me with it, then we will be equal on both sides and will not have to speak of it again."

He offered his bow to Bold Fox, but Bold Fox did not take it. He merely looked into Black Cloud's eyes. Red Wing said from the shadows: "He does not hear you. It is only the voice of Many Flowers that he hears." But Black Cloud persisted, saying: "My brother, try hard, listen to my words. I never wished for you to lose your daughter. I have never wished for you to have any misfortune whatever. Many times our people have been together as good cousins. You and I never had hard words for each other. Let there be no bitterness between us now. I cannot bring Many Flowers back. I can only bring these things to show you how my heart feels. I wove the blankets and the bridal shawl on my own loom. The shawl was for my own daughter, Glistening Shell. I have brought sacred tobacco and meal, and also these prayer feathers. Take them, so that we can go on living."

Bold Fox looked intently into Black Cloud's eyes, but he did not say anything. Red Wing said: "He does not hear you. Take up your presents and go away." Black Cloud meditated, then he said: "My heart understands. How can blankets compensate for a daughter? What do I have that would be enough? Only my own daughter, Glistening Shell. Therefore I offer her to you. Take her into your house. Be her father. Let your wife be her mother. Let the young man be her brother. In this way your family will become whole again, and it will be my house that is broken. Ash Hill and Yellow Cliff will be able to live on in harmony and balance. Yet, if you accept, will I then care anymore whether Ash Hill and Yellow Cliff live on? Now I have said everything."

Bold Fox still watched Black Cloud's face, but he did not speak. Instead, in a quiet voice he began to sing his song about what Many Flowers had said from her grave. Red Wing said: "Can you not understand? It is useless. It is not just a daughter he wants. It is Many Flowers. I also want Many Flowers. Can you give her? No, you cannot do anything. It is too late. What has to be done, only Hair Cutter Kachina can do it."

Black Cloud arose, picked up the presents he had brought and returned to Yellow Cliff wondering what it was that Hair Cutter Kachina could do. He went to the kiva and said to Great Pine: "I was there in Bold Fox's house. I spoke from my heart but he did not reply. I offered him blankets into which I had woven peace and serenity, but he did not want them. I offered the bridal shawl I had made for my own daughter, into which I had woven patterns of the whole universe. He did not want it. He looked into my eyes as if he were saying, 'More, I want something more,' but he did not speak any words. I said, 'My brother, I have nothing more to offer except my daughter, Glistening Shell. Take her into your house, make her your daughter. Then it will be my family, not yours, that will be broken.' He did not accept. He began to sing again. Red Wing spoke ominously, saying that only Hair Cutter Kachina could do what had to be done. So I departed from there. It was useless. As you can see, I have done everything possible, and now I am finished with this affair." Great Pine acknowledged that it was so.

Even while such questions occupied the minds of the Yellow Cliff leaders, things appeared to be going well for the Grey Fox Clan. Some of their houses were now finished, and the people were in a relaxed mood. Still Water's roof beams were not yet covered, but whenever other Grey Fox old ones came by he went in and out of his doorway, saying: "You see? Why do I have to climb ladders? I have learned from my older brother, the field rat." Everyone was busy trading leggings, moccasins and other things for corn, which was plentiful in Yellow Cliff, and the people were confident that they would not be hungry when winter came. Women made new pots to replace the ones they had had to leave behind at the canyon, and men repaired their stone tools and made new flint blades. Almost all of the Grey Fox families made friends among the Yellow Cliff people, and already Grey Coyote had invited some of the Grey Fox old ones to participate in some of the kiva councils.

One afternoon Black Cloud stood on the roof of his house, which was near the chief kiva, and called for the young men of the village to assemble. Young people hurried to the dance court to hear the announcement. Black Cloud called for silence and began his statement. "You young people, are you ready? Tomorrow the kachina racers arrive! They come to see if you are swift. They come to see if you are strong. They come to see if you have spirit and courage. So be here, young people, and accept the challenge. Run! Show them how fleet you are. Let them see the soles of your feet on the trail ahead of them. If you win, there will be gifts for you. If you lose, you will have to accept the penalty they demand. But either way you will bring a blessing to the village. So run, young people, that the sun will rise again, that the rain clouds will come, that the corn will grow, and that the entire earth will be fertile! Do not fear anything! Be here waiting for them tomorrow, let them know what kind of people we are in Yellow Cliff!"

As they left the dance court, Falling Snow asked Young Antelope: "How are the races run? What are the punishments for losing? I have never seen a kachina contest before." Young Antelope answered: "Have I ever seen it? Until we came to Yellow Cliff I never heard of it. I know only what people are saying. They say the runners will come from Ash Hill dressed as kachinas. They will challenge us, saying, 'To that butte out there and back,' or 'Around that cottonwood grove and return.' You accept, you start running. A kachina racer tries to catch you. If you get back to the chief kiva first, the people will give you gifts because of the honor you bring to the village. If your opponent catches you he will punish you. Every kachina gives his own form of punishment. He may whip you with a yucca branch, or blacken your face, or cut off some of your hair." Falling Snow said: "I would not like to have some of my hair cut off. I would rather receive the gifts." Elk Horn said, "I too prefer the gifts."

That night Elk Horn's family and Falling Snow's family were together in White Moccasin's house, and White Star demanded to hear a story about foot racing. Elk Horn's grandmother, Yellow Hair, laughed, saying she did not know any such tales. White Moccasin said: "I remember a story my grandfather told about the races between Tall Mound and Broken Rocks, two villages back there on the Eastern River where our people once lived. Have you heard it?"

They answered no, they had not heard it, and White Moccasin said: "Very well, I will tell you a little. If you do not believe it, it is only because I do not have the art of telling that my grandfather had, or perhaps because you are too sleepy to listen, for this story really happened, and the places were real and the people were real, and the proof of it is that Spider Grandmother had a part in it. Tall Mound was the larger village, and Broken Rocks the smaller. Tall Mound had many good runners, Broken Rocks only a few. The chief of Tall Mound came to Broken Rocks and said to the chief there: 'My people want to have a race with you. Let us agree on a day.' The chief of Broken Rocks said, 'We do not have many runners here to compete with yours.' But the chief of Tall Mound persisted. He said: 'Now, all the time our two villages have been living here we have not had any races. How can it go on forever like this?' The chief of Broken Rocks answered, 'Yes, but our people do not own many things that they could bet on the races.' The chief of Tall Mound answered: 'Let them bring what they have. It does not matter. Come on the fourth day after today.'

"The chief of Broken Rocks said, 'Very well, we will come,' but he was not happy about it. He called the young men to the kiva and told them: 'In four days we have to run races at Tall Mound. Let us prepare.' So the young men went running every day to toughen their sinews, and the old ones watched them, saying, 'Our young men are not ready, they will not be swift enough to win.' But on the third day the crier chief's daughter also went out to watch the young men training themselves. She said to them, 'I will run with you.' They said: 'What is this? A girl wants to run with us? Run then. We will go out to that piñon grove, and when we are coming back we will meet you going the other way.' They began running. Soon the girl was in front of them. When she reached the piñon grove they were behind her. Already she was coming back and they were not yet at the grove. She arrived at the place where they had started. She sat down to wait. After a while she went home to grind corn. Only then did the young men reach the place of starting.

"The old ones had watched the young people running, and they said, 'Let us keep this a secret. When we get to Tall Mound we will know what to do.' The day for the race came, and the whole village of Broken Rocks went to Tall Mound carrying the presents that would be wagered. The Tall Mound people said: 'Let us begin. Your best runner will race against our best runner.' They put down corn and leggings, saying, 'You do the same, and whoever wins will take it all.' The Broken Rocks people put down corn and leggings. The chief of Tall Mound pointed to a young man, saying: 'He is our best runner. Where is yours?' The chief of Broken Rocks answered, 'Why, our scouts came over here to watch your runners practice. They told us your young men are too slow, and that it would not be any pleasure to win against them. So they are not going to run. But our crier chief's daughter says she will run. So let us begin.' The chief of Tall Mound said, 'Our best runner, he will race against a girl?' The chief of Broken Rocks said, 'Yes, otherwise we will go home.' The people of Tall Mound said, 'Look, they have brought things to bet, so let us win these things from them and then we also will go home.'

"This is the way it was, and the girl ran a long race against the Tall Mound runner. When she returned to the starting place he was still running far behind. The people of Broken Rocks won many gifts, but the people of Tall Mound were angry. They said, 'It is some kind of a trick, let us race again.' So the girl raced against another Tall Mound young man. When she returned to the starting place he was still far behind. Again the people of Tall Mound had to give up gifts. The Broken Rocks people put their winnings in a pile. One after another the young men of Tall Mound raced against her, one after another they lost, until the people of Broken Rocks had a very large pile of winnings and the people of Tall Mound did not have anything left. The Tall Mound old ones went to one side and had a council. They said: 'Let us have one more race to get our wagers back. This time we will use medicine to make sure our runner arrives first.' Now, Spider Grandmother was at that place in the form of a spider, and she overheard everything. She went in her human form to the Broken Rocks people and told them what was being planned. She said: 'Whatever they want, agree to it. I will help your daughter win. I will make myself small again and sit on her shoulder.'

"So the Tall Mound chief said, 'Now we will have one more race.' The Broken Rocks chief said, 'Very well, but you have nothing to bet.' The Tall Mound chief said: 'Yes, we will bet all our unmarried young women. If your runner wins, you will take them all. If our runner wins, we will take everything that is in that pile of presents.' The Broken Rocks chief said: 'Very well. Then after that everyone will be done with betting and we will go home.' Spider Grandmother made herself small, and in the form of a spider she sat on the girl runner's shoulder. The Tall Mound people selected the son of their crier chief to run for them. The race began. Now they were still going out toward the piñon trees, and the girl runner was already ahead. The medicine men of Tall Mound performed sorcery and turned their runner into a swallow. This swallow flew very fast and took the lead. Spider Grandmother saw what happened. She called for rain, and rain fell heavily. The rain made the swallow's wings very heavy and it fluttered to the ground. But the ground was now slippery, and it was hard for the girl to run, so Spider Grandmother caused the sun to shine again. The girl was running swiftly, but the swallow also was flying again. Soon the swallow was leading. Spider Grandmother called for a hawk to come. The hawk came and knocked the swallow down. Now again the girl was in front and the swallow behind. As the girl rounded the piñon grove the swallow overtook her and was leading the race. Now Spider Grandmother caused a cloud to come down and envelop the swallow so that it could not see where it was going, and the girl went ahead. After a while the swallow came out of the cloud and began to overtake the girl runner. Now they were approaching the finish line. This time Spider Grandmother changed the swallow back into the form of the crier chief's son. He was very tired. He dragged his feet. He could not finish the race. So the girl runner of Broken Rocks came in first.

"The Broken Rocks people said, 'Now give us the presents you pledged.' The Tall Mound people said: 'Let us forget it. You take your things and we will take ours and go home.' But the Broken Rocks people demanded, 'Give us what you pledged.' So the Tall Mound people gave up all their unmarried daughters. When the people of Broken Rocks arrived in their village, Spider Grandmother transformed herself into her human shape and said: 'Because Tall Mound has many evil persons in it, what has happened will not be forgotten. They will come and make war on Broken Rocks. You people must abandon your village and go to some other place where they cannot find you.' They did what Spider Grandmother told them to do. They departed and went westward. Only the ruins of their village remained."

White Star said, "My grandmother, did it truly happen?"

White Moccasin answered: "Why should you doubt it, my grandson? Did I not say it was told by my grandfather? Everyone knows that ordinary people can sometimes be seen as bears or deer. Why not as a swallow?"

White Star said: "Yes, that part I believe. I believe that the boy runner turned into a swallow. I am asking only about the girl. Could she truly run faster than boys?"

White Moccasin laughed, saying, "What I told you is the way it was. If you doubt it, go ask my grandfather and he will confirm it." White Star seemed to be wondering where to find White Moccasin's grandfather, and everyone joined in the laughing.

The morning of the Yellow Cliff races came. Falling Snow, Elk Horn and Young Antelope went together where the people were gathering near the chief kiva. Half the village was already there. Women and girls were standing on the rooftops, and the men crowded along the edge of the dance court. Two blankets had been laid out near the kiva, and as the people arrived they went there and put down corn and other prizes that would be given to winners of the races. Everyone looked expectantly toward Ash Hill, watching for the kachina runners. Here and there a boy who hoped to win something pranced around to keep his muscles supple.

The sun rose higher. At last there was a hum of excitement as a line of running figures appeared in the distance. They came up the southern trail and burst into the dance court, where they ran wildly back and forth shouting and making strange sounds. Every runner was masked and costumed to represent a kachina. They were led by two Mudheads, whose bodies were painted brown. The Mudheads had brown calabashes for masks. Round lumps of mud attached to the calabashes gave them a comical appearance. There was much laughing at the antics of the Mudheads. They fell, stepped on each other, chased grasshoppers, scratched themselves indecorously, and picked invisible insects from their heads. One of the Mudheads mounted to the roof of the chief kiva and proclaimed, in the manner of the village crier chief: "Laugh, you people of Yellow Cliff! You are looking at yourselves as you were when you came from the lower world. Even the pretty maidens looked like this, except for something a bit different here and there. Now their lumps have slipped a little lower. I am sure some of you young men have noticed it. Well, we are here now, and we are ready to begin." He jumped from the kiva roof and chased his Mudhead companion across the dance court.

A Whipper kachina bounded up to the kiva roof, a threatening yucca whip in his hand. He announced: "You people of Yellow Cliff, we are here so that you can show us how fleet you are. Race with us. The races will be a blessing to the village. Yet be determined to win, for if I

catch you I will make you regret that you did not run faster!" He held
his whip up ominously to make his meaning clear. "We begin now
with the short races, from the chief kiva to the far end of the court,
around the shrine and back. Challenge if you dare!"

A racer kachina representing Dragonfly stepped forward, looking for
a challenger. A small boy ran out of the crowd, signalled, and began to
run with Dragonfly in pursuit. Dragonfly made a great display of running hard, but he held back to allow the boy to reach the kiva safely.
The crowd applauded the outcome, aware of Dragonfly's generosity. A
larger boy came forward and signalled. He began to run with Dragonfly
at his heels. This time Dragonfly did not hold back. He caught the boy
and smeared his face with soot that he carried in a buckskin bag attached to his belt. The Whipper kachina moved forward and waited for
a challenge. A young man came out of the crowd, signalled, and began
to run. He remained ahead of Whipper most of the way, but he was
caught just as he was getting to the area of sanctuary. Whipper struck
him across the back four times with his yucca whip. Then Elk Horn
went out and challenged Whipper. Elk Horn was fleet, and Whipper
could not catch him. When he arrived back at the chief kiva, people
gave him corn for his prize. After that, Rabbit Hunter kachina raced.
He caught his opponent and struck him with his throwing-stick.

When Hair Cutter Kachina took his position to await a challenge
there were excited calls from the crowd, for Hair Cutter's punishments
were more lasting than some of the others. He was challenged, and
they began running. Hair Cutter moved swiftly and caught his opponent, and with his sharp flint knife he cut off a handful of the young
man's hair and tucked it into his belt. Falling Snow also raced Hair
Cutter. He finished safely and received his prize. The short races went
on until the sun was nearly overhead. Women brought food to the
visiting runners. Whipper then stood on the kiva roof and called out,
"Well, we have been practicing. Now bring out your best runners. We
will go from here to that small hill where the mesa juts out to a point.
We will run around the hill and return to the dance court. To win this
race a person must be strong as well as swift. So run, you young men of
Yellow Cliff, for when we catch you we will not hesitate to lay on the
punishment. Make your strides long, make your steps sure, for now the
real running begins."

Whipper came down from the kiva roof to await a challenge. A
young man stepped forward, saying, "Were you a diving hawk,
Whipper, you would starve before catching me!" They ran down the

eastern trail, fast yet reserving something for the return. They reached the point of the mesa and turned back. The Yellow Cliff youth was in front, but the racer kachina was close behind. The distance between them diminished. Just as they reached the edge of the village, Whipper caught his opponent and held him firmly until they reached the dance court, where he whipped the young man vigorously with his yucca whip. The next kachina runner received a challenge from Falling Snow. As they began, he heard Young Antelope call out, "Run well, younger brother!" It was the kind of running Falling Snow liked best, testing speed, strength and endurance. He heard the racer kachina behind him and lengthened his stride. The distance between them remained the same. After a while the racer kachina was breathing hard, but he stayed with Falling Snow. As they came to the point of the mesa the kachina said, "Ah, but you are a runner!" And Falling Snow answered, "Cousin, now the running is just beginning." He maintained his stride but moved his legs faster, and the distance between them increased. He, also, was breathing hard, but he felt his legs moving smoothly. As they approached the village Falling Snow no longer heard the footsteps of his opponent. When he reached the dance court he turned and saw the racer kachina walking dejectedly. There were calls of praise for Falling Snow from the rooftops, and someone said, "Look, he makes the kachina's heart cry!" People pressed gifts of corn into Falling Snow's arms.

There were more races to the point of the mesa, then Hair Cutter stood on the chief kiva and scanned the rooftops where the women and girls were standing. He looked intently at those who occupied Black Cloud's roof. He said, "Now we will truly see a race to remember. Let Yellow Cliff give me a runner to pursue. We will go to that place in the valley where a rock stands up like the point of a lance." He descended from the kiva roof and stood in a starting position. This time it was Young Antelope who stepped forward. He said, "Cutter of Hair, let us begin." The two runners went swiftly out of the dance court and down the south trail. Because the valley was lower than the village, spectators on the rooftops could follow the progress of the runners, and they called out from time to time, "Young Antelope remains ahead. . .! They have reached the rock pointing up like a lance. . .! Now they are coming back. . .! Young Antelope seems to be slowing. . .! They are coming up the south trail. . .!" And when the runners were halfway up the trail, people called out, "Ah! Hair Cutter has caught him!" A few moments later the racers came walking into the dance court, Hair Cutter holding Young Antelope's arm firmly.

They approached the chief kiva and stood quietly. Everyone awaited the cutting of Young Antelope's hair. Hair Cutter took out his long flint blade deliberately. Then, suddenly, he went running toward Black Cloud's house and mounted the ladder. People wondered what antics the racer kachinas still had in store for them. Hair Cutter reached the roof. He seized Black Cloud's daughter, Glistening Shell, by the arm and threw her down. The women and girls on the roof were surprised, thinking Hair Cutter was going to take some of Glistening Shell's hair. Instead, he cut off her head. He ran to the edge of the roof holding her head up for all to see. He took off his mask so that people could recognize him. He was Red Wing, Bold Fox's son. Now he turned and jumped to the next roof. Running with the head in one hand and his mask in the other, he went from roof to roof and leaped to the ground on the far side of the houses.

Yellow Cliff was in turmoil. Women were screaming and jumping from the roofs into the court. Some men went over the rooftops in pursuit of Red Wing. Others went to their houses for weapons. Soon a large party was running after Red Wing toward the wall of the cliff. He bounded up the steps that had been carved in the cliffside. The pursuers followed. When Red Wing reached the top he paused and held the head up so it could be seen by the people down below, then he went racing across the mesa top toward Ash Hill. He arrived at the place where a trail descended to his village. There he set the kachina mask on a tall stone, and after that he went on. His pursuers reached the place where the mask had been placed, and there they stopped. Elk Horn asked, "Why are we stopping here?" And someone answered, "We cannot go beyond where the mask is sitting." Elk Horn asked, "Is it medicine?" And the person answered: "No, we do not fear the mask, but it marks a boundary. If we go past this place with our weapons the Ash Hill people will come out and make war. We are not looking for war with Ash Hill. That is something that must be decided in council. We only want to kill Red Wing. We have not been able to do it. Now we have to go back and see what the old ones are saying." Someone said, "First let us shoot arrows down the trail so that Ash Hill knows we are angry."

They shot some arrows down the trail, and then they returned to Yellow Cliff. One of the pursuers said to Great Pine: "We went as fast as we could, but Red Wing left his mask on a rock at the top of the village trail. We halted there, saying, 'It is only the old ones who should tell us to invade Ash Hill.' We shot arrows down the trail so the Ash Hill people would know we have a claim against Red Wing. Then we returned." Great Pine said: "Yes, it was good that you turned away. We need time to ponder what has happened."

The body of Glistening Shell was buried the next day, and when that was done Great Pine went to Ash Hill to speak with Standing Bear. The two men descended into the kiva and smoked. Standing Bear said: "My brother, the killing of Black Cloud's daughter hurts my heart." Great Pine replied: "My brother, I do not question it. But my people are angry now. Your racer kachinas came into our village saying the contest would be a blessing for us, then one of our daughters was slain." Standing Bear said: "Yes, the evil is apparent. Yet it began in Yellow Cliff, came to Ash Hill, and returned to Yellow Cliff. If one of your sons had not killed one of our daughters, what happened at the races would not have occurred. Once an evil force has been launched there is no telling what it will do before it has exhausted itself." Great Pine said: "I do not say who is right and who is wrong. I say only that something must be done. We are the fathers of our villages. We are the ones who must teach the meaning of harmony and good living." Standing Bear said: "Yes, your words are good. Before the races took place there was anger and resentment in Ash Hill because of what Lone Peak did to Many Flowers. Now, since Red Wing killed Glistening Shell, there is not anger anymore. The people say everything has been made equal. Both our crier chiefs have lost their daughters. Our people say let the matter end here."

Great Pine said: "My brother, that is what I want, let it end here. But things are not in balance. The anger bounces from one village to another, so that when we have sorrow in Yellow Cliff your people are happy, and when you have sorrow in Ash Hill our people are contented. One act of reprisal only prompts another act of reprisal. In this way we nourish evil and give it new strength. I tried to stop things. I sent Black Cloud to make peace with Bold Fox. Black Cloud offered him blankets and a wedding shawl into which had been woven the patterns of the universe. He offered his own daughter to replace the one Bold Fox had lost. Bold Fox rejected everything. Had he accepted, the evil would have been brought to a halt, it would have withered and died. We have one more chance. Send Bold Fox to speak with Black Cloud. Let them exchange presents. Let them be in harmony, two men who have lost equally." Standing Bear said: "My brother, if this can be done I will be glad. I will talk to Bold Fox about it, but will he hear anything? For his mind has been touched by a spirit and he does not seem to know one person from another. I will do what I can, but if I cannot move him, then you yourself must find a way of calming the anger in Yellow Cliff."

Great Pine answered: "Good. That is where we begin. Yet there is something more. I will tell my children, 'Here the evil force must wither and die.' They will say, 'Yes, let it come to an end. But where is Glistening Shell's head, so that it may be buried with her body?' My brother, give us back Glistening Shell's head. Only if this is done will my people listen." Standing Bear said: "The head, I myself did not see it. I know only that Red Wing ran through the village holding it by the hair. He brought it to his house to show to Bold Fox, then he came out with it and ran through the village again. People say he went to the top of the mesa with it, where the shrine to Death Old Man stands. From there he went somewhere, still running as if the races in Yellow Cliff had not ended. When he returned in the night he no longer had the head in his hand. Perhaps he buried it. Perhaps he flung it away. No one knows. I will speak with Red Wing. We will try to find the head so that we can return it." Great Pine said, "That is good." After that he returned to Yellow Cliff.

The following night a group of Yellow Cliff youths gathered on top of the mesa and went to the place from which they could see Ash Hill directly below. They threw many stones down on the village and shot some burning arrows as well. The night after that, Ash Hill youths came to the mesa edge above Yellow Cliff, and they also threw down stones and shot burning arrows. The old ones on both sides considered what might be done to cool tempers. People in Yellow Cliff were saying: "Over there in Ash Hill they claim that the village is innocent of Red Wing's wrongdoing. If so, let them return Glistening Shell's head. When will they do it?" People in Ash Hill were saying: "When Many Flowers was killed in her grinding room, did we then hear any cries of anguish from Yellow Cliff? Now they are complaining about a missing head." In Yellow Cliff some said: "Their crier chief's daughter was killed, our crier chief's daughter was killed, therefore the crimes are even and the matter should come to an end." But others said: "No, it is not the same. Ash Hill's racer kachinas came as friends promising a blessing. While we sought harmony they were planning a bad deed. The circumstances were not the same. We should not have anything more to do with those people."

Among the young men who had pursued Red Wing without catching him there was frustration. Some of them urged that they should ambush Red Wing on the trail or in the fields and kill him. Most people in both villages went calmly about their daily affairs, but an invisible cloud of uneasiness and uncertainty hung over the Mesa of Flowers.

In their houses on the western slope, the Grey Fox old ones had a special concern. Still Water said: "Is this what we journeyed so far to find? It was told to us that at the Mesa of Flowers our flight from evil would be over. We arrived, we built our houses, then we discovered how things truly are. Will we ever escape from quarreling? I do not think so. Dissension came out of the underworld with us and now it is to be found everywhere. This is the place that was prophesied to us. Now that we have found evil living here, what can we do? We can not run away anymore. We must contend against it the best way we can. When the two Warriors undertook to make the land safe for humans, they went out and killed the giants, the monsters and other evil things. They killed things that were evil, but evil itself they could not kill. How can we do what the Warriors could not do? We must stand where we are and not think of any more journeys. Let the cliffs fall, let fire scourge the land, we must remain where we are and contend with contamination, for wherever people may go, evil precedes them or follows them."

Flowing Spring said: "What you say, I believe it. Yet how do we contend? One cannot pierce evil with an arrow, or destroy dissension by throwing it from a cliff. Are the young men of Yellow Cliff contending when they rain stones on Ash Hill in the night? No, they are merely soaring in the air on an evil wind. Prayers, you say? How many prayer feathers will it take to turn away the wind of evil?"

Yellow Corn spoke then, saying, "My brothers, we once lived on different levels inside the earth, and then we were born into this world. Perhaps after our long travels we have arrived at a new level of experience. Perhaps we are now more human than we were when we departed from our first village, Red Cliff. Perhaps that was the purpose of our many journeys, who can say? Now we are part of a large village at the Mesa of Flowers. Our lives have been blended with the lives of other clans. Once we were the whole of something small, while now we are a small part of something big. Things that happen in Yellow Cliff today are like the tail of a lizard that passed through the village before we arrived, just as what is happening now will leave its mark on tomorrow. We cannot control everything, yet we must live with everything. We cannot make other people strive, but we ourselves can strive for what is good. As to what things are good, we already know them: Recognition of all living creatures as our brothers and sisters. Honor to the old. Hospitality to the stranger. Veneration for Father Sun and Mother Earth. Balance. Harmony with rivers, trees, mountains and men. If there are yet more such things we will learn what they are. In pursuing harmony we are contending with dissension and evil. Is there any other way to go?''

As Flowing Spring has said, people in the villages were soaring on an evil wind, and one harsh act followed another. Some young men from Yellow Cliff who had participated in the kachina races crept into Ash Hill in the dark of night and threw brush and flaming torches into Bold Fox's house. People came quickly to put the fire out. They found Bold Fox sitting quietly on his blanket looking at the flames. Several nights later young men came to Yellow Cliff from Ash Hill on a reprisal raid. They drew up the ladder from the chief kiva to trap whoever might be sleeping there, then they threw down burning brush and hot peppers, shouted insults, and quickly disappeared into the darkness. No one was in the kiva at the time, but the fire scorched the whitewashed walls and left acrid fumes that lingered for a long while. The next day some Ash Hill people killed a Yellow Cliff dog that had wandered into the village. A few days after that a small group of Yellow Cliff youths caught an Ash Hill woman out in the valley and forced her to submit to them. One thing followed another without any end.

Great Pine went again to Ash Hill to see Standing Bear. He said: "My brother, I waited for you to come with words that would help our villages. You did not come, that is why I am here." Standing Bear answered: "Yes, things are very bad. The last time you and I spoke together I listened carefully to your words. I went to Bold Fox, I sat with him in his house. I said: 'Only you can prevent things from getting worse. I know that you yourself had nothing to do with Glistening Shell's death. You are a father who has lost a daughter and Black Cloud is a father who has lost a daughter. Let us go to Yellow Cliff and speak with him. What has happened to you and to him has made you brothers.' Bold Fox looked into my eyes, but he understood nothing. He did not know me."

Great Pine said: "Yes, but there was another thing. Where is Glistening Shell's head?" White Bear answered: "We did much searching on the mesa and in the ravines, but we did not find it. Red Wing would not tell anyone what he had done with the head. I did what was possible. I sent Red Wing to Reed Spring and told him to remain there. Thus there will not be any expeditions from Yellow Cliff to kill him. And you, my brother, what are you doing to discourage those who are looking for trouble? What are you going to do to punish the young men who took our daughter by force out in the valley? I, also, thought that my brother Great Pine would come to say he was doing something. But you did not have anything to tell me."

Great Pine replied: "That is true, I could not tell you anything because I have not found out who the persons were. Are we not like two men throwing sticks at rabbits in the dark? I speak to my children sharply, I scold them, but like Bold Fox they seem unable to understand my words. How can our villages go on this way?"

When they parted, the two chiefs felt discouragement in their hearts.

The days were becoming shorter, and thoughts in both villages were turning to the cold months that lay ahead. The men hunted so that dried meat could be put away for the winter, while the women searched for roots or chinked up cracks in the house walls to make their rooms weathertight. Children gathered firewood and stacked it in front of the houses or on the roofs. In Yellow Cliff the kiva societies prepared for a New Fire Ceremony to set into motion the forces of germination for the coming year. In Ash Hill, also, the kiva societies were preparing for the ceremony, which was to take place on a different day from the one designated in Yellow Cliff. But now that feelings between the villages were tense, Ash Hill did not invite the people of Yellow Cliff to come to its rituals, and Yellow Cliff, likewise, did not invite the people of Ash Hill. On the day that the ceremony began in Ash Hill, a brush fire swept across the top of the mesa above that village, disrupting the ritual activities. Two days later, as the New Fire Ceremony was beginning in Yellow Cliff, some heavy boulders were dislodged at the top of the cliff stairway. They did not strike any of the Yellow Cliff houses, but they severely damaged the retaining wall of the spring and destroyed a shrine at the base of the cliff. After that, if people of the two villages encountered one another while foraging for wood, one group or the other would turn away and no greetings would be exchanged.

One morning Lame Badger appeared in Yellow Cliff wearing his One Horn headdress. He went first to Yellow Corn's house, and when Yellow Corn greeted him he said, "Interrogate me so that I can cross the line." Yellow Corn said, "My brother, who are you and where do you come from?" Lame Badger replied, "I am the one that comes." Yellow Corn said, "Enter then, and be welcome." Lame Badger said, "No, no, first you must ask me if I am worthy." So Yellow Corn asked, "What have you done that is good in this world?" Lame Badger said: "I have done a little of everything that is good. I have directed the people to come or not to come, according to their character. I have told them to go or not to go. I have guarded the kivas from intruders. I have sent the spirit out of my body to supplicate for rain when the people needed it. I have tended my corn faithfully." Yellow Corn answered: "My brother, that is good. Now enter my house."

Lame Badger said, "No, no, you must ask me if I committed any wrong actions." Yellow Corn replied, "My brother, I do not think you could do a bad deed." Lame Badger said: "Why, everyone commits bad deeds, though he sometimes calls them good deeds. When I was a young boy I was to be initiated so that I could be taken into the Horn Fraternity. I heard that when a boy is initiated the kachinas whip him. So at night I crept into the kiva and stole all the whips. Therefore, they could not find any whips to whip me with, and they only scolded me." Yellow Corn smiled, saying, "My brother, that was long ago when you were a small boy." Lame Badger said: "Yes, small boys do not know how to perform truly bad deeds. When I was older I learned. Well, when are you going to judge me? Do I go to the Village of the Dead or to the fiery pit?" Yellow Corn answered: "I am not the one who stands on that trail making such decisions. Enter my house." Lame Badger said impatiently, "First you must wipe out the line of meal." Yellow Corn scraped his foot through the dust. He said, "The line is wiped out." Then Lame Badger entered. He took the One Horn headdress off and put it on the ground. The two men smoked.

After a while Lame Badger said: "It was Death Old Man who lighted the grass fire on the mesa above our village. I saw him walking there, the flames coming from his mouth. He breathed on the grass to make it burn. After that he loosened the boulders above Yellow Cliff and caused them to fall." Yellow Corn answered, "My brother, I hear you." Lame Badger said: "He is still there, walking on the mesa where he lived before people came. Perhaps now he wants all the land back. You cannot reason with Death Old Man. If you want him to touch you he laughs and goes away, but if you run from him he pursues you. He is not reasonable. Also, he does not understand the difference between good and evil. When I spoke with him he said, 'Good and evil, they are the same, I do not distinguish one from the other.' I said: 'Then you yourself are evil, old man. If you do not know good when you see it, you must be evil.' He said: 'Those things do not concern me. Evil and good are things for you humans to worry about. Perhaps you have nothing better to do.' I said, 'Because I am old do you imagine I do not know anything?' I said: 'You, old man, you are always hungry. You are like a person with a handful of sweet corn ears, first eating one, then another. You are afraid that the ears will get away from you.' He said, 'The ears are mine.' I said, 'Yes, you claim all the corn, but you do not know a good ear from an evil ear.' He said, 'Yes, it does not make any difference.' You see how Death Old Man is." Yellow Corn said: "Yes, I see how he is. But was it truly he, not men, who fired the grass and caused the boulders to come down?" Lame Badger answered: "Have I grown old and become wise for nothing? Why do you doubt my words? Is it because I hobble and drag my feet? If you cannot crack the shell off my words to see what is inside, then I am wasting my time. People are waiting for me in Ash Hill. They must be told which way to go, to the Land of the Dead or the fiery pit." He replaced his One Horn headdress and departed from Yellow Corn's house.

It was the season for gathering pine nuts, and the women of Yellow Cliff went out searching in small groups. They picked the nuts from the ground in piñon groves and probed into burrows where chipmunks had already stored seeds for the winter. On one of these nut-gathering days, two young girls came running to the village saying that a band of Ash Hill men with bows in their hands had captured two old women in the valley and were threatening them. Young men who were in the village at the time took weapons from their houses and went into the valley where the women had last been seen. Falling Snow went with his bow and Young Antelope carried a lance. The Yellow Cliff party arrived at a place called Spider Mound, and there they saw a circle of Ash Hill warriors, and in the center of the circle were Yellow Hair and White Moccasin with their baskets. The Ash Hill men were shouting and gesturing at the old women. When they saw the Yellow Cliff men coming, they turned and prepared to fight.

The Yellow Cliff spokesman said: "What! Are you Ash Hill warriors now battling old women?" The Ash Hill men shouted back, "No, not just old women, but sorcerers!" Falling Snow called out, "They are not sorcerers, they are my grandmothers!" An Ash Hill man responded: "A grandmother can be a sorcerer! Two babies died in our village last night. It was told to us that the sorcerers were out here gathering pine nuts. We found the old women whispering together and preparing bad medicine. It is clear that they are the ones." The Yellow Cliff leader said: "They are not witches. Leave them alone." In response, some of the Ash Hill men shot arrows. The Yellow Cliff men also shot arrows. The Ash Hill men fell back, but one of them struck Yellow Hair with the shaft of his lance as he passed her. Both sides exchanged arrows again, then the Ash Hill men retreated toward their village. Falling Snow carried Yellow Hair back to Elk Horn's house and gave her to Buffalo Girl to take care of. Great Pine met in his kiva with the old ones. He said: "It seems that now we have gone from one place to another without any way to get back to where we began. What brought us here I do not know, merely one thing following another thing. How can we be friends with Ash Hill anymore?"

Grey Coyote said: "It is an old story. The Bear Clan resents us. It hates the Coyote Clan and the Fire Clan because it was we who were given the secret of fire, and because Death Old Man is our sponsor. When the Bear Clan arrived here Death Old Man told them: 'I am waiting for the Fire Clan to arrive, but they are long in coming. Therefore, use the land until the Fire Clan appears.' When we came, they did not say, 'Death Old Man, let us keep the land in trust for you,' they said, 'This is our land, it was given to us to hold forever.' Because they lied they do not want us here in Yellow Cliff. Their lie chokes them. They want us to leave. We will not leave. Let the Bear Clan leave."

Twisted Spruce said to the Council: "What Grey Coyote says is true. Let the Bear Clan and all of its relatives leave, for one village or the other must go. Now they are beating old women and shooting arrows. We also will shoot arrows." Great Pine said, "Let us not yet release the bowstrings. For what has been happening, perhaps only a few are responsible. Also, let us not say to ourselves that persons in Yellow Cliff have not done anything at all to make Ash Hill angry. What has been happening, I know that White Bear did not want it. Let us have a council with him. Let us explore everything. Let us try to keep things from getting worse."

Grey Coyote said: "Have we not already spoken with the Ash Hill old ones many times? They cry, saying, 'Our hearts are sore,' but they do not do anything. Where is Glistening Shell's head? They keep it there somewhere as a trophy. When we had the races we sought blessings for the village. They deprived us of the blessings and made the races into an evil encounter. They tried to kill our old ones in the kiva. They rolled boulders down on us from the cliff. They beat our old

233

women and call them sorcerers. Now, if it is only a few bad persons who are doing such things, why cannot Standing Bear stop them? If he cannot stop them he should not be chief. Our village has suffered enough from their actions. It is time for us to behave with courage." When the council ended, the men of Yellow Cliff began to repair their bows and make new flint points.

That evening Great Pine came to Yellow Corn's house. He said: "Now it is up to you and me to find harmony with Standing Bear if we can. The Coyote and Fire clans are too angry, they are ready to fight. Let us go to Ash Hill together. You are a small clan. You are new in Yellow Cliff. Standing Bear trusts you. I have seen you talking with Lame Badger as with an old friend. Standing Bear will understand that you speak from your heart."

So they went together to Ash Hill and met with White Bear in his kiva. They smoked. Then Great Pine said: "My brother, it has come to shooting arrows and beating women. Where are we going? The evil things are getting worse. Will we have to fight? The Coyote Clan and the Fire Clan say there is nothing more for us to talk about. I have tried to keep them in a peaceful path. I have urged you to discipline your people. Perhaps my words were too feeble. You and I are the fathers of our villages. Can we not find a solution?" White Bear said: "Here also the people are angry. They too say there is nothing more to discuss." Great Pine said: "Let us hear what Yellow Corn has to say. Perhaps he can lead us to a better trail."

Standing Bear's eyes turned toward Yellow Corn, who said: "I do not have any wise words. I cannot say whether Ash Hill or Yellow Cliff is more at fault. Does one village have two baskets full of grievances and the other four? It helps nothing to measure out the offenses. Surely the two murdered girls have paid for everything. Both of you are men of good heart. You both want harmony. It is for you to say what must be done. I can only speak of the Grey Fox Clan, of where we came from and what we were looking for. Long ago it was told to us that we would come to the Mesa of Flowers. It was said that our life would be hard and our journey long but that the Mesa of Flowers would be something truly worthwhile. Our grandfathers who began the journey are gone. Our fathers who continued the journey, they also are gone. We who are still living have spent our entire lives looking for the Mesa of Flowers, stopping here and there along the way to rest and grow corn. We made friends on the trail and left them behind. Again and again we saw the signs pointing to the Mesa of Flowers.

Again and again we were told that here we would find the world in balance. We arrived. We looked around us.

"We said to one another, 'It is true, the Mesa of Flowers is a beautiful place.' We built our houses. After that we saw that an evil wind was blowing over the villages. We asked ourselves, 'Can this truly be the Mesa of Flowers, or are we back once more in our original village that was destroyed by dissension?' If people cannot find harmony here, where will they find it? If the old ones cannot show the people what is right and what is wrong, who can show them? The Mesa of Flowers is a place to remain in forever. Do not let these villages become ruins. Do not let the houses turn into ghost houses. That is all. I am finished."

Standing Bear said: "My brother, my heart hears you. Yet can I hold back a river with my hands? The water flows between my fingers. If there is medicine to stop what is happening, I do not have it. I admonish my children, but they admonish me, their father, saying, 'You are not treating us well, you want to prevent us from doing what is honorable. Because Yellow Cliff abuses us, we abuse Yellow Cliff. Was it not a Yellow Cliff person who began everything?' This is the way they speak to me. I admonish them again, saying, 'What Lone Peak gave to us, Red Wing gave back to Yellow Cliff. Why did we not stop there and let it rest?' They say: 'You, our father, are not telling us anything good. If you cannot tell us something good, do not tell us anything.' This is the way it is in Ash Hill."

He turned to Great Pine. He said, "Our trail has been covered by blowing sand and I can no longer see any landmarks. Your people do not listen to you, my people disparage my words. So how will it be? Shall we call on the kachinas to send us judgment by fire? Shall we ask for a flood to destroy every house and every living thing? No, we love our children too much. Yet if this is not to be, I see only one other way. Either your people or mine must abandon their homes and find some other place to live. If we do this, one village will become a place of ghosts. If we fight, both villages will become ruins." Great Pine answered, "I hear your words, my brother. I accept. Let one of our villages depart from here. But which of us is to leave?"

Standing Bear said, "Why, let us gamble for it. Whoever wins will stay, and whoever loses will go."

Great Pine said, "Have we truly arrived at this point of the trail?"

Standing Bear answered, "Yes, that is where we are standing."

Great Pine and Yellow Corn returned to Yellow Cliff. Great Pine said, "We will bring the affair to the council. As Standing Bear sees it,

I also see it. There is no way back to the beginning. We can only go on from here." When they arrived at the kiva, someone came to tell them that Yellow Hair, Elk Horn's grandmother, had died from the lance blow she had received while hunting pine nuts. Great Pine assembled the council. He said: "You see how it is with us. The monster of evil is smothering us. In Ash Hill it is the same. Standing Bear cannot do anything. He says, 'Shall we burn our villages to the ground and destroy them both? Or will one of us depart from here forever? Let us gamble to decide who will go and who will stay.' I see it the way he sees it. Once fighting has started it will never end. Hunters will be killed by other hunters' arrows. Women will be seized and abused at the springs. Stones will rain down on the villages from above. People will be ambushed in the fields. Let us debate the matter now and come to a decision."

So the council sat throughout the night discussing what should be done. Some said: "Let us proceed slowly. Let us live day by day. Perhaps the anger will cool." Others said, "We already know how it is. We do not have to wait for the sun to set to know that it has risen. Let us fight Ash Hill. Let us defeat them, then they will stop making trouble." But some looked back on the histories of their clans and said: "It has happened before that a village moved from one place to another to avoid violence. The mesa is endless. A new village can be built elsewhere. Therefore let us play the gambling game with Ash Hill to determine who goes and who stays." When the first light appeared in the east, no decision had been made, and the men of the council went to their homes to sleep.

Then, just as the sun was appearing over Bow Height, people began to call out that a man was standing up above on the edge of the cliff motioning with his arms and talking to them. They could not recognize him or make out what he was saying. Men, women and children came from their houses and stood on their rooftops. And when most of the people were outside looking upward, the person on the cliff threw something down and quickly climbed out of view. The falling object landed near the spring at the base of the mesa wall, and everyone ran to see what it was. They came to the place and saw the object lying there. It was Glistening Shell's head.

The people fell silent. Black Cloud went forward, picked up the head and carried it away without saying anything. Anger surged through the village that the head had not been carried back with respect, but thrown with contempt from the mesa top. After a while people began to say: "Those Ash Hill people are no good. Why are we living here?"

The old ones who had sat up all night went again into the kiva. They debated again, and this time they concluded that one village or the other would have to go away and leave its ghost houses behind. Great Pine sent a message to Standing Bear saying that the people of Yellow Cliff were ready for a contest to see which of the two villages would be abandoned. He proposed that the elders of each side should come to a certain mound the following day, bringing with them a young boy dressed in the manner of a kachina. And Standing Bear sent a return message to Great Pine saying it would be done.

The next morning people from the two villages began to gather near the mound. Those from Ash Hill remained a little to the west of the mound, and those from Yellow Cliff stayed somewhat to the east. There were relatives and friends on both sides, but they did not call out any greetings to one another. Among the old ones, the delegation from Ash Hill arrived first, and they had with them a young boy dressed as a Morning Kachina. When the old ones from Yellow Cliff arrived they had with them a young boy dressed as a Snow Kachina. Great Pine addressed Standing Bear, saying, "My brother." And Standing Bear answered, saying, "My brother." Great Pine said: "What we are about to do now will be done in peace. Let no one point a lance or bend a bow. Let us all be known as people who seek harmony in the world. Let the kachinas be our witnesses." Standing Bear said, "Yes, let it be that way." Great Pine said: "The contest will be the throwing of the split reeds. Our kachina boys will do the playing. Thus no one will ever be able to say that Yellow Cliff or Ash Hill played the game falsely. And in years to come people will not say the old ones did this and that, for they will be reminded that the playing was done by children and judged fairly by the kachinas. The players will throw until both have scored, and whichever side has the most points will win the contest." Standing Bear said, "Yes, it is agreed."

Standing Bear instructed the Morning Kachina how to hold the reeds and drop them. Morning Kachina dropped the reeds, and two of them lay with their painted sides showing, and one with the plain side showing. He did not score anything and passed the reeds to Snow Kachina. Snow Kachina dropped the reeds. All three of them lay with their plain sides showing, and Yellow Cliff had scored two points. He dropped them again, and this time they lay with one plain side showing and two painted sides showing, so he passed the reeds back to Morning Kachina. When Morning Kachina dropped the reeds they all fell with their painted sides up, giving Ash Hill three points. Ash Hill had won.

Standing Bear said, "My brother, it is done." Great Pine answered: "Yes, it is done. Ash Hill will stay. Yellow Cliff will depart. Let it be inscribed on this rock, so that other people who may come this way will know that our troubles were resolved without war." Standing Bear said, "It will be inscribed."

The people returned to their villages. In Ash Hill some were saying, "Well, now at last we will be rid of those Coyote and Fire Clan troublemakers." Yet not everyone was happy about it because they had sons, daughters and grandchildren living in Yellow Cliff. In Yellow Cliff people were saying, "The Bear Clan over there in Ash Hill wanted everything. They claimed everything for themselves. They attended our ceremonies, they stole our rituals and carried them back to their kivas. The kachina masks we brought with us, now the same masks are in Ash Hill. They even claim our springs, saying, 'Do not forget that these springs were given to the Bear Clan by Death Old Man.' It is good that we are leaving."

The men who belonged to the ritual fraternities spent much time in the kivas packing the paraphernalia that they wanted to take with them, and whatever had to be left behind they burned in the kiva fireplaces. In every house the people sorted out their belongings and filled their carrying baskets. Each clan discussed where it would go and who its travelling companions would be. Part of the Coyote Clan thought its people should go to Round Rock and Reed Spring in the west. Another part believed the people ought to return to the Eastern River. There were also those who said: "We will leave the village because we lost the reed throwing game. But why should we let Ash Hill drive us out of the country altogether? Let us build a new settlement somewhere along the mesa."

The Grey Fox People were downcast. They were saying, "What is the meaning of all this? We have just arrived at the Mesa of Flowers. We have just finished building our houses. We are making ourselves secure for the winter. This is the place to which we were told to come. Why do we now have to leave?" Yellow Corn told them: "My children, have you never watched eagles as they begin to make their nests against the wall of a cliff? They begin in one place, and if they see it is not right for them they look for another ledge. When they find the place that is right, there they make their nests and there they remain, on the cliff that they have chosen. We must leave Yellow Cliff because it is becoming a ghost village and no one can go on living here. But we will not make another long journey because this mesa was given to us as a destination. Do you see that small butte standing out there in the south? Let us go to that place and build for the last time. From there we will always see the Mesa of Flowers in front of us. Children will be born and we will thrive if we live by what we know to be good. Other villages will look toward our butte and say: 'That is where the Grey Fox are living. Let us be their friends. Let our sons marry their daughters, and let our daughters marry their sons.' " For two days the Grey Fox old ones sat in Yellow Corn's house and talked about where they would go, and at last they agreed that they would build their new village in the valley on the rising ground below the butte.

On the morning of the fourth day the people of Yellow Cliff started down the trails that fed into the valley. They carried their blankets, their tools, their weapons, their firebows and baskets full of shelled corn. As more and more families departed, the lines of people on the trails grew longer and longer. By the time the sun was halfway to the crest of the sky there was one living line extending as far as the eastern point of the mesa, and another stretching out toward the southern horizon. When the Coyote Clan families reached the valley, some of them turned westward toward Round Rock and Reed Spring, while others branched away toward the Eastern River. On the top of the mesa there were many persons from Ash Hill who watched the dispersal. They saw the people of Yellow Cliff fanning out in all directions. Forgetting the anger that had created this event, they said in wonder, "How could it be that two small boys throwing reeds could cause such a thing to happen?"

When all the Grey Fox people were ready, Yellow Corn gave the signal to move. They picked up their loads, put them on their backs and carefully adjusted the carrying straps on their foreheads. In addition to other things, Burning Tree, Falling Snow and Young Antelope had the buckskin bundles containing the kachina masks from Red Rocks Place. Some of the young women carried babies in cradleboards. White Blanket, whose belly was swelled with the living child within, helped White Moccasin take up her heavy basket of corn.

Falling Snow saw how frail White Moccasin was. He wanted to take the load of corn away from her, but already he had everything he could carry. He wondered if White Moccasin would be able to walk as far as the butte. He said: "My grandmother, let us leave the basket here. I will come back for it." She answered, "My grandson, do you think the old ones are not good for anything?" Falling Snow said, "My grandmother." He turned away without saying anything more. He saw Elk Horn and Buffalo Girl already moving out. Elk Horn grinned at him, saying, "Ka ka ka ka!" Falling Snow answered, "Ka ka ka ka!" The Grey Fox people departed from Yellow Cliff, Yellow Corn and the other old ones leading the way down the south trail.

They approached the mound where the reed throwing game had taken place. Standing there, wearing his One Horn headdress and holding his lance, Lame Badger was waiting for them. As the Grey Fox old ones arrived, he made a line in the dust with his lance and motioned for them to stop. Addressing Yellow Corn he said: "Oh, you people, why should you cross my line? What have you ever done in this world that was good?"

Yellow Corn answered: "My brother, we have done what people ought to do. We have fed the hungry and cared for the old, and we have lived in harmony with the land."

Lame Badger asked, "Are you departing forever?"

Yellow Corn answered: "No, we are merely leaving this ghost village behind. We will settle in the valley from where we can see the Mesa of Flowers every morning as the sun rises."

Lame Badger said: "Yes, that is good. Well, do not stand there, but cross the line. I give you a safe and true trail."

Yellow Corn said, "My brother, may your trail also be safe and true."

Then the Grey Fox people went south toward the butte that they had chosen. From the mesa top they could be seen for a while, and after that they blended with the colors of the desert valley.

Badger Boy	A Grey Fox elder
Black Cloud	The crier chief of Yellow Cliff
Bold Fox	The crier chief of Ash Hill
Broken Lance	The village chief of Bow Height
Buffalo Girl	A young Yaya woman, Elk Horn's wife
Burning Tree	A Grey Fox elder; later, a kachina priest
Butterfly Cloud	A Grey Fox woman, older sister of Badger Boy
Butterfly Woman	An old woman from the Yaya village
Crooked Pine	A Yaya youth
Crying Wolf	A Grey Fox elder, the group's crier chief
Elk Horn	A Yaya youth
Falling Snow	A Grey Fox young man, grandson of Limping Deer and White Moccasin
Flower Mountain	A Grey Fox woman, daughter of Yellow Bird
Flowering Gourd	A deceased uncle recalled by Limping Deer
Flowing Spring	A Grey Fox elder
Glistening Shell	A girl of Yellow Cliff, daughter of Black Cloud
Great Pine	The village chief in Yellow Cliff
Green Corn	A Grey Fox woman

Grey Badger	Leader of the wandering Bean People
Grey Coyote	Chief of the Coyote Clan in Yellow Cliff
Lame Badger	An aged One Horn priest in Ash Hill
Laughing Crow	A younger brother of Badger Boy
Limping Deer	Leader of the migrating band that becomes the Grey Fox Clan
Lone Peak	A young man of Yellow Cliff, son of Black Cloud
Long Arrow	The village chief of Red Rocks Place
Many Flowers	A girl of Ash Hill, daughter of Bold Fox, sister to Red Wing
Red Sky	A Grey Fox young man
Red Wing	A young man of Ash Hill, son of Bold Fox, brother to Many Flowers
Running Buffalo	The chief of the Yaya village
Sleeping Bear	An old man of Red Rocks Place
Sleeping Hawk	The kachina priest at Red Rocks Place
Sleeping Wolf	A Yaya man
Small Buffalo	An elder of the Earth House People
Standing Bear	Village chief of Ash Hill
Standing Rock	A Grey Fox elder
Still Water	A Grey Fox elder
Stretching Bear	Elder of the wandering Bear Clan family
Sun Caller	An old man of Red Rocks Place
Tall Chief	A medicine man recalled by Limping Deer
Twisted Spruce	The Fire Clan chief in Yellow Cliff
Walking Bear	A young Grey Fox man

Walking Buffalo	A young man of Red Rocks Place
White Blanket	Elk Horn's sister, later Falling Snow's wife
White Moccasin	Limping Deer's wife, Falling Snow's grandmother
White Star	Grandson of Green Corn
Wolf Child	A man of the Yaya village
Yellow Bird	A Grey Fox elder
Yellow Corn	A Grey Fox elder, successor to Limping Deer as the Grey Fox leader
Yellow Hair	Elk Horn's grandmother
Young Antelope	A Grey Fox young man

SOME OF THE TRIBES
MENTIONED IN THIS NARRATIVE

Coconino	Havasupai, a northern branch of the Yuman-speaking Hualapai tribe that settled at Grand Canyon in the 12th century.
Kawaika (also Kawaik)	A Keresan language group of Eastern Pueblo clans, now represented by Laguna Pueblo.
Kwikapa	Cocopa, one of the Yuman-speaking peoples of the southern Colorado River region.
Paiute	Semi-nomadic Shoshonean-speaking people, some of whom once ranged through parts of what are now Arizona, Nevada and Utah.
Tewa	A group of loosely related Tewa-speaking villages and clans of the Rio Grande region.

Tinneh, Apachu	Apache, an Athabascan-speaking tribe that entered the Southwest some time after the 10th century, following the trail of buffalo and other game.
Utaheh	Ute People, a Shoshonean-speaking people who entered the Southwest in small bands as hunters and gatherers. Town-based Indians regarded them as predators.
Yayatu, Yayaponcha	Yaya People, a small group whose affiliations and language are not known. Traditions of Third Mesa Hopi say the Yayatu once had a village north of Oraibi, that they spoke a strange language, and that they were very strong in medicine. (See H. R. Voth, *The Traditions of the Hopi,* 1905, pp. 123-24, 241-44.) The Hopi Yaya secret society, now extinct, seems to be based on these recollections. Who the Yayatu really were, however, remains a mystery.